THE
DAVID
CONNECTION

BASIL TAHER

ISBN: 978-1-7752033-0-8 (sc)
ISBN: 978-1-7752033-1-5 (e)

Lulu Publishing Services rev. date: 03/08/2018

"…the sins of the father are to be laid upon the children"
The Merchant of Venice, Act III Scene 5

PROLOGUE

Standing stark naked, her head spinning, exhausted with fear and anguish. The girl dropped the gun on the floor and quickly walked to the other side of the bed ignoring the moans and groans coming from Hans lying injured on the floor, she put her clothes back on and ran outside. Her old bicycle was still there leaning against the wall where she normally leaves it after every use. She jumped with difficulty, still shaking from the terrible ordeal.

The girl started to pedal the bicycle as if her life depended on it, leaving a thin tire mark on the muddy path. Remnants of a late March snowfall were still visible on one side of the long driveway. She glanced behind to see if Hans was coming after her. With no sign of him, she focused on the main road a few hundred feet away. Ingrid veered behind the tree line and waited; after a few more seconds when there were no approaching cars she crossed the intersection and continued along the path on the other side pedaling as hard as she could, but Mr. Hendrix's house was still a good twenty minutes away. She was now struggling, her legs were stiff with pain, the cold breeze was hitting her face like needles but she didn't care. It was only a matter of time before they find Hans and launch a search. She would rather die than to get caught by the Gestapo; what Hans had done to her would pale in comparison.

The last four hundred yards were the hardest; she propped herself up and pedaled faster until she reached the final rise, finally relieved to see the familiar dark orange tile roof with the two distinct brick chimneys. Ingrid groaned in agony as she got off the bike and leaned it against the fence. She entered the yard through the side gate and hurried toward Madam Yvonne's suite at the back of the house, then knocked on the door ever so gently, mindful not to make too much noise.

Madam Yvonne opened the door and gasped, "Come inside!"

PART 1

CHAPTER 1

Rachael Lieberman was born on the third day of September, 1921; it was a warm Saturday morning, in the town of Stettin, on the shores of Lake Dabie in Pomerania, a Prussian province of Germany close to the Polish border. Her father Amram Lieberman was a very strict Orthodox Jew, who spoke both German and Yiddish at home and also spoke Polish with relatives who came to visit from his native Krakow. Amram was a hardworking man who left early in the morning and rarely returned home before mid-evening, just in time to kiss his little daughter goodnight before she went to sleep. He owned a store in downtown Stettin; business was tough but provided an adequate living for his family. Although he usually kept to himself he was very close to the town Rabbi, David Goldstein and participated occasionally in the Jewish community functions, attending weddings and bar mitzvahs only with close family or synagogue friends. He was however, a well-liked person and enjoyed respect among the members of the wide Jewish community.

Amram met Mildred Hirsch, who was a year younger than him at a synagogue function. She was a very gregarious girl with flaming red hair and freckled face, of medium height and had a slender figure; she was pretty but not strikingly beautiful. Amram had known her parents since he was a child helping his father at the family grocery store and Mildred caught his eye when she came with them to the synagogue. Amram's interest in Mildred was met with approval from her father, yet her mother wasn't exactly sure he suited her daughter; she thought him a little too reserved for their Mildred. But her father ignored his wife's apprehension and agreed to marry his daughter to Amram when he came to ask for her hand in marriage, believing the young man to be good for her and able to provide a stable home where she can bring up a family.

Although Mildred expressed the same ambivalence as her mother, consent had already been given and she conceded to her father's wishes. With the blessing of Rabbi Goldstein, Amram and Mildred were married in late October and within few months Mildred was pregnant with their first child.

Amram's modest means didn't afford Mildred the same standard of living she was used to, but considering the times they lived in after Germany's defeat in the First World War, things were hard to come by. She had problems adjusting in the beginning, Amram was out all day, she hardly had any friends visiting and the only time she had chance to meet people was at the synagogue where she and Amram attended every Saturday.

Rachael was a pretty little baby weighing 5 pounds and 10 ounces, she had a smidgen of black hair and her eyes turned dark blue when she was two weeks old. Amram and Mildred were elated with the new baby and eight days after her arrival they took her for the customary name giving at the synagogue. Rabbi Goldstein held the baby in his arms as he gave her blessing and affirmed her as a new member of the temple.

Germany at the time was reeling from the effects of the First World War defeat, jobs were scarce, food and other essentials were in short supply and a new nationalistic fever was gripping the country. Disaffected army officers took advantage of the situation and tried to rally the German people to their cause, drumming nationalistic fervor and calls for revenge against those who allegedly betrayed the country and signed the articles of surrender. Nobody had as much success as a petty corporal from the southern region of Bavaria, Adolf Hitler. Hitler began his career making speeches highlighting Germany's past laurels and the superiority of the German people; he visited beer joints in the Bavarian city of Munich where he started his movement. Initially rebuffed, he continued unabashedly until people started to listen, followers trickled in from the ranks of the unemployed and from the Prussian army.

In a short span of time, Adolf Hitler managed to amass enough members to form a semi military organization dedicated to uniting Germans in a collective effort to re-build the country and restore its past glory. He based his beliefs on the racial superiority of the Aryan people and the racial purity of the German nation; proclaiming no place for outsiders in Germany, he concentrated his hatred against the Jews blaming them for Germany's humiliating defeat and surrender. From this the Nazi party grew within a span of just a few years.

Jewish people across Germany ignored the menace of the Nazi party, they thought it was a passing fad at the beginning, but by the time Rachael was four years old, people started to take notice. The Nazi problem was initially confined to the southern state of Bavaria, but the influence was creeping slowly to the north and as the situation deteriorated Amram started to think about his own safety and that of his family. He discussed the situation with Rabbi Goldstein.

"You need to stand firm with the community," the Rabbi advised, "the only way is to persevere and ride out the storm, Amram. There is no wavering now, we have been living here for generations, but these thugs will disappear one day when this nation is back on its feet again."

There was one more thing bothering Amram however; he started to notice in the last few months a distinct change in his wife. She appeared to have lost interest in him, there was even a feeling she didn't care for him anymore; she hardly made any attempts to talk to him when he returned home from work in the evening. He blamed himself for her lack of interest; he worked long hours and was always tired. She had been sitting alone all day long, money was tight and there was a feeling of despair among the Jewish community.

When Rachael turned six, a birthday party was given for her at the home of her grandparents, Dora and Sal Hirsch. Even there, the guests felt the tension; everybody noticed Amram and Mildred hardly spoke. Rabbi Goldstein was among the few people who were invited; the Rabbi was particularly fond of this child because he had no children of his own. He made fuss of her when she came with her parents to the synagogue. By this time Mildred and Amram were no longer living like man and wife. Mildred was sleeping in her daughter's bedroom; she was also missing her Saturday service and spending more time outside the house when Amram was at work.

The last time she went to visit her family her mother asked her outright, "Is there anything wrong between you and Amram?"

Mildred's eyes moistened before she admitted, "Mother, Amram is a decent man and I don't want to criticize him, but I don't love him. I shouldn't have married him in the first place."

"But Mildred, he is your husband now and you have a daughter with him, you need to reconsider how you feel!"

"No mother, I have made up my mind, I am planning to leave him. To tell you the truth, there is another man in my life, I have been seeing him for a while and I am planning to leave Amram. We plan to marry and immigrate to the Holy Land. At some point I will bring Rachael there, but for now I want to leave this awful country forever and settle in a place we can call our own, where Jews are welcome."

Mildred's parents were stunned but couldn't make her change her mind, she was adamant about leaving her husband. As expected, Amram was devastated to return home one evening and find a note from Mildred sitting on the kitchen counter"

> *Dear Amram,*
>
> *After going through an agonizing time for the last two years, I can no longer bear it. My heart belongs with somebody else and somewhere else. I regret causing you any pain and wish you well. Rachael may stay with you for the time being or if you wish you may have my parents take good care of her. I have decided to move on to Palestine and start a new life there. I will send for Rachael after I settle down.*
>
> *Goodbye. Mildred*

Amram calmly put the note on the kitchen table. Tears welled as he wondered where his wife had gone, with whom and about his very manhood. And what did she tell Rachael? He lay awake all night thinking about what went so horribly wrong with his life, why did he deserve this? He could not remember a time when he hurt anybody, so why is God punishing him?

In the morning he dressed Rachael, took the bus over to his in-laws, kissed her on both cheeks and said goodbye to her. He didn't bother to go to his shop; Amram returned home and closed the door behind him.

Rabbi Goldstein was in his living quarters at the back of the synagogue when he heard a knock on his front door. A cheerful elderly man was standing at the door.

"Good afternoon Rabbi."

"Well, good afternoon to you Herr Goldman. It is rather unusual to see you at such a time, is there anything I can help you with?"

"Yes, to tell you the truth I needed some help with paying my debt to Herr Lieberman, I went round to see him at his shop this morning as I normally do at the beginning of each month but the shop was closed. I thought perhaps Herr Lieberman must have an emergency and had to leave before I arrived, but to my surprise the shop was still closed after lunch when I visited him again. In all the years I have known Herr Lieberman, I don't ever recall visiting him and finding the shop closed, so I thought of bringing the money over to you. Maybe you will be kind enough to pay it on my behalf? You see I am leaving town later this evening to Warsaw to be at our grandson's bar mitzvah."

"Yes," the Rabbi answered, "that is rather unusual, Herr Lieberman is a very reliable man. But I will indeed give him the money on Saturday when he comes for prayer with us."

The following morning, Amram's father in-law was waiting in front of the synagogue. "Good to see you Herr Hirsch, there is a worried look on your face; I hope nothing bad has happened."

"I am glad you are here Rabbi," Sal Hirsch started. "Amram brought Rachael to stay with us yesterday and promised to pick her up last night, but he never showed up. I assumed he had forgotten so I went down to talk to him at the shop this morning. I know he must be feeling bad, you see Mildred has left him. She is going to Palestine. But to my surprise the shop was closed, and this is unusual; Amram never missed a day at the shop all his life! I stopped at his house and knocked at his door several times but there was no answer. I know he was very close to you, I wonder if you have any idea where he might be?"

Rabbi Goldstein was an astute man, and he knew something extraordinary must have happened to prevent Amram from opening his business two days in a row. "Let us go check on him," he said to Herr Hirsch, "maybe he is sitting at his house feeling sorry for the loss of his wife."

The Rabbi knocked at the front door, waited a minute and then knocked again. Still no answer "Just wait here," he ordered Herr Hirsch, trying to hide his growing alarm. He went around the house and pounded loudly on the back door. It jerked opened with the force of the knock, so the Rabbi walked in through the kitchen and into the living room. Unprepared for the scene in front of him, he froze for a moment, said a prayer and let himself out of the front door. So shaken when he emerged into the sunlight from the darkened house, he squinted trying to find Sal Hirsch. "Let us just go." he mumbled.

The police arrived and the lifeless body of Herr Lieberman was transported on a stretcher to a waiting ambulance. In a brief note sitting on the table next to an empty box of rat poison, Herr Lieberman professed his love for his child: *All my worldly belongings are now yours my love, I hope your life will be better than my own*, he wrote. Rachael was sad for the loss of her father. Only six years old she asked her grandparents, "Why did papa want to be in heaven with God and not with me?" Her grandparents couldn't reply; they were trying to find an answer themselves.

Rabbi Goldstein came to visit quite frequently; the little girl touched his heart. He asked Dora Hirsch when her daughter, Mildred was coming back for Rachael. There was a brief silence before Dora Hirsch answered, "We have no exact date. 'I'll be back after I get settled in,' is all she said before she left for the Holy Land."

Mildred and Haim boarded a train bound for Italy after they said goodbyes to her parents. As she kissed Rachael on both cheeks, she said, "Don't be afraid, Rachael, Mummy will be back for you soon and Mummy loves you very much."

They arrived in Italy the following day and they boarded a ship bound for the port city of Haifa on the Mediterranean coast of the Holy Land. Haim Ashkenazi was originally from Poland but had lived in Germany since childhood with his parents. He was a very motivated man with lots of determination. Life in Germany had little appeal for him; he believed the nationalistic fervor gripping the country was going to get worse. "This is not a passing fad, it is here to stay," he told Mildred when he first met her at his sister's house. "I am not staying in this place; in fact I am preparing to begin a journey to our ancestral land in Palestine. This is where we belong, not in Europe where we have been treated with hatred and suspicion ever since we arrived here more than a millennium ago." Mildred was attracted to this fiercely independent and outspoken man, he seemed to know where he was going and she felt the same way about Germany.

Soon after their arrival in the Holy Land, they were greeted by the Jewish agency officials who provided them with the necessary identification and then transferred them into kibbutz Gvat in northern Palestine. The kibbutz was an agriculture outpost consisting of thirty-four families clustered together on a hilltop and surrounded with barbed wire all the way round. The view from Mildred's kitchen window was absolutely beautiful, endless rolling hills meeting the sky at the end of the horizon, with tracts of green land in between. She could see a man in khaki shorts sitting on top of the wooden watchtower, rifle nozzle leaning on the side. She didn't understand when they first arrived, but she quickly caught on about the hostile people out there. Don't worry, she was told, we will defeat them one day, and our great country Israel, will emerge from the ashes! Mildred experienced a great rush of adrenaline at this, she felt great love and attachment with the people and the place and she wanted to be part of the fledgling community that finally arrived to settle the land of their forefathers. She sat down that evening and wrote her first letter to Rachael and her parents: *I am so happy to be here, I feel I was born new again, answering the call of our Lord. I cannot wait to see you here with me soon.*

Life wasn't easy for the new settlers, there was work to do; tilling and tending the fields, teaching in the classrooms and cooking and baking in the kitchen but above all there was the endless duty to protect the commune. Palestine was under British control and the Jews arriving from Europe and Russia were at first met with casual indifference. But as their numbers increased, the indigenous Arab people became hostile and skirmishes flared up all the time. It wasn't only men who did the protection, but women too had to do their share.

"We are back after 2000 years in exile. This where we belong and this where we will stay!" Haim proclaimed.

Rachael was told when the first letter arrived, "Mummy is now in the Holy Land. She will be coming soon to take you with her."

"What is the Holy Land, Grandma?" the little child asked.

"This is the land where King Solomon built his great temple from pure gold and where little David slew the evil giant Goliath. God has given this land to the Jews, they have been absent for so long, but now they have returned!"

When Mildred received the first letter from her parents she sat down crying, sad about the news of her husband, the father of her child.

"Perhaps I shouldn't have left him," she sobbed, "it was I who pushed him to despair."

"Stop blaming yourself, Mildred," Haim ordered. "This crying isn't going to bring him back; you need to focus on your new life in order to bring your child where she belongs."

Mildred wrote a long letter to her parents explaining the situation. *I need nothing more in life than to see you again Rachael*, she added, *I miss you and love you with all of my heart, I will be there for you when the situation improves a little, but now is not the right time.*

Sal and Dora Hirsch loved their only daughter, but also loved their granddaughter very much. She was no trouble at all, in fact she brought so much joy to their lives and they didn't mind looking after her. Rachael was now enrolled in the neighborhood elementary school. The first grade children in her class were predominantly Christian girls; there were however, a few Jewish families in the affluent district where the Hirsch family lived. The school's long serving principal, Jacob Myers, was Jewish however; he and Sal had been friends for years.

Haim and Mildred were married in a simple ceremony at the Kibbutz. All the families gathered for the occasion. Mildred wore a white dress and a veil to cover her face and her long red hair, and when the local Rabbi pronounced them husband and wife, Haim removed it and gave her a long kiss in front of the cheering crowd.

Haim was an ardent Zionist who believed strongly in the need to resettle the ancient promised land and turn it into the land of milk and honey again so he joined the Jewish militia organization, *The Hagenah*, set up for the defense of the Jewish communities in Palestine. He quickly acquired the necessary training to lead a small unit in the kibbutz.

"We must not only defend our community," he told his followers, "but we must launch counterattacks in retaliation against those who try to kill us!"

He developed a reputation for bravery and leadership, and on a trip to the near town of Nazareth, he and a group of eleven men came under attack, where he sustained a direct hit to his left eye. Haim was rushed to the city of Haifa for treatment but doctors at the hospital were unable to save his eye, however, the patch was a badge of honor he wore for the rest of his life.

CHAPTER 2

A year had passed since Mildred and her husband arrived at the Kibbutz. Arab attacks against the Jews intensified; there were skirmishes virtually every week and the cycle of violence never stopped. Mildred desperately wanted to bring Rachael over but she feared for her safety. She wrote back to her parents again, this time imploring them to immigrate to Palestine: *The larger community needs you father. Things in Germany will get worse; please remember what happened to the Jews in Russia, they suffered and died in the pogroms there, not for any reason other than they were Jews. I'm afraid the same fate will come to the Jews in Germany so please come here before it is too late.* Mildred also informed her parents of her career plans to become a nurse due to the great need in Palestine, as well as Haim's injury.

"No way, I don't fancy going to Palestine," Dora Hirsch told her husband when she finished reading her daughter's letter. "We are very comfortable where we are. Nobody gets injured every week here. I think the Zionists have a pipe dream, the Arabs will not allow them to settle! They too say the land is theirs. There will be endless conflict and war between them."

"I think you are right," Sal agreed, "I don't fancy sending Rachael there either. Needing her mother is one thing but having to live in a very hostile environment is another. The poor girl needs to get proper education in Germany; she doesn't need to spend her life in the middle of nowhere, with no schools and no future. I think you are right Dora; Mildred is under the spell of this revolutionary guy, Haim. He has not only lost his eye, he lost his brains also!"

Rachael, who was now in her second grade at school, was a petite and slender girl with nice straight shoulder length black hair, pale white skin and a round face. Her most striking feature was the color of her eyes; they were piercing blue and danced with energy. She would rather spend hours in the backyard with her toys than working on her school books.

"Come on in," her grandmother used to shout, "time to set down and read your books!"

"I'll be there grandma!" But it was not until dark when she entered the house, starving and demanding to be fed.

Dora read Mildred's letter to Rachael when it arrived.

"What is a patch grandma?" the little girl asked. Her grandmother explained that Haim was injured in the eye; he is now covering his eye with a piece of leather so nobody can see his injury. "Why doesn't he want people to see it?" the little girl wondered.

"Because it is not pretty."

Due to the economic conditions, attacks against Jews started to increase in numbers and intensity, the police and the average person in the street looked the other way as gangs of Nazi youths terrorized the Jewish population. The Jews' sense of security started to wane, some stayed in their houses, doors and windows shut, many lucky ones fled to any country which permitted them to stay. North America was a favorite destination, South America, and the Holy Land had their share of immigrants, but the unfortunate hapless majority remained in a country they had once considered their own, feeling powerless .

The Hirsch family lived in the northeast part of Germany in an affluent section of Stettin, far removed from the Nazi's regions of influence and traditional assault locales. They hardly experienced any physical attacks or verbal abuse, and thus far had no reason to leave. Dora Hirsch sat and wrote down a long letter to her daughter:

> *Dear Mildred, we are sorry to hear your husband was injured. We sincerely hope to see him again one day. We also hope life will get better where you are. Your father and I constantly fear for your safety and look forward to the day when you finally return and be with us again. Rachael is growing by the day and she misses you so very much. I don't want you to be too concerned about her; she has grown to be a beautiful little lady and is doing well in school. She settled in well with us and she is no trouble whatsoever. We only hope the security situation will improve in the Holy Land soon but please don't send for Rachael until all things quiet down. We love you and miss you and you will always remain in our heart and prayers.*
>
> *Sincerely*
> *Your loving parents*

PS: we hope you like the attached picture of Rachael, please send us some of your pictures.

Mildred's heart melted when she opened her parents' letter. She kissed her daughter's picture and placed it close to her heart, then immediately wrote a response to her parents. She told them how much she missed and loved Rachael:

I am now counting the days before she can come here and be with me. I don't believe the situation here is getting any better, quite the contrary it's getting worse. The other day we lost a dear friend, shot dead on his way back from the field. Haim found him lying on the ground in a pool of blood but the man died before we had a chance to take him to the hospital. His death affected us all but hit Haim the most, he was very close to him. The good news is that we will have a whole bunch of new immigrants coming soon to our commune. We all look forward for their arrival and we will take more comfort in the safety of a larger community. I will be going to Haifa next week for six months in order to get my practical training at the hospital. I have passed all my exams and this is the final requirement before I become a certified nurse. Everybody here is waiting for me to finish; we don't have a resident nurse at our kibbutz and one is greatly needed.

Mildred stuffed two photos inside the envelope, one of her standing alone, the other one was of her and Haim holding hands. Haim was wearing the now familiar eyepatch on his weathered face and he had a gun strapped to his waist.

CHAPTER 3

Rachael turned eleven just after school started in 1932. Now in fifth grade she was full of energy and eager to learn, but one month after the school term began tragedy struck. Ingrid Schroeder, a girl in Rachael's class became gravely ill and in a matter of few days she was dead, the victim of a vigorous form of tuberculosis. School was shut down for a few days, and all the children had to be examined. Dora was so scared her grandchild was infected, but the school principal, Jacob Meyers, came to visit a few days later bearing good news-- none of the other girls at the school had any signs of the dreadful disease.

Rabbi Goldstein, on the day after his seventy-third birthday, was walking on the street when he saw half a dozen youth running away from the synagogue. He picked up his pace and went around the temple, looking for any signs of trouble. There, on the back wall, a swastika, the emblem of the Nazis was sprayed with red paint. He hurried back to his living quarters and brought detergent and a bucket of water. He tried in vain to scrub off the paint but all he could achieve was to make the emblem look like an unsightly red smear.

The Rabbi was a genteel man, six feet tall with broad shoulders and a radiant face. He easily won friends and gained the trust of subordinates and never for a moment thought trouble might come to his community in Stettin. Others told him he was in denial but when the Rabbi looked around all he could see were ordinary citizens going about their own business. "You are mistaken." he used to say to the people who were afraid to go out of their houses and to those who were planning to leave Germany. This last incident however made him think again.

The Nazi party steadily gained strength and popularity. Large crowds of people came to see Hitler delivering a speech in Brandenburg, and an even larger crowd packed Grunewald Stadium in Berlin. A general election was held in March of the same year; the Nazi party didn't win it, but made an impressive showing. In July, 1932, yet another election was held, this time to elect deputies to the Reichstag, the German Parliament. The Nazi party made an impressive showing again, but didn't win outright. Hitler, however was determined to rule Germany. General Paul Von Hindenburg, the president of the country appointed Kurt Von Schleicher to head the government. The man had no chance to survive; the concentrated onslaught and the muscular tactics of the Nazis forced him to resign. After a mysterious fire was staged at the Reichstag by the Nazis, the communists were implicated for the crime instead. Hindenburg had no choice but to appoint Hitler the chancellor of Germany, as of January 30, 1933.

Hitler's ascent ushered in a new era in Germany. The first thing he did was to introduce temporary emergency powers, this was one way to consolidate his control over the country and have all the reins in his hand. The German people weren't too enthralled at the beginning but slowly started to adapt to his ways. Dissension and criticism were not tolerated. People were urged to work hard, play by the rules and show no resentment. Jews on the other hand weren't considered average German citizens; on the contrary, they were viewed with suspicion as foreigners whose presence was malignant to the society and a taint to the purity of German blood. Hitler ordered a campaign of systematic terror against the Jews, the *"Untermenschen"* or sub humans. Jewish people walking the streets were stared at; some were made fun of and ridiculed while still others were roughed up.

The economic conditions in the country at the start of the Nazi rule were in a terrible state. Unemployment was very high, production was at a standstill and the general feeling was one of despair. By the beginning of 1935 the out lash against the Jews was in full swing and the Nuremburg laws were introduced. Jews lost their right to German citizenship, they could not marry outside of their faith, Jewish organizations were proscribed, shops and homes were vandalized, and people had to display the mandatory yellow Star of David. Shops too had to display the word *"Juden"* to indicate Jewish ownership, and storm troopers stood outside to deter people from shopping there; this was carried out by the Nazi authorities in a deliberate attempt to bankrupt the Jews and force them to leave.

Rachael didn't encounter any such demeaning incident until she turned fourteen. She arrived at school late one morning. The teacher made her stand in the corner; students threw crumbled papers at her, they taunted and made fun of her. "You dirty Jew, go home!" they chided. This was done in front of the teacher who was in fact enjoying the scene and cheering the kids to do more. Principal Herr Meyers was powerless to do anything; he feared for his own safety, and all he did to the teacher was to give him a perfunctory reprimand.

Rachael came to hate school and hate the teachers, she cried every morning when her grandmother forced her to go.

"Don't cry my Rachael; you need to show some toughness in life. One little incident like this should not make you hate the school, go out there and show them you are better and smarter than they are!" Rachael walked into the classroom with poise, but deep down she was terrified; she couldn't wait to get back home and shield herself in the comfort of her bed, the door shut behind her and curtains drawn.

Attendance at the synagogue had been in decline in the last few years. Many people moved out of Germany, either voluntarily or forcefully. The Rabbi was getting old and frail but never lost his will to persevere, his belief that one day the decent German people will return to their senses was unshakable--until the day the synagogue was fire bombed.

Tuesday, the fourteenth of September, 1937 was Yom Kippur or the Day of Atonement, a beautiful sunny morning. Congregants started to arrive early to the temple for the *"Shacharit"* or Morning Prayer; Rabbi Goldstein started the solemn service with a reading from the Torah, and about the time he began to offer incense on behalf of the Jewish people a loud noise interrupted the service followed by a deafening explosion. People were thrown out of their seats, items were strewn all over, and many lay injured on the floor. By God's grace there were no fatalities, but the malicious attack brought the service to a complete halt and the synagogue sustained extensive damage. It was more divine intervention that the synagogue didn't burn to the ground.

A little over a year later, November 10, 1938, came the night of broken glass, "Kristallnacht". Hitler ordered a campaign of violence and terror against the Jews; seven days later when it was over, more than ten thousand shops and businesses were completely destroyed. Homes and synagogues were torched and left to burn, personal belongings and contents stolen. Police and fire departments never responded to emergency calls, and afterwards the Jews were left to clean up all the mess and pay retribution.

Rachael turned seventeen a little over a month before Crystal Night.

Walking home from school on a cold afternoon at the end of November, she saw a plume of smoke in the distance. An acrid smell tainted the atmosphere and there were particles of ash flying in the air. She proceeded with caution, careful not to draw attention to herself. When she was closer to her street she could hear sirens, but she was not prepared for the horrible scene awaiting her when she turned the corner. A group of people were gathered in front of her grandparents' house; a large fire truck parked over the pavement was obscuring her view but as she drew closer she could see the house was in flames. The roof had totally disappeared and the smoldering house was gutted. She dashed with all the strength she could rally towards the house, crying hysterically for her grandparents. "Grandpa! Grandma! Are you alright?"

Officials at the scene restrained her from going any closer. She fell to the ground shivering with fear and trepidation; after the fire truck left the scene all that was left was the smoldering shell of the home she lived in for the last eleven years.

A kind, elderly woman who lived next door to the Hirsch family came over to her and whispered, "I am sorry Rachael, but your grandparents have died."

Rabbi David Goldstein never thought it could come to this, the country he was born in and loved so much now disintegrating before his eyes. He remembered when his mother sat next to him in bed and told him biblical stories about the Hebrew prophets, the story of how Joseph was picked up by the caravan and brought to Egypt, and how Moses' mother hid him behind the bulrushes. He also remembered the stories she told him about the great Bismarck, who defeated the French and unified all the German States and made them one great nation of Germany, she instilled in him the love of country as much as the love of religion. Now he looks at the country he loved so very much and cannot begin to fathom what really went wrong, why the people are turning against him and his fellow Jews. What did he do to deserve this kind of treatment?

More to the point, what did the young lady lying in bed in the other room do to lose her grandparents? Sal and Dora Hirsch were the epitome of good and hardworking people who looked forward to a peaceful retirement; why did they deserve to have their house firebombed when they never hurt anybody? Why did their lives have to end in such a horrible and undignified way? The Rabbi's heart ached for Rachael; the poor girl lost her father twelve years ago, her mother disappeared from her life, and now the only close relatives left have been murdered. Herr Goldstein got up and walked to the kitchen; he prepared a bowl of soup and took it over to Rachael.

"Here you are my child, you better have something. You haven't eaten in two days." There was no answer.

Rachael lay trancelike in bed. Her entire life had been turned upside down and she looked very frail and vulnerable. The Rabbi sat down on the edge of the bed, put her hand in his and started to say a prayer.

"Repeat after me Rachael,

Sh'ma yisro-ayl, adonoy

Elo-haynu, adonoy echod.

Hear, O Israel, the Lord is our God, the Lord is One.

Blessed be the name of the glory of his Kingdom forever and ever.

God is the Lord.

The Lord is King, the Lord was King, and the Lord will be King forever and ever."

Rachael softly repeated the familiar words after the Rabbi and she was sound asleep when he finished.

In bed that evening the Rabbi tossed and turned, he was at a loss what to do. He felt Rachael was now his responsibility. He thought immediately of two people who also cared for the poor girl: Jacob Meyers, the retired school principal who was making the final preparations to leave the country, and Doctor Albert Wiseglass, a cousin of Dora Hirsch. The doctor was well known in the community before he retired six years earlier. He too was making plans to leave Germany. Rachael knew both men, they were familiar and trusted. The first thing the Rabbi did in the morning was to invite them over for an informal sit down in order to debate solutions for Rachael's tragic situation.

CHAPTER 4

The news of the fire and of the Hirsch family murder hit the Jewish community like a ton of bricks. They had heard terror stories before about what the Jews were experiencing, but now it was close to home; two of their community members were murdered and a poor child was left behind without any family and without any means of support. Everybody in the community felt for her yet they were powerless to help. Under normal circumstances they would have stood by her, but these times weren't normal, their resources were depleted and everybody was holding tight to what little money left in his or her possession.

The Rabbi got up early the day after he met with the doctor and the school principal; he dressed and quickly left the house, hurried to the post office and put a letter in the mail addressed to a Rabbi in the city of Lyon in France. Inside the letter he stuffed another envelope addressed to Mildred and instructions for the Rabbi to forward the letter to Mildred at Kibbutz Gvat, in Palestine. Rabbi Schumer and Rabbi Goldstein were old friends; they met in Salzburg during a rabbinical seminar before the First World War. Rabbi Schumer was active in the Zionist movement and enjoyed many connections. During the meeting Rabbi Goldstein held with the school principal and the doctor, the three men decided after several hours of deliberation to inform Mildred about her daughter and about the tragic loss of her parents. They also devised a plan to get Rachael out of Germany and send her to the Holy Land. Albert Wiseglass agreed to have Rachael stay at his house until they hear back from her mother, but time was of the essence for Dr. Wiseglass as he was making preparations to escape Germany himself.

Rabbi Goldstein sat with Rachael after he and the other men had their meeting. "All children are precious in God's eyes, and God loves you my child. What happened to your grandparents is absolutely monstrous; these Nazis have taken over this decent country and turned it into hell on earth. But you must remember, we Jews have been around for thousands of years and many attempts were made against us, yet we have always triumphed in the end. Sal and Dora, your beloved grandparents, were fine people who tendered nothing but decent service to this society, they didn't have to die the way they did at the hands of these hooligans, but now they are in heaven with God. You can grieve their death but don't bemoan the injustice; you must move on, live your life and then get even with those who perpetrated the heinous murder. Germany is now going downhill and this crazy Fuhrer is taking everybody down with him; the situation here is very bad and is likely to get worse, so we believe it is in your best interest..."

"Excuse me, Rabbi, but who is 'we'?" Rachael was beginning to tear up as her future was being laid out.

"Herr Doctor, Herr Meyers and I believe it is in your best interest to leave Germany and join your mother in the Holy Land. I have sent a letter to inform your mother about the tragedy that killed your lovely grandparents, and I also informed her of our intention to send you to her. I am so sorry Rachael you have to go through this terrible experience at your tender age, but you must show resolve and determination to succeed. There are no alternatives for you my child, this country is doomed, most Jews have left or are planning to leave, their journey out of here is not easy, and not too many countries are welcoming them with open arms. But in your case it is even more difficult. We must smuggle you out of Germany to a friendly country where you can board a ship heading to Palestine; France is the only logical option, it has a regular ship service to Palestine and we have people who will provide you with assistance. You need to get ready now because tomorrow I will be taking you over to Dr. Wiseglass where you will be staying until all the necessary preparations are made. The Doctor and his wife Elsa will also give you some education which will help you fare better along the way. Do you understand all of this Rachael?"

"Yes, I do Rabbi Goldstein; I will be happy to go to Palestine and be with my mother. I hate this country and hope not to see it ever again."

The Rabbi dropped Rachael at the Doctor's house in the morning as planned and then hurried to meet Jacob Myers; arrangements were made to meet somebody on the outskirts of the town.

Binyamin Komlin was a short balding man with reddish blotches covering his face and neck. He spoke slowly with a deliberate no nonsense voice. He was on the run for several years, hiding during the day in the woods around Stettin and sleeping in different safe houses at night. The Gestapo were looking for him because of his Jewish background and communist affiliations. Considered armed and dangerous, orders were given to local authorities to shoot him dead if they found him. Binyamin was a friend of Haim Ashkenazy. The two grew up together, joined the communist party at an early age, and both of them foresaw what was coming to Germany. Haim decided to emigrate to the Holy Land; Binyamin however, decided to dedicate his life to helping the Jewish community in their quest to leave the country. He began his political career with a solid conviction that Communism was the answer to human equality and the spread of wealth among all the people, but with the rapid rise of the Nazis and their hidden agenda to eradicate the country of its Jewish population, he changed course and now dedicates his time to urge his fellow Jews to rise against them. As leader of the Jewish underground in the Stettin area, he maintains close contact with other groups in the country both Jewish and none Jewish. They were all united in their pursuit to help persecuted people escape.

Benyamin was happy to oblige when Jacob Meyers approached him to help Rachael. "Yes, we can provide her with forged identifications. All you have to do is give us a photograph of her and a possible name and leave the rest to us. I will have a new picture identification made up within a week. If you don't have a specific name we will have to research death records to find a suitable alternative, a dead person of a similar age would be best."

Jews who had the financial means simply paid their way out of Germany, others who were able to find a country to accept them legally were also able to leave without problems. Rachael however, neither had the financial means nor valid immigration papers. The only available option in her case was to be smuggled out of the country and the only logical destination was France. Once there, she could travel unhindered to the port city of Marseille on the Mediterranean coast, and catch a ship bound for Palestine or use other clandestine ways to reach the Holy Land through the help of the Jewish Agency and other Jewish organizations.

Jacob Meyers and Rabbi Goldstein arrived in the woods on the outskirts of town for their scheduled meeting with Benyamin. "We are sorry to have you involved in all of this," the Rabbi said to Benyamin.

"Do not worry, Rabbi, all I care for right now is to get this poor girl out of here as soon as possible. I have good people who will be able to help once she makes it close to the French border, and I will send messages to associates in the area to expect the girl in a month or two. I am confident our people will deliver. Do you have all the information for her new identity ready?"

"Yes, we have," the Rabbi responded, and he handed him a photograph of Rachael. "We have given her the new name, Ingrid Schroeder."

"We thought the name was a perfect choice," Jacob Meyers said, "Ingrid was in Rachael's school and the poor girl came down with tuberculosis and subsequently died of her infection. She and Rachael were very close in age; Ingrid was born in August, 1921, while Rachael was born in September the same year."

"Very well, gentlemen, this is a perfect choice indeed. If a search was ever done on her for any reason, the information on her new identification will match perfectly."

Dr. Wiseglass made a call to an old acquaintance, a lady who used to work at his office as a nurse's assistant before she moved to Stuttgart after she was married.

"Is this Janet Vasco?" the Doctor asked.

"Yes, this is she, how may I help you?"

The Doctor proceeded to tell Janet about Rachael, and what happened to her from the death of her father to her mother going to the Holy Land and finally to the murder of her grandparents.

"Janet, I want a favor of you, would you be able to help this girl? She doesn't have anybody in this world and she is in a desperate need!"

"I am so sorry to hear all of this about Rachael, of course I can help. Anything you ask doctor. I am on maternity leave right now and I know Dr. John Heinrich, where I work, is looking for a receptionist, Rachael can come and stay with us until we find her somewhere close to the French border. In the interim she can be working for doctor Heinrich to earn a living."

"I know I can count on you Janet, and I will not forget your help. I hope one day I can return your favor."

"You don't have to mention it doctor, you have done so much for my husband and me."

"Bless your heart Janet, I wish you all the best. By the way, Rachael will be issued new identification papers; she will go by the name Ingrid Schroeder. Please don't mix up the names."

Janet Vasco was a tall woman with long curly black hair. She was originally from the Stettin area before she made the move with her pharmacist husband to Stuttgart. She was not happy about leaving the city of her birth, but she knew Dr. Wiseglass was retiring and her husband Frank had a good job offer, therefore, she decided to go. Frank was an intellectual, a few years older than her. He joined the communist party when he was young but had to quit after the communists became the target of the new power sweeping the country. He hated the Nazis and what they stood for, however he kept his sentiments to himself for fear he would earn their wrath.

Mildred was busy with her new nursing career in the Holy Land. Jews and Arabs launched guerilla warfare against each other, and the situation was deteriorating so much on the ground, there wasn't a day without news of yet another Jewish settler gunned down or a Jewish family ambushed and killed. Hostilities on both sides were simmering for some time but eventually came to a head when the Arabs revolted in 1936. The British, who were given a mandate over the Holy Land by the League of Nations, tried to implement an even handed approach, but neither party trusted them. The conflict turned into three-way front and Kibbutz Gvat came under fire. Mildred was constantly busy tending to the injured; it was hectic life for her and her husband, and the day she received the letter with the French postmark she thought the mail was delivered to her by mistake. When she opened it she nearly collapsed with grief.

"What is the matter?" Haim asked when he returned home and found his wife in a terrible state. He tried to soothe her pain but the hurt was deep.

"I must go right now to bring Rachael here! She is my baby, Haim!" she cried.

"Oh, no, Millie. It's too dangerous. I think it's best to leave it for the Rabbi and our brothers in Germany, Rachael will be alright. They will give her whatever help she needs to safely make it out of there. I will use all my connections to see this through; I have many friends who can help Rachael once she crosses into France."

After discussing it with Haim, Mildred sat down and wrote a long letter to the Rabbi, in which she expressed her profound appreciation for the help he afforded her daughter. *Regrettably, I won't be able to come back to Germany to fetch Rachael, but Haim will be making arrangements to bring her to the Holy Land once she arrives in France. Her best option is to go directly to Lyon. We will provide Rabbi Schumer the names of the people who will take her from there and bring her safe and sound to us. Please pass all my love to Rachael and tell her how much I miss her and look forward to seeing her soon.* Mildred mailed the letter to

Rabbi Schumer in Lyon with a note to forward the letter to Rabbi Goldstein in Germany.

Rabbi Goldstein was happy and relieved to receive a response from Mildred; in fact her letter arrived in the nick of time. Dr. Wiseglass had already received his immigration papers and was making the final preparations to leave.

The Rabbi went over to see Rachael at the doctor's house. "I am so pleased to tell you, your mother is waiting for you in the Holy Land! She loves you so much and she is looking forward to seeing you again. But now my child, I want you to get ready, because I am coming for you tomorrow. We will take you to the train station so you can begin your journey out of this horrible country. You will first go to Stuttgart and my friend Janet Vasco will help you cross the border into France. Once there you will be taken to the city of Lyon and Rabbi Schumer will make the final preparations for you to get to the Holy Land and unite with your mother. You must cooperate fully with all the wonderful people who will be trying to help you, listen to their advice and don't despair! Do you have any questions, Rachael?"

"What about you, Rabbi Goldstein? Everybody is leaving and I don't want you to get hurt staying here on your own."

"How kind of you, my child. Don't worry about me. I think the Nazis will spare me, I don't think they will harm an old man like me!" Rachael needed to hear his assurance.

Dr. Wiseglass took Rachael to say goodbye to the Rabbi at the synagogue the following morning.

"I will never forget your kindness, Rabbi Goldstein, I am forever in your debt. But I wish you would please come to the Holy Land and be with us again. We will be like your own family and we will look after you in your old age.

The Rabbi was nearly in tears. "I will miss you my child, and I will pray for your safety. Please pass my best wishes to your lovely mother, and remember to always obey our Lord. I have also prepared a little gift for you my dear." The Rabbi reached behind his desk and pulled out an old duffel bag. "This belonged to my dear wife, but now it is for you, Rachael. May God be with you and give you the resolve to come through this." He leaned over and kissed Rachael on her forehead, turned his back and walked away. He didn't want her to see the tears.

Dr. Wiseglass dropped Rachael a block away from the station mindful not to be seen with her for fear somebody might recognize him and the whole escape plan might unravel. When Rachael boarded the Stuttgart train, she did so under new identity, Ingrid Schroeder.

"Please don't forget to use your new name, you must be careful not to make any mistake! Somebody may pick up on it and your journey to the Holy Land will be in jeopardy." These were the last words of advice from Herr Doctor.

Ingrid Schroeder sat in the train feeling sad to leave the city of her birth forever; she was sorry to leave all the wonderful people behind, yet happy for the chance to unite her with her mother.

Janet Vasco was a tall woman with long, curly black hair. She was easy for Ingrid to recognize at the train station in Stuttgart.

As her husband Frank took Ingrid's duffel bag, Janet asked, "How was your train ride, dear?"

"It was fine. Dr. Wiseglass sends his sincere regards to you. He and his wife asked me to give you their heartfelt appreciation for the help you are providing me."

"Oh, don't mention it, Dr. Wiseglass had done many favors for me, he is a wonderful man! But now we need to sit down and explain how we will proceed with your escape plan." They found a bench in a quiet area of the station where Janet could continue in privacy. "I have told everybody that you are my niece. I have also got you a job with Dr. Heinrich. He is a very kind man you will be working as a receptionist in the front answering the phone and making appointments. I will escort you tomorrow to the office and introduce you to everybody and also explain your responsibilities in detail."

"We are also in contact with the people who will help with your escape, and as soon as they tell us the time has come, we will let you know. These people know the border area very well and they will only act when they determine it is safe to do so. I know at the present the time is not right; there is a lot of troop movement in the area we were told."

Rachael liked the tone of her new name, 'Ingrid Schroeder', she knew it sounded very German and should remove any suspicion about her Jewish background. She also felt comfortable with Janet and Frank; they looked like very decent and sincere people. Maybe I shouldn't feel the same way about

German people any more, she told herself, there are many good people among them.

In the evening after she retired to her bedroom she opened the old duffel bag. The rabbi had put in it a small bundle of money, a chain with a gold Star of David attached, a prayer shawl and the Torah. There was also a note and a short prayer scrolled in his own hand writing:

Dearest Rachael,

You will always be in my heart and will remain there forever. Have a safe trip home. See you in Jerusalem.

Rabbi Goldstein

Ingrid was crying when she finished reading the note and the prayer. She kissed the Torah and went to sleep.

CHAPTER 5

A month after Ingrid arrived in Stuttgart there were no new developments with regard to the escape plans. Janet could sense Ingrid's frustration.

"Please be patient," she told her, "the time is not right yet, and I am sure the underground group who are helping you will be in contact when they determine it is safe enough to move you."

Another month passed and the underground group told them the German army tightened security on all the country's borders after Germany invaded Czechoslovakia. That night Ingrid went to bed wondering what the future may hold for her since chances of crossing into France were now significantly reduced.

Janet had been home with her baby girl for a few weeks now, but her maternity leave was nearly over and Ingrid wouldn't be needed at the Doctor's office anymore. Aware that Ingrid had to work since sitting at home doing nothing was not only boring but unhealthy, she contacted a friend of hers, Madame Yvonne Fischer, who was working for a family in the countryside near the town of Offenburg. Janet asked if she knew a family in need of live-in domestic help and explained the circumstances of her 'young niece'.

"Yes, I do know a family," she answered without any hesitation. "General Karl Schneider's live-in help, Gretchen, is quitting next week. Frau Schneider asked me if I knew somebody to replace her, and I told her I will ask around. If you want I can tell her about your niece."

"This is wonderful, Yvonne. Ingrid is almost eighteen years old and a very smart young lady; I can get a letter of recommendation from Doctor Heinrich if they wish."

"I don't think that will be necessary, Janet. The General and his wife are in poor health and they desperately need someone right away, I'll call you back after I have the chance to visit with them."

Madame Yvonne Fischer originally came from Strasbourg where her French roots run deep. She married Friedrich Fischer, a truck driver from Offenburg who was a gregarious wine drinking German. His upbringing was harsh; he started early in life picking wine grapes and by the time he turned fourteen he was driving the vineyard's tractor back and forth from the field to the winery compound. He developed a reputation for good and reliable work ethics. Friedrich joined the communist party not for ideological reasons but because his best friends joined before him and they subsequently lured him in. He met Yvonne while making delivery runs between Offenburg and Strasbourg, She had a similar background, born in servitude and employed as a maid for various rich land owners, a job she despised but was unable to escape as she had no other training. Her employers in France often belittled and overworked her and she, too, thought the communist party could provide an escape from such a miserable life. Their brief marriage ended when the truck Friedrich was driving rolled down the side of a mountain in heavy fog, and after his death, Yvonne came to work on the German side of the border.

Yvonne, like Janet, hated the Nazis with a passion. Her brother Simon was a member of the underground group who provided help for Jews and others who wanted to escape Nazi Germany. The group consisted mainly of French nationals and some local Germans who were dissatisfied with the regime in Berlin. The leader of this communist faction in Strasbourg was Marcel Lalonde, a tall, handsome and charismatic man in his forties. He and Benyamin Komlin knew each other, having met several times in Berlin before the Nazis took over. It was Marcel to whom Benyamin delivered the message about the impending arrival of Ingrid.

Doris Schneider was panic stricken when her domestic help announced she was quitting. It would be difficult to find a replacement considering where they lived in the countryside outside Gengenbach, not too far from Offenburg. She and her husband Karl were in failing health and needed somebody to look after them as their two grown children were married and live in different cities. She couldn't thank Yvonne enough when she dropped to see her over the weekend.

"I have good news for you Frau Schneider, I found a young girl who is interested to work for you. She is the niece of a dear friend of mine. She was temporarily employed at a Doctor's office, but her services are no longer needed. If you wish, I can arrange for her to come down for an interview."

"I am very interested, but how old is she?" Doris Schneider asked

"She is eighteen years old, and her aunt told me you will be very impressed with her, she is reliable and diligent and doesn't mind to live out in the country!"

"Very well, have her come for an interview, the General and I would like to see her."

When Janet told Ingrid about her new placement near Offenburg, she stressed how close it was to the French border as well as the beauty and tranquility of the area.

"But the most important advantage for working at the retired General's house is it will provide you with the perfect cover. Nobody will ever suspect or go looking for you there. You will feel very safe."

Janet escorted Ingrid for her interview at General's Schneider's house. On the way, they stopped first at Madam Yvonne's place of employment, Colonel Hendrix's home, right at the edge of the Black Forest. Colonel Alexander Von Hendrix was retired from the Prussian army where he served for almost forty years. He lived first in Leipzig where he was originally from, then moved to his present house in the vicinity of the little village of Haigerach, not too far from the General's house. Yvonne had been in his employ for the past four years. Ingrid immediately liked the affable French lady; she felt genuinely happy when Yvonne told her about the underground group.

"I will take you up to the forest to meet them when you get settled down. These guys know what they are doing and they will help you cross to safety in France."

Ingrid's interview went very well. Doris Schneider was concerned over Ingrid's age at the beginning but felt comfortable after she asked questions, and she was impressed with the way Ingrid answered. She found the young lady was mature beyond her years, looked motivated and had a friendly disposition. Ingrid also liked the Schneider's house. The General and his wife were getting old, they didn't look much trouble and seemed dead set in their ways, and the property was pretty and secluded just off the main road.

Offenburg is a road and train junction at the foothills of the Black Forest, about 25 miles from the French border city of Strasbourg. The forest itself is almost rectangular in shape and has a growth of conifers so dense it blocks out the light hence its name since Roman times. General Schneider and his wife lived in an old stone farmhouse with a dark grey tiled roof, set in a clearing with few scattered trees and surrounded by woods on three sides.

A small dry creek bed separated theirs from the neighbor's dairy farm on the east side; the picturesque rolling pasture land was ideal for grazing cattle.

Ingrid started her job few days after the interview; Janet came down with her on a lovely spring morning. The air was still cool as they drove through Offenburg, and then continued to the General's house. Ingrid fell in love with the charming area with its vineyards dotting the sides of the roads.

Her living area was very much like Madam Yvonne's. It was a small room attached to the back of the house. It had no windows but there was a bathroom, a small metal frame bed, an old wooden wardrobe and two chairs. It was all she really needed, considering she wasn't planning to stay long. Her purpose was to lie low until the time was right to execute the escape plan.

Her duties were mainly to keep the house tidy and clean, help in the kitchen and look after the old General and his wife. The house needed very little work, there was hardly any traffic inside, and the General and his wife loved to sit in a small sunny enclosure off the living room to read books and newspapers. A nurse came from Baden-Baden once a month to check on them. She left them medicine and checked their general health and gave additional instructions to Ingrid. Ingrid liked the General very much; he was very good with her, always courteous and never too demanding.

The General and his wife's two grown up children, Fredrick and Freda, were both married. Fredrick and his wife lived in Stuttgart, were childless, and not particularly close to the General. Freda on the other hand was very close to her parents; she was an elementary school teacher and her husband was an army officer working at the Projectile Testing Laboratory near Dresden in East Germany. They had two children, fourteen year old Hans and nine year old Elizabeth.

Ingrid easily settled into a routine at the General's house. She diligently did her housework and tended to her employers' every need. Doris and the General were pleased with her performance and felt very comfortable with her.

Ingrid liked to go for walks in the forest while they were resting in the afternoon. She also liked to chat with George, the old farmer and his wife when they were in the vicinity of the barbed wire fence separating the dairy farm from the General's property. Ingrid also enjoyed sitting on the swing the General's grandchildren made from a rope dangling down from a thick tree branch close to the farmer's fence where she could watch the cattle grazing in the field.

Either Madam Yvonne came to visit at least once a week at the General's house or Ingrid walked all the way to the Colonel's house to visit with her. It was a long walk, so Yvonne told her she could use the old bicycle in the shed, but first she must take it to Gengenbach to have the chain and flat tire fixed

"Once you have it repaired, it will make your life easier and you can make it here from the General's house in a little over twenty minutes. You can also come with me in the future to visit the guys out in the woods. It's fun to go out there, sometimes they ask me to get them supplies from town or deliver messages to some of their people around the area." Ingrid was curious; she desperately wanted to meet the men who were supposed to help her escape.

Several months passed since Ingrid began her employment at the General's house and she was getting very frustrated with the slow pace of her escape plan.

"What seems to be the problem?" she asked Yvonne.

"I am sorry but the guys don't believe the time is right," Yvonne was quick to answer. "They will not take any chances and will act only when it is safe. They are telling me both Germany and France are amassing troops at their borders and declared the area a military zone. They don't see any way to get you out of here at present. They are sorry you left it to the last moment to come here; had you arrived a year earlier or even a few months earlier, then it would have been easier to take you across. They also believe the winds of war are gathering in the distance, both England and France have signed an agreement with Hitler, but if Hitler is foolish enough to violate the terms of the agreement he will drag this continent into a big war. God only knows when or how bad it will be, but all the guys believe war is inevitable, if the crazy Nazis are foolish enough to test the resolve of France and Britain."

By this time Ingrid became like a fixture at the General's house. She didn't mind the easy work and the friendly atmosphere. Fredrick, the General's son and his wife sometimes came to visit over the weekend. They were very friendly but rather a boring couple and Ingrid had the distinct feeling the General and his wife were happy when their son left on Sunday morning. Once, she overheard Fredrick telling his father that war is unavoidable at this stage. The General however dismissed his son's remarks.

"I think Hitler is too smart to fall in the trap and create an excuse for France and Britain to attack us."

Doris walked in the kitchen that same evening after she finished talking on the phone with her daughter. She sounded so happy when she told Ingrid that her daughter and her family were coming from Dresden for a visit next week and gave Ingrid a list of things to buy from town in preparation for their arrival. Ingrid mentioned the bicycle at the repair shop.

"Now, I think I will ask the repairman to fit it with a shopping basket when I go tomorrow to pick it up. The bicycle will be a great help especially when I do shopping in town, I can go there faster and carry more things back!"

Freda and her husband Herman arrived on a beautiful afternoon. Herman, in an army uniform, looked remarkably tall and had an imposing figure, but he had a kind face nevertheless. Freda was a rather plain blonde woman wearing horn-rimmed glasses, and she too looked very kind. Little Elizabeth was adorable; she came running over to Ingrid.

"Hello, are you the new lady helping grandma, what is your name?"

"I am Ingrid, what is your name?"

"I am Elizabeth, and I am nine years old."

The boy, Hans, was rather an odd child. When he met Ingrid for the first time, he just stared at her and made her feel uncomfortable. She felt his eyes follow her wherever she went. She tried to make friends with him. "My name is Ingrid Schroeder, what is your name?" she asked him politely. He didn't answer; he just kept staring at her. That evening she went to her living quarters after finishing the housework and as she entered her room she heard a noise outside. When she looked out the door, Hans was there, lying on the grass. It appeared as if he had tripped. "Are you alright?" she asked. Wordlessly Hans got to his feet, picked up a small rock and threw it in the air, staring at her the whole time. Then he turned around and ran away.

Ingrid went to visit Yvonne the day after Freda and her family went back home.

"You look so tired Ingrid," Yvonne commented, "what is the matter?"

"I had a rough week. It wasn't the amount of work but that grandson, Hans. He made me so uncomfortable, staring at me all the time. I tried to talk to him but to no avail. I don't know what I could have done to alienate him so much."

Yvonne sighed, "Ah, yes, this boy is the apple of his grandfather's eye. The boy was close to Gretchen, the lady who used to work for the General and his wife before you started working, so perhaps he misses her. But don't take it personally, and they only come visiting once a year, normally around this time in the middle of the summer."

"By the way, I see you already picked up your bicycle, how do you like it?" Yvonne asked.

"It's fine but a little old so the seat is hard and uncomfortable, but I can jump on it easy. See how I had it fitted with a shopping basket?"

"Well this is great, now we can go to the forest and meet the guys, how would you like that, Ingrid?"

"I cannot wait; I am so looking forward to leaving this place!"

The two of them rode on their bicycles for almost an hour in the Black Forest before they left their bikes and walked the rest of the way to where the fellows were waiting under an outcrop of rocks. Ingrid was shivering with excitement when she came face to face with the rough looking men with guns slung on their shoulders. Marcel, their leader spoke German well but still had a strong French accent. He welcomed Ingrid warmly and introduced the rest of the guys. All of the men smoked heavy and smelled of French cigarettes; they looked like they hadn't have a shave or a wash for a long time but seemed happy and jovial nevertheless, cracking jokes with each other.

"So tell us about yourself, young lady?" Marcel asked.

"What do you want to know, monsieur?"

"We would like to know more about you; we have received a request to help you cross into France, but no other information."

Ingrid gave them a quick summary of what brought her here. "They burned our house to the ground and murdered my family," she recounted through tears. "My mother emigrated to the Holy Land more than ten years ago and I am trying to join her there. Would you help me please?"

"But of course," Marcel answered, "you can count on us, we will get you out of here as soon as the situation allows. You must be patient young lady. We are not in business to jeopardize your life or ours, but we will act when the time is right, do you understand?"

"Yes, I do, I promise to cooperate fully and promise not to harass you."

The guys broke out in laughter at her choice of words. Simon, Yvonne's brother pulled out his gun and fired a shot in the direction of the nearby creek. The sound nearly knocked Ingrid to the ground, and they all laughed again.

"Don't frighten the poor girl," Yvonne shouted at him.

"Oh, no, I am not trying to frighten her, but she better get used to the sound of guns, she will hear it along her way to freedom. We don't want to fail in a critical situation. The noise may cause her to panic and draw attention to her and to us." He turned to Ingrid. "Would you like to try the gun young lady?" She nodded and he handed it to her. "This is what you need to do. First you release the safety pin, then you aim at your target and then you pull the trigger. Easy, no?" Ingrid took the pistol in her hand, Simon placed his over hers, and he directed her finger over the trigger and helped her pull. Another deafening sound nearly threw Ingrid to the ground, and they all started to laugh again.

"You are so cruel Simon; leave her alone!" Yvonne ordered.

"No, it is okay, I am not frightened," Ingrid answered, "can I have another go please?" She held the gun herself this time, aimed at the water in the creek, and fired, falling to the ground to great applause from the men.

That evening she couldn't sleep, she was so excited and thrilled about the events earlier in the day. She never imagined in her life she would be holding a gun in her hand let alone firing one, but she was proud of her achievement. She was also pleased with the guys, they seemed fun to be around, and she felt comfortable and reassured the end was within sight. She thought about her mother and wondered what she was up to. She knew her mother would have been proud had she seen her using a gun, and Ingrid imagined her saying, 'You will need it here in Palestine.'

At night Ingrid dreamt about the Holy Land, the biblical rolling hills dotted with palm trees, shepherds roaming the land with herds of sheep and goats and the beautiful blue skies with shining stars, I am finally going to the land of milk and honey, the land of my forefathers; oh God I cannot wait.

Ingrid was bored sitting in the house on her own. The General and his wife had been gone for a week visiting their son in Stuttgart. The General hadn't been feeling well, and he decided to see a specialist over there. So with the afternoon free, Ingrid jumped on her bicycle and went over to see Yvonne. She wanted to convince her to go to the forest, to the group's hiding area. She had been thinking about the gun and wanted to try it again. Ingrid found Yvonne in a state of panic when she arrived.

"What is it Yvonne?"

"You haven't heard yet? Hitler sent his troops to invade Poland! The monster has been lying to us all along; I think he and Stalin had worked it between them, each country will take a portion of poor Poland and the country will be no more. This is absolutely diabolical; this crazy man is pushing the whole world into war! I am very concerned this war will be worse than the last, and it is us the average people who will suffer the most. The leaders will be living in cozy palaces eating big meals and drinking fine liquor, and they expect all of us to sacrifice. I am sick and tired of them all!"

Mildred sat in her clinic the day after France and Britain declared war against Nazi Germany. She had not felt this bad in all her life. It looks like war will break out any day in Europe, and she didn't know where her daughter was. She didn't even know if she was dead or alive. "Oh God!" she lamented, "What did I do! I lost my parents, and I don't have the slightest idea where my daughter might be. Please God, help her and stay with her."

Rabbi Goldstein was so happy the day he received a letter from Rabbi Schumer in France, he couldn't wait to get to his office to open it. Rabbi Schumer explained the phone call he received from the Jewish Agency, advising him that Rachael will be crossing the border from France soon. The people who are involved with her escape were told to bring her over to his Synagogue in Lyon. He assured Rabbi Goldstein that Rachael will be in good hands and he will do exactly what was required to help 'Ingrid' travel to Palestine to be with her mother. Rabbi Goldstein thought about Rachael, or Ingrid as she is called now, wondering if she was out of Germany yet. He pulled out a pad and wrote a letter back to Rabbi Schumer, to thank him for his service. He also wrote a letter to Mildred to let her know that everything was done to ensure Rachael's safety and ended the letter by finally expressing his desire to immigrate to the Holy Land. *I am fed up sitting here on my own,* he wrote. *Most of our community has departed and I don't even have a handful of people attending Shabbat, so I have decided to come home to the Holy Land. As a matter of fact, I have made arrangement to meet Binyamin Komlin in the next few days to work out the necessary arrangements just like the ones we made for Rachael. I hope to see you and Haim soon.*

One of Binyamin Komlin's associates came to the synagogue two days after the Rabbi failed to show up at the planned meeting. He found the letter on the floor next to the mutilated body of the Rabbi lying behind the Synagogue door. It was clear he was tortured before being shot in the head. There was widespread damage to the synagogue and Nazi graffiti was everywhere. The man covered the Rabbi's body with his own jacket; he said a prayer for him and left the synagogue with the letter in his hand.

CHAPTER 6

Hermann Schmidt grew tall on the shores of Starnberg Lake. As a teen-ager he was sent to a school for the gifted, because he showed remark-able abilities in the academics, and after completing high school, he went on to the University of Munich. He graduated in mechanical engineering in record time and soon found a job with the State of Bavaria Department of Road Authority, a job that provided him the opportunity to be out in the open most days, something he enjoyed and appreciated. Freda, Hans's mother was originally from South West Germany, and like her father before her was born in the city of Baden-Baden in Wattenberg State, close to the French border. She was a slim woman who was dedicated to her profession and to the students at the school where she worked. She grew up in a military family; her father was a high ranking officer in the Prussian Army, and they lived in various parts of the country. Both Hermann and Freda were skilled skiers and they enjoyed nature, music and the arts, so it appeared from the start they were destined to be together.

WWI started not long after the Grand Duke of the Astro-Hungarian Empire was assassinated in Sarajevo by a Serbian nationalist. Germany found itself on the side of its neighbors to the south and against its traditional foes, France, Britain and Russia. Hermann was drafted into the army after com-pleting a brief military training and he was assigned to a unit on the western front to defend Germany from the French. Morale among the troops was very high and the camaraderie was strong.

During the war, German troops showed remarkable courage and deter-mination; they were winning one battle after another against the retreating French, and German troops from the other war theatres in the east and south were reporting similar gains; the Germans knew they had better training and superior technology against their enemies.

The western command under Officer Karl Schneider was stationed on the outskirts of the town of Baden-Baden, close to the French border, and the Germans built a trench line to deter the newly introduced mechanized tanks from crossing into Germany. Hermann was indispensable to his unit especially with the kind of engineering knowledge he possessed, and General Schneider came to appreciate Hermann as well, frequently summoning him to do repair work at the base or at his own residence in town. It was during such repair visits to his commander's residence that Hermann and the General's daughter Freda struck up a relationship, with approval of the General and his wife.

Although Hermann's unit came under fire many times during the initial period of the war, the Germans were well equipped and determined, and Hermann managed to survive the war with hardly any serious injuries. But Germany's fate was different, and on the 11th, of November 1918, Germany signed the articles of the armistice treaty after the Kaiser himself slipped out of the country into exile in Holland. Germany was declared a republic the following day and the victorious Allies enforced harsh terms on the defeated Germans. Nobody was more stunned by this defeat than Hermann; because the army division his unit belonged to under the command of General Schneider won battle after battle he was sure that Germany would be victorious.

When Hermann stopped at the General's house to say goodbye, the mood inside was bleak and dark, but the family were pleased to see him. They had a little chat and exchanged the usual pleasantries, then the General who was known to be a man of few words stood up in the middle of the room and with his strong military voice proclaimed, "The day will come when the German people will rise up again and reclaim our lost honor!"

Freda was sad to see Hermann leave for Bavaria the following day; she had grown accustomed to his visits and would miss him terribly, but for now, she resolved to concentrate on studying the requisite courses at the teachers training college.

The train journey back to Bavaria was sheer agony for Hermann; he sat at the edge of a crowded seat surveying the passengers around him. Many were in fact discharged troops just like him. It was dark and eerie and the air was stale inside the carriage. Most passengers were just looking down at the floor with blank stares, the weak and hungry twitched and convulsed with the train's motion, and some had visible scars of chemical infliction from mustard gas. In an instant they gasped for air, and then choked after each breath, their irritated eyes tearing. Many of the injured received little or no treatment at all, there simply weren't enough medical supplies, and so many walked aided by a cane, while others leaned on fatigued friends.

Hermann was bitter, the proud German nation was humiliated and broken, and as the train traversed the land at a steady pace, slowing down only for bends and turns, the familiar countryside became a sad landscape muddied by drizzle and despair.

Hermann's father and mother rushed to greet him when he walked through the door; it was a pleasant moment after an otherwise awkward journey that had had a promising start, full of optimism and triumph. Hermann's parents wanted to hear about their son's experience on the western front, but he was in no mood to talk, the memories were still raw and painful and the gaudy details of the war were still vivid. He was hopelessly tempted to tell them what he saw: friends standing in the trenches adjusting their masks to cope with the horrendous mustard gas to no avail, then moments later the familiar drop of death; the churning sound of an empty stomach, and the screams of the badly injured receiving treatment with nothing to dull the pain. But alas, it is over, it is all behind him now, his parents needn't know.

Marshal Hindenburg took the reins of power after the king went into exile, and he steered the country forward, but there were many problems, especially the large number of discharged and now unemployed troops. The government worked hard to turn the economic tide around, and invested heavily on infrastructure as a means to revive the stalled economy. Hermann like everybody else around him needed a job, and because of his background he was able to return to the state's road department. The huge increase in the use of automobiles before the war started required the rapid construction and repair of roads in different parts of the country. Although the job took him all over the state and occupied his time, there was one thing still fresh in the back of his mind.

Freda and her family were relocated to Stuttgart after the war ended. Her father, General Schneider was still on active duty and a member of the general staff high command. Freda started her last year at the college and she was hoping to get a job at an elementary school close to home.

"A letter came in the mail for you, today," her mother announced when she came in one afternoon.

"Who possibly could have written to me, mother?"

"It seems to be from Hermann; he mailed it from Munich two days ago," she answered.

Freda was speechless, she thought they had parted ways when he came to bid farewell after he was discharged from the army, what could he possibly want? She picked up the envelope and went to her room, shutting the door behind her. Her mother knocked at her door when she failed to show up for supper that evening, "What is wrong darling? You look like you have been crying." She sat next to her and stroked her back.

Freda bashfully told her mother, "Hermann is interested to continue a 'cordial relationship' with me, and he said maybe we can begin by writing to each other." Her mother just smiled and understood her daughter.

Hermann couldn't open the envelope postmarked from Stuttgart fast enough, and he felt overjoyed as he walked home after work. Both parents sensed a different attitude as he sat at the long dining table. They were fidgeting with anticipation to learn the reason behind the sudden change and were relieved when he told them about Freda's letter, and she too would like to maintain a friendship with him.

Their relationship prospered and by the middle of 1923 he took his family over to Stuttgart to meet Freda and her family. The two families sat round the dinner table reminiscing about the good times before the war, and this new phenomenon sweeping Bavaria, Adolf Hitler and the Nazi Party. There was a consensus among them that Germany belongs to the Germans and there is no room for outsiders in their country. During the trip, Hermann asked Freda if she would like to move to Munich one day and she accepted without hesitation. They were married in a little chapel in her home town of Baden-Baden. Her father escorted her down the aisle; she looked lovely and radiant in a simple white dress with a small flower tucked in her hair, and everybody cheered when Hermann placed the ring on her finger, a symbol of his love and devotion to his bride.

The newlyweds rented a home in the outskirts of Munich. He continued to work for the road department and she easily found a job teaching young students at an elementary school. Life was rather hectic at the beginning, he left for work early in the morning and didn't return until late evening, and she too had to work at the school until late afternoon then rush home to prepare dinner. Almost a year later during a visit to Munich, the general and his wife were very happy to learn their daughter was pregnant with their first grandchild!

Hans Gunter Schmidt was born on a cold January day in 1925 in his father's hometown just outside of Munich. He was a big baby with enormous blue eyes and a golden tuft covering his head. Right from when he was born, he was the pride and joy of his parents. He quickly grew to be a big baby who could almost outpace his mother just by crawling on the floor, he was an adorable boy full of energy and he brightened the mornings for his parents with a smile radiating from his rather big and round face. Hermann and his family settled into a routine, he and Freda got up in the morning and went to work leaving Hans in the care of his doting grandparents.

When the child turned four years old, he enrolled in the school where Freda taught, and that arrangement worked best for the family since she was pregnant again. Baby Elizabeth when she was born had gorgeous golden hair and chubby cheeks, and Hans was thrilled when he saw his sister for the first time. He put his arms round her and planted a big kiss on her face to the cheers and laughter of his parents.

The new baby however, came to this world when the economy took a turn for the worse, following the stock market crash in New York in 1929. The economic malaise spread to Europe and the rest of the world, but hit Germany rather hard, and businesses were failing at an alarming rate again leaving many unemployed. Hitler and his Nazi followers were well organized, and took advantage by encouraging new recruits to join the party. Their ranks multiplied with the disaffected and the unemployed, and the Nazi mantra was that the elites in Berlin were corrupt and inept and beholden to the Jews.

Hermann's luck came to an end when he lost his job in the middle of 1930. The country, like the rest of the world, was going through an economic meltdown; prices sky rocketed, national institutions were rocked to their foundations, jobs were vanishing, lines at food banks sprouted everywhere and the general mood was that of despair and foreboding. The government simply didn't have the resources to keep people employed and it was burdened with war reparations. Hermann was dispirited, he had no choice but to go out and look for work. After several months, his search still came up empty, there were simply no jobs available, and everyone was frightened and unsure what the future holds.

He came home late one evening with a smile on his face. "You look like you found a job," Freda began while they were at the dinner table.

"No, I have not," Hermann replied. "But I have come up with an idea today, and it has the potential to salvage our future!"

"You have my full attention, what idea are you talking about?"

Hermann expressed his desire to open up a mechanic shop, citing the rapid increase in the use of automobiles in the country and the lack of specialized people and shops that cater to the growing needs of motorists. "We must take the reins into our hands and chart our own future!" he declared firmly.

"And how are you planning to achieve this? This sounds like a great idea, Hermann, if only we had the resources to pay for the expense of setting up a business. You must be fully aware that you need money to rent a shop, buy tools and equipment, money we currently don't have," she said with a little frustration.

"You are right darling, but I thought about going to the bank to see if I could get a loan to help me with the startup cost."

Hermann was on time the following week for his appointment at the bank; he was all dressed up and sat in the lobby waiting until a bald elderly man came over to greet him.

"I am Simon Rosen," the bank manager courteously introduced himself, "What can I do for you Herr Schmidt?"

Once settled in the office, Hermann stated, "I am here to apply for a business loan. Our city and the area at large have a paucity of specialized mechanics with enough expertise to repair and refurbish automobile engines, and I am glad to inform you that I have both the knowledge and experience to make a successful business."

"That sounds very interesting," Herr Rosen answered, but went on to inform Hermann that the bank would loan money for a new business only if the owner provides a collateral equivalent in value to the loan amount. He agreed with Hermann about the need for this service and admitted that the business proposal has merit and a good chance to succeed, but quickly cautioned that things out there feel a little unsettled and everybody is keeping what little cash they have for more essential purchases.

When Freda came home from work with Hans trailing behind her, she found Hermann in a sour mood sitting at the kitchen table. He was bemoaning his luck with the bank and the lack of job opportunities in his beloved hometown.

She sat on the chair next to him, held his hands in hers, and gently consoled him. "This is not the end of the world Hermann. There must be other things you can do,"

"I have spent days upon days looking for a job but came up dry. I don't think there are jobs out there anymore," he said with a chill.

"You could be right, honey. I suggest you go and see another bank, maybe they will be more amenable to help."

The following day was Hans' sixth birthday and Freda invited Hermann's parents to come over to celebrate the occasion. Hermann couldn't mask his mood when his parents arrived in the evening; they were looking forward to visiting the grandchildren and brought a present for each one, and Freda hoped for a light atmosphere with special cake and decorations.

Hermann's father however could feel his son's frustration. "How did your meeting at the bank go?" he asked quietly.

"It didn't go well at all," Hermann answered with a flat voice.

"Why? They didn't like your business proposal?"

"The funny thing, the bank manager believed my business proposal has merit and he agreed the mechanic shops are in great demand," Hermann said.

"Well, I don't understand, what seems to be the problem? Why couldn't he loan you the money?"

"The problem wasn't with the business model, but according to the bank's manager, it has to do with the bank's policy and the current market conditions, and he wasn't prepared to take any unnecessary risk. He wants to have collateral. I think this bank manager is a little too conservative, I think I should try my luck with another bank."

"Don't waste your time son!" Hermann's father jumped in. "Banks are owned by Jews; if one turns you down, the rest will definitely follow suit, they all tell each other, and you have no chance for now. But listen, if the bank manager wants collateral, I am willing to put my house up. It is worth more than the amount you were asking, and therefore you should meet the bank's requirement."

Freda was dead set against this, and she made her opinion heard loud and clear. "What if the business fails, your parents stand to lose their home! I think it is unfair to expect them to go through this possibility, no matter how remote."

"I didn't ask him to put his home up, he offered and I accepted. God forbid, but if my own son ever happens to go through a situation like the one we are going through, I will not hesitate for one moment to put my home up for his sake!"

Hermann and his father arrived at the bank on time to sign the loan documents, and Herr Rosen was thorough and detailed in explaining the terms of the loan and the implications should the loan fail to perform.

"Are you sure, Herr Schmidt, you want to go through with this loan? Your son may have a good business idea but the situation out there is not encouraging and you may lose your house if the business doesn't succeed." Hermann's father however, signed the loan documents without uttering a word.

Hermann wasted no time setting up his business. He rented a building on a major route going in and out of Munich, he purchased and installed the necessary equipment, and opened the shop for business after the sign adorning the front of the store reading *Schmidt Auto Repairs* was installed Hermann and Freda were thrilled with the revenue the business generated by the end of the first month; the location proved a good choice and the demand for auto service was steady and consistent. They both felt optimistic despite the uncertainties around them and purchased a gift for Hermann's father as a token of appreciation for helping with the bank loan. Hermann's parents were excited when told how well the business was doing, and his father felt the gamble he took on his house was well worth the risk.

Hermann received a letter from the bank on the first anniversary of his opening, with an accounting breakdown of the last twelve payments as well as a thank you note from the bank manager, Herr Rosen, congratulating him on the success of his business and to thank him for sending the payments before their due dates.

It was hard work and a bit of luck that changed Hermann's fortunes, but for the rest of the country the story was rather mixed. Hitler too started to see his fortunes change for the better; by the beginning of the nineteen thirties the number of delegates representing the Nazi party in the Bundestag increased substantially but the increase wasn't large enough to form a majority yet. Hitler's message was simple, blame all of Germany's problems on the Jews and the communists, and use scare tactics and intimidation against his enemies, and in time, these tactics worked very well. The rest of the country however, took a sharp turn for the worst and the economy was in a free fall. Unemployment was rampant and the Deutsch currency was fast losing its value, making inflation worse and credit unavailable.

By the beginning of 1932, riots aided by the Nazis broke out in many parts of the country, people were protesting the austerity measures the government had to put in place and the majority was left with little to survive on. Hermann's business also started to suffer and revenues plummeted, yet he continued to make the payments to the bank until his account dried up. In April he missed a payment for the first time. A letter from the bank arrived warning of the dire consequences if the payment was not received promptly; Hermann had no choice but to ignore the letter and continue to work hard in the vain hope things will improve in the future, and he can make it up. After several more missed payments and subsequent demands that he pay the outstanding balance, there came a final ultimatum from Herr Rosen, warning that the bank under the terms of the loan will exercise the option of foreclosure. Hermann ached with pain, overwhelmed with grief at the thought of being the cause for his father to lose his home.

Hans was present when a representative from the court served his grandfather with the notice to vacate his home.

"I am sorry to inform you, Herr Schmidt," the official began to say, "but the court has ordered you to hand over your home to the bank and you have only until tomorrow morning to vacate. Failure to comply with this order will land you in jail."

William Schmidt, the proud German who worked all his life to provide honorably for his family was now marked to be thrown out of his home and into the street with nowhere to go. He was understandably bitter, and chose to vent his anger against the Jews. He used derogatory words to refer to them, *"Judenschwein"* or Jew pig. He looked at Hans and said, "These are the true enemy of the German people and you must do all you can to avenge these Jews who make their money out of the misery of ordinary Germans! May the Lord put a curse on them from now till the end of times!" His neck turned bright red, sweat poured down his face and he collapsed on the floor. Hans was terrified and started to cry; the ambulance came and took away his grandfather.

Three weeks later he died as a result of this massive coronary. It was a sad end for a decent man who was loved by his family and gave everything until he could no more. Hermann couldn't stop blaming himself for this tragedy and he felt utterly hopeless. Hans, just seven years old at the time, couldn't stop crying when his beloved grandfather died.

Freda's father General Schneider traveled to Munich to pay respects to Hermann for the loss of his father and found his daughter and her family devastated both financially and emotionally. He sat at the dinner table and turned his face towards his son-in-law and in a firm and charged voice told him, "I have fought many battles in my lifetime. Life is like a war consisting of many battles, some you win and some you lose. What matters most is when you lose a battle you get up and stand on your feet again so you can fight another day and win the war." He reached and grabbed Hermann's hands and looked in his eyes and said, "This is what you must do from now forward." The General also told him that he was fully aware of their financial situation and without a hint of empathy said, "I want you to know I am here for you if you need help, but I also suggest you rejoin the army. To tell you the truth, they can do with somebody like you; you have discipline, intelligence, experience and the qualifications to make you among the best officers. I therefore would like you to come and see me at the War Ministry in Berlin in two weeks. I will see what I can do to help you establish a career in our armed forces. As you know I will turn seventy in few years and the army will not let me serve past that age; you might as well take advantage of my contacts and this opportunity will only last while I am still in active duty."

Hermann took his family and drove to Berlin to meet with General Schneider. Christmas was just two weeks away but nobody was in the spirit of the season, a grim mood prevailed instead, the worldwide economic depression hit Germany harder than anywhere else, but Hermann was luckier than most. General Steinmotz, the head of the recruitment department at the War Ministry, approved his employment after the great introduction by General Schneider, and Hermann was assigned to the military testing facilities in the city of Dresden in Saxony, East Germany.

Hitler, now Chancellor quickly rounded up his foes, consolidated the reins of power, purged the government of the old guard and brought in his Nazi henchmen. He further passed legislation based on German racial purity and superiority and relegated non Germans to second class citizens with special restrictions on the Jews and Jewish institutions.

Hermann and his family settled in Dresden in early spring after he completed the mandatory officer training. The pretty city lies on the banks of the river Elbe in the historic kingdom of Saxony. Its baroque style architecture features buildings dating back to medieval times and it is situated not too far from the Czech border, about 125 miles south of Berlin. Hans loved the area and settled in rather quickly. The main attractions were the many skiing facilities in the mountains nearby, and the abundance of parks and lakes for summer escapades. Hermann started his first day of work at the army testing range in the outskirts of the city, and Freda easily found a teaching job at an elementary school. Their new routine was interrupted rather abruptly when Freda received an emergency call from her mother to advise her that her father, General Schneider, had been rushed to hospital with severe chest pains. Freda's mother, who was sick herself, urged her daughter to come to Stuttgart to attend to her father.

General Schneider was a frail man when he walked out of hospital, aided on one side by his son Fredrick and on the other side by Hermann. They drove home to his house in Stuttgart, where Hans and his sister Elizabeth were waiting, and when the General stepped out of the car, both children ran towards him with open arms.

"Grandpa," they shouted, "how are you? We were worried about you! Please don't get sick again, we hate to see you feeling unwell."

The General wiped tears from under his glasses and with a forced a smile and open arms, told the kids, "I am just fine, I am just fine, my boy and girl, I will be alright, and I promise not to get sick again!"

The General was not well at all; he had suffered a debilitating heart attack that made him weak and slow, and he had no choice but to end his illustrious career with the army and take early retirement. He and his wife Doris, and Albert, the young Alsatian dog, moved to a country residence. The house, which they bought many years earlier was located near the town of Offenburg close to the edge of the Black Forest and not too far from the spa city of Baden-Baden where the General was originally from. That is when the elderly couple decided to hire Gretchen to look after them.

Hitler and the Nazi Party moved quickly and systematically to consolidate their power in Germany and to oversee the gradual removal of the last vestige of the democratic institutions. He introduced a very ambitious plan to turn the country around and to strengthen the military in contravention of the agreements Germany was forced to sign after its defeat at the end of WWI. Many wealthy industrialists were happy to oblige and offered their resources in the service of the state, and after two years in power, Hitler declared himself absolute leader, "Fuehrer" or Leader of the country. He also appointed members of his Nazi Party to be in charge of the military and civilian departments. The German economy started to show signs of improvement and by 1936 Hitler's popularity soared and Germany started to feel more confident about itself.

Hermann rose quickly through the ranks and became a researcher in the army's projectiles and rocket development center. He, like his father-in-law had predicted was very bright, dependable and loyal, and was totally committed to the service of the state and the Nazi party; he collected many commendations from his superiors as a result. Hermann and his family welcomed the change in their life and shared the prevalent feeling among the German nation that things were improving under the leadership of the Fuehrer. This feeling of course was the result of the intense propaganda the state practiced on the average people but there were also many signs of progress. The country's employment rate started to climb steadily, the industrial output increased significantly and the currency stabilized. There was law and order everywhere and the political stature of Germany increased substantially in Europe. Hitler often spoke about German laurels and past glories, and promised to lead the German people to greater prestige. Many believed him when he talked about the sinister and treacherous Jews--he urged the nation to boycott them and not to intermarry with them, they were regarded as collaborators with the outside enemies of Germany who would not hesitate to suck the blood of Germans when it comes to their money and interests.

CHAPTER 7

Now ten years old, Hans was a big and strong boy and he was looking forward to doing two things at the end of the school year. The first was their annual trip to see his grandfather, General Schneider, at his farm house, (and to see his favorite lady, Gretchen, their domestic help), and the other thing he wanted to do was to join in the *Jungvolk* or Hitler's Youth for young boys under the age of fourteen. The summer trip went as planned and the General enjoyed seeing his daughter and her family, and as usual nobody enjoyed it as much as Hans. Both the General and Gretchen made a fuss of him and he spent hours playing with Albert. Even the farmer next door took him for rides around the farm on his tractor.

Soon after they returned home, Hans fulfilled his desire and joined the Jungvolk, where he and the other boys received firsthand indoctrination in Nazi ideology, German superiority and hatred of the Jews. They also received scout and semi-military training, and at the end, each youth must perform a loyalty oath to the Fuehrer. There Hans befriended a fellow by the name of Claus Schwarz from the Alsace region of western Germany. The two boys competed in sports and stayed in the same dorm, often ventured out in the woods and played soldier games with their homemade toy guns and by the end of the summer they were inseparable.

At the beginning of 1939, Gretchen informed General Schneider and his wife that after several years of working for them she was retiring at the end of the month due to ill health. Her friend Yvonne Fischer, house maid for Colonel Alexander Von Hendrix, an old army colleague of General Schneider, was a regular visitor at the General's house, and upon hearing Gretchen was quitting her job, told Frau Schneider that she knew of a young lady in Stuttgart who was looking for a live-in position. Doris Schneider asked for more information about the girl, but Yvonne couldn't provide many answers, all she knew about her was through a friend, Janet Vasco.

"I know her name is Ingrid, and she was working at a doctor's office in Stuttgart. Yvonne suggested you ask Ingrid to come down for an interview."

Janet Vasco brought Ingrid Schroeder from Stuttgart to meet the General and his wife. They first stopped to see Yvonne, and Ingrid liked the French lady, especially after Yvonne told her about her brother Simon, a member of the underground group who will help her to escape Germany. After they finished with Yvonne, they continued to the General's house. The interview went well and Doris hired her on the spot.

Ingrid settled in her own private room attached to the back of the General's house. It was cozy with just the essential furniture to make her stay comfortable. The first day, Doris Schneider spent some time explaining the work responsibilities and familiarizing her with the property, and at the end of the day Yvonne dropped by and the two ladies had a friendly chat.

On the evening of September, 1ˢᵗ 1939 Ingrid decided to go over to visit Yvonne and when she arrived, she found her in a state of panic.

"What is it Yvonne? You look in a terrible state. You are making me dizzy pacing back and forth, please sit down and tell me what is wrong," Ingrid ordered.

"Haven't you heard?" Yvonne snapped back at her.

"No, I haven't heard anything; would you please calm down and tell me what is going on?"

"Germany invaded Poland this morning, and do you know what this means?" "Well, Germany and Poland are going to fight another war I guess!" Ingrid answered nonchalantly.

"Wrong! There will be another world war and it will be worse than the Great War!"

"What you mean another world war?"

"Oh yes, there will be another war. Both France and Britain warned Hitler they will not stand idle and let him gobble yet another country, and this man is foolish enough to test their resolve."

Yvonne's prediction was very accurate indeed; both Britain and France declared war against Germany two days after the invasion of Poland. Yvonne sat with Ingrid to explain the consequences of this war on her escape plans. "You will not be able to go anywhere now with the war raging throughout the continent. It will take the underground time to adjust to the new realities before they figure how to help you escape. You are no longer at the top of their priorities, and all you can do for now is lie low and see how events develop."

Ingrid was devastated, she was trapped in a country she no longer likes, and worse, she will not be able to join her mother in the Holy Land any time soon. She went to her room that evening not knowing what the future may hold for her.

As a military family they were happy the war broke out. "This is our opportunity to exact revenge on our adversaries," Hermann told Hans, "Germany will be victorious, and we will restore our lost honor and show the whole world this nation is made of steel! Hitler our leader will take us from one victory to the next until our enemies raise their hands and surrender in defeat." Hans was very excited about the prospect and asked his father if he could join the army. "Not now son," Hermann answered lovingly, "you are only 14 years of age but maybe when you reach 17, you will be eligible to enlist. But I am so proud of you for showing the courage and the determination to defend the land of your ancestors!"

However, Hans was now of age to join the *Hitler Jugend* for boys between 14 and 18. He was looking forward all year long to begin training with the grownups, and to join his best friend Claus Schwartz. The two had grown both in size and strength and they were eager to prove themselves. They trained in the basics of military fighting and physical fitness, and were subjected to more brainwashing with Nazi propaganda and they were taught to believe in the superiority of the Aryan race. Those who prove themselves and show outstanding performance and allegiance to Hitler are selected to join the SS or the elite fighting units most loyal to the Fuehrer. Claus was very aggressive and strong, showing himself early on to be a shining role model with great potential.

CHAPTER 8

Ingrid was relieved when Hans and his family returned home after their weeklong visit; she couldn't understand Han's hostility towards her, but now he is gone, she can relax a little and get on with her life.

Europe however, was ablaze with the war raging across the continent, Germany, Italy and Japan joined in a military alliance called the Axis, while France and Britain joined forces to counter German ambitions in Europe. Reports coming from the front were not so good for Ingrid; the Axis forces seem to have the upper hand as the British retreated and the French capitulated in record time, and precisely as Yvonne predicted, Ingrid's escape plan was placed on hold for the time being.

After a day full of bad news from the war theater, Ingrid settled in her bedroom and locked the front door behind her. She was none too happy with the course of events in Europe and she felt discouraged and dispirited, so she pulled the duffel bag from under the bed and poured the contents on the mattress. She picked up the prayer book and started to read, and soon felt a degree of inner peace. But her mind was in a trance, imagining life with her mother in the Holy Land under clear night skies full of shining stars. At least her mother was surrounded by Jewish family and friends, in sharp contrast to Germany, where Jews are considered the enemy with no choice but to hide their true identity in order to survive. She collected the shawl, the prayer book and the gold Star of David, pulled them close to her heart and item by item, she kissed each before putting them back in the bag. She placed the duffel bag on the floor under her bed, turned the lights off and went to sleep.

Jews were feeling the full brunt of open hatred and discrimination against them; it was illegal for a Jew to become a citizen or marry a non-Jew, sell his property or work for the state; Jews who remained behind in Germany were apprehensive about the future and feared for their lives. They jostled to survive the onslaught of hate and propaganda perpetrated by the authorities and the general public and had no alternative but to hide. The state sponsored effort to rid Germany from its Jewish population was transformed into a policy called the Final Solution, the Nazi plan to physically exterminate them. Jews were rounded up and hauled by the trainload to concentration camps throughout Eastern Europe erected for their mass annihilation.

Hermann and Freda brought the children to visit her parents over Christmas and New Year. Ingrid was instructed to go to town and get groceries and other items the children cherish and she saw an opportunity to improve her tenuous relationship with Hans by baking him a cake for his 16th birthday. Hans didn't even attempt to speak to her, or even acknowledge the delicious cake she baked for him. When she met him face to face at the back of the house, he turned around and walked away, but seconds later she felt something hit her on the back. She turned to look and saw Hans with a snowball in his hand. As she wiped off the remnants of the slush, she admonished him sternly. "What did you do that for!" Hans stood there without saying a word. "Don't ever do that again, or else I will tell your father!" Hans was piqued by her tone; he turned and walked away in disgust.

During their ride back home, Freda asked the children if they had a good time.

"I don't care for Ingrid that much," stated Hans. "I preferred Gretchen instead."

"Oh, why not, what did she do to upset you?" Freda probed.

"Nothing in particular," he responded with indifference,

"Freda pressed on, "Both grandpa and grandma speak highly of her, and she seems a good worker and has good manners; you have no reason to dislike her, do you?" Hans didn't answer and kept quiet for the rest of the journey.

This untoward incident with Hans bothered Ingrid, and she repeated the events to Yvonne the following day after Hermann and his family left for Dresden. Yvonne didn't attach any significance to what happened; she simply dismissed the incident as immature behavior by a teenage boy. But Ingrid was not so sure, and told Yvonne she was thinking of telling the General about this bad behavior by his grandson.

"Just give the boy a little time; he will grow out of it eventually."

By the middle of 1942, the war was still simmering in Europe; Germany had opened two new fronts, one in the East, and the other was in North Africa. A few months earlier, Hitler decided to renege on promises he made to Stalin and ordered the invasion of Russia; the country was in the grip of a nasty war on all fronts.

As the conflicts escalated, Ingrid's patience waned and her confidence in the escape plan started to abate. She was in desperate need to alter the course of her life, but what options did she have? The very people who were supposed to help had their hands tied. She felt down and unmotivated to do anything; she went to her room, shut the door behind and started to cry, but then in a moment of mental confusion she pondered other choices. Could she just take matters into her own hands? Can she go it alone and cross the border into France by herself? Should she reveal her true identity to her enemies and let them decide her fate? She had enough of the whole thing; at this point she didn't care if she lived or died and cried out loud, "Oh God, I am so desperate! Please help me, please help me God!"

The following morning when she awoke, she got dressed and took Albert for his usual walk. It was starting out a beautiful sunny day and George, the farmer next door waved when she came close to the fence. She enthusiastically waved back; she always admired the old farmer and his wife for their energy and dedication, and wished with all her heart all Germans are as good as this honest couple. *I don't know why they hate us so much? I never hated anybody growing up in Stettin.*

On her way back to the house she thought about Yvonne and the underground group. Ideas in her head start to swirl so fast it made her dizzy, but she felt better when she made up her mind to visit the rough bunch hiding up in the forest, and after she finished her duties for the day, she hopped on her bicycle and peddled to Yvonne's house. Yvonne was tending to the flowers at the entrance; she waved from a distance and the two girls sat outside enjoying the autumn sun.

"What made you come by today?" Yvonne asked.

"I have been feeling so down for the last few months, and I never thought I would be here for as long as I have. But here I am, four years later and no end in sight, I don't know how much longer I can tolerate this!"

Yvonne hastily responded, "I hear you loud and clear, Ingrid, the question is what other choices are available at this juncture? The war is still going strong and this crazy Hitler has made a huge blunder by invading Russia. Mark my words, this war will be over soon. Hitler didn't learn from history; Napoleon before him failed to conquer Russia, his army was nearly decimated by the Russians and the brutally cold weather. I strongly believe this adventure in the East will mark the end for Germany."

"You sound like a school teacher, Yvonne, but I suspect you cannot give me a date for when this happy occasion might take place? I am rapidly losing confidence in the whole thing. I don't even know if the guys are still interested to help me leave this awful place!"

"Of course I don't know exactly when this war will end, but I can see the light at the end of the tunnel; it is already in plain view," Yvonne answered emphatically.

"I hope you're right, Yvonne, but I'm not too optimistic. I'm thinking I should go it alone and cross the border to France at night. The border isn't that far and I think I will be able to walk the distance on my own."

"You must be out of your mind! France is under occupation by the Nazis, and even if you manage to cross the border safely, what then? You still are in a German controlled area, and you will be arrested and cut to pieces by the Gestapo when they determine who you are. Actually, they will make mincemeat out of you and throw it to the guard dogs! You have to be sensible, Ingrid, and don't let your frustration rule your decisions," Yvonne warned.

Ingrid couldn't control her emotions. "I miss my mother so much, I miss being normal and I am fed up with it all!"

Yvonne felt a surge of sympathy for this young lady who had been through so much in her life. She reached out and put her arms round Ingrid and lovingly said, "Alright my dear, let me see if I can make arrangements to meet the guys next week. I will ask outright if they can take you to a safe country where you can board a boat to the Holy Land."

The following week Yvonne accompanied Ingrid to the regular rendezvous spot under the rock outcrop. Simon, always the joker, spotted them from a distance and hid behind a tree, and when they approached he jumped in front to scare them.

"What did you do that for?" Yvonne yelled.

"Just giving you some practice for when we take you across," he said with a broad smile.

"Stop it Simon!" Marcel, the group leader ordered. He turned his attention to Yvonne and Ingrid. "What is the happy occasion that brought you here today?"

"We came to talk to you about Ingrid's desire to cross to France on her own; she is fed up waiting for you guys!"

They all broke into laughter at that. "Are you serious or just out of your mind?" Simon sarcastically asked.

"Don't be horrible!" Yvonne shouted at her brother. "You are so heartless, this poor girl has been waiting for four years, and she wants to be with her family again. What is wrong with that?"

"Nothing is wrong with that," Marcel interjected, but taking her across is not as easy as you think. Troops are crossing the border back and forth all the time, France is under German control and I see no point to go there, it is not going to do her any good."

"But Spain is not under German control, is there any chance you can take me there?" Ingrid pleaded.

"To tell you the truth, we do work with other underground groups operating all over France, but we have no contacts inside the Spanish terri-tory. The logistics can be daunting to take you undetected all the way to the Spanish border; the distance is more than a thousand kilometers, and needs careful planning and coordination with different groups. I don't believe we can accomplish the mission successfully, I personally cannot guarantee your safety, and I recommend you stay here until the situation on the ground changes," Marcel cautioned.

"When exactly do you think the situation might change?" Ingrid asked softly.

"You never know for sure, it could be a month or a year from now, God only knows. But while you are here, you may wish to practice shooting a little," Marcel said in an attempt to change the course of the conversation.

"Yes please, I would love that." Marcel handed her his pistol, and began to show her how to fire it. "I know how to do it on my own," Ingrid confi-dently motioned him away.

The other members gave a big round of applause, and with whistles and claps ringing in her ear, she took aim at an empty can and fired. She pulled the trigger and fired again and again to even louder cheers.

Ingrid was rather disappointed when Doris told her that her daughter Freda and the children were coming to spend Christmas and New Year with them again; she was not looking forward to another encounter with Hans. She thought the best way was to avoid him and get out of his way. When the family arrived from Dresden she was surprised to see Hans was now over 6 feet tall, very masculine with big arms and a sturdy hulk of a body; he was a good looking young man indeed, with short blond hair and big blue eyes. She greeted him like she always did in the past, but again he never responded and just walked away. She didn't have the courage to bring the subject up with his grandmother; leaving him alone was the best thing to do for now, she told herself.

Hans's curiosity made him watch Ingrid with keen eyes, things however unintentionally developed in the wrong direction. Doris had a little accident inside the house and asked Hans to go over to Ingrid's room and summon her to clean the mess on the kitchen floor; Hans hurriedly ran to the back and knocked at Ingrid's door. There was no response coming from inside, so he knocked again. Still no response; he thought for a moment and instead of going back to inform his grandmother that Ingrid was not in her room, decided instead to have a quick look inside. Ingrid was in fact in her bathroom bathing, and she didn't hear the knock on the door, but just as she stepped out of the bathroom with only a towel wrapped round her, Hans opened the unlocked door and came in. Ingrid stood motionless when she saw him then gasped with indignation. However, she inadvertently dropped the towel and there she was, stark naked standing in front of him.

"What are you doing in here?" she angrily asked as she quickly bent down to pick up the towel and cover herself. Hans was red in the face and couldn't take his eyes off of her, but before she could say anything else he was already gone.

Hans turned eighteen years old in January, 1943, and like everybody his age he was called on to serve in the army. He used both his father and grandfather's connections to help him get assigned to the western front close to his best friend Claus. He and Claus were enlisted at the same time and had to undergo the requisite military training before they were sent to the front. Claus was commissioned with the SS, most loyal to Hitler, while Hans was sent to northern France.

As the tide of the war was appearing to ebb for the Germans, the Nazis began to accelerate their plan to exterminate all the Jews in Germany and Europe, they were out in force to apprehend and incarcerate them. Jews were used as forced labor in the most inhumane manner one can imagine, they were reduced to skeletons due to starvation, and when the time came, they were ordered to strip naked, herded inside death chambers and lethal fumes were released. The corpses were then collected and cremated in ovens constructed for this purpose. During the period between 1941 to the end of WWII, several millions people were gassed and burned to death. They were mostly Jews, but Gypsies and other undesirables, like the mentally ill and the handicapped met the same fate.

In late 1943 Nazi Germany started to feel the economic pinch; food was in short supply, and production of fuel and military hardware was severely reduced due to air raids on production facilities. The Red Army was in hot pursuit of the retreating Germans who suffered massive losses in the east and lost their vital fuel producing areas. The United States joined the Allies and by the beginning of 1944 the Italian army was overwhelmed by US and British forces. Hitler had no choice but to divert much needed troops and supplies to rescue his ally Italy. Morale among German troops began to show signs of strain and the average person in the street found store shelves almost empty. It was a trying time for the German people.

But by June 1944 the momentum had totally changed in favor of the Allies, General Eisenhower, the supreme commander of the Allied forces, ordered the successful invasion to liberate France. For the Germans the situation was bleak after the Allies achieved air superiority, and without adequate air cover, they couldn't withstand the fire power hitting their positions from land, sea and air. They retreated to the German border to defend the fatherland and Hans joined Claus when his unit reached neared Baden-Baden. He was unhappy with his new assignment to guard the ammunition depot in the outskirts of the city; he would rather participate in the defense of his beloved country with his brave comrades on the front. Nonetheless, the new assignment provided him the opportunity to be close to his grandparents.

Claus was pessimistic about the country's future, but Hans was still hopeful, still believing in the superiority and technical know-how of the Germans. Rumors were circulating that London, England, was attacked with a German super weapon called the V2 Rocket; this was a powerful rocket fitted with warheads which inflicted great damage to the British capital, and Hans proudly told Claus that his own father was involved in the production of these rockets at the Dresden facilities. He believed these rockets will turn the tide and make Germany victorious again. Claus on the other hand applauded the use of this new technology but believed it was too late to save Germany.

In February 1945, both the British and the Americans launched a massive air raid over the city of Dresden in retaliation for the indiscriminate rocket attack against London, and in a matter of few days, more than 3,500 allied planes and heavy bombers dropped thousands of tons of bombs on the city. It was the greatest firestorm to hit any city in Germany, and when the air campaign was over, the entire city was in ruins with more than 25,000 people dead. Hans, upon hearing the news, was concerned about his parents and sister; he waited anxiously to hear of his family's fate.

The General and his wife were also panicking about their daughter and her family, and when Hans came to visit, they asked if he had any information from the city. Hans was unable to tell them anything other than the grim news of massive civilian casualties. The General, despite his failing health, decided to travel to Stuttgart in a desperate effort to find his daughter.

Hans was awakened in the early hours of the morning with gunfire all around. A group of enemy infiltrators attempted to breach the storage depot he was assigned to guard and half asleep, he jumped out of bed and joined his fellow soldiers in a pitched battle that lasted more than an hour. Reinforcements arrived and the infiltrators either were killed or escaped, two of his own comrades were lost and scores were taken for treatment. His thoughts after the battle were with his injured friends, but he was worried numb about his family in Dresden still, and he couldn't wait for his grandfather to come back with news.

Claus came over to visit, and he too was not in great mood. He was worried about the fate of the country and conceded that the situation was very grave. There was talk among Gestapo and SS officers to organize an escape plan in the event Germany was defeated. He explained the reasons behind the talk; there will be a manhunt for the SS officers if Germany falls, and, they will be brought to justice for alleged crimes against the Jews and others. The two friends sat down with a bottle each of homemade schnapps, and drank one glass after the other and by late afternoon they were totally inebriated. Hans got up and said he'd hitch a ride to his grandparent's house, just to be away from it all and have a rest until they return the following day. Maybe they will have good news about his family.

He arrived at his grandparent's house just as Ingrid emerged from her room to take Albert for a stroll. When she was out of sight, Hans decided to have a quick look inside her room. He found it very neat and clean, nothing looked out of place. He opened the wardrobe and went through her clothing, everything was tidy and organized. In the bathroom, again nothing was out of the ordinary. He took his shoes off and lay on bed for a moment and decided to wait until she comes back. I am going to have fun with this girl, he told himself. Images of Ingrid's naked body were flashing in and out of his head, her pale white skin, her beautiful round breasts and her nice long legs, now he was aroused. He propped himself up and sat on the edge of the bed, fidgeting with anticipation, then decided to go to the main house and see if there was any beer or alcohol there. As he bent down to reach for his shoes under the bed, he could feel something else. He pulled out Ingrid's duffel bag and poured the contents on the bed. Hans was not ready for what was inside; he unraveled the prayer shawl and there they were--a Jewish prayer book and a gold chain with a Star of David attached. There was also a handwritten letter addressed to Rachael, and signed at the bottom by Rabbi Goldstein.

Hans was enraged, "This fucking bitch is a Jew! She has been spying on us!" Then he heard Albert barking outside.

As Ingrid approached her room, she wondered why the door was wide open, so she picked up her pace and hurried inside. She was surprised to see the raging face of Hans waiting for her behind the door. He was wearing his uniform, which was unusual.

With a trembling voice he started, "You fucking Jew! You have been deceiving us for so long, but you can't con us anymore, you fucking Jewish bitch!"

Ingrid instantly noticed the duffel bag and its contents scattered on the floor, and she realized her life was in mortal danger, and she was no match for this raging animal. And there was a gun tucked on his side. This is the end for me, she thought.

"Take off your clothes you filthy whore!" he ordered. Ingrid stood trembling with fear, unable to comply with his demand. "I said take off your clothes you fucking Jewish bitch!"

"I ca…ca…can't…"

He slapped her across the face and with his powerful hand threw her on bed and lifted her skirt. He was very aroused now as he removed her clothes until she was totally naked, then struggled to take off his own while keeping her pinned down. He was intent on humiliating her.

"You are just a Jew cockroach! Worth nothing! Nobody gives a damn about you!"

His weight crashed down on top of her and she could smell the alcohol as his teeth were bared over her face and he tore into her. Then he was pushing as hard as he could, his sweat dripping in her eyes. His hot stinking breath caused her to gag and the power of his thrusts slammed her head against the headboard. Then his body tensed and she could feel him gripping her hair and her breast tighter but she could barely breathe, let alone scream. Suddenly it was all over and his body slumped to the side.

She was finally able to inhale as he rolled off the bed, swearing, "There you go, you fucking Jewish bitch! Did you like that? Because I can do it to you again, you whore!"

Hans got up too quickly, reeled and staggered towards the bathroom. She could hear him cursing and swearing; it sounded like he was having trouble urinating. She was sure he intended to kill her when he was finished. Looking at the door, she wondered if she could escape. Probably not, she was stark naked, and even if she could, where would she run to? He'd outrun her and wrestle her to the ground, and then...

Ingrid searched the familiar room from one corner to the other until her eyes fixed on his uniform, his holster dangling on the side of the chair where he had thrown his clothes recklessly in a moment of passion and temper. She slipped out of bed and inched on her hands and knees towards it. Grabbing the holster, she flipped the side open and drew out the gun.

She could still hear him in the bathroom, loud and drunk, pushing to finish; the intermittent splash was now a trickle, he'd be out soon. As she held the gun in her hand her entire body was trembling, her face and hair were drenched and her hands were sweaty. With warm blood sticky between her legs, she felt like a cornered animal, but she was ready to kill this son of a bitch. Ingrid couldn't imagine what a Jewish girl would face for shooting a Nazi officer, but she had heard things. The images sent a shudder down her spine and brought her to alert. She ducked down beside the bed, hands firmly gripping the weapon.

Suddenly his massive arm flung across the door jamb, and the rest of his hulk emerged a second later hunched under the creaky bathroom door frame, his eyes glistening red, sweat streaming down his face. Hans looked eager for another encounter with his prey. Squinting into the dark room, he spotted her crouching on the floor beside the metal bed, gun in hand. As he considered the situation, she got into a better position and took aim. Nervous but intent, her eyes locked his in a death stare.

"Drop the gun, you fucking whore!"

Ingrid gripped the gun a little tighter with both hands, finger twitching on the trigger.

"Drop the gun, you fucking Jewish bitch! I will skewer you!" His hands demonstrated his intent as Hans took a small step towards her.

As the deafening sound of the gunshot echoed in the small space, his body jolted back against a wall and slid to the floor. Blood came sputtering out of his right thigh all over the room.

"You fucking bitch, I will kill you with my bare hands!" he shouted.

In agony, he managed to turn his body around and attempted to stand up. With his hand over the thigh wound he briefly regained his balance, but as he lunged towards her, there was one more deafening sound. Hans dropped, screaming like a gored bull.

Ingrid stood up, her body cold and trembling. She could see his body slumped over in front of the bathroom door, blood pooling around him. He was still murmuring faintly. She grabbed her clothes and quickly dressed, collected the items on the floor and put them back in her khaki duffel bag and bolted out of the room, leaving the door wide open.

Her old bicycle was leaning against the weathered stone wall where she'd left it, under the oak tree. She turned the bicycle around and straddled the painfully hard seat, duffel bag swung over her back.

CHAPTER 9

George was on his way out to the field when he heard the noise the first time Ingrid fired; he turned towards his wife and asked if she heard it too. The second time, they had no doubt it was a gun and it was coming from the direction of the General's property.

George was in a state of panic when he arrived at the scene. He found Hans' naked and bloody body on the floor and he immediately alerted the police. Hans was clinging to life when paramedics took him to hospital, and since he was a non-civilian, the case was turned over to the Gestapo to investigate possible underground activities in the vicinity.

The Gestapo quickly concluded the old farmer didn't know who was responsible for the shooting. But they found out the owner of the residence was none other than Hans' grandfather, and the General was away in Stuttgart. They also learned the General employed Ingrid, a live-in young lady who was hired to help with household duties. The farmer further told them that Ingrid was at the house earlier on, as he saw her walking the dog not too long ago, but she was nowhere to be seen and Hans was lying on the floor with a gun wound to his leg when he arrived.

The Gestapo officer in charge of the investigation asked the farmer where Ingrid could have gone; she obviously was a suspect and the police would like to talk to her.

"Oh no," the farmer told them, "Ingrid is a very nice girl. She has been with the family for six years, and everybody likes her. But her only close friend is Yvonne, who works for Colonel Hendrix."

The colonel answered the door when the Gestapo came round. "No, I haven't seen her today," he answered politely, "She normally comes here to see Yvonne, my maid. "She lives in her room at the back of the house; please follow me and I will take you down to talk to her." The officer determined after interviewing Yvonne that Ingrid was not there and Yvonne had not seen her at all that day. Yvonne however echoed the farmer's description of Ingrid as a very nice girl, who in no way was capable of committing a heinous crime.

Light rain started to come down as Ingrid was racing away from the Colonel's house after she stopped to tell Yvonne what Hans did to her.

"Where have you shot him? Is he still alive?" Yvonne asked sympathetically.

"I think he is still alive, he was murmuring and making noise when I left the room. I think I shot him in the leg," Ingrid answered with anguish.

"This boy hates Jews, and he probably would have killed you and nobody would have given a damn because you are Jewish. You must not come inside my room; the Gestapo will come looking for you once they discover Hans was shot. You better leave right away and head to the forest, and ask the guys to help you. I will stay here, because the Gestapo no doubt will come looking for you at my place, and it would be suspicious if I was gone, too. Be brave and be safe, dear Ingrid, and may the Lord come to your rescue in your hour of need."

As the silhouette of a person approached the rock outcrop, they stood at guard with hands on their guns, but they soon realized it was Ingrid, struggling to make the last few hundred yards. They were horrified to see her in the condition she was in; the poor girl must have taken several hits falling off of her bike in the slippery rain. She was bleeding all over, her skin was lacerated and her body and clothes were absolutely drenched and muddy, and she could barely stand when she finally reached them. The guys sprang into action the moment Ingrid finished telling them what happened.

"We better take her out of here, before she passes out," Marcel ordered. "The Gestapo will have their dogs on her trail and will be here soon."

Claus was in the hospital when Hans woke up after surgery. He was anxious to hear from his best friend what happened, and who in fact shot him and why. Hans, still weak and tired, proceeded to tell his friend about Ingrid. "I accidentally found a suspicious bag under her bed, and when I emptied the bag, it became apparent this slut was a Jewish whore hiding in plain sight, and probably passing information to our enemies! I was so mad, I lost control, and all I wanted at that moment was to humiliate and degrade the bitch. But she stole my pistol and shot me when I came out of the bathroom. Please, Claus, find her for me, I want to kill the whore with my own hands!"

The Gestapo indeed went looking for Ingrid; the person who was of most interest to them was Yvonne. They interrogated her once more, but she was adamant she knew nothing about Ingrid's whereabouts, and she expressed shock and alarm when told Ingrid was in fact Jewish. The Gestapo believed her after the colonel corroborated her story. Claus suspected Ingrid maybe hiding out in the Black Forest, or could be lying low at a safe house somewhere in the area. He instructed his men to keep an eye out for her, and he also organized a search party in the Black Forest nearby but came up empty.

Hans was released from the hospital once his wounds healed somewhat. The doctors told him he was barely clinging to life when paramedics brought him in due to the massive loss of blood, but they also assured him his injuries were no longer life threatening. However his ankle was shattered, and it's likely he will walk with a limp for the rest of his life. Hans was taken to his grandparents' house to recuperate, but when he arrived the mood was utterly grim and sad. The General and Doris were devastated after they found out Freda, Hermann and Elizabeth had all died when the house they lived in sustained a direct hit during the blitz over the city of Dresden. Hans wished he, too, was dead when told about the fate of his family. He felt utterly helpless.

The group scrambled to find a place to hide Ingrid. The French border was the new front after the Allied forces pushed the Nazis back to Germany, so crossing there was no longer a consideration. Marcel suggested they keep moving around in the woods until the Nazis give up on their search, but Jean, the French farm hand with the yellowing front teeth suggested a different idea, "Why don't we hide her in the big barn close to Willstätt? I worked in the area and know it well. The farm backs all the way to the edge of the woods and when night falls you can reach the barn without being noticed." Marcel knew exactly the farm Jean suggested on the other side of Offenburg, and it lay in the opposite direction to where the Gestapo was expected to concentrate their search. He thought it was a splendid idea and they could hide Ingrid there for few days while coming up with another plan.

That evening Ingrid was taken to the rear of the farm and they waited until the farmer turned off the lights in the house. The big red barn was near the edge of the woods and it was stacked high with hay bales stored for the cattle's winter feed. There was a wide double door at the front and a small door in the back. If Ingrid was behind the bales of hay nobody could see she was hiding there.

The girl was utterly exhausted by the time they dropped her at the barn. It was dark and eerie inside, and she was in so much pain she began to cry and lamented her bad luck. She raised her hands in supplication, "Oh God, I beg you oh, Lord, to see me through this ordeal. Please, God help me, all I want is to get out of here and be with my family again, please, please God, I beg you for help."

Ingrid was sound asleep when Marcel came in the following evening with some food and drink. He told her they weren't quite ready to take her out of this place yet, but assured her they were actively looking for ways, and as soon as they work out a plan they will be back.

"But how long before you come back, Marcel? I am very afraid at night here on my own."

"Be patient my dear," he answered reassuringly, "just be patient and we will get you out, that I promise."

Only two days after Hans was shot, the Gestapo abandoned their effort to search for Ingrid. They concluded that she must have had an accomplice, and had been smuggled out of Germany. They did all they could under the circumstances, and given their resources, she was not a priority. Claus went to visit Hans and informed him of this.

"What the hell?" Hans was furious.

Claus explained, "The Gestapo wasted precious time before they even launched the search and she just disappeared into thin air." He continued, "But I believe Ingrid was hiding somewhere in a safe house waiting for the right moment to escape. She's still her, I'm sure. We'll find her."

Claus was getting disenchanted with the whole thing; he knew some of his SS comrades were discussing escape plans, and they were all resigned to the fact the Allies and the Russians will invade Germany soon. South Tyrol, an autonomous area of German speaking people located in the north of Italy was the focus of their secret plan. It enjoys a considerable level of self-government and shares borders with Switzerland and Austria and is dominated by the Alps; they carefully chose the location because the population are fiercely pro Germany and likely to come to the aid of German escapees. However, Claus was torn between staying put and fighting the enemies till death or the opportunity to leave his beloved Germany behind. He can see the chances for victory are next to none, but ultimately decided he wasn't ready to go anywhere; he was going to remain and help his Fuehrer, his country, his family and his friends in their hour of need.

Ingrid's patience wore thin as she sat tucked up between bales of hay not knowing when the end will come, or if at all, but suddenly she heard the back door open and the familiar voice of Marcel.

"Get ready right now! We're taking you out of here right this minute!"

Ingrid jumped up, picked her duffel bag and ran, hand in hand with Marcel. It was raining and a thin layer of fog blanketed the fields for as far as the eye can see. "We deliberately chose a day like this," he explained, "because the reduced visibility will increase our chances of success." Ingrid looked composed that evening but was very nervous and frightened inside. The plan involved an accomplice with a small farm truck who was supposed to pick them up at a pre-arranged location, then, drive north to the liberated part of Germany using small unpaved farming lanes not frequented by the Nazis. But there was one hurdle on the way; the Nazis have erected road blocks to search motorists for infiltrators and army deserters and in order to bypass the last road block, they must hide in the woods until the accomplice driving the truck goes through the barricade. He would then pull over after the second bend in the road, then get out of the truck and lift the hood cover, pretending he was looking into an engine problem. The waiting party will recognize the signal and quickly make their way out of the woods to the waiting truck, at which time the driver was to speed off and use country lanes to reach safety in the liberated areas.

"Halt!" the truck driver was ordered by the troops manning the road block. "Your papers." The driver was ready and handed his identification to the Gestapo officer as the other soldiers looked around the vehicle and in the back. "Where are you heading tonight?" The officer demanded.

"I am going home," the driver calmly answered.

"And where have you been this late in the evening?"

"I was trapped in Stuttgart because of the air raid, but when the raid was over, I decided to come home."

"Very well," the officer said, and sent him on his way. But the Gestapo officer thought the answers the truck driver gave were rather rehearsed, and felt he wasn't genuine; he immediately called the Stuttgart office, to verify if there had been an air raid earlier in the evening. When learning there hadn't been, he gave orders to follow the vehicle; he instructed the troops to turn off their car headlights and keep their distance.

Marcel and Ingrid saw the truck coming from a distance. It stopped and the driver got out and left the hood up as planned.

"Time for us to run, Ingrid!" Marcel ordered.

The Gestapo officer in the lead car stopped when the truck stopped. Hunched behind his car to watch, he saw the driver get out and go to the front of the vehicle and lift the hood. His heart started pounding when he saw two silhouettes running from the edge of the wood towards the waiting truck, and he ordered his troops to move in.

Marcel saw the German troops coming, and he shouted at Ingrid, "Turn back! Turn back!" Ingrid didn't understand his command, she simply was too eager to run.

Marcel made it back to the woods and quickly disappeared. But Ingrid was now in the hands of the enemy.

CHAPTER 10

Claus was at his best friend's house the following morning. "We got her last night!" he proudly announced.

"Got who?" the still sleepy Hans replied.

"Ingrid. The bitch was with members of the underground and a suspicious officer followed the getaway truck that was supposed to pick her up; when she emerged from the woods, the officer arrested her. I told you she was hiding somewhere, but the bitch is in our hands now! I'm going to make that dog scream…" Claus gestured his intent.

"No, you won't!" Hans announced with excitement, "She's mine. I am the one who will torture the Jewish scum with my own hands. I will take enormous pleasure in every shriek and moan she makes after what she did to my foot."

They made their way to the holding cell where Ingrid was kept. She didn't recognize either of them when they walked in, her face was already bloody, her eyes and face were swollen, and she was lying on the floor of her cell barely aware. Hans used his uninjured foot to flip her over, and then with all the strength he could garner, kicked her again on the face and all over her body. He knelt down and started punching her face. The more she screamed the more ferocious he became. He picked her up in his arms and lifted her over his head, and with all his power slammed her down on the cell's hard floor. He jumped on top of her once more, pummeling her face and chest. Then he lit a cigarette, took a couple of draws until it was glowing red, and stamped it on her neck. The smell of burning skin filled the air. Ingrid screamed until she lost consciousness.

Hans walked out of the cell satisfied. "The Judas whore got what she deserved," he sighed. "You should bury that bitch alive, Claus, I don't ever want to see her again. She is a dirty scum. Or you could break every bone in her body and throw her out with the garbage where she belongs, I don't give a damn what you do with it."

"Don't you worry Hans, she's on her way to Dautmergen. They will gas her first, then incinerate her in the oven like the rest of the filthy race she belongs to."

Later that day Ingrid's almost lifeless body was thrown in the back of a military truck and taken to the prison facilities at Dautmergen, but unknown to Claus, the gas chambers had already been dismantled on the orders of the third Reich, in order to eliminate any evidence of the atrocities. Therefore, Ingrid's body was dumped on the floor of a large room full of other prisoners. A guard walked in with a bucket of ice cold water to dump on her naked body; her body twitched a little in response, but Ingrid was so severely beaten, she couldn't offer any resistance. Another guard dragged her by the hair to one corner where other prisoners were sitting. Her buttock was bleeding profusely and left a trail along the floor.

Two days later she regained consciousness; she squinted through her swollen eyes, but all there was to see was death and carnage around her. Men and women so thin their ribs were visible. She could hear the screams and moans of the starving women and children, and she noticed the guards discarding the bodies of the ones who didn't make it through the night. The most sadistic guards came in and lashed at the prisoners with thick sticks and leather whips for no reason other than the pleasure of hearing them scream.

General Dwight Eisenhower, the Allied Supreme Commander in Europe had almost ninety divisions of a multi nation task force amassed at the German border and ready for battle, and on the first week of March, just few days before Ingrid was captured, the field commanders received orders to cross the border into Germany to begin the liberation. Claus was there at the front, but he knew, like the rest of his Gestapo comrades, it was futile. Nevertheless he fought to the bitter end, satisfied with the knowledge that if he falls, at least, he would have fallen with honor and his blood will soak into German soil where it belongs.

Hans was worried for the fate of Germany and his own future, but he was in no condition to fight because of his injury. He wanted to be there at the front line with his comrades and was sad he wasn't able, but both his grandparents were old, sick and almost totally deaf, and he needed to be with them. It was clear his grandfather's health took a steep turn for the worse after the loss of his much loved daughter and her family. Hans saw him lying in bed most of the time staring at the ceiling with a vacant expression as if he was asking God, why are you keeping me alive, please hurry up and take me off of this earth. The last few months had been the worst in his life; he had a brilliant military career and fought many battles, and he saw death and destruction, but nothing like the misery that had now befallen Germany. Yet despite all his misery, he was thankful to God; at least Hans was still alive.

Ingrid woke up in the middle of the night to the horrifying sounds of women who were being beaten by a group of guards. The rest of the prisoners just sat watching but were powerless to help. She was cold and shivering, every twitch and turn was sheer agony, and she was very hungry and thirsty. She turned to the girl who sat on the floor next to her and asked, "When will they feed us?" The lady, who was obviously in as much pain as she, looked at her with shock and bewilderment, she could not even muster the strength to laugh at the absurdity of the question.

"You're lucky if they give us something every three to four days," she warily answered. Ingrid gazed at her in disbelief, but when she looked around, she understood why. The prisoners were like skeletons, fleshless skin stretched over bones. She knew she was going to die, she could smell the stench of death. All she could hear were the cries of starving women and children. She didn't care about anything now except food; her stomach was cramping and she kept swallowing her own saliva to keep the hunger pains at bay, but to no avail.

The following morning one of the women guards came in with a bucket full of leftover food and dumped the whole thing on the floor of the cell. Ingrid had never seen people move faster in her life, it seems they all just dove at the pile at once. Ingrid's hunger forced her to do the same, and she was shoving whatever bits her hands could catch in her mouth, but it was all over in a matter of seconds, and every morsel disappeared. She managed to swallow just few mouthfuls, it was meager but it did help curb her pains a little. She stayed awake all day long thinking about her life and if she will ever get out of there alive. The prisoners could now hear bombs exploding not too far away, and they seemed to be getting nearer by the hour.

Claus' platoon was finally overrun after a heroic fight and his unit disintegrated all at once. The commanding officer came and told his men, "You guys have been terrific, but you are now on your own." Claus like many of his comrades shed his army uniform fast, and ran to hide somewhere; many comrades surrendered, others went home or escaped to the countryside, and a few were able to cross to Switzerland. Claus, who didn't have anywhere else to go, headed to the General's house to meet up with Hans and try to convince him to run.

"I have no choice but to stay here," Hans answered his friend. "I will not leave my grandparents to fend for themselves. If I leave them, they will die very quickly."

The bomb explosions were now loud and clear, and the prisoners who were still alert determined the fighting must be just a few miles away. Ingrid didn't know the cause, but there was a lot of bizarre activity at the prison. The guards didn't seem to conduct their business as usual, and she saw weird goings on in the courtyard; filing cabinets were taken out from offices and hauled away to waiting trucks, documents were burned and office furniture was smashed to bits. Because of her starvation she couldn't keep her eyes open for any length of time, her spirit was low, and the other prisoners around her were dropping dead faster than she could count. All she was thinking about was food, she never imagined the acute pain of hunger could be so severe, but there was nothing to be had and she was slipping in and out of consciousness. When darkness fell, the only sounds were the moans of the hungry and the awful racket of gunfire outside the prison walls.

CHAPTER 11

Sergeant André Chevalier with the First French Army was the first to enter the prison cell at Dautmergen. What he saw inside made him run out immediately; he was so sick, he bent over and threw up on the pavement. His commanding officer rushed over, "What is wrong, André?"

"You better put your mask on sir," André replied, "the place is full of bodies and the stench is unbearable."

The pair put their masks on and went back in, but they weren't truly prepared for the scene before them; the dead and dying prisoners left behind by the escaping Nazis were beyond description, the conditions were appalling. Children, men and women's bodies were strewn everywhere and the few who were still alive were so hungry and sick, the officer immediately called in the field medical team as well as a photographer to document the misery and the sheer hell these people had endured.

The French commander who entered the Offenburg area was in no mood to compromise; he gave strict orders to his units to respond with vigor against armed resistance. He also issued orders to arrest all males between the ages of 16 to 60 with no exceptions, and all escape routes were to be sealed, including the Black Forest. When the soldiers came round to the General's house in their wider effort to rid the area of Nazis, both Hans and Claus were arrested against the General's protest. Hans felt so sorry for his grandfather who once was a powerful figure, now reduced to beg just an average soldier to save his grandson from being arrested. But the French ignored his pleas and Hans and Claus were taken down to a schoolyard in Offenburg where the French army converted the school compound into a detention facility. When they arrived, there were hundreds of other men standing in line waiting to be admitted.

After being processed, both guys were pushed inside the courtyard. French soldiers stood on guard round the perimeter wall with orders to shoot anyone attempting to escape.

On April 30 1945, two weeks after Hans and Claus were arrested, the prisoners heard a joyful celebration when the news of Hitler's suicide reached the French troops. The detainees realized this was the end, the collapse of the Nazi regime. A week later, when the French troops spontaneously began to sing La Marseillaise, outside there were hugs and tears and firing of weapons in celebration of Germany's unconditional surrender, but it was disheartening for the guys in prison to experience this incredible defeat.

A short time later, George the farmer came to see Hans at the temporary detention facility and informed him his grandfather passed away the night before from heart complications, and was buried earlier that morning. Hans dropped to his knees and started to cry.

"Come on, Hans! Your grandfather was a fine soldier and a noble man. He had a good long life, and you should be proud of him," George advised before he left.

The French troops turned the POWs into laborers to remove dirt and debris from the streets, work on farms to help with food production, and whatever menial jobs were required; the western allies didn't have any intention to keep the German prisoners longer than necessary; they realized most of the soldiers were ordinary people forced to serve in the army. SS officers however, were treated more harshly and kept in seclusion, and the few who were suspected of pervasive ideological Nazi leanings were deemed not eligible for release. After months of incarceration the POWs had to appear before a review tribunal. Hans, who was young with no known records of impropriety, was among the lucky ones slated for release. But since Claus lied about his true identity at the beginning, and was suspected of involvement in war crimes, he was not eligible.

Ingrid was in a coma for a few days after the French troops found her near death on the floor of Dautmergen prison camp. It was sheer luck and the skillful effort of the field medical team that saved her life, but her condition remained grave indeed. Her heartbeat was almost flat when she was found, and doctors gave her little chance to survive. Malnutrition, broken bones, heart failure and septic wounds were some of the afflictions the doctors had to deal with, but a few days after intensive treatment she started to show small signs of improvement.

The condition of the prisoners when they were found was indeed beyond description. The few who were lucky enough to survive were in desperate need for medical attention; the field doctor could only administer rudimentary, yet vital treatment to save them before he ordered their transfer to hospitals in the French city of Strasburg. The troops documented the scene before them, cleaned and disinfected the whole compound and closed the facility pending further investigation. The prisoners were in such a state, the majority were unconscious and the few who were too sick to speak, had no identification.

Ingrid finally opened her eyes after two weeks in intensive care. She was bandaged from head to toe and was fed intravenously, and nurses constantly checked the monitors for signs of progress. Several days later her condition was such that the doctors were able to treat her bone fractures and skin infections.

The doctor who treated her when she first arrived at the hospital came to check on her, accompanied by a woman.

"Hello, I am Doctor Edward Foster and this is Dr. Jane Foster my wife. Can you speak?" he asked through an interpreter.

"Yes," Ingrid faintly answered.

"What is your name?"

"Ingrid."

"Hello Ingrid, I hope you feel a little better now. We want you to know you are safe now, in a hospital in Strasburg. We have treated most of your wounds and I can see the swelling in your face and neck has gone down considerably. I am pleased you are getting a little more color in your face. Dr. Jane and I will continue to look after you until you fully recover. Do you have any questions, Ingrid?"

"No," she whispered.

Ten weeks passed since Ingrid was admitted and her condition improved significantly. A hospital administrator came to the ward and obtained all her personal information, her full name, last known address, date of birth and the events that led to her capture and imprisonment at Dautmergen.

"How are you Ingrid?" Dr. Foster asked later that day while checking her pulse and looking at her chart.

"I feel much better doctor, thank you so much."

"I'm so glad to hear that. I expect you to recover completely, but we have two pieces of information for you Ingrid; I have one good and one not too good, which one would you like to hear first?" Doctor Foster always tried to keep it light and personable with his patients and his manner went a long way to aid in their progress.

Ingrid thought for a minute, "I haven't had any good news in a while, and I had my share of bad news, please start with the bad one, hopefully the good one will cheer me up at last!"

"Well, I am sorry but it looks like you will have a permanent scar on your neck, it will shrink a little bit and behind your pretty dark hair, it's not too conspicuous."

Ingrid was relieved; the bad news was not too bad. "Oh, and what is the good news, Doctor?"

"You are pregnant, you are approximately 12 weeks into your term; it is a miracle you didn't lose your baby given the ordeal you have been through. By the grace of the Lord, your baby was saved."

When that registered, Ingrid's face turn red and contorted, and she began to cry. Dr. Jane was a little baffled and didn't expect this reaction, she held Ingrid's hand and asked her, "What is the matter, Ingrid? We thought you would be so glad to hear this?" But Ingrid was inconsolable, she simply pulled the bed sheet over her face and her cries turn into sobs.

Dr. Edward Foster was born to a wealthy Quaker family in Santa Barbara, California. He met his wife Jane, also a devout Quaker, at a hospital in Los Angeles where they both worked and they were married few months before WWII started. When the United States entered the war, they both volunteered to work with a field unit accompanying the troops. After their unit swept through France and continued east to liberate Germany, the two doctors were asked to remain in Strasburg to attend to more complex cases. The majority of their patients were American GI's, French soldiers and members of the resistance, Ingrid however was the first Jewish victim they treated. Dr. Jane and her husband were particularly upset to see Ingrid in the condition she was in when she arrived, they couldn't believe how cruel the Nazis were and how much this girl endured. Dr. Jane nearly cried when she read her report for first time; Ingrid touched her heart and she promised to give all she could to save her.

They enlisted the service of a psychiatrist to help her overcome the psychological scars; the girl was still so young with a whole life ahead of her. But she had no one left to go to once released from hospital. She had nowhere to sleep and her pregnancy added to the dilemma. Doctor Jane knew of a

Quaker organization based in New York City who offered assistance to war refugees to immigrate to the United States to start a new life, and she decided to write to them to find out if they would offer help to Ingrid.

Her husband, interestingly argued against helping Ingrid immigrate to America, Palestine is where he thought Ingrid should go, he attempted to convince his wife.

"Didn't Ingrid say she has a mother in Palestine?" But before he continued with his argument, Jane interrupted; she could see where this conversation was going.

"Yes dear, she did say that, but Ingrid has not heard from her mother in seven years, and you know the situation in Palestine between Arabs and Jews is so volatile. Would you under the circumstances send her to another troubled area with so much turmoil? This girl has suffered enough with war and strife, and it is high time she leads a normal life. She may want to go to Palestine in the future, but now is the wrong time." Jane did receive a reply from the Quaker organization, signed by the organization's secretary Drew Ingram, stating her willingness to help Ingrid when she arrives in America. She also mentioned in the letter the list of potential families who are willing and able to take in refugees fleeing war-torn Europe.

Ingrid's recovery was in short, miraculous. The use of her arms and hands came back remarkably well, and she could walk on her own unaided. Her weight increased significantly, and all her functions returned to normal. After six months in the Strasburg hospital she became part of the family; everybody loved sweet Ingrid and offered help when she needed it, even the dour faced physiotherapist went out of her way to lend support and assistance. Her conspicuous pregnancy stirred extra sympathy, and nurses stopped to give her love and advice yet there was an underlying feeling of guilt among them all that this beautiful girl was subjected to the most inhumane treatment by fellow Europeans.

"What would you like to do when you get out of here?" Dr. Jane asked.

Ingrid hesitated for a moment, she really did not know. Looking at the doctor, she admired this lady and wished she could be like her. "I really don't know what to do with myself. I came to Offenburg almost seven years ago in the hope to escape Germany and unite with my mother in the Holy Land, but I was trapped... I still would like to join my mother over there but I have no money or the resources to go on my own. I don't even know where and how to search for her when I get there..."

Dr. Jane listened intently and felt a great surge of sympathy. "I understand how you feel and I am so sorry you have been through so much hardship. Ingrid, I feel we can help you settle somewhere where you have the opportunity to regain your life and prosper in the future, and I strongly suggest the United States. It's the only country in the world that welcomes you and can provide the ideal opportunity to move up in life. I also suggest, once you settle down there, you can search for your mother in the Holy Land and reunite with her in the future, how does this sound?"

"I don't know much about America and I don't speak English. How do you expect me to communicate with people there?"

"That is a valid point, but many people from around the world have immigrated to America. At first they didn't speak English, but they learned along the way and made a success of their life. I am confident you can do the same. And right now the situation in the Holy Land is rough and likely to get worse, so please think about that. I can help you settle in America if you wish and help find you a job, so you can provide for yourself and your baby. Let me know what you decide."

Dr. Jane stopped to see Ingrid the following week. She handed her two books, one was about America with photos and illustrations, the other to help her learn English. "These books will give you an idea about the United States and maybe help you make up your mind!"

"That is so kind of you doctor, but I decided America is where I want to go for now. I always wanted to visit the country and see the skyscrapers and the statue of the woman in the harbor, and I believe Americans like you are very nice people and easy to get along with."

"You are so nice Ingrid, I am so glad you made up your mind, and I believe you made the right choice. By the way, we call the woman statue in the harbor the Statue of Liberty. It was a present from France to the United States to mark America's independence."

After this conversation, Dr. Jane saw to it that arrangements were quickly made for Ingrid to travel to America after her release from hospital. The Quaker organization agreed to help the young pregnant girl settle in Michigan with a Quaker family. Travel documents were obtained from the US consulate in Paris and the US Navy consented to let Ingrid cross on one of the passenger ships leased to bring the troops home from Europe.

CHAPTER 11

Hans was released after a few months of incarceration in the makeshift prison. A scene of complete devastation greeted him on the streets: collapsed buildings everywhere, piles of rubble and debris, snapped electrical lines, empty stores and hardly any food available for the starving population. Hans went home to ponder the next chapter in his life but when he arrived he found his grandmother sick and bedridden, with sores all over her body. She survived her ordeal after the death of her husband with the help of George and his wife. Hans was horrified to see her in the terrible condition she was in, with hardly any medicine left to treat her, but the food situation was his first and foremost concern. With many of the working age male population still incarcerated, there was severe shortage of laborers and farms were left fallow. When the occupying force realized the only way to feed the defeated people was to release some of the prisoners to work the land, Hans saw his opportunity and he was one of the lucky few to find a job at a farm not too far from home.

Claus, however, remained in prison for the time being. He regretted not listening to his SS comrades who slipped out of the country before they were captured. He heard many made it to South America where they settled and built new lives, and when Hans came to visit him as he often did, he mentioned the idea to his friend, but the timing wasn't right. Life in prison was monotonous for Claus with no outlook for release, so he and several of the former SS officers started to talk about escape. It involved help from the outside, and Claus assured the co-conspirators they can count on Hans.

The plan was to take advantage of the time when the prisoners were working in the field, and the guards who had become lax after so many outings with the compliant prisoners, could be easily distracted. One group of inmates would pretend to engage in a physical fight among themselves to which the guards would respond, providing the opportunity for the other group of inmates to come from behind and overpower them, escaping in one of the vehicles that brought them to the field. Hans will have made arrangements for them to hide out at a safe house until the time was right to slip out of the country on forged documents he had secured from one of his connections.

As planned, Claus and his comrades made it to Austria and then to the sympathetic region of South Tyrol. From there it was rather easy to obtain travel documents, based on the Red Cross assumptions the prisoners were stateless and therefore eligible, and of course with assistance from the local people and some clergy in Rome who had Fascist leanings. By the end of 1945, Allied forces had moved their troops to the Far East War Theater with Japan, therefore, it wasn't hard for Claus and his friends to make it to the Port of Genoa on the Mediterranean coast where they purchased tickets to travel on a passenger ship heading to South America.

CHAPTER 12

The time finally arrived for Ingrid to leave the hospital. She was sad to say goodbye to Dr. Jane Foster and her husband, and so grateful to these wonderful people for the help they gave her. It made her regain hope in the decency of human beings after the incredible trauma she had been through. Dr. Jane gave her another book with many photos of America as a parting gift.

"All the best, Ingrid, We hope you like the United States and settle well, our sincere wishes for a safe journey."

Ingrid cried with joy for these wonderful doctors who went out of their way to help a total stranger. She kissed many of the staff with whom, she had become so familiar, and hugging Dr. Jane and her husband, promised, "I will never forget your kindness doctors, I will be forever in your debt."

She was taken to the port town of Calais to board a boat full of American GIs returning home from Europe. They stopped at Southampton in the south of England to pick more GIs before going on to New York City. Ingrid blew a kiss as they sailed away from the English coast as a token of appreciation to the brave British who stood against all odds to fight Germany alone.

The returning GIs were a very happy bunch, who smoked and drank and laughed. The mood was merry and friendly, and everybody was anxious to get home and get on with their lives. Still, Ingrid's limited English made her feel lonely, she was not yet used to the American culture, it was certainly different from the traditionally more conservative culture found in Germany.

After more than four days at sea, the ship approached the American coast and Ingrid recognized the New York City skyline from a distance. She was so excited when the boat sailed past the Statue of Liberty before it eventually docked at Pier 88 on the Hudson estuary. Passengers filed down the gangway and ran with open arms towards waiting relatives. Men and women embraced, there were kisses and tears and everybody seemed so happy to reunite with loved ones. Soon Ingrid spotted her name written in orange on a piece of cardboard and ran towards the lady who held the sign.

"I am Ingrid!" she excitedly told the lady.

The woman shook her hand and introduced herself. "I am Drew Ingram, welcome to America, Ingrid! The land of the free!"

Drew was an overweight lady wearing big black glasses and carrying a large manila envelope in one hand and the sign with Ingrid's name in the other. She moved with purpose and energy, "Are you ready? Let's pick up your belongings." But Ingrid didn't understand. Drew pointed at the terminal building and gestured to pick up her bags.

"No, no," Ingrid declared in broken English, "No luggage."

"You don't have anything whatsoever?" she asked, until it dawned on her all this poor girl had was the clothes she was wearing and nothing else. Drew took Ingrid to a waiting car and drove off to a small office building on the outskirts of the city. The whole time, Ingrid was looking out of the car window fascinated with the New York skyline and the distinctly different architecture. She couldn't help but notice how wide the streets were, and how friendly the people were with whom they engaged. She genuinely felt at ease with Drew, although a bit nervous as she completed all the necessary interviews and filled the pertinent documents to make her stay in the US legal. Drew explained about the family in Detroit, Michigan, where Ingrid would work as a live-in maid and stay until such a time when she can go it alone.

The next morning Ingrid was taken to the Greyhound bus station, and after Drew said goodbye she was on her way to Detroit, almost a thousand miles away. As she had been told, sure enough there was a black man carrying a sign with her name on it at the Detroit bus depot, waiting to drive her to the residence of Mr. Russell Eaton, his employer.

Russ Eaton was a partner with the prestigious law firm Green, Towbridge and Eaton in Detroit, specializing in corporate and real estate law. The youngest of three children of immigrant parents, Russell graduated from school with honors and received a scholarship to study engineering at the University of Philadelphia, but two years into the course changed his major and pursued a degree in accounting. He worked for a chemical company for a while but quit his job to enroll at the University of Maryland where he obtained a law degree. He found a job at a law firm in New York City which depended on real estate transactions for most of its income, and worked diligently for five years putting in long hours and cultivating new clients. Single at the time, he shared a small apartment with Zac Green, also a lawyer and a native New Yorker. In a matter of a few years he saved enough to purchase a single family house, but by 1920, he amassed real estate holdings worth hundreds of thousands of dollars.

Zac recommended Russell to his brother, who was a partner in a law firm in Detroit, Michigan. Russell accepted the partnership proposal David Green made to him and soon fell in love with the thriving industrial community. He enjoyed working with his new partners in a modern office downtown, looking across the Detroit River into Canada. The firm had three partners: David Green was the senior partner, a well-known figure in the vibrant Jewish community and Edmond Towbridge was a tall and lanky lawyer originally from the Ohio, and now, Russell Eaton. Detroit prospered in those days and Russell knew it would due to Henry Ford's contribution to the automotive industry.

At the turn of the 20th century, Henry Ford, an industrialist from the Detroit area, established the Ford Motor Company. He introduced a new concept in the manufacturing of cars based on the moving assembly line and by means of mass production he was able to produce them cheaply enough for the average person to afford. By 1915, sales rose to almost a million cars with an average price tag less than $400.00, and by 1920 almost half the cars in the U.S. were Ford Model T. It was because of this economic upswing Russell invested all his money again in industrial stocks and real estate holdings.

Phil Evans, a real estate developer dropped in at the law office one day to discuss a problem collecting from a company which hired his service to build an industrial park in suburban Dearborn. After Russell won the lawsuit, a friendship between the two men blossomed, based on their mutual Quaker ethics.

Russell invested money with Phil Evans and received hefty returns on his investment, and by the mid nineteen twenties he became a rich man. Russell occasionally visited Phil's house in the very affluent Detroit suburb of Grosse Point, where he met and fell in love with Phil's only daughter, Mary. Within a few months, Russell proposed and Mary accepted, Phil gave his blessing, and the couple married in 1925.

But by the end of 1928, the economy in the United States went through a difficult period and steadily slowed; smaller banks showed serious signs of financial stress, the situation gradually deteriorated and by the middle of 1929 the economy was in a free fall. The great depression hit the country with a vengeance; banks collapsed, wide spread unemployment ensued, home foreclosures tripled and the stock market was under severe pressure. Russell and

Phil Evans however predicted the calamity; both men were astute enough to liquidate their assets at prime value before the New York stock exchange crashed on October 29, 1929. They kept the cash in the office vault.

Russell's family grew in the 1930s; he and wife Mary had their first son Russell Jr, then daughters, Meredith and Wendy and purchased a large house close to Phil Evans' in Grosse Point. The house was spectacular, with a circular driveway, large terrace in the back overlooking a swimming pool set in the middle of a manicured garden with mature trees. They were now in a position to hire a gardener, a personal driver and later they added a maid.

With Detroit's booming post WWII economy, Russell Eaton's law office expanded significantly and revenues poured in; he used his increased income and the cash he stored away before the depression wisely; he re-invested in major real estate developments, industrial parks and farm land and became a very wealthy man.

When Drew Ingram's office contacted him about the poor Jewish girl who almost died at the hands of the Nazis, he didn't think twice before he accepted their request, even with the knowledge Ingrid was almost seven months pregnant.

"Yes, of course we can help," he responded without a trace of hesitation. "I can offer her a job and a room to live in. I owe it to these people," he said, "they have suffered untold misery at the hands of the Nazis. Besides, Rita can do with extra help in the kitchen. Considering the size of our family, it's become too much for one maid now."

CHAPTER 13

Claus and his friends arrived at the port city of Rio de Janeiro eight days after they set sail from Italy. Some of his comrades continued to Argentina, but Claus thought Brazil was the better option. When he went through customs at the port terminal he emerged with a new name and identity: Ricardo Palatine. Ricardo spoke not a word of Portuguese, the language of Brazil, but he felt blessed to be there on this warm summer day at the end of December, 1945, almost nine months after his capture by the French. He didn't have much money and couldn't afford a room in a hotel, yet he felt happy to be alive and free again in his new country. He walked around fascinated with this bustling metropolis, studying his options and planning his next move. He came across a Catholic church and decided to walk in and have a talk with the priest, thinking perhaps he might glean information about the German community in the city. The priest didn't speak German but with sign language Ricardo was able to learn of another church where there was somebody who spoke German. The helpful priest stepped out to the street to hail a taxi and explained to the driver where to take Ricardo.

Father Roberto Vicario answered the door when Ricardo rang the bell. Father Vicario, an Austrian, also changed his name upon arriving in Brazil at the turn of the century. He allowed Ricardo to stay temporarily at the church until the coming weekend; he explained one of the parishioners who attends mass every Sunday may be able to offer help. Ricardo offered to clean the premises as a token of appreciation.

Two days later he was introduced after mass to Walter Vogel, an older man with thick white hair. He told Ricardo he was an electrician, originally from the town of Graz, in southern Austria, and he worked in different parts of Brazil for almost thirty years, eleven years in Rio. Now he is thinking to retire after a long time in business. He also told Ricardo about a machine shop in the city of Porto Alegre whose owner was German and may have work; he asked Ricardo to come see him the following day so he can initiate the contact.

Ricardo was delighted the next morning when Walter Vogel told him Martin Bauer was willing to offer him a job if he was willing to learn the trade. But Walter had a wide grin on his face when Ricardo asked if he could take a taxi to Porto Alegre.

"No, you cannot take a taxi down, the city is in the south of the country, 1500 kilometers from here!" He dropped him at the bus depot the following morning, and gave him little money before he wished him luck and said goodbye.

Martin Bauer was waiting at the bus depot when the very tired Ricardo emerged; he recognized Martin right away from his curled up mustache and Bavarian hat. Martin drove to his shop at an industrial park in a rundown part of the city and the two sat to talk. Martin was from the alpine area of Bad Kohlgrub in Bavaria; he arrived in Brazil penniless after WWI and settled in Porto Alegre because of its large German population. He worked as a machinist in his native country and the experience helped him find a job quickly, and several years later he opened his own successful business. But as much as he loved Brazil he found work ethics different from Germany, and when Walter called him to tell him about Ricardo, he didn't hesitate to help, he knew it was the right thing to do, helping a compatriot. Martin was still very German at heart and preferred his own people.

"What brought you here to Brazil?"

"Well, as you know, Germany is destroyed and still under occupation. The French bastards rounded up all the men and threw us in jail. But during one of the regular outings to the field, we overpowered the guards and escaped to Austria. We were all excited when Germany had the upper hand at the outset of the war. I don't understand what happened and how we lost!"

"I am sure you guys fought bravely, it was all over the newspapers here, but what happened to Dresden was shocking; we saw images of a flattened city, the poor residents must have suffered terribly."

"Don't mention Dresden, my best friend, Hans, lost all his family there."

"Do you think the country will recover from the state it's in?"

"It all depends how long this occupation will last. I have confidence in Germans, and I believe the country will one day become great again."

"Do you have any knowledge in the machine shop business?"

"I'm afraid not, but I am good with my hands and I am willing to learn!"

"Very well Ricardo, you can use the room in the back to sleep and tomorrow you can start afresh!"

Hans came home after a long day at work on the farm. He was depressed with no friends in the area anymore. The French of course came looking for Claus after he escaped; they knew he and Hans were friends and took Hans down for interrogation, but Hans stood his ground and lacking evidence the French had no choice but to let him go, but they kept him briefly under surveillance before finally concluding he was not involved. After a year, Hans still wondered if his friend safely made it to South America.

He came home from work one day to find his grandma in a terrible state, her condition worsened during the night and Hans didn't have the medicine to keep her alive. She died the following morning and was buried next to her husband. Hans felt so lonely after her death, he didn't know what to do and he had no more friends or blood relatives, he wished he was gone too, but he had no other option than to stay and continue to work.

One day he received a letter postmarked from Brazil that changed his life. The letter was from Claus, or Ricardo as he became known; he gave a detailed narrative of the escape, and the momentous day when he arrived in Porto Alegre. Ricardo praised his employer, and described how much he enjoys the sun-drenched country.

> *You must see this beautiful city on the Atlantic coast! The people are nice and friendly, and although I miss Germany, there are no opportunities at the present, and I am glad to have made the decision to come to Brazil. I believe it was the right decision, and I hope you too consider immigrating. The country is booming and work is plentiful.*

CHAPTER 14

Mary Eaton's heart leapt out of her chest when her husband came home from work the day he received the call from Drew Ingram. He asked his wife and children to come to his study and told them about Ingrid. "I made a prompt decision to have this poor girl stay with us; she has been through the most inhumane treatment at the hands of the Nazis in her native Germany, and she was left to die in the most dreadful conditions you can imagine. But the Lord saved her and the baby she is carrying, and it is now our duty to help. We will welcome her and make her part of our family. Because of what she has endured we must all do our part to make her stay with us as pleasant as possible. And remember when you talk to her, she speaks very little English!"

Mary cried when he finished, she was genuinely sad to hear what happened to Ingrid, and she was proud of her husband for taking a stand and demonstrating the kind of person he truly was. Mary did her part too, she asked Fred the driver to come to the kitchen where his wife Rita was busy preparing dinner. "I have some news for you. We will have a new girl coming to live and work at the house with us, her name is Ingrid." And she recounted the story of what happened to the poor Jewish lady.

Rita was also in tears when Mary Eaton walked out of the kitchen. "I can never understand why people do such horrible things to each other, why can't we all get along and become friends all over the world? There will be no wars and no conflicts if we just respect each other's space, but I guess the Lord must have different plan for us, and I hope and pray one day peace will come to the whole wide world."

Fred was listening and when she finished he said. "Amen."

Ingrid rested in her room the morning she arrived, and in the evening, Russell and Mary Eaton introduced her to the rest of the family and the staff. When she entered the kitchen the following day, Rita, who was in charge of the kitchen and the house cleaning explained her duties.

"You start here in the morning after you take the newspaper from the front door and leave it on Mr. Russell's desk in the den. You come back here when you're finished and help me prepare breakfast for the family, and after the children leave to school, you go upstairs and clean their rooms and Mr. Eaton's den. Be careful not to touch any of the papers on his desk. You start on the main floor after you finish upstairs, the usual mopping, dusting and so forth, and the last thing you do is the basement. Clean your room but don't bother with mine, I like to do that myself. Fred has allergies and I don't use detergents. Do you have any questions?"

"No I don't," Ingrid replied with a smile.

Rita was a very kind lady indeed. She began life in rural Louisiana, where her mother worked in the fields picking cotton on the Banks of the Mississippi. Rita was nearly 14 years old when her mother died, and her father finally disappeared and never came back. Relatives looked after her for a while but people were very poor; she was placed in an orphanage where she worked in the kitchen and learned the art of Southern cooking. She eventually found a job working at a restaurant in New Orleans and gradually became in charge of the kitchen. She met Fred, the Eatons' driver, at the home of a mutual friend. Six months later Fred traveled from Detroit and proposed to her, they married and she moved back with him. The Eatons instantly liked her big smile, and Mary offered her a job and the couple was given a room in the basement. All the children loved her and considered her part of the family; and they especially loved her Cajun cooking!

Ingrid was almost seven months pregnant when she started work. She was determined to learn the customs and how to prepare food American style; it was funny at the beginning, Rita explained things in sign language and then followed it with slow and deliberate English, and the two girls often broke out in laughter, and mimicked how they sounded to one another when they spoke. They bonded well, and Ingrid despite her advanced pregnancy was eager to learn and help. Rita often ordered her to go put her feet up in her room but Ingrid didn't listen.

One unseasonably warm day at the end of November just few weeks after she started Ingrid decided to take a little walk in the back garden. She had already finished her work inside and the baby was giving her trouble, so she put a light sweater on and with her arm firmly on the back of her hip she strolled around the swimming pool.

"Hello, hello, you must be Ingrid?"

She turned around to see who was talking to her--a man wearing a wide rim hat came over and put his hand out. "I'm Greg McKay, the gardener."

She shook his hand and replied, "Hello, I am Ingrid the new girl, nice to meet you."

"Yes, I know who you are," Greg answered with a broad smile, "I was told all about you, and I hope you are enjoying your walk out here."

"Yes I am," she answered with a smile of her own. "I like to go out when the baby starts kicking, I guess he wants to go for a walk."

Greg laughed out loud, "How do you know the baby is a boy?"

"I don't, but only boys behave badly."

Greg just roared laughing, "You are funny, you are funny!" he repeated. "Why do you say that about boys, how about girls, are they all good like you?"

"I don't know if I am good or bad, but boys are naughty sometimes. I think we should change the subject if you don't mind."

"No problem, what would you like to talk about?"

"Why the pool is empty; it had water last week."

"Well, I normally look after the garden and the pool but I was away in Texas, and I emptied the pool the day I returned. In fact this should have been done earlier, but I was away for my sister's wedding."

"But it looks prettier with water in it, why do you have to empty it?"

"It gets cold here and it freezes in winter, and to prevent damage, we empty the pool, clean it and cover it with a vinyl liner until the next season."

"When is the next season start?"

"I usually refill it with water at the end of spring, the last two of weeks of May."

"Thank you for the information Greg. I better get back in; I enjoyed talking to you."

"Yes, it was nice meeting you, Ingrid, and I enjoyed talking to you, too."

CHAPTER 15

Porto Alegre, Ricardo's adopted city in Brazil lies on the shores of a very large lagoon navigable by ships, and situated at the confluence of numerous rivers converging together to create an inland lake connected to the ocean by a narrow passage. Because it was so well protected from the open waters of the Atlantic, the Portuguese settled the area in the late 18th century and waves of new immigrants from Europe and elsewhere arrived in large numbers, particularly from Germany and Poland. Ricardo described this beautiful setting along the coastline with forested mountains as a backdrop at the end of the letter he sent to his friend back in Germany.

The letter Hans received from Ricardo finally changed his mind about emigrating to South America, and after the loss of his grandma, he felt adrift on his own, not knowing what to do or where to go. He was tired of the misery that had befallen the country and the foreign occupation with its degrading treatment of ordinary people. He contemplated his future and concluded he desperately needed to change his own course, and when the letter arrived, painting such a rosy picture of Brazil, it didn't take him long to sit and write a response to his friend 'Ricardo'. He liked the sound of Claus' new name and understood the reasons behind the change.

Ricardo was happy to receive a letter back from Hans yet sad about Germany's situation. He calmed his friend's fears about immigrating, and explained in his response how easy it is to go through the process; the economy is booming and the country desperately needed more workers, he assured.

Hans decided to discuss the future of the property he inherited from his grandparents with George; he went to visit and found the farmer with his son Fritz at the back of the barn getting hay for the cattle. Hans was surprised when George immediately offered to buy it from him on condition he pays for it in installments. The deed of transfer was signed the following week in Offenburg. Hans was a little sad to get rid of the last remnant tying him to his family and country, but he was ready and eager to go, and after filling out the necessary immigration papers, he put them in an envelope and sent them to the Brazilian embassy in Bern, Switzerland.

Ricardo was not surprised when Hans very soon after sent him a letter to advise him the application was approved and travel plans were already made for him to come to Brazil. Hans traveled to the Marseilles on the Mediterranean coast and boarded a passenger ship to Brazil. He sat on the deck admiring the view as Europe faded out of sight when the ship went through the Strait of Gibraltar. It was the spring of 1947 and Hans was just over 23 years of age, tall, masculine and full of energy.

CHAPTER 16

Ingrid had not been feeling well; her unwanted pregnancy gave her little physical discomfort but enormous psychological complications. She wanted to get rid of her baby at any cost, but was unable. Early on she tried several times in her bedroom to punch her belly hard to trigger a miscarriage and when that failed, she tried to use a coat hanger. That painful attempt made her bleed, but did not have the desired outcome. She sat in bed feeling sorry for herself and wished she had never met that bastard Hans, and given that hatred, she made her mind up to put the baby up for adoption as soon as it arrives.

Ingrid celebrated her first Christmas in America and to everybody's delight it snowed the night before. She was ready to give birth any minute and Dr. Healey assured her the last time Mary took her to the maternity clinic it would be healthy, yet the doctor could see Ingrid was having serious emotional issues. But he mistakenly attributed the problem to the terrible experience she had been through at the hands of the Nazis. Ingrid was careful not to confide what happened with Hans to anybody, the shame of it kept the secret locked in her heart.

Rita was concerned too, she had become like a big sister to Ingrid over the short time they'd known each other, and saw how agonizing the pregnancy had become. The girl was struggling to get out of bed but forced herself to help in the kitchen, always dutiful, always ready to please.

Mrs. Eaton took it upon herself to ask, after Rita expressed her concern, "Is there something bothering you, Ingrid?"

"No, I am fine," she answered.

Ingrid's mind was in turmoil, she knew the subject of the baby's father will come up, and she dreaded the day, what will she tell people? "I am proud to be carrying the baby of the man who raped me, and by the way he was a Nazi bastard, and the enemy of the Jewish people?" She even prayed, "Oh my God, please help me get rid of this baby before it comes, I cannot live with the shame. I hate myself and I will hate this baby forever!" Wild thoughts spun out of control in her mind and kept her awake at night.

Christmas day was nice; there were many presents for her but the one from Greg the gardener was the one she liked most. It was a nice coat for her and a blue suit with small white shoes for the baby. It looked so adorable it made her cry, and she wished her baby was conceived under different circumstances. The thought Greg put into it when he purchased the presents touched her. He was a man of modest means, yet he took the time to buy her something. When he came to the house, she thanked him warmly.

"I am headed to Texas," he told her with his usual unassuming smile.

"You just come back from there last month, why are you going again?"

"I like to go fishing," he gestured with his hands clasped together, "I love to go deep water fishing with my friends in Corpus Christi." Greg showed a childlike enthusiasm. "My best friend has a shrimp boat and he takes me on board with him, it is so peaceful at night in the middle of the ocean, and I enjoy it so much with my friends!"

"You are a lucky man to be able to go every month, Texas must be close."

Greg broadly smiled and explained Texas was another state, and more than 1500 miles from Detroit, but he didn't mind the drive in his old truck. "I daydream while I am driving and I don't give a hoot about anything in the world, it is so relaxing. But I don't go there every month like you suggested, I only go once a year during the off season in Detroit, and the reason I visited last time was for my sister's wedding in Abilene."

Ingrid was rushed to the hospital on New Year's Eve, and after 21 hours of sheer hell, a healthy baby boy came to this world on the first day of the year. Rita was with her in the delivery room holding her hand during birth, and when the nurse came back and handed the little boy to the mother, Ingrid looked the other way; how odd, the nurse thought. Most women are filled with joy, but this woman is filled with disgust at the sight of her new baby.

The moment Ingrid dreaded the most finally arrived. The nurse pulled a seat up and sat next to Ingrid's bed. She had pen in hand and was filling out an official looking form.

"Today is the 1st of January, 1946," she mumbled under her breath, and then she turned towards Ingrid. "Do we have a name for the boy?" she asked.

"I haven't thought about it," Ingrid answered shyly.

"Well, I have to fill in this form for the birth certificate if you don't mind; you better think of a name quickly my dear."

"Call him David if you want," Ingrid said with little interest.

"Is this what you want to call him?" the nurse said from under her glasses.

"Yes," Ingrid answered, her eyes looking down, frightened to lock eyes with the nurse.

"Very well, David Schroeder," she entered on the form and added the baby's gender, and race; male, Caucasian.

"What is your husband's name?" the nurse continued.

"My husband? I don't have a husband, he is dead," she answered swiftly.

"I mean what was your husband's name before he died?"

"David Schroeder," she answered, her voice quivering.

CHAPTER 17

Hans arrived in Porto Alegre on a drizzly Friday morning at the end of April, 1947, and when he finished his immigration papers he was a transformed man with new identity in his adopted country of Brazil. He was now Oscar Silva.

Ricardo was waiting for him at the port terminal; the two guys embraced, shook hands and hailed a taxi to Ricardo's new apartment. They sat up all night long talking and reminiscing about the war and its aftermath. Luckily it was the weekend, and the following morning they went out to explore the city that has been home to Ricardo for less than two years. They stopped at the central public market, a neoclassical building constructed in the middle of the nineteenth century and one of the most recognized landmarks in the city. Oscar was mesmerized with the enormous displays of unfamiliar tropical fruits, and the aroma of exotic foods. They sat in the ice cream parlor enjoying the landscape and watching people pass by, they went to the main square in the historical downtown area; they visited the palace of justice, the metropolitan cathedral and Saint Peter's Theater before they ended the tour at Mario Quintana's culture house where many of the locals meet. The two young men genuinely enjoyed their time and each other's company and when they returned home, they were exhausted.

Ricardo has been working for Martin Bauer at the machine shop ever since he arrived in Brazil. Hans' name came up many times in conversations Ricardo had with his boss. "I have a wonderful friend back in Germany," he used to say to Martin, "Hans was a fine solider, a good comrade in arms and a fierce nationalist."

After Hans made up his mind to immigrate to South America, Ricardo enthusiastically asked Martin, "Do you still remember my friend Hans?"

"Of course I do," replied Martin, "what about him?"

"Well, he is coming to Porto Alegre next month. He is too tired of the situation back home and wants to seek a different opportunity here in Brazil."

"Very well, please bring him over when he arrives, I would like to meet him," Martin answered with his usual smile.

Hans, or Oscar as he is called now, escorted his friend when he went to work on Monday morning. The first thing Martin noticed was Oscar's dialect.

"Are you from Bavaria originally?" he asked.

"I sure am," Oscar answered with pride. The two struck up an instant kinship because of their heritage.

"I see you walk with a limp, was it a war injury?"

"It most certainly was," Oscar answered quickly, "as a matter of fact shrapnel tore my ankle to pieces and the hospital where I had my wound treated didn't have the medical supplies available at the end of the war, so the result was the permanent condition you see now."

"How terrible!" Martin said with sympathy, "does it still bother you?"

"It did for a while but it has completely recovered; the limp will remain a constant fixture in my life I guess." Oscar obviously avoided any reference to what actually transpired with Ingrid; it was part of the past he so desperately wanted to forget. Hans told Martin his first priority was to find work and asked if he knew anybody looking to hire somebody like him.

"I don't know for sure, but I will be glad to ask around."

Hans enrolled in a language school to learn Portuguese in order to improve his chances to get a job. Almost a month had gone by and his search didn't turn up any positive results, but his luck changed when he received a message from Martin, who asked Ricardo to bring Oscar to the shop.

"I may have some news to cheer him up."

"Why, are you going to offer him a job?" Ricardo probed.

"No, answered Martin, but I have somebody else who might."

Gustave Doda was born and raised in the city of Porto Alegre at the turn of the century, his grandfather, also named Gustave, emigrated from Gdansk, an industrial port in West Prussia in the 1850s to avoid conscription in the army. He settled in Sao Paulo and invested the money he raised from the sale of the considerable property holdings he owned in coffee plantations. His investment made him a very rich man, however, in 1888, the Brazilian government outlawed slavery and coffee production which depended on cheap slave labor plummeted as a result. Gustave lost his fortune, and unable to cope, ended his own life with a gunshot to the head. His son Emil moved south and settled in the city of Porto Alegre, where he started from scratch, and by the beginning of the century when young Gustave was born, Emil was the proud owner of a medium size construction company which Gustave inherited after his father's death. Gustave was an able man with foresight and acumen; he diversified the company's activities and made land excavation and drilling a profitable part of the operation. The business took off like a rocket since the services it offered were in great demand in the swampy terrain. Gustave developed a business relationship with Martin Bauer and for the last twenty years all the tooling for his equipment and spare parts were done at the machine shop Martin owned. When Gustave stopped at the shop last week to discuss business, Martin mentioned the new immigrant from Germany.

"I can always use good help; send him over for an interview!"

Oscar arrived at Gustave's construction yard on time, anxious to meet the man who may offer him a job. Gustave was standing in the yard with a group of employees when he spotted the tall blond man going inside the office building, and the first thing he noticed was the limp. "I wish Martin had mentioned the man was an invalid, I wouldn't have bothered to talk to him," he muttered to himself before going back to the office. Gustave, however, was in for a surprise. Not only did Oscar have the essential experience to operate different kinds of machinery, a trade he picked working at the farm back in Germany, but has the drive and the right personality for the job, Gustave determined the leg injury was not a detriment. He offered him a job on the spot.

"You can start tomorrow, and be here at 6 am sharp," he ordered.

CHAPTER 18

Eight weeks after David was born, jet black hair covered his head, the birth wrinkles on his face all but disappeared, and the grey blue eyes that twinkle with every smile, very much like his mother's, turned deep blue. Ingrid emotionally rejected her son from the day he was born but was dutiful towards the baby's needs, pending completion of the adoption process. She was waiting for the right opportunity to talk to Rita first, who no doubt would want to know the reason behind her decision to give up her beautiful and healthy baby. She debated in her mind what to say; I don't have the wherewithal to bring up the baby on my own after the death of my husband, or, the baby was a mistake, my husband and I never planned to have one in the first place. Perhaps: this child is so beautiful and deserving a better life with a father and a mother to give him a proper family life. However her mind was not yet set on how to rationalize her decision. She was unsure and felt uncomfortable with how to proceed. The true reason however, must never ever be revealed; this is something eternally locked in her heart and mind and shall not be told to anybody, not even to her own mother. This overwhelming sense of shame suppressed the rape in her subconscious and sealed it there forever.

Rita observed a change in Ingrid after the birth of her baby. She noticed how miserable and forlorn Ingrid turned, crying all the time, her eyes puffed up and her energy waned. Rita passed on her concern to Mary Eaton. "I don't know what happened to Ingrid, but she didn't want to have this child. I remember she turned her face away when the nurse handed her the baby after birth. She just hasn't been her usual self. What should I do?"

Mary was sympathetic. "Just give her space, she probably has post-natal problems, but she will get over it. I know some women suffer after they give birth, but let me know if the problem lingers, would you, please?"

One day when Rita came to check on Ingrid, she found her hugging the baby ever so close to her heart and a stream of tears was cascading down her cheeks;

"What is the matter?" Rita asked with concern.

Ingrid turned her face the other way and admitted, "It is not his fault, it is not the baby's fault, it is my miserable luck in this life, and I shouldn't take it out on David! He is my baby and I love him so very much! Oh, Rita, he flashed me the biggest smile you can imagine, with both arms and legs flailing in the air; he looked so beautiful, like a little angel! It made me so happy just to see he was happy to be with me. I love this boy, Rita; I love him with all of my heart!" Both girls sat crying, holding hands and not saying a word.

Letting Ingrid release some of the tension bottled inside worked like magic. Rita was so happy when Ingrid once again became the girl she was, happy, jovial and pleasant to be around.

Little David loved Rita to pick him up when his mother brought him to see her, sitting in the stroller the Eatons gave her for Christmas. The little boy put on a show with his gorgeous smiles and baby talk, wriggling in her arms and tenderly kicking with his feet, he was truly a bundle of joy. Ingrid bestowed so much love on her baby and left him in Rita's care while she was doing house chores. Even Mary Eaton doted on David and she told her husband, "The boy looks like an angel, and I bet he will be a heart throb someday!"

Greg made it back from Texas in time to begin the spring preparations around the garden. There was the usual pruning of the trees and the rose bushes, the mulching of the dead leaves left behind from last fall and of course the pre-season coordination with the nurseries for ideas on what to plant in the flower beds.

Ingrid was pleased to see him come to the kitchen with his usual smile and high pitched laugh. "This is the first time I see you not wearing your hat," she said with a giggle, "You have thick red hair and it looks good on you."

"I got my red hair from my father and so did my sister, we all have red hair and freckles. My background is Scottish and my grandfather was born in the highlands."

"You haven't told us about Texas, how was it down there, did you have a good time?"

"I had a blast, the weather was out of this world and I caught enough fish to feed an army! I love that place, it is booming so much after oil was discovered; there are oil derricks as far the eye can see."

"Wow, you made me want to see this place, perhaps one day I get to go!"

"So where is the baby?" he questioned, "I heard he is bonny; I cannot wait to see him!"

"He's asleep right now, but I will bring him out when he wakes up. I think he would like to meet you, too!"

Summer was a week away, and Mary Eaton suggested they go to New England for a vacation when the children finish school. Russell was against the idea, "Let's just go to the cottage this year, I have a little surprise for you!"

"You have got me curious, what are you surprising me with?"

"Oh no, I'm not saying anything now, wait until we get there. But I am sure you will love it!" he teased.

Greg normally went with the Eatons when they vacationed at the cottage. The children loved to have him, he was so much fun and they liked to go fishing with him on the lake. There was no problem with accommodation; the outbuilding at the entrance of the property has a loft and two rooms on the main floor. Greg loved the loft and often sat looking at the farmland out back or the passing motorists in front of the property. Fred and Rita stayed in the large room next to the kitchen and Mary told Ingrid she can stay in the spare room. Ingrid asked to be excused because of the baby, but Mary wasn't having it.

"No Ingrid, we are not leaving you here sitting on your own. God forbid, you may have an emergency with nobody available to help. Russell will not allow it dear."

The cottage the Eatons owned was in reality a big house sitting on several acres of land covered with tall grass and few trees, and located close to the town of Holland, on Michigan's west coast. The children were excited when told they were going, but Ingrid was a little confused and she asked Greg, "Are we going to Holland next week?"

"Yes we all are. "You and the baby will ride in the truck with me, and we will set out early in the morning. Rita and Fred will drive in the little blue sedan the night before to get the cottage organized for the family."

"But Holland is in Europe, how do you drive there when there is an ocean between us?"

Greg fell on the floor laughing his head off. "What is the matter with you, Greg? Why are you laughing at me?"

"Wait until I tell Mary and the children," he could barely finish the sentence.

"Now, now, you are making me feel like a fool, what is wrong with you? Will you please quit laughing or else I am walking out of the room!"

"No, don't go please; Holland is a small town in Michigan and not the same Holland as in Europe. They call it Holland because the people who settled the area were from the Netherlands and gave the name to the town in honor of the country they originally hailed from, but you made my day, that was so funny!"

Mary Eaton was really surprised when she saw the present her husband purchased. "Oh my God!" she said when the family went to the marina the day after they arrived in Holland. "What a beautiful boat!" The children were even more excited than she, and Russell tossed the key to Greg.

"There you are, you told me you can ride this baby like a pro, let us see how far you can take us!" The family spent the whole day on the boat; they moored up the coast and had lunch on a secluded beach. The children loved to jump overboard into the cool water of the lake. For dinner, Rita prepared the trout and the yellow perch they caught fishing. Ingrid too was happy to see little David enjoying all the fuss the family made of him. When his mother took his socks off and dangled his feet in the water, the little boy wanted more and attempted to leap out of her arms.

CHAPTER 19

Oscar had now been with Gustave a year, and though the job was demanding and the schedule was always busy, he was nevertheless happy to be working and making ends meet without relying on anybody but himself. Gustave was also pleased with Oscar's performance; he was the first to arrive at the job site and the last to leave.

"Reliability aside, this man is worth his weight in gold," Mario, the construction manager told his boss, "he is a good operator and gets things done with no hassle, he gets along well with the rest of the crew and surprisingly his Portuguese has improved considerably. I do recommend him to lead the crew when we start the new Villa for Helmut Spiegel. I am confident he will do us proud and I am sure Mr. Spiegel will be happy with his performance. Plus the two can talk in their native language."

"I agree with you, Mario, this man is as good as it gets. He is like a sponge, always wants to learn and suck up all the knowledge in one go, I wish the rest of our guys are half as good."

Helmut Spiegel was born in 1894 in Düsseldorf, Germany; he was a teenager when his father Manfred accepted a teaching position at the University of Sao Paulo. The family decided to stay permanently in Brazil when Manfred, given the economic situation, saw no good reason to return to Germany after WWI. "Brazil on the other hand is on the ascendance, opportunities are abound, people are friendly, and the notion of being a part of building a new nation appeals to me greatly." None of the family objected; Helmut was doing well in school, and his mother was content leading the life of privilege her husbands' job affords. Manfred instilled in his only son the love of learning and the pursuit of excellence; Helmut graduated from university with honors and immediately found a job in the city of Santos, where he worked for a shipbuilding yard. When the company he worked went public, Helmut used all his savings and the money he inherited after the death of his father to buy shares in the company. He also kept a large tract of farmland his father purchased in California at the recommendation of an American colleague.

The largest shareholder of the company was a rather sullen person of Greek background, Alexander Theodopolis. Alexander was a very adroit businessman who amassed a fortune in the cargo shipping business with a fleet of more than a dozen ships. He recognized Helmut's talent and lured him to work in his own company, and in span of few years elevated him to the position of General Manager, eventually rising to junior partner. During the great depression however, the shipping industry suffered substantial losses. Mr. Theodopolis who suffered from chronic health problems saw no point to continue doing business, and sold the company to Helmut for a fraction of its true value.

Helmut worked hard and traveled the world in search of new venues and opportunities for his company and in a matter of few years he was able to make the company profitable again, but his big break was when officials from the city of Porto Alegre came to his office and made him an irresistible offer; relocate his company to Porto Alegre and receive an attractive incentive package.

It was two of these incentives that made Helmut accede to the city's proposals; a ten year tax break; where the company is exempted from paying income tax on profits it generates for the next ten years, that was the first incentive, but the important second proposal was what tipped the scales. The city offered to grant premium ocean front land for him to develop into modern cargo storage and handling facilities. It was a win, win situation for both the city and Helmut; the city will benefit from the creation of jobs and business spin-off and the development of vacant land at the expense of the private sector. For Helmut it was a proposal worth many millions and he was getting it for free.

Helmut retained the services of Gustave Doda when the plans for the port transformation project were approved by the city; Gustave and Helmut worked unceasingly to finish the development, and in a matter of a few years the project was completed successfully. Helmut was not only satisfied with Gustave's performance; he was impressed by his honesty and dedication. The two developed a business relationship and Helmut's future construction projects were automatically awarded to Gustave, including the construction of his dream house on the hills overlooking the city.

At the pre-construction meeting Helmut attended with Gustave, Oscar was also present as project leader. The two met again days later at the proposed building site so Oscar could explain the layout and the family got a firsthand feel of the location. Helmut's wife and daughter were full of praise for the tall blond guy; they were fascinated with the details and impressed with his knowledge. Their beautiful daughter Gretchen didn't escape Oscar's eyes, either.

Construction on Helmut's house began in earnest. Oscar became the foreman and equipment began to break ground to connect the secluded site to the main road. Underground utilities were installed and excavation to lay the foundation followed immediately. Helmut made it a habit to drop by on weekends to check the progress. All went as planned and the building footprint started to take shape. Oscar was doing one heck of job and Helmut lavished praise and told him he was a hardworking man. This compliment meant the world to Oscar; he desperately wanted to succeed in his adopted country and make a name for himself and the acclaim was an affirmation he was going in the right direction.

The construction took almost a year to finish and at the end Oscar was busy supervising the interior's last finishing details and the placement of the furniture in the rooms according to the client's preference. When it was time to hand the project over to the owners, Gustave and Oscar were there to walk the family through their new home and show them its many attributes. They particularly loved the split level family room with cathedral ceiling and glass front permitting a splendid view of the city below. A giant vase containing a spectacular arrangement of fresh cut flowers greeted the family when they finally moved in the following week, Oscar's way of expressing sincere best wishes and congratulations.

CHAPTER 20

Ingrid's ambivalence towards David completely turned into love and devotion and the little boy was happy when they sang for him in the kitchen on his second birthday. Greg took the time to buy him a cake and have it adorned with two small candles, and everybody cheered when he blew out the flame.

Ingrid settled well, working at the house and rearing her child, but there was something from the past still bothering her immensely. She often woke up with nightmares and with scenes of the rape and the torture still vivid in her mind. Her body squirmed with every slap to her face and every lash on her back, and images of Hans stamping the cigarette in her neck made her scream. She kept the pain hidden deep inside her and found it hard to talk about events from her past when prodded by Rita or Mary, for fear it will haunt her when she went to bed.

There was one more thing nagging at her and it made her feel helpless. She recalled Dr. Jane Foster's last words before they parted ways, "I hope you will enjoy America when you get there, you can always look for your mother in the Holy Land after you settle down."

By now Ingrid felt established and the desire to reunite with her mother was still strong, yet she felt helpless to begin the search. The fear of the unknown was on her mind, and the shame of having baby David out of wedlock was also a factor. Maybe she was a little afraid to go to the Holy Land so soon after the fledgling state of Israel was created only a few months earlier. Perhaps she should wait.

The Eaton family wanted to talk to Ingrid about the past; so did Greg and Rita who occasionally asked a casual question about the Nazis and life in the concentration camp. Ingrid typically dodged the question or gave cryptic answers like, "I don't really remember what happened, I was semi-conscious most of the time." The question she hated most was about the baby's father, it was an open sore in her heart and all attempts to enquire were shunned. "David's father died, and I am still grieving his death, I would appreciate it if you don't bring the subject up again." The family appreciated the healing power of talk to release the tension and therefore couldn't grasp why she was so afraid. They respected her wishes however, and the subject was not broached again. Mary Eaton understood the girl must have had a terrible time during her ordeal and told the others to leave her for now; she will open up when she is ready.

Ingrid made sure when the weather was nice to put baby David in his stroller and take him out for a little run in the garden, and she liked to go out there and sit by the pool to admire the landscaping. Greg often stopped and fussed with the baby and talked to Ingrid about gardening. He didn't ask personal questions, he sensed her vulnerability, saw her sad at times and felt compelled to protect her. In order to cheer her up he asked if she was busy this weekend.

"No I am not, why do you ask?"

"There is a movie playing in the theater everybody is raving about and I wanted to see if you were interested to go see it with me."

"What is the name of the movie?"

"Best Years of Our Lives," he answered quickly, "and from what people say about the movie you will be impressed," he added in an effort to raise her interest.

"Yes, why not, I will go with you," she answered eagerly.

Rita couldn't help but notice Greg's interest in Ingrid was growing by the day, he often comes to the kitchen looking for her, and looked disappointed when she wasn't there. If he asked where she was Rita routinely answered that she is busy changing the baby or she is cleaning the rooms upstairs.

"Please tell her to come for lunch outside and bring David with her,"

When Ingrid returned to the kitchen, Rita used to tease her, "Guess who was here looking for you?"

"You don't have to tell me, I know who," she would say with a smile. Occasionally she bundled the baby up, prepared a sandwich and went out for a little break in the garden.

"There you are, take your favorite ham and cheese; don't you get tired eating the same thing over and over?"

"I like to eat turkey and other cold cuts but ham and cheese is my favorite. I don't see you eat a lot yourself!" Greg observed.

"Yes I do, I nibble all day long, I hate to gain weight and become fat."

"You look just fine Ingrid, as a matter of fact you look beautiful, really beautiful!" he added with a grin.

Ingrid blushed, picked up the baby and hurried back in. She liked Greg as well; he has such an easy going personality and puts everybody who comes his way at ease. But the last few months she noticed Greg wanted more, and though Ingrid didn't mind the attention, she was not quite ready yet for a relationship.

Ingrid was meticulously dressed the evening Greg came in the kitchen to pick her for their date.

"You look marvelous," he started saying, beaming from ear to ear.

"And you too," she answered with embarrassment, "and you are not wearing your hat! I am so used to seeing you wear it all the time; it is like a permanent fixture on your head!"

They all laughed and Rita noticed they were holding hands when they left the house. After the movie they walked for a while along the river's promenade until Ingrid announced, "I better get going; David will be waiting for me and Rita is going to bed soon."

"I have something to tell you," Greg said. "I usually take my vacation in Texas at the beginning of the winter, but I've decided to remain in Detroit this year."

CHAPTER 21

Oscar has been in Brazil for four years now, working hard for the same company. His boss elevated him to a higher position in charge of several crews and provided him with a work truck to move between job sites. Ricardo, too, became second in command at the machine shop and virtually ran the business for his boss who was seriously thinking of retirement. Both guys worked all hours of the day and many weekends too. They lived frugally together in the same apartment and saved most of the income they generated. Oscar was pleased with his job but wanted more out of life. He told his best friend one evening after work he was thinking of moving on from his job to try going it alone.

"Are you nuts?" responded Ricardo to this most foolish idea.

"No, I am not stupid Ricardo, but I cannot see myself doing the same thing forever. I want to be somebody and build a life for myself instead of doing the same thing day in and day out."

"I can understand your frustration Oscar, but you don't have the resources and the contacts to make it on your own. You will enter uncharted territory if you follow through with this idea, and I strongly advise you to stop thinking about it and continue with the same job, the job that pays for the food on the table."

"I am not quite sure your argument has any merits Ricardo. When you arrived here in Brazil, you didn't know anybody. This is what you call uncharted territory, but you made it and I don't see why I cannot do the same and try my luck. If all else fails I can always go back to work for Gustave, but I am more confident now than ever before of my chances. For the last four years I worked hard to learn the business. Many in the construction industry know my name; so do many of the suppliers and clients. I got to know this city and how the system works and I speak decent Portuguese. Please Ricardo, examine the facts and tell me why wouldn't I succeed?"

He felt confident he had acquired enough knowledge and experience in the trade and it was the right time for him to make a move. Oscar resigned from his position at the construction company against the advice of his best friend and the protestations of Gustave.

"Why do you want to resign Oscar?" Gustave asked with irritation, "I have treated you well, increased your salary twice and gave you many perks."

"I have made up my mind, Gustave. I want to be my own boss and explore if I can make it in construction on my own. It has nothing to do with you personally, in fact you treat me well and with honesty and fairness and for that I am thankful, but I have this burning desire to establish a company I can call my own." Gustave was furious. He was unable to change Oscar's mind, so he got up and stormed out of the office.

Oscar learned the essence of the trade and honed his construction skills over the years he worked for Gustave, but he desperately lacked the knowledge required to set up a company and more importantly he didn't have sufficient financial resources. He was able to save most of the money he earned and what he received from the sale of his grandfather's house, but in real terms what he saved didn't amount to a great deal and without the help from the bank he stood little chance to succeed. There was one more complication he had to contend with and decided to talk to his friend.

When Ricardo got home that evening, Oscar was waiting for him and before his friend sat down he asked him if he knew anything about setting up a company in Brazil. He admitted that in addition to needing more capital than what he had accumulated, he really didn't have the business background necessary.

"Not a damn thing," Ricardo answered quickly and without hesitation.

"Do you think your boss Martin Bauer might be able to help me?"

"I wouldn't even ask him, Oscar; even if he knew, I still wouldn't ask. Please don't forget it was Martin who recommended you for the job at Gustave. Do you think he will be happy to give you information to set up a construction company so you will be in competition with one of his major clients?"

"You can look for a lawyer in the phone directory; I think this will be your best option." Ricardo added.

Oscar indeed thought about getting a lawyer but decided the cost might deplete his resources and leave him with insufficient amount to start a business. He felt discouraged and a little helpless after the attempt to get free advice from Ricardo's boss went down the drain, but then he thought about Helmut Spiegel, and decided to pay him a visit at his company's head offices.

Helmut and Oscar had not seen each other since the day the construction at Helmut's villa was completed, but Oscar distinctly remembered Helmut's last words when they said their last goodbyes. "This is my business card with all the contact information; don't hesitate to call if you needed help or advice." Oscar picked up the phone and dialed his number.

Helmut sat behind the desk listening intently to Oscar giving details about the construction company he proposed to establish, and without hesitation agreed to help.

"No problem, I can put you in touch with our in house legal department, they can offer you free advice on how to register your company and obtain the necessary permits. I can also put you in touch with a good bank manager. But a word of advice, son--the bank manager would want to see your idea in writing, this is called a business plan, or a detailed account of how you intend to establish the company, why you need the bank to give you money and how you intend to spend it. I must also point out it is difficult to obtain credit, especially for a beginner, and the criteria for approving a loan may be insurmountable in your case, but it may be worthwhile to try."

Oscar was confounded after the meeting; he had no clue where to start and he never thought there was so much involved.

Helmut found out from the legal department that Oscar had not called in to set up an appointment. He knew the reasons why; it was evident during the meeting Oscar didn't have the knowledge to write a business plan. Yet he had witnessed firsthand the zeal with which this man operates and the way he carries himself and Helmut understood what it takes to make a successful business. He identified in Oscar the talent, dedication and the character essential for success. He picked the phone.

"I have a proposal to discuss with you Oscar, please come to see me tomorrow."

After the first meeting Oscar held with Helmut, he couldn't stop thinking about the business plan. He had a solid idea how to proceed and dabbled with ideas and numbers but couldn't articulate his thoughts on paper. When he arrived for the meeting Helmut called for, he didn't anticipate what Helmut had in mind. The conversation began to take a serious tone when Helmut asked for details.

"To tell you the truth Mr. Spiegel, I have a darn good idea how to make a success of this endeavor, but I am unable to translate my thoughts on paper. If you wouldn't mind, I will be thrilled to tell you verbally."

Helmut sat back in his chair and said, "I will be delighted to hear about it, Oscar."

After two hours, Helmut said, "You convinced me Oscar, and I am pleased to tell you of my decision to finance the cost. But I have one caveat; I want to partner with you and become part of the deal. Each of us will own half of the business. I put up the money, you execute the work and we split the profit down the middle. In addition to the financial resources I am offering you to tap on my knowledge and contacts in the city. How does this appeal to you?"

Oscar couldn't believe his luck! He thanked Helmut for his confidence and agreed promptly to the generous proposal.

CHAPTER 22

Mildred failed to reach Europe before WWII started and blamed herself for not being able to bring her daughter safely to the Holy Land, but she was relieved Ingrid was hiding in Germany and good people were working earnestly to help her escape as Rabbi Goldstein assured her in his last letter. Nobody thought at the beginning the war it would last five years, and her hope to reunite with Ingrid turned from hope to despair and then to dread.

There was no more news about Rachel since the last letter written by Rabbi Goldstein before his murder; that letter was in fact sent to her by Binyamin Komlin, whose associate found it lying next to the mutilated body of the Rabbi. But now the war was over she told her husband Haim, "I am going to Germany to look for my Rachel, I cannot bear to wait any longer. I want to see my baby."

Haim however suggested she first write to the Red Cross to find the whereabouts of Rachel. "Germany is in utter chaos now, and you cannot travel across a military zone, the roads and railways are destroyed and the Red Cross is your best bet," he soberly told his wife.

Mildred learned from the Red Cross in Switzerland her daughter was captured by the Nazis and imprisoned at Dautmergen. However, the Red Cross mistakenly believed she died of starvation at the camp; there was no record of her alive. Mildred was so upset; Rachel was her baby, the only baby she ever had. She cried for days until she had no more tears to shed.

After the war ended, the Zionist movement in the Holy Land received more sympathy from world leaders in recognition of the horrible treatment the Jews received at the hands of the Nazis and the subsequent extermination of a large segment in Europe. More money and guns poured into the area, and the Zionists organized themselves into a paramilitary force fighting both the Arabs and the British. Haim was elevated to the post of commander for an elite unit to fight the Arabs, while Mildred was assigned to a field medical team to provide treatment to the injured during fights. This was their life now.

Ingrid's life in America dragged on at the same pace working for the Eatons for six years. Quite the contrary, the family recognized she was essential, both in the kitchen and helping with the cleaning of the large mansion, and her English proficiency improved considerably. She was looking forward to going to the cottage in Holland before David starts school in September. This trip was a tradition the whole family enjoyed; last summer little David had so much fun playing in the water with Greg and with the Eaton children.

Yet Ingrid still felt a vacuum in her heart. She was brought up Jewish and feared her attachment to her faith slipping away. She confided her fears to Greg one day.

"What is your religious background? I mean which church do you go to?" she asked him.

"I am not a religious person," he quickly answered. "I haven't been to church in a long time. The Eatons invited me to join their Quaker church but I declined. I was brought up Presbyterian like my father, my mother however was Catholic and neither of them went to church regularly. How about you Ingrid, did you go to church often when you were young?"

"Yes, I did, I had a religious upbringing. My family went to synagogue every Sabbath and I miss that now. By the way, we call our church synagogue and our priest is called a rabbi."

"Yes, yes I already know all of that; I pass a synagogue every day going to work."

"Do you really? What is the name of the Synagogue and where is it located?"

"It is in Dearborn close to where I live, and I haven't paid much attention to the name, but since you mentioned it, I will look for it."

"I really, really want to visit the Synagogue you are talking about; I feel this urge to reconnect with my faith."

"I didn't know you were religious or noticed spiritual inclination before, why the sudden change?"

"Nothing important I suppose, but in my family tradition we gather in the synagogue for our newborn's religious celebration, and I was under so much stress when I arrived in this country, I failed in my duty towards David."

"I don't quite understand, I haven't seen a woman more engrossed with her baby than you, and I was under the impression you must have given him the necessary ritual rites. But I would be happy to take you."

"I wish I had, but to tell you the truth I haven't. David was not afforded the proper religious ceremonies Jewish babies typically receive at the synagogue, ceremonies like the name calling and *Brit Milah* for boys. You see in our religion we take these ceremonies seriously, it is considered *Mitzvah* or God's commands."

"That is so interesting; I suppose in Christianity we have something similar. We take our babies for baptism at the church, an act similar in nature to what you do at the synagogue."

"What is baptism? I heard this word before but I don't understand what it means."

"Baptism is the washing of the baby with holy water as a sign of purification and religious rite, and it is an important religious ceremony for Christians. If you wish, I can take you to the synagogue one day and you can talk to the priest there."

"You keep forgetting Greg; it is a rabbi not a priest and yes, I would love to go to the synagogue but it has to be on a Saturday if you don't mind."

Rabbi Efraim Abramson of El Beth Shalom Congregation was pleased to see Ingrid when she came to his office with little David trotting behind. He was so touched by her story after she finished telling him about her ordeal at the concentration camp and about the good Samaritans who gave her so much love and support.

She also confided, "When I arrived in this country I was in so much stress and neglected my duty towards David. Please forgive me rabbi, but I am here seeking to amend my indiscretion and do what is right for my boy."

"It is never late in the eyes of the Lord; all babies are the children of the Almighty and we should love and cherish them just as the Lord loves and cherishes you and I. Please come with your husband and the baby next week and I will be glad to bless him and perform all the things he missed when he was a baby. I recognize your circumstances are not typical of other Jewish women and the Lord must have wisdom behind events that shape our lives."

"I am sorry Rabbi, but I omitted to mention my husband died at the hands of the Nazis before David was born. I am bringing the child up on my own. The family I work for are God-sent; they are so wonderful and they are like family to David and me."

"God bless you my child, and may God bless this Christian family for looking after you."

Greg was dozing off in the truck outside the synagogue when Ingrid finished. Her eyes were swollen red and tears were still trickling down when she approached the truck.

"What is going on Ingrid, why are you crying, are you okay?"

"I am not upset, I am very happy, really happy, and so is David," she answered softly.

Ingrid had been thinking about Greg for a long time. She thought he was nice and genuine the day they met, but over the past year she felt really close to him. He wasn't the best looking man in the world but he was handsome in his own way, though he needed to improve his wardrobe or even comb his unruly hair instead of wearing a hat on his head all the time. But this is who he was, always casual, always there to help others, never late for work, and David truly loved him.

Rita observed how close Greg and Ingrid were getting. He takes her out regularly for something to eat and to the movies on weekends, and she always prepares sandwiches for him when he is outside. She even offered to do his laundry and press his shirts. Rita wasn't surprised at all when Ingrid wanted to ask questions about him.

"How long have you known Greg?"

"Oh, gosh, I have known him a long time I suppose, maybe fifteen years, even longer I guess. Why do you ask?"

"I really like him, he is nice and interesting, and I find it easy to talk to him."

"I can see that, you cannot wait for lunch time to take sandwiches out to him and you offered to do his laundry; I believe you are in love with him, Hon!"

"How did you and Fred meet, were you in love with him before you married him?"

"Don't change the subject Ingrid; I can see why you fell in love with Greg, he is a good man, very much like my man Fred and I can tell you one thing for sure, Greg likes you. He likes you a lot."

"How do you know he likes me, what did he do to make you say that?"

"He said so himself."

Ingrid was on Greg's mind also. It wasn't only her placid nature and unassuming personality that attracted him, but the girl was beautiful! Her long, thick black hair and slender figure, not to mention her blue eyes and the tone of her skin, and that lovely accent of hers when she speaks in English was an attraction on its own, and Greg cannot stop thinking about her.

It was the summer of 1953, and the country has a new president, Gen. Dwight D. Eisenhower, and the prevailing feeling in the United States was one of happiness and optimism. Greg had just arrived home when he received a call from Russell Eaton. "I would like you to come over to the house this evening. Mary and I decided to have an impromptu party at the house tonight for Russell Jr. He graduated from college and he is flying in from New York this evening. We would like to gather round the pool for a surprise party for him and I'd like you to be here to help."

"Yes sir, I will be there," Greg said before he hung up. He had indeed planned his evening differently, he in fact was looking forward to a surprise of his own, but Russell always meant the world to Greg and he couldn't tell him no. He jumped in the shower and when he finished he put his best suit on, fastened his shirt and put on his bow tie. He jumped in the truck and drove downtown; he had an important stop to make before going to his employer's house.

Ingrid was in her room getting ready to come to the kitchen when she heard a knock on the door. "You better hurry up," Rita called from behind the door, "we have guests arriving in a couple of hours and we need to get the kitchen ready for the caterers, they well be here soon!"

"What are you talking about, who is coming?"

"Mrs. Eaton came down a little while ago and told Fred to go to the airport to pick up Russell Jr. We're having a surprise party for his graduation. You and I will help with the drinks, and the caterers will serve the food."

"Okay, all I have to do is put my apron on and I will be out in a minute."

Ingrid and little David walked to the kitchen in a hurry; she sat David on the chair and gave him a piece of paper and crayons to pass his time, and she sat with Rita polishing the glasses. An hour later, the kitchen was crowded with frantic people from the catering company bringing in stacks of plates and serving dishes. Mary Eaton came down dressed in a beautiful evening gown, her hair coiffed in a nice style.

"Are we all ready yet, the guests will be here any minute, and where is Greg, hasn't he arrived yet?"

"Yes Ma'am, I just got here!"

Ingrid was speechless when she raised her head to look. She saw an utterly different Greg; he was all dressed up in a three-piece suit, his red hair washed and combed to the back, his shoes all shiny and his round face happy and radiant.

"Wow, wow, wow!" Ingrid and Rita hollered together, "You look spiffy, like an English country gentleman! What is this all about?"

"Nothing important," he said with his usual giggle, "I have to be here for my buddy, Russell Jr."

The party started soon after Russell Jr. walked in to the cheers and the congratulation of the guests. Servers with hors d'oeuvres trays walked between the guests while Greg was uncorking the wine and champagne bottles and pouring their contents in the glasses. Both Rita and Ingrid dressed in their black uniforms were in and out carrying trays of drinks. It was a gorgeous summer evening in Detroit and the atmosphere in the house was merry and convivial. After everyone finished eating and tables were cleared, Russell Eaton put on Hank Williams' new song, Honky Tonk Blues and everybody was on their feet dancing.

Exhausted, Rita and Ingrid walked back to the still crowded kitchen for a little respite before going out for the next round of drinks. When the two girls came in, Greg asked everybody in the kitchen. "May I have your attention everybody? I have an announcement to make, please." The men and the women stopped and formed a circle round him.

He went down on his knee, took Ingrid's hand in his and said, "I love you Ingrid. Will you marry me?"

Ingrid was speechless and shaking all over. "I love you; I love you with all of my heart Greg McKay! Yes, I will marry you!" She threw her arms round him and they kissed to the cheers and whistles of all in the kitchen.

PART 2

CHAPTER 23

O scar received his first business call while applying the final touches to the new office he rented on a busy street in the city center. The blue and yellow neon sign was scheduled for installation in the afternoon. They called the business H&O Construction, using the initials of their first names, Helmut and Oscar.

The caller, Mr. Rodriquez, was the general manager of a real estate management company with property holdings across the city. He wanted to invite Oscar to bid on a new project, a multi-storey mixed use building for commercial and residential tenancy. Oscar had been forewarned by Helmut to expect the call, and made arrangements to drop by his office to talk about the project and pick the plans up for pricing.

One of Helmut's best friends, a regular at the country club, owned the real estate company, and the last time they met, Helmut informed him about the new construction company in town. The man agreed to give them a chance to bid on his upcoming project once the design drawings were complete. His level of interest rose after Helmut told him about Oscar, his new partner. "You have to see this man in operation; he is knowledgeable, dedicated to his work, meticulous with the details and knows how to get things done correctly." Mr. Rodriquez had actually seen Oscar's work when he visited Helmut's new villa on the outskirts of the city and heard him boast about the tall blond man from Germany who was in charge of the construction team which built it.

Oscar was well prepared when he visited the real estate magnate at his plush offices in a tall building close to the city center. The man was impressed with Oscar and promised to give him the job if he submits a competitive bid. Oscar wasted no time and prepared a cutthroat offer after a thorough investigation of the plans and as a result was awarded the contract over the rival offers. Oscar was pleased to get his first break and was adamant to do all he could to showcase the project for all to see as well as make an impact on the city's architectural landscape.

Work started promptly after the ceremonial signing of the contract. The survey crew marked the coordinates for the structure, and excavation began immediately to prepare the underground work. The profile of the building started to take shape a few months after breaking ground. Helmut and the owner dropped by the building site every once in a while to check on the progress, and after fourteen months of nonstop work the tall building was ready for its first tenant. Helmut was happy with the result but not as much as the owner. The cost came below the initial estimates and the building was completed in record time, much to his satisfaction.

H&O construction developed a reputation for efficiency and good quality work and job contracts poured in. Oscar worked long hours without breaks and Ricardo complained to his friend how frustrating it was to come home every day to an empty house and all the conversation was about construction on the rare times when Oscar was indeed there! Oscar responded to his best friend's accusations with some irritation, "You are right Ricardo, I have been really busy and have been staying late to supervise work at the job site, but the city is growing fast and there aren't enough qualified people to do the work."

"Why don't you hire a construction manager to help take some of the burden off of your shoulders?"

"That is easier said than done, Ricardo. So far I interviewed half a dozen candidates but none impressed me. They all claim great knowledge and experience during interviews but their performance in the field suggests otherwise, and I am left with no choice but to ignore my social life in favor of building a solid foundation for my future. You've got to have discipline to succeed because if you don't others will overtake you and leave you out in the cold. I even turned down Helmut's invitations to meet him and his family at the country club; I simply don't have the time."

Helmut did ask again when he dropped by to see Oscar at his office one day. "My family and I will be with friends at the country club on Friday evening. Why don't you join us for dinner and cocktails?"

"Let me see what I can do Helmut, but I am so busy, even my roommate Ricardo was complaining how long I work every day."

Yes, he is right. I also noticed how long you work every day, which is a good thing, but you need to meet and talk to people. I attribute my own success to hard work, but socializing with people added to my success a great deal. You see, meeting people to widen your circle of friends will reflect positively on your business in the long run; this is what you call networking. It is so very important in life because you get many business leads through friends and acquaintances, especially when people get to know who you are and become familiar with what you do."

"Alright, you convinced me Helmut. I will be there Friday evening but I have a small request to make; may I bring Ricardo also?"

"Bring whomever you wish, and you don't need to ask for my permission!"

Friday evening started with a light drizzle but the rain stopped by the time Oscar and Ricardo arrived at the country club. The maître d' escorted them to Helmut's table on the covered terrace overlooking the pool in this very opulent place. Ricardo couldn't help but notice the expensive décor with plush carpet and fancy linen coverings, beautiful tropical flowers arranged tastefully in crystal vases and placed on tables. The guests sat on expensive rattan chairs and music was playing softly in the background. As they made their way to where Helmut was seated all eyes were on them, many were curious; who were those two good looking guys? Especially the tall blond one.

Helmut stood up to introduce them to his guests and family, "You still remember Erika, my wife and Gretchen, my daughter..."

"How can I forget them!" he said with a laugh after he gently shook their hands.

Helmut ordered a round of drinks and the music volume was turned up a notch. The dance floor was getting busier by the minute and Helmut asked his wife for a dance. Hans and Oscar stayed at the table talking to the guests and when Helmut returned he noticed Oscar was talking to Gretchen; he had a pen in hand and was drawing lines in the shape of a building on a piece of paper.

Helmut teased his daughter, "Is Oscar boring you with his construction, dear?"

"No dad, he is so interesting," she replied demurely.

"You need to stop this Oscar. Work is work and fun is fun and the two don't mix! Why don't you take Gretchen for a dance instead?"

"Would you like to dance?" Oscar asked her.

"I would love to," she answered, and the two got up and walked hand in hand to the dance floor. Gretchen couldn't help but notice how well he danced despite his limp.

On their way back to the apartment Ricardo commented how beautiful Gretchen looked this evening. "You lucky devil, you scored big tonight! Gretchen turned away all the men who asked her to dance, but she was on her feet the minute you asked!"

"I sure was lucky tonight, the girl is a knockout, and she is dripping with class and charm. I hope I get to see her again."

H&O Construction experienced phenomenal growth with each passing day. Oscar now has a personal secretary and in house engineering and accounting departments with scores of employees. With more projects on the way, much to the respect and the envy of competitors, H&O moved to new premises with multiple offices and a big conference room littered with construction drawings. The work volume was getting too large for one man to handle and Oscar was looking for a reliable person to take some of the load. His search produced potential candidates but none matched his expectations, so he picked up the phone and called Helmut.

"I wonder if you can help? I have a problem finding the proper person to carry some of my work load," he asked with a hint of frustration.

"There must be many people available out there who surely can meet your requirement. I fail to understand why you are unable to find the right person," Helmut answered with encouragement.

"You are right about that, many people are available," Oscar responded, "but the person I am looking for has to be extremely reliable, hardworking and close to my way of thinking. Somebody I can operate with on the same wavelength, and someone who can understand me in an instant and relate to my way of thinking. You see, we built a good reputation over the last few years and I don't want to lose it if I hire the wrong man for the job. It is absolutely critical to have someone who completely understands me."

"You don't have to explain any further Oscar, but you already have the person you are looking for. Ask Ricardo to take the job."

Ricardo was not too unhappy getting a job offer from his friend, but he explained his commitment to Martin Bauer at the machine shop. "The man took me under his wing when I arrived penniless in this country. I cannot in all honesty turn my back on him now. He suffers from diabetes and last month the doctor informed him the condition is affecting his limbs. I'm afraid something will happen to him if I leave, and I will not forgive myself if it turned out I was the cause."

"This is very honorable Ricardo, and I admire your stand, but it won't hurt to ask the man and see what he says. Explain to him you have an opportunity to work with me and build a better life for yourself. He is a fair person and he probably will not stand in your way."

Ricardo was stunned when he approached Martin with the subject.

"You can go, with my blessing Ricardo. I don't have the strength to carry on with this business anymore and I have been thinking to put it up for sale ever since my condition worsened. As a matter of fact I was going to offer it to you first but you deserve better in life. You and Oscar will make a good team together, but may I please ask a favor of you? Can you stay with me until the business is sold?"

Ricardo became Oscar's right hand man soon thereafter. The plan was for Ricardo to supervise the site jobs and the outside work, and Oscar to manage the company and the huge clientele he built over the years. The two young men made a dynamic pair and things were off to a good start.

CHAPTER 24

Greg and Ingrid were married in the same church he used to go to with his parents on the few occasions they chose to be close to God. The pastor didn't even remember Greg when he came in to discuss his wedding plans; it was that long since he saw him. The ceremony was attended by a small number of people: the Eaton family, a few friends, Rita and Fred. Little David handed Greg the ring when the pastor ordered and pronounced them man and wife as Greg slipped the ring on Ingrid's finger. The Eatons paid for the reception at a nice hotel as a wedding gift.

Ingrid didn't mind the church ceremony as long as the marriage was also blessed by the Rabbi at the synagogue, to which Greg readily agreed. There were other things the couple addressed before their union.

"I want to bring David up in the Jewish tradition because of my obligation towards him, and in the future when we have more children my religion dictates they become Jewish like their mother," Ingrid insisted.

Greg fully understood her desire to have David brought up in the Jewish tradition but he was ambivalent about future children. "My parents didn't shove religion down my throat," he told her, "they let me choose between my mother's Catholic church and my father's Presbyterian church, and I seriously believe this be the best course for our children. We should make both options available and let them choose the one that best suits their spiritual needs." Ingrid reluctantly conceded.

The new 'Mr. and Mrs. McKay' left David in the care of Rita and headed to Texas for their honeymoon. This was Ingrid's suggestion, she had always wanted to see the place her husband talked about so much, and on the day after David's 8th birthday they put their suitcases in the back of the truck and hit the road south in the direction of the Lone Star State. It was snowing lightly in Detroit but the snow stopped by the time they crossed into Indiana; the weather remained cold though. They arrived exhausted in Memphis in the early hours of the morning after a long drive from Detroit. During the trip her eyes were eager to explore; she never stopped looking out of the car windows willing to ask and happy to listen when Greg explained landmarks along the way. Ingrid gasped when they drove by the Mississippi river; she had heard of it from school and was excited when the actual river came into view!

The newlyweds made it to Corpus Christi after that much needed rest in Memphis and a stop in Abilene to see Greg's sister. Ingrid was amazed how Greg and his sister look so much alike, both have flaming red hair, round faces and that silly but infectious giggle. Ingrid loved the Texas coast with miles of unadulterated sand, but she particularly enjoyed the excursions on the boat with friends and the Texas style crab boil on the beach around the fire at night. It was utterly enjoyable and Ingrid couldn't get enough; she was sad to say goodbye to all the new friends she made. Greg and Ingrid returned to Detroit happy and eager to resume the normal routine working for the Eaton household, but on the way back from Texas, Greg had one important thing he wanted to discuss with Ingrid.

"Last November," he began, "I stopped at the Duran Nursery in Dearborn, and I was baffled when the old man told me he was thinking to put the business up for sale. I have been a customer for a long time, my dad used to take me there for all his landscaping needs and I continued to go there after my dad passed away, and I buy most of the stuff for the Eatons' gardens from there still. I was curious why Mr. Duran wanted to sell it when the business was doing so well. The old man gave a big sigh and confessed his children, whom I know all on a first name basis, don't want to continue with the business. Their preference is to go to college. He also admitted the business was making a good profit, but the hard work and the long hours is what concerns his children, in his opinion."

"Okay," Ingrid said impatiently, "what is your point?"

Greg had been thinking about the Duran Nursery ever since the old owner expressed his desire to sell, so he approached him before the wedding to discuss the sales particulars. "Well, it's a little more than I can afford, so I am thinking to ask Russell Eaton to go in partnership and buy the business jointly with me. Do you think it is a good idea?"

"It is entirely your decision, I don't know much about business, and you know the man better than I do."

"Yes, I do know Russell well; I have been going there with my father since I was a little boy. My father started at his old house and continued when they bought the mansion in Grosse Pointe. I think the man will accept my proposal and I intend to have a word with him when we arrive home."

Ingrid however expressed some caution. "You need to consider if the business is viable and will generate enough income to pay the rent and put food on the table, especially after the loss of my small income. You assured me the salary you are making every month is more than sufficient to cover all our expenses, and there was no need for me to continue working at the Eatons."

"I am not at all worried, the business has many established clients and I will continue to provide the same service if not a better one," Greg said energetically.

Greg approached Russell about the business but was surprised how fast Russell answered him. "No, I wouldn't be interested to go into the nursery business, but if you wish to buy it, I will be glad to help. I can loan you the money to pay for the business and you can pay me the loan back on monthly installments until it's all paid off."

Greg couldn't believe his luck. "You have a big heart Mr. Eaton, I cannot thank you enough!" Greg answered excitedly.

"But wait a minute," Russell continued, "There's one condition: will you continue to look after our garden, Mary is very fond of you!"

Ingrid wanted to rent a two bedroom apartment but Greg insisted they needed three bedrooms. "There are only three of us, you, me and David. Why in God's name do you want three bedrooms, what will you do with the extra room? You must take the extra cost into account, particularly when you are starting a new business with an uncertain future."

"You are right, Ingrid, but I would like to have one or two more children in the future, and if you consider the expense associated with moving from one place to another it makes more sense to get three rooms now. I also have great hope for this business, I believe in it and hopefully we will become prosperous like the Eatons."

It was time for Ingrid to say goodbye to her heroes, the Eaton family. She stopped in the kitchen first but couldn't get herself to speak, she put her arms around Rita and the two women embraced for several minutes crying. Then she, Greg and David walked hand in hand to the breakfast nook where the family gathers in the morning and with a trembling voice full of emotions she bid this wonderful family her farewells. "You will remain in my heart for the rest of my life, you are true angels and it has been my honor to serve you the past years. Greg, David and I will forever be in your debt, may the Lord bless you and stay with you forever."

Old man Duran was not wrong in his assessment about the nursery business; the first nine months after Greg purchased it, he never returned home before 9 pm. Ingrid expressed her displeasure, "What takes you so long every day? David only sees you on Sunday afternoons. You leave before he is up and you return when he is in bed, too tired to have a conversation."

"Yes dear, but work never stops all day and when we close our doors at 7 pm, I work on the books so nobody is around to disturb me. The old man's last words when he handed me the keys were, 'son, you need to do two things if you want to succeed, look after clients well and look after your books even better,' and this is precisely what I am doing."

Ingrid was none too impressed, "Is this how we are going to live for the rest of our lives, work and sleep and do nothing else? Maybe you need to get a bookkeeper to look after the books, Hon."

"Yes dear, I will. In the future when things get better and our loan is paid off."

David's 11th birthday was coming up soon on New Year's Day 1956. He was a handsome boy now and doing very well in school.

"What would you like to have for your birthday?" Ingrid asked her son.

She, herself, was in for a surprise. "I would like to have a record player," he answered promptly.

"What do you need a record player for, David?"

"I love music and I want to play Elvis."

"Did you get this idea from school?"

"No mother, I didn't. But I was in the truck with dad last Sunday and Elvis was playing his new song on the radio. Dad was singing along and I really enjoyed it."

"And what song was that, David?"

"Don't be Cruel is the one I liked most."

"Why how many were there?"

"Oh, there was another one about a dog, but I cannot remember the title."

"Very well David, when your dad comes home we will discuss it, but I have another present to talk to you about."

"Oh Mom, will I have two presents then?" David asked with excitement.

"Yes dear, you will this time. You will have a new brother or a new sister. Which one would you like to have?"

"I would like to have the record player," he answered innocently.

Greg was thrilled with the news when he came home in the evening. "I have been to the doctor's office this morning," Ingrid greeted him when he walked in the kitchen, "and I have a little surprise for you...I am pregnant!"

Greg couldn't believe the news. He rushed towards his wife, put his arms around her waist and lifted her off her feet in the air. "This is the best news I heard all day!" The couple laughed so much at David's request for a birthday present, and Greg promised to get the boy what he wanted for his birthday.

"By the way, which Elvis song was about a dog?" she asked with a smile.

"Do you mean, 'Ain't Nothin' but a Hound Dog'?" Greg said, whistling the tune.

CHAPTER 25

Porto Alegre, last big city in the south before you reached the frontier of another country, was expanding rapidly due to the influx of business and people. Oscar and Ricardo enjoyed this unseasonably sweltering Saturday afternoon in their new high rise office building on the city waterfront overlooking the bay; cigar smoke filled the air.

Signora Alvarado walked in, "Can I do anything before I sign off for the day sir?"

"No, have a nice weekend and I will see you Monday morning."

The minute the secretary walked out of the office Ricardo started, "What are your plans for the evening?"

"I think I am meeting with Gretchen tonight. Helmut and Erika will be there; do you want to join us?"

"I don't know yet. Lauretta talked about the movies for something different to do, let me see if I can convince her to come to the country club tonight."

H&O Construction was doing very well indeed; the high quality work and consistent performance earned them a good reputation, made them the envy of their peers and propelled them to the ranks of the best in the region. The company widened the scope of its activities, doubled its work force and became large enough to sign big construction jobs all over the south of Brazil. Helmut through his wide circle of business associates and friends was instrumental, but the field work was managed by Oscar and Ricardo, and the outcome was invariably good. The increased business volume compelled the company to move again, this time though to a brand new building owned and constructed by the company itself. Oscar in particular turned out to be a good and smart manager and his office occupied the top floor of the building. The two guys were inseparable, they worked together as a team and the results showed as they moved up in life and developed wide circle of friends and acquaintances. In addition they both purchased new homes and each was involved in a romantic courtship.

Oscar was still in the office after Ricardo left; he lit another cigar, grabbed a drink from the office refrigerator and sat on the couch pondering his life. *If only my family could see all of this, they wouldn't believe it. But they would be proud of me. I really do miss them. My sister Elizabeth would have been in her mid-twenties by now, very beautiful like she always was, probably married with children. Oh, I miss that opportunity to be an uncle to her children. I guess I will never be with Elizabeth, gone forever, but I feel blessed and lucky to have my beautiful Gretchen. What a lady, in a class of her own, always caring, always loving, and always giving with that big heart of hers. She brings me so much joy and I wish I had more time to spend with her. But I have to continue working on my business, one day it will be one of the largest in the country...*

Oscar's thoughts were interrupted with the sound of the phone.

It was Gretchen on the other end. "Why don't you come to the house and have dinner with us tonight? We have visitors from out of town, and dad cancelled the country club for tonight."

"Who is coming?" Oscar asked inquisitively.

"Friends from Sao Paulo, but originally from Dusseldorf in the old country. They are really fun, you'll like them."

"Very well, I will be there," he confirmed. Then he called and left a message for Ricardo to meet him there.

The people Oscar met at Helmut's house were indeed very nice and fun loving. Gerhard Foch was an industrialist in Sao Paulo who became rich in the mining business in central Brazil. He was an overweight man in his late sixties and enjoyed a glass of good ale, and after few pints he was off talking about his adventures and telling great jokes along the way. The evening started with Gerhard telling everybody about the trip he made to Germany last year, and how proud and full of wonderment he was at the country after the massive destruction it suffered during the war, how it was able to turn around its fortunes and become at the forefront of nations. The German miracle he was referring to was achieved by none other than Chancellor Conrad Adenauer who completely rebuilt the country from the ground up and brought unprecedented prosperity. He made the country respected around the world again. Nevertheless, Gerhard's favorite hero was still Adolf Hitler, and he, like many of his fellow countrymen widely share the same sentiments of German pride and superiority. After dinner was finished, Gerhard told Oscar, "When you are in Sao Paulo come see me, I would like to introduce you to some great people in our area."

Ricardo did come with his girlfriend to Helmut's house that evening; the two have been going out with each other for over a year now, but the relationship was unraveling. Lauretta was the jealous type, always suspecting Ricardo of impropriety with other females. Gretchen's relationship with Oscar on the other hand was getting stronger by the day. Even Erika commented how well the couple suited each other. Oscar was a leader in life, he was a go getter and secure enough to provide for her daughter and afford the life to which she was accustomed. Gretchen confessed to her mother that Oscar was the man she loved to be around. Yes he is serious sometimes but he is also fun loving and a good dancer, too.

The day finally arrived Oscar was thinking of for some time. He buzzed his secretary. Ramona's familiar voice came on the intercom, "Yes sir, I will be over right away."

She took some notes and walked out, but before she closed the door behind her, Oscar shouted, "And cancel all my appointments for the rest of the day!"

He took the elevator to the underground parking garage, jumped in his convertible Mercedes and sped off to pick up the two items he ordered from the prestigious store, and then he drove home, and made two calls the minute he arrived.

Helmut answered the first call. "I would like to invite you, Erika and Gretchen to dinner at Pueblos this evening."

"I don't believe we have anything planned for this evening," answered Helmut, "Yes, we can meet there, but what is the occasion?"

"Nothing special, but we will enjoy the evening together. I know Erika and Gretchen love the food there, Ricardo is coming, too."

"Alright I look forward to a nice evening."

Ricardo also accepted the invitation when his friend called. "Lauretta will not be with me though; she and I are going through a rough patch now."

When Helmut and his family arrived at the highly acclaimed restaurant overlooking a spectacular view of the bay, they were ushered to the round table Ramona had reserved for her boss. A stunning arrangement of red roses was sitting in the middle of the table and a band playing soft music was sitting on the small stage in the corner of the dance floor. Oscar and Ricardo rose to greet the guests.

They all enjoyed their aperitifs in this elite setting, followed by appetizers and then the main course and lastly came the dessert. Oscar, who was especially handsome dressed in an expensive suit and tie, whispered something in the waiter's ear. Shortly, an expensive bottle of Dom Perignon was brought over to the table.

Oscar stood up next to where Gretchen was seated and then he went on his knee. He held Gretchen's hand in his and said, "My darling, I wanted everyone we care about to be here tonight for a special reason. I want them to witness how much I love you and want to spend the rest of my life with you. Will you marry me, beautiful Gretchen?"

The whole restaurant erupted in applause and cheers when Gretchen said, "Yes, yes I will!"

Oscar opened the jewelry box he picked up earlier in the day and slipped a stunning ring on Gretchen's finger, then a diamond encrusted gold watch round her wrist. The waiter poured the champagne and Ricardo stood to toast his best friend and his future bride. Gretchen and Erika were crying and the mood was one of sheer happiness and enjoyment.

Oscar and Gretchen were married at the main Lutheran church in town; hundreds of guests came to this elegant place. The wedding was performed in a traditional German ceremony. Erika was seated in the front row next to Ricardo and many of her family members were also present. Oscar and Pastor Hinkle stood at the altar busy talking. When the band was given the signal to begin, Gretchen entered, dressed in a gorgeous satin wedding dress, her blonde hair done up in soft waves and curls with a veil round her face. Walking down the aisle with her father, she looked like an angel, glowing and beautiful. When they reached the altar, Pastor Hinkle began the ceremony.

"We are gathered today in the presence of God and in the presence of loved ones and friends, to celebrate one of life's greatest celebrations and to give recognition to the holiness of the union between a man and a woman, and to add to the Lord's blessing which shall unite this bride and groom in holy matrimony. May this marriage be adorned with true and lasting love. Who brings this woman to this man?"

Helmut said, "I do," He then turned to his daughter and kissed her on the cheek and walked back and sat next to Erika.

Pastor Hinkle continued, ordering Oscar to step forward and take the hand of Gretchen and with his slow deliberate voice he continued, "This moment, you bring the love of your hearts as a treasure to share with one another. We rejoice with you now as you celebrate this union which has already been created by friendship, respect and love."

He picked up the two rings and held his hands up to display them, "Let us bless these rings, oh God. These rings are circles, symbols which remind us of sun and earth, symbols of holiness and peace that has no beginning and no end. In this moment bring your blessing to these rings to also be symbols of unity, of joining and commitment and for the love Oscar and Gretchen have for one another. These rings that Oscar and Gretchen will wear for the rest of their lives as an expression for the love and commitment they have for each other. Oscar and Gretchen, as you dedicate yourselves to one another we are reminded of the presence of God amongst us." The pastor hands the first ring to Oscar; he slips the ring on her finger.

"Please repeat after me, I Oscar, take you Gretchen, to be my wedded wife, to have and to hold, from this day forward, for better or worse for richer for poorer, in sickness or in health, to love and to cherish till death do us part. I promise to show you all the same kind of love that Christ showed the church when he died for her, and to love you as part of myself in his sight we will be one."

The pastor hands the second ring to Gretchen. She picks up the ring and slips it on Oscar's finger.

"Gretchen please repeat after me, I Gretchen take you Oscar to be my wedded husband to have and to hold from this day forward, for better for worse, for richer for poorer, in sickness and in health, to love and to cherish, till death do us part. I will live first unto our God and then unto you, loving you and obeying you caring for you and ever seeking to please you. I lay down my life for you and as of this day I submit myself to you."

Pastor Hinkle continued, "Oscar and Gretchen, we, your family and friends, wish for you the very best and we wish that you be filled with joy. Oscar, you may kiss the bride."

Oscar lifted Gretchen's veil, "You are the most precious thing in my heart, I love you Gretchen," and then he kissed her on the lips to the roaring cheers of the attendees.

At the end of the ceremony, the bride passed white ribbons for the guests to tie to their cars' antennas. The couple and their guests formed a procession and drove through the streets honking their horns. Many motorists honked back wishing the couple the best of luck. The couple after several hours of dancing and receiving the customary congratulations at the country club retired for the evening.

The following day the newlyweds stopped to say goodbye to her parents before heading out on their honeymoon at the superb Iguazu Falls on the border with Argentina. Tears were coming down Erika's face; she was truly happy her daughter had become the wife of this wonderful man.

CHAPTER 26

Baby Sonia was born on a beautiful sunny July day. She was a healthy baby with a trace of her dad's red hair, and when the nurse came back and handed the baby to her mother, Ingrid couldn't contain her emotions. Greg was crying also, the proud parents were so overjoyed with their new baby.

The following day the couple went home with Sonia in Ingrid's arms. They stopped at the Eatons' house to pick up David who was in the care of Rita.

"David, this is your sister Sonia, isn't she beautiful?"

David stood on tiptoes in order to reach his sister and plant a big kiss on her cheek. Rita took the little baby in her arms, "Dear God, she is so beautiful! You are going to be a pretty girl, aren't you?" she said lovingly.

The Eaton family also came to give their congratulations and Greg explained the name they chose for the girl was after his mother's first name. Eight days after Sonia was born, Ingrid and Greg took her for the traditional baby blessing at the synagogue. Rabbi Abramson placed the holy book on her crib and recited the traditional blessings for Jewish girls.

The nursery business was doing well and Greg was very happy with the purchase he made two years earlier. He retained the majority of the clients the old man had accumulated over the years and Greg devoted much of his time to add more. He tripled the number of his employees during the height of the season in the summer and by the end of 1959 he saw further increase in his business. The U.S. Congress approved the Federal Highway Act President Eisenhower proposed three years earlier, and many of the now completed roads were in need of landscaping and he was awarded a major government contract.

Greg came home very happy one evening. He picked up little Sonia and put her in his arms, "I have these two earrings for you my little girl, you are the joy of my life!"

Ingrid who was in the kitchen came in and asked what was this all about.

"What do you mean?" Greg responded.

"Well I mean the earrings, what is the occasion?"

"I don't have to have an occasion to give my daughter a piece of jewelry. Neither do I need to have a reason to give one to my wife also!" He pulls a small jewelry bag from his pocket and hands it to his wife.

Ingrid looked at the beautiful long gold chain featuring a Star of David. "Oh my God, Greg McKay! You still surprise me after all of these years and I love you so much!"

Greg had recently been thinking of buying a home instead of paying for rent. The loan Russell Eaton has given him to purchase the nursery business is now fully paid, his bank balance looks healthy and the business has been doing well for several years. Ingrid was not so sure about the idea at the beginning.

Greg was incredulous. "I thought you would be jumping for joy at the idea of owning your own house, what seems to be the problem?"

After a long sigh, Ingrid stated, "Haven't you heard the news yet?"

"What news?" he said impatiently.

"We will have a big war with the Soviets. President Kennedy announced yesterday the United States will enforce a blockade around Cuba, because the communists have nuclear warheads stationed there and the missiles are directed at us. The Soviets said they will retaliate if we attack their ally Fidel Castro. There will be another big war like the war we had in Europe and our house will be destroyed!"

"This is nonsense my dear! If they attack us with nuclear bombs we will retaliate and we will utterly destroy each other! I think the leaders will come to their senses and work out a solution before the whole world go up in smoke. I don't think we need to worry about it, but for now we need to buy a house we can call our own home."

Ingrid finally relented. She and Greg decided the Dearborn area is where they'd like to remain because of the business, and he contacted a real estate agent and provided him the criteria for the house that best suits their taste and budget.

Ingrid was taken aback when David, now 16, came home from school at the end of the missile crisis, "Didn't I tell you mother? The communists will always back down when they are threatened. Our country is far stronger than they are and I knew they will flinch first. I told my teachers during the safety drills at school, there is no need for any of this nonsense of hiding under the table. There will be no war at all, the commies are a bunch of cowards!"

"Where do you get all this David? You sound like an adult!"

"Mr. Wurzbach, my Geography teacher, held a discussion in the school yard with a bunch of my friends about the Cuba crisis. He didn't care for the communists and neither do I. I have been reading about them for a while. They are mischievous and cannot be trusted."

Ingrid was utterly mesmerized by her teenage boy, he was more advanced in his thinking than many twice his age. She was aware her son reads quite a lot and his father constantly takes him to the public library to pick up books, but it was incredible how much this young man knows for his age!

Sonia was seven when news of President Kennedy's assassination hit the airwaves. Ingrid like the rest of the nation was sad, but nobody was more upset than David. He sat in their new home watching TV as the president's casket was unloaded from Air Force One into a waiting ambulance. The sight of his grieving wife was very touching, it made his mother and father cry.

But David, who was in his senior year at school sat stone faced. He felt angry, very angry. His parents were surprised when he got up and said, "One day the communists will be implicated for the plot to kill our president because he valiantly stood up to them. But the United States will avenge this crime!"

David was doing incredibly well at school; he was always at the top of his class and deservedly earned the spot to deliver the graduation valedictorian speech. His ambition was to continue his education and become a lawyer, but he decided first to apply for a finance and management degree at the University of Chicago because of the great program and subjects offered.

Ingrid took David regularly to synagogue and he felt at home there; he developed an intense attachment to the religion of his forefathers and was very proud of his Jewish heritage. As he grew older he never missed the opportunity to attend salient religious celebrations.

Rabbi Abramson was very pleased Ingrid brought up her son Jewish, but he was mystified when he noticed little Sonia was coming one Sabbath and skipping the next. He attributed this behavior to Sonia's age so didn't approve when Ingrid told him about the arrangement she made with her husband. "My husband and I agreed before we were married to bring up our children in both traditions, and this is why Sonia comes to the synagogue every other Saturday. She is with her father at his Presbyterian church the week she misses the synagogue. Our philosophy is to let her choose the faith that appeals to her soul. The Rabbi didn't believe that wise, but thought it was not his business to interfere between husband and wife.

Ingrid was for the most part very happy with her life; she has a wonderful husband who loves her very much and two children whom she adores. Everything seemed perfect, but she felt incomplete. She often over the years confided in her husband, "I miss my mother so much, and I have a strong desire to see her and show her how happy I feel living in America with my wonderful family! I wish to go to Israel one day," she told Greg. "This will mean the world to me. My mother will get to see her grandchildren, Sonia and David will see their grandmother and I will be very happy to see my family united again."

"Yes dear, I'd love to go too and meet your mother, but with the purchase of our new home we simply cannot afford a trip across the world right now. Besides, Sonia is still too young, maybe we should wait a couple years until she is old enough to appreciate and remember the trip?"

But when Sonia turned seven, Greg lived up to his promise. He came from work one evening feeling happy. "This morning we signed two large commercial contracts with the city of Dearborn, and I called that travel agency on Greenfield Road to get information about a trip to Europe and Israel. Honey, I would like to cheer you up and satisfy your ambition to go to the Holy Land to see your mother! And it could also be a present to David for graduating with honors. How does that sound?"

"I love you Greg McKay, I love you so much darling! I can't wait to tell the children, they will be so excited!" But while hugging her husband, Ingrid remembered something. "Oh. I've never flown before and I don't think I'd like it. To be honest, I am very afraid of flying. Is it possible to take a boat instead?"

"Everything is possible for you darling; let me see what I can do."

The children were indeed very happy when Ingrid told them about the trip.

"Where in Europe are you planning to take us?" David inquired, "May I suggest Germany; we will have a chance to see the old country where mum came from!"

"No we will not go there," Ingrid quickly interrupted, "I don't want to see the country ever again!"

"Okay Mum, where else do you suggest?"

"I would like to see England, I've heard so much about it and the country has a special place in my heart. The English people stood up to the Nazis, and had it not been for them, I probably would be dead by now."

"You forgot America mother, England wouldn't have won the war if it wasn't for America!"

"You are right David, America came in later, but England stood its ground since the beginning against the Nazi monsters."

Greg came home late one evening and he looked frustrated. Ingrid greeted him with concern. "What is up honey, you look like something is bothering you?"

"Yes indeed," he said, "I have been at the travel agency for the last four hours, and the agent made more than a dozen calls to passenger liners working the route between England and Israel with no luck at all. There are few passenger liners operating between the two countries and they are booked solid. But I was able to book two cabins to England, however we have no other option but to fly to Israel when we reach London. I am sorry darling, but I tried my best."

The Queen Mary, Cunard's flag ship passenger liner operating between New York and England, was waiting for them at Pier 88. They arrived in the nick of time that early morning in June and although the area looked a little different from the time when Ingrid first arrived in America, it brought back fond memories. The family was impressed; Greg didn't spare any cost to give them a nice holiday. The ship was majestic indeed with beautiful cabins and a plush interior. As the ship pulled up its anchor the whole family, like the rest of the passengers, were on the upper deck to observe the view of the New York skyline as the ship sailed down the Hudson River. Ingrid and the children waved goodbye and stayed on deck until the city faded from view. She was emotional when they passed Lady Liberty, yet full of pride, and the family took many photos with the new Kodak camera David bought with his own money for the trip.

Four days later the ship eased its way through the English Channel and the rocky coast of England was on full display covered in a thin layer of morning mist.

"Are we going to see the white cliffs of Dover?" little Sonia wanted to know.

"No we are not, we will get off at Southampton. Dover is still further east," David informed her.

"This is my boy, he is so smart," Ingrid whispered to her husband.

The family took the train to Waterloo station in central London. Greg was nearly run over by a passing car; he looked the wrong way when he tried to cross the street. "Be careful," he shouted to his children. "They drive on the wrong side!"

The McKay family had a wonderful time the following day and made the Palace of Westminster their first stop, the gothic building containing the houses of Parliament and seat of an empire overlooking the River Thames. This majestic place is full of history and works of art, and in the corner stood Big Ben, the iconic clock towering above the Palace. Before they finished for the day they stopped at two more of London's most iconic landmarks, Westminster Abby and St Paul's Cathedral. During the rest of their stay in London, they visited Buckingham Palace the residence of the Queen. Sonia loved the pageantry and was thrilled to see the traditional changing of the guards. They ended the day at a restaurant overlooking Trafalgar Square where the naval hero, Horatio Nelson is perched on top of a tall marble column in the middle of a busy square, and the family enjoyed a quick meal of fish and chips wrapped in newspaper served British style with salt and vinegar. Ingrid threw a coin in the fountain to offer the friendly English people her best wishes.

They loved and enjoyed their stay in this beautiful and verdant country, but it was time to say goodbye. They headed to Heathrow Airport the following day to catch a plane to Tel Aviv. Ingrid brought with her the name and phone number of a person who may be able to help find her mother. After more than twenty years since she heard from her, Ingrid was up all night thinking and preparing for the encounter.

"I cannot tell you how excited I feel! I cannot wait to see my mother and give her a hug, she will be pleased to meet you and the children!" she said to Greg. "And I cannot wait to see Israel, the home our forefathers, the land God promised the Jews. It is a miracle the country came into being and I am eternally thankful for all the Jews and the many good people who helped bring it about."

A little under five hours later the plane started its descent over the eastern Mediterranean. The ancient land of Israel in plain view from the airplane's window looked beautiful from a distance with white waves crashing along the coast. The weather was sunny and ground temperature was 91 degrees, the captain announced.

Before she traveled to the Holy Land, Ingrid asked Rabbi Abramson if he knew anybody who might be able to help find her mother.

"My mother immigrated to the Holy Land with her new husband after the death of my father. I was 7 years old when she left and I have not seen her since. She was expecting me to join her there, but because of my ordeal in Germany we lost all line of communications and I don't have the slightest idea where she might be now. All I know is her husband's first name and that she lived in a Kibbutz in the north, but this is before the creation of Israel." The rabbi nodded in understanding; he'd heard similar stories before. Ingrid continued, "I know my mother wouldn't have given up searching for me and will have attempted to find me after the war, but her search must have been inconclusive and she may have assumed I was killed."

The rabbi was touched by her plight. "I was sad to see Sam Gershan, one of our dear congregants leave us to make *Aliyah* to Israel seven years ago. He was a dear friend and a much loved member of our community, but after hearing your story, I realize how much the Lord does things we fail to understand at the time. But He always has the wisdom to show us why later, doesn't he? I think your story is befitting to His wisdom and Sam will be there to help you my dear. Come after prayer to my office and I will look for his address and phone number."

The following morning Ingrid picked up the phone in their hotel room and dialed the number. "May I speak to Sam Gershan, please?"

"This is he, who is this please?"

"My name is Ingrid McKay. I am from Detroit, Michigan. Rabbi Abramson gave me your name and number, and he said you may be able to help."

"Yes, the rabbi is a dear friend indeed, how may I help you, Ingrid?"

"I came to Israel to look for my mother…" and Ingrid repeated the same story she told the rabbi to Sam.

"Ingrid, I am so stirred by your story, please tell me where you staying? I will be glad to come by to talk to you."

The next day Sam Gershan took the family out for lunch and a tour of the city and before dropping them back at the hotel he took all the pertinent details about her mother. "What is your mother's name?"

"Her maiden name was Mildred Hirsh, and she was married to my father Amram Lieberman, they lived in Stettin. The city used to be in Germany but I believe after the war it became part of Poland."

"You said your mother came to Israel with her husband; was Amram Lieberman her husband?"

"No, my parents were divorced and my mother married another man, his name was Haim. I have searched my head for his last name, but I came up empty. I am sorry but I don't remember his last name."

"Do you remember anything about the man, anything that will help me at all, a photo will definitely help."

"I don't have any photos if either him or my mother, I lost everything when the Nazis found me. But I can give you description: my mother was tall with long red hair. Haim was tall also with dark hair and complexion. He had a black beard and wore a patch on one eye; my grandparents called him 'the revolutionary one'."

"My last question, do you know where they lived?"

"No, from what I remember, they lived in a kibbutz somewhere in the north of the country, and it looked like rolling hills behind where they stood judging from the photo my mother sent to us."

"Very well, let me see what I can do. You will be here for a while, won't you?"

"No, we arrived here yesterday afternoon and we will be flying back home in just six days."

The first thing Ingrid wanted to do is to go to Jerusalem, and she explained to the family the significance of the city. "Jews lived in the Holy Land from time immemorial.

King Solomon built a magnificent temple in the city, a house of God and the gate to heaven. It housed the Ark of the Covenant until the Babylonians came from the east and destroyed the temple and took the Jews into exile, the Jews wept by the Rivers of Babylon when they remembered Zion, They hoped to go back to Jerusalem and with the grace of God they returned and built the Temple once more. But again the Temple was destroyed and the Jews were exiled. The hope to build the temple stayed with us all of those years and when Israel was established in 1948 they chose "Hope" or 'Ha Tikvah' for the new national anthem.

The tour guide took the family all over the western part of the city. They visited the Kennset, the Israeli Parliament building and 'Yad Vashem', the Holocaust History museum. Greg and David had to support Ingrid, who nearly collapsed with emotions. The memory was so fresh and painful she broke into tears and couldn't look up at the pictures on the walls, they were too graphic for her.

When they returned to the hotel that evening there was a message from

Sam Gershan. Ingrid couldn't get to their room fast enough; she picked the phone and dialed his number.

"Hello Sam, I see you called."

"I have indeed, may I come see you tomorrow? There are things I would like to discuss with you."

"Sure you can see us tomorrow, is there a problem?"

"No, there is no problem, but I have some information for you."

The family was in the hotel lobby having coffee when Sam and another uniformed man came in the front door.

"Do you remember me Rachel?" The man had a patch on his eye and spoke German to Ingrid. "I am Haim Ashkenazi."

"Sorry, I didn't recognize you, but yes I remember you from the photo my mother sent to us. The uniform threw me off a little. Well, how are you doing and where is mother?"

"I am doing very well. I am a colonel in the IDF, The Israeli Defense Force. Please allow me to tell you about your mother." Ingrid was becoming nervous about his manner. He went on, "Mildred was the love of my life. She and I immigrated to the Holy Land together as you already know. Your mother became a nurse and she was very active in the building of our Kibbutz, during our war of independence. I was a captain in the army and our unit was dispatched to the hills of Jerusalem to fight the enemy and secure a lifeline for our besieged communities in the area. Mildred was assigned with our unit to offer medical help for the injured. When our unit came under intense bombardment from the enemy, a mortar shell exploded close to where your mother was standing, she suffered a direct shrapnel hit to the chest. I'm sorry, Ingrid, she was loved so much..." Ingrid was beginning to understand what he was telling her. "Everybody ran to help, but it was too late. Her injuries were fatal; Mildred died a hero in the defense of the land of Israel."

Ingrid nearly collapsed with sadness and grief. She was sobbing loudly, as were David and Sonia. Greg was stroking her back as she hunched over crying.

Haim continued, "I want you to know something important, Rachael. Your mother never ever stopped loving you. She tried to bring you here, but the situation was difficult for us and it was dangerous as you were in Germany, but God knows how much she loved you and how much she wanted to bring you here. When WWII was over she was making arrangements to go to Germany to bring you, but the report we received from the

Red Cross indicated you died in a concentration camp at the hands of the Nazis. Unfortunately, your mother went to her grave thinking you weren't alive and when I got a call yesterday from the Jewish Agency to inquire if I was married to a woman by the name Mildred Hirsh, well…I said yes I was, of course. The caller then informed me Mildred's daughter is here in Israel looking for her. I broke down and started sobbing like a baby, we had no idea you were alive, but thank God you are alive and well! I recognized you the minute I walked in the hotel, although you are older now. But you haven't changed a bit from the photos we received from your grandparents. It is a miracle you are alive and well, and I am sure Mildred is looking down from heaven with a big smile on her face. Please let us all say a prayer for your mother."

A military jeep came to the hotel the following day to pick them all up. Haim arranged for Ingrid and her family to visit Mount Herzl, the national cemetery for the state of Israel where Mildred was interned. Haim was there waiting when they arrived. Ingrid brought her prayer shawl and covered her hair, Greg and David held her by the arms when they reached the grave and when Ingrid saw her mother's name she broke down once more. Haim saluted the grave and led a prayer in honor of his fallen wife.

CHAPTER 27

O scar met with his father-in-law at his sprawling business offices the day after he returned from Iguazu Falls.

"How was the honeymoon, young man?"

"Fabulous, Gretchen and I had a wonderful time, and the Falls were spectacular, they blew my breath away!"

"And how is work going nowadays?"

"The construction business is doing well, but I can see signs of weakness building up, I have a funny feeling we might be in for a slowdown."

"Funny you should say that; I feel the same way about it, but future events will prove us right or wrong, let us wait and see."

"I don't believe this is the right attitude, Helmut. We need to look for different options just in case. We have lots of equipment and we must keep it humming; they won't make us any money setting idle in the yard. I came to your office to discuss the conversation Ricardo had with this big investor from Rio De Janeiro. Apparently this man called when I was away. He wants to see if we are interested in a project to build three office buildings in Brasilia. Ricardo made arrangements for both of us to meet him in Rio. I thought about asking your input and opinion to do a project so far from home base."

"Who is this big investor? Do you know his name?"

"I didn't catch his last name, but his first name is Luciano."

"I think I know who you talking about' if it is Luciano Ricci, the man is a shrewd businessman. I don't think it's a bad idea to meet with him and widen our business reach. Showcase our company in the federal capital and secure future government contacts, etc! Let me know when you're planning to go, I am very interested.

Oscar arrived home from work one evening, kissed his wife on the cheek and grabbed a bottle of beer from the refrigerator. Gretchen had not been feeling well the last few days, suffering with morning sickness all day long.

She told her husband. "I couldn't stand it any longer; I made an appointment to see the doctor. I hope it isn't stomach flu but I really don't feel well and I lost my appetite."

"I don't think it was the food at the club last week. You and I ate the same thing and I would be sick too if that was the case," suggested Oscar.

The next morning, Ricardo was in a buoyant mood; he entered the office singing at the top of his lungs.

"What makes you so happy this early, big man?" Oscar asked.

Happy is not the right word, Mister! I am ecstatic, and I feel on top of the world! I finally finished with Lauretta and I am seeing a new girl, Bridget is her name. She's German, but born in this country, just wait until you meet her! She is a classy lady, but has one big problem. She lives in Sao Paulo. Her father is on a business assignment in Porto Alegre, and they are planning to go back when he is finished in two months, and guess what? She knew Gerhard Foch, he is a good friend of the family apparently, isn't that a coincidence?"

"It sure is, bring her over for drink; I would like to meet her."

Oscar arrived home late Friday evening after staying late in the office to catch up with paperwork piled up during his honeymoon absence. Gretchen looked stunning with in a white dress, and when he walked in, she looked at him adoringly and said. "I have made us reservations at Pueblo, just for you and me."

"For when, honey?"

"For tonight, darling."

"Oh, I have been out all day and I haven't stopped since the moment we got back from honeymoon three months ago. I was hoping to have an easy night."

"I promise it will be easy tonight, and I have a little surprise for you, a very sweet surprise I must add."

Oscar reluctantly agreed and as soon as they settled down in their restaurant booth, he said to her, Okay Hon, what are you surprising me with tonight?"

"Let's wait until after we eat, and the surprise will be sweeter than dessert."

"You already said it was a sweet surprise and now you have my full attention, so come on and tell me!"

"I am pregnant!"

CHAPTER 28

Greg and Ingrid took the children to visit their old employers, Russell and Mary Eaton, who were very happy with the souvenir Ingrid brought them from Israel.

"How was your trip to the Holy Land?" Mary asked.

"It was very nice, the children had a great time, but the trip ended on a sad note unfortunately." Ingrid continued to tell them about her mother and what happened after she arrived in the Holy Land, and the memories made her cry again.

The Eatons had some news of their own. Rita had retired and moved back to Louisiana with her husband. Greg asked them if they were buying another house because he'd seen the for sale sign on the front lawn.

"Yes we are, actually, we're leaving Detroit." Russell explained he was retiring this year and they were moving to Los Angeles to live close to Russell Junior who works with a big investment firm out there.

Russell turned towards David, "What are your plans for the future, young man?"

"I would like to be a lawyer eventually, but for now I am going to the University of Chicago. I am hoping to sign up for a combined course in finance and management." David gave the answer in his customary firm, professional sounding voice.

"Very good choice David, I am really pleased for you. You look like a smart and determined young man and I wish you all the best." He then turned towards Sonia. "And how about you little princess?"

"I will be in second grade when I go back to school at the end of the summer," she answered, "but I don't want to be a lawyer like David. Law degrees are for boys!" They all laughed at her cute answer.

David was indeed a very gifted student, reading books and watching sports were his two favorite pastimes, and he passionately loved the Detroit Tigers. His reading interests were broad and diverse; he was a ferocious reader and in the last year at high school he read nearly fifty books. The family used to drop him off at the library when they went out shopping and found him deep in concentration when they picked him up several hours later. He also developed a knack for debating other students. Many were no match for him; he always came prepared with a good grasp on the subject of the debate. What struck his mother's attention most was how much he knew about domestic and international politics at his young age, and he didn't care one little bit about communism. One day he told his mother the communist system sounds fair on the outside but it is rotten from within and serves the interests of the elite and the party members only. "It will eventually collapse and vanish forever in the future," he told her.

"Where do you get all of this knowledge, David?" Ingrid proudly asked.

"Mom, all you need to do is to look at the how the Soviets chose to run their country. The leaders live in lofty mansions and the proletariats the system is supposed to be helping are getting poorer and poorer by the day. Look at us Mother! The system here in the US, is not perfect, but the people are improving from one year to the next; it isn't difficult to discern which is the more superior system. We have liberty in this country, you come and go as you please, we have freedom of expression and when our leaders make mistakes, they get voted out of office. Over there on the other hand, their leaders are dictators and stay in office for life."

David started the first term at the University of Chicago with hope and determination. He was a handsome young man, with short black hair and blue eyes, always clean shaven and neatly dressed. He shared his dormitory room with a lively student from Alabama who spoke with a pronounced drawl and his main interest was the pursuit of pleasure more than the academics, unlike David who was focused on his scholastic career and was not into what he considered a waste of time attending social events. Girls found him attractive and some even pursued him but he showed little interest to engage in serious relationships. His teachers, however, wished all their students were like him. He engaged them in intelligent discussion, always seeking to enhance his knowledge and understanding. His study habit was systematic and consistent and many who interacted with him predicted he will go somewhere in life.

Sonia was the inquisitive type, doing well in school and very popular among her friends. She was passionate and helpful and seldom turned down her mother's request to help with household chores. She was genuine and bubbly and brought so much joy to Greg and Ingrid. Although Greg was not the religious type, he nevertheless infused Christian values in his daughter and made it his obligation to take her to church every other Sunday to attend mass. Her mother too instilled Jewish values in the ever eager to learn young girl, and she, too, never missed taking her Sonia to the synagogue when it was her turn on the Sabbath. Greg and Ingrid at the outset of their marriage decided to introduce Sonia to both faiths and let her determine the one she feels most comfortable with. Both Pastor Adams and Rabbi Lieberman were aware of this setup, but never expressed any opinion; they saw no wisdom in trying to influence this unique situation, but were very welcoming when she came in with one of her parents.

David on the other hand was the religious type, always eager and yearning to go to the synagogue, and on many occasions stayed behind to speak to the rabbi after the service. The rabbi fondly repeated to Ingrid how mature the boy was for his age. "He asks questions and engages in discussions people twice his age don't even know about. Your boy is very smart and I predict he will make a name for himself!"

Greg's nursery was doing well, and he no longer worked late into the evening after the business loan was paid off. He felt it was important to spend quality time with his family; he took them to the beach often in the summers and to the indoor community pool and ice rink in the dead of winter. Ingrid too was happy and content with her life. Greg bought her a car when they returned from the Holy Land so she can be independent, and it made her happy not to ask him to run her around when he came home tired from work. She was very proud of her children and she loved her husband with all the fibers in her heart.

CHAPTER 29

At the beginning of 1956, President Juscelino Kubitschek became the president of Brazil, bringing unprecedented growth and prosperity to the country. He was a much loved and admired politician who presided over the relocation of the country's capital to the newly formed city of Brasilia.

That same year, Gretchen was unexpectedly rushed to the hospital in the early hours of the morning on a cool July day. She was in such pain and Oscar couldn't wait for the ambulance to arrive. He put his wife in the passenger seat and sped off to the emergency room where the doctors immediately took her to the operating room. She had internal bleeding and the medical team decided to perform a caesarian section on her in order to save the baby she was due to have in three weeks. It was a miracle the baby survived; the newborn was placed in an incubator for further medical observation. When the doctor emerged from the operating room, he found Oscar pacing in the hallway. "I have two pieces of information for you Mr. Silva," the doctor began. "You are the proud father of a baby boy, but unfortunately your wife will not be able to carry again. She has a medical condition which threatens her life if she becomes pregnant again. You are allowed to go into her room now."

Oscar was overtaken with joy when he came to Gretchen's bed side. But as he kissed her on the forehead, she was crying softly. The nurse escorted him to the unit where the baby was in a glass incubator with oxygen mask and wires attached to his body. Oscar wept at the sight of his first born, "Oh my God, he looks so marvelous!"

Karl Joseph was the name the parents chose for the baby. Helmut and Erika were waiting at the house when Oscar and Gretchen brought him home from the hospital three weeks later. Gretchen handed her bundle of joy to her mother.

"Dear Lord!" she said, "He looks gorgeous! So much like you Gretchen! His hair is exactly like yours when you were born, right Helmut?"

"Yes dear, he sure does have her hair! What a handsome little boy!"

The baby, in fact, looked the double of his father when he was the same age, with the same big round face with sparse golden hair covering his head, and his big blue eyes sparkled when Erika passed the infant back to his mother.

"You should look at some of the photos when I was a baby and you won't be able to tell the difference," Oscar said with pride, "This boy is almost identical to how I looked. I wish my mother and father were here to see their grandson, they would be so happy and proud." Oscar also explained the boy was named after his beloved granddad, the general.

Oscar and Helmut boarded a plane to Brasilia, the new federal capital. Planners chose the site in the Brazilian hinterland because of its central location and suitable topography. They were hoping to have the construction completed by the beginning of 1960, but progress was slow and it became evident the target date might be missed. The government gave incentives to the developers to speed up the pace of construction and avoid further delays, and when Ricardo received the call from Luciano Ricci, he voiced readiness to cooperate and take some of his workload. Helmut and Luciano knew one another and shared many common friends, however, when Luciano contacted H&O he wasn't aware Helmut was involved in the company. Nevertheless he was pleased to see him with Oscar, and he took the pair for a tour of this huge construction site. When they finished, the two parties agreed to have H&O construction engage in some of Luciano's work. During the plane ride back to their home town the same evening they decided on Ricardo as the man in charge of the project in Brasilia.

Ricardo accepted the assignment to manage the construction work; he assembled a contingent of some of the most qualified personnel and equipment and dispatched them to the city to begin the construction work. However, he decided to take a detour to Sao Paulo to see Bridget, the new girl in his life. They were calling each other almost every night since her father finished the assignment in the city and she returned home to Sao Paulo. Ricardo was hoping to convince her to move in with him in Brasilia, but she explained her conservative family wouldn't permit this, But she was still willing to go out with him when he visits Sao Paulo.

Ricardo had a wonderful time in this very large and modern metropolis and during a visit to her house one evening Gerhard Foch was among the guests in attendance. Ricardo recalled the enjoyable evening the two had when they first met at Helmut's house. Gerhard was impressed with Ricardo after he learned of his SS background, and decided to offer an invitation to him and Bridget. "You two should come to our camp this weekend, a whole bunch of people will be there. We normally sit down and enjoy each other's company and have some food and wine. The ladies prepare all sorts of traditional dishes from back home and I will bring excellent quality Wiener schnitzel from a German butcher here in town."

"Sounds interesting, but who will be there at the camp?" Ricardo inquired.

"It varies, but usually more than four dozen people come. The majority is from Germany, but we have few Danes, a couple of French and a nice gentleman from America, who comes often."

Ricardo picked his girlfriend up on Saturday morning and drove the winding road to the wooded mountain area outside of the city. He followed the directions Gerhard gave him; take the highway in the direction of Santa Ines, and 3 kilometers after the sign for Juquery, take the dirt road on the right immediately after you pass the Esso gas station. He turned into the dirt bumpy road until he reached a large white stucco villa with a red adobe roof. The villa had a large courtyard and a swimming pool lined with chairs, loungers and tables with red and white umbrellas. It was all obscured from the main road by a thicket of pine trees.

Ricardo was pleasantly surprised to find all the people present harbored strong attachments for the fatherland and equally strong sentiments for Nazi ideology. Hatred for the Jews and everything Jewish is what united them; this hatred ran deep in their souls, they blamed the Jews for controlling the world and its finances, and believed they have complete leverage on all western governments.

Martin Fleischer, the leader of this group, was a colonel with the SS during WWII under the direct command of Heinrich Himmler, the SS top leader responsible for the murder of millions of Jews. Martin was one of the few lucky men who managed to escape from Berlin on the day Germany signed the unconditional surrender. He disguised himself dressed as a woman and was lucky to slip through the Russian defenses encircling the city. Martin arrived in Brazil with little money but survived by working odd jobs until he came in contact with the likeminded Germans who are now his current backers.

This group of the well-heeled people was working on a plan to restore Germany to its past glory and rid the world of all the Jews, and in order to bring their aspiration to fruition, they enlisted Martin Fleischer to recruit and train old Nazi comrades to build the Fourth Reich from the rubble and ashes of Hitler's Third Reich. Their strategy is to start a nucleus in Brazil and then spread the activities to North America and Europe. Ultimately they hope to unite all the Aryan people under one umbrella to fight the forces aligned with their enemies.

The day baby Karl turned two years, Helmut and Erika came to celebrate their grandson's birthday. Erika picked up the playful boy in her arms. "Mother Mary" she exclaimed, "this boy looks the double of you Oscar! I wish your parents were alive to see him, I am sure they would be proud."

"I am flattered," Oscar answered, "but he is a handful for his mother. The part- time maid we hired after he was born is inadequate. She is unable to handle him and look after house cleaning as well; we are thinking to get another maid to help."

"I have a better idea," Erika suggested, "why don't you get a live-in maid? She will be there all the time to babysit Karl should you decided to go out in the evening."

"What a wonderful idea," Gretchen agreed, "what do you think, honey?"

"I think it is a splendid idea; let me see what I can do to find the right girl!"

Before Helmut said goodnight, he asked Oscar to drop by to see him at his office the following day. "I have something important to discuss with you."

The following day, Oscar was in a good mood when he arrived at Helmut's office. He passed along the good news to his father-in-law on how well Ricardo was doing in Brasilia. "It looks like this man is on a mission! He organized his people to work three shifts round the clock and the efforts are producing remarkable progress in such a short time. He anticipates having the project completed two to three months ahead of schedule. What a man when he feels challenged!"

"Yes indeed," Helmut answered with disinterest, "Luciano called the other day and he was all praise for Ricardo's performance, but I forgot to mention it last night when we came to visit. But the reason I wanted to talk to you Oscar is something personal. You and Gretchen have been married for three years now and her mother and I can see you love one another and seem happy in your life. You also gave us Karl; this little boy is the apple of Erika's eye, and words are not enough to describe how much love and affection we both have for him. Having established all of this, I summoned you here to discuss my retirement. As you know, my father traveled by boat through the recently opened Panama Canal to Los Angeles after WWI. The purpose for that trip was to purchase a tract of farm land on the advice of an American colleague, a botany professor at the university where my dad also taught. He convinced my father Southern California had the ideal climate to grow Brazilian citrus fruits, particularly oranges, and he indicated the demand for the fruit in the United States exceeded supplies. He recommended my dad establish a fruit farm close to Los Angeles, and he insisted the farm will be profitable once the trees mature in few years. My dad agreed with his friend's assessment after finding out he could buy property below market value because of the depressed demand at the end of the war. He was fortunate enough to have the funds available after he inherited a considerable amount following the death of his father.

My father wanted me to come with him to California, but my boss wouldn't allow me to take a break from work. However, when my father returned, he told me the land he purchased was flat and full of weeds and needed a large amount of capital to establish the working farm, money he didn't have since he spent most of what he got to buy the tract. But he was adamant to do something and spent too much time looking for somebody to partner with. There were, apparently, two serious people willing to invest but my father died before he realized the dream. So, I own this piece of land now and I intend to build a retirement home on it and move to the US to spend my golden years there. I am very fond of the country and Erika loves the weather and the city's tempo. I will be sixty-five in a few months, and after a long career in business I think it is time for me to call it quits. This brings me to why I want to talk to you, Oscar. Broadly, I have two options available to me at this moment; I either sell the business or else keep it going, and obviously each option has merits and drawbacks. But deep in my heart I hate to let go of my baby, even after the many years it took me to build it up and make it what it is now. I therefore want to make you an offer. What if you take over my seminal position as the chief executive officer and oversee the day to day running of the company and in return I will give you 49% of the company's shares, on condition you are not allowed to sell them and they go to Karl in the event something happens to you?" Oscar nodded attentively. "However, you are allowed to cash dividends at the end of each profitable year. I will remain the chairman of the company and I will make myself available for advice and consultations, and I will attend events you deem important, but otherwise I don't want to be bothered with the day to day running of the operation. We have very competent staff and I elevated my top producer, Manuel Alvarado, to the position of deputy general manager, despite his young age. I think this man is worth his weight in gold and I groomed him over the past five years to run the company and so far he's doing a superb job. He is intelligent, loyal and trustworthy; I recommend you keep him as your right hand man. Of course should you come across a problem beyond his expertise, I am only a phone call away for advice. I know you need time to digest my offer, but please try to give me your answer at the end of the week."

"No, you don't have to wait a week to hear my response," Oscar blurted, "I accept your offer unconditionally, and it will be my distinct honor to take over your position and continue on the same path you charted. And it will give me great pleasure to pass it down to Karl when he reaches the right age!" The two gentlemen shook hands to seal the deal.

Helmut also informed him they are already booked on a flight to California the following week. "Erika and I will travel to Los Angeles to talk to a developer and to a real estate agent about building a nice home for us. We are looking forward to going and to begin a new chapter in our life. California is so beautiful with its different seasons. It's not like the constantly hot climate of southern Brazil. We'll be near the ocean and our house will be large enough for you and Gretchen and of course baby Karl to stay as long as you wish. It will give Erika and me great pleasure to see our daughter and grandson as often as you can visit.

CHAPTER 30

Greg and Ingrid were waiting for Sonia to come home from school one afternoon near the end of her school term. A violent storm had just passed through the area leaving the streets littered with broken trees and roofing materials in its aftermath. The family had plans to drive to Chicago to attend David's graduation from University, and the car was packed, waiting.

"What took you so long?" Ingrid asked her daughter with an edge to her voice.

"Mom, be patient, I couldn't just get up and leave. We had to go in the school basement when the storm was overhead, and I came as fast as I could."

"Very well, hurry up and change your clothes. We will be out in the car."

The family drove west and arrived in Chicago five hours later. Traffic was particularly heavy all the way from Gary, Indiana to Chicago. David was there waiting when they arrived to explain about the next day's graduation ceremony. They were excited to learn the University chancellor would personally hand the diplomas to the eligible graduates.

The family arrived early the following day in order to walk around the campus of this prestigious university built in the late eighteen hundreds. The land was donated by Marshal Field, a wealthy merchant from Chicago with contributions from philanthropist John D. Rockefeller. When they finished their tour, they walked to the large auditorium behind the administration building for the ceremony. The large hall was full of students and attended by family members and faculty staff.

David did not forewarn his family he will be receiving a special accolade for merit and achievement on his outstanding academic performance and for attaining the highest grade point average. Ingrid was indeed surprised her boy's name was called first. He walked on the stage wearing the customary robe and mortar and when the chancellor handed him the degree the whole auditorium erupted in applause.

Ingrid was crying loudly, "My boy fills my heart with so much pride! I don't know where he gets it from, he is so smart!"

Greg surprised David with his gift; he made a reservation for the whole family to spend a week in Niagara Falls. "This is your present David. You have made us all proud, son, and I want you to enjoy your break before you start your professional career!"

A few days later, the family drove from Detroit across the Ambassador Bridge into Canada and continued east to the town overlooking the spectacular falls. There had been a brief shower before they arrived and a huge rainbow hung over the river gorge.

"Oh Lord!" Ingrid gasped, "I have never seen anything more beautiful, this alone is worth the trip!"

During the drive back to Detroit, David asked Sonia if she had any ambition to continue with her education. He got an earful back from his little sister! "Don't think you are the only smart one in the family! I'm doing really well in school and I came in first this year in my class, too, so there!"

CHAPTER 31

Gretchen picked up the phone when it rang at the new villa Oscar bought for his family.

"I have found a house maid for you ma'am," said Oscar's secretary, Ramona. "She has a good reference from her previous employer, a banker who was relocated to Belo Horizonte. If you want to interview her I can send her over with the driver right away."

Yes, please do that. I am taking Karl to the doctor later this afternoon. He wasn't feeling too well and I would like to talk to her before I leave."

"Very well ma'am, I will send her right away."

When the girl got out of the car, Gretchen noticed she was very young. Although she blamed the secretary for sending inexperienced help, Gretchen ushered the girl to the living room where Karl was lying in his crib. "Please sit down," she commanded, "what is your name?"

"My name is Elsa Montez, ma'am."

"How old are you, Elsa?"

"I am 17." Elsa sat up straighter in her chair.

"You are a little young for the job, have you finished school yet?"

"I had to quit school when my father died, ma'am. He fell from the top of the building he was working on and died instantly. My older sister and I had to go out to work to support our family."

Gretchen changed her mind. Originally she was apprehensive when she saw the girl stepping out of the car, and impulsively thought, no way, this girl is too young, but now she felt bad after hearing the circumstances. She decided to at least give her a try. The letter of recommendation from Elsa's previous employer helped; it was full of praise, and it recommended her for this kind of work without reservation, and it specifically mentioned her skills with little children. "Okay, you can start tomorrow. Please be here at 8 am so we can go over details." Gretchen told the young girl.

Elsa was born in Porto Alegre; her parents came to this town looking for work from their native Ciudad Del Este, a town across the border in Paraguay. They spoke Spanish at home but also had good command of Portuguese, and when their daughters were born they made sure to give them strict Catholic upbringing and taught them to speak Spanish and Portuguese. Gretchen learned from the reference letter that Elsa, after the death of her father found a job cleaning the house of a rich banker. The family already had a nanny to look after their two young children but she quit because the children were unruly and too much to handle. Elsa volunteered for the job, but the banker's wife, like Gretchen, had reservations about putting the children in the care of a 15 year old girl. But given her demeanor and the quality work she does round the house the banker himself argued in favor of hiring the young maid. The family was so surprised to see how well she did, the children loved their new nanny and over time they became more disciplined and well behaved. When they were transferred out of the city, they offered to take Elsa to Belo Horizonte but she declined, citing her mother's ill health.

Elsa was there first thing in the morning when Oscar came down to the kitchen for his morning coffee. He stood at the door to observe the new girl; she was singing a soothing song for the baby and waving a toy at him. Karl was all excited and laughing and was happy to take his bottle.

"Good morning sir, I didn't see you come down, can I get you anything to drink?"

"Yes Elsa, please bring me a cup of coffee, black no sugar. I'll take it with me."

Gretchen called him in the afternoon. "Hello darling, how is your day?"

"I'm doing great, how is Karl doing?"

"He's fast asleep. He was playing with Elsa for the last hour nonstop. This girl is so good with him and you should see little Karl, he took to her so much! He's just full of smiles when she sings to him!"

"Yes dear," Oscar said with a grin, "I think this girl might surprise both of us."

Ricardo was putting the final touches on the project in Brasilia when Oscar came in for the handover ceremony. "Where is Helmut? I thought he was coming with you." Ricardo asked.

"He's in L.A. for the next three months. He decided to take early retirement this year. I guess he needs to take it easy, he is been working hard for forty years, nonstop."

"I guess so," Ricardo agreed, "but who will take over his position now he is gone?"

"That will be me," Oscar answered, "I will run the shipping company and you and I will jointly run H&O construction."

"Well, then, good! I'll look forward to it. I am full of ideas and I would like to see how far you and I can take this business."

The two men decided to stop in Sao Paulo before heading back home.

"I would like to meet your new friend Martin Fleischer and the rest of his men at the camp," Oscar requested.

"Okay, this will work out fine. I haven't seen Bridget for a while; I guess we can stop at her folks' house before we head to the camp."

"You haven't told me how you two are getting along?"

Ricardo took a deep breath. "Yes, my friend, I think this is the right girl for me. She is beautiful and comes from a good family' I am thinking about her very seriously nowadays."

Ricardo drove the now familiar mountain road up to the building site, he really liked the company last time he visited and the atmosphere was merry. Oscar was introduced to Martin.

"I heard a lot about you Oscar, welcome to our camp. Please let me introduce Richard Woodruff, our friend and associate from America. He was away last time Ricardo visited." The three of them walked towards a very kind looking man wearing a Hawaiian shirt and a pair of shorts. He was sitting at the edge of a lounge chair reading a book and looked from underneath his glasses when Martin approached.

"Mr. Woodruff, I have these two gentlemen I'd like to introduce to you." Richard stood up and shook their hands.

"Very pleased to meet you."

Richard explained he had been coming to the camp over the last four years, but the past six months he was away in the United States to look after his dying wife. Cancer finally took her just few weeks ago; he is now back in Sao Paulo for the last time before he goes back to the US for good when his tenure at the University comes to an end.

"Sorry to hear about your loss," Oscar said. "I hope you enjoyed your time here in Brazil, Mr. Woodruff?"

"I have indeed; this country will be a part of me for the rest of my life. But I have to go back home to be with my family. I have two daughters and a son, all of them married. And as of next month I will be the proud grandfather to seven grandchildren! They keep me going!"

"Will you retire completely from teaching when you return home?" Ricardo asked.

"No, no, not yet. I started with a two year sabbatical here in Brazil, then my university in the states granted me two more years, but I guess all good things in life must come to an end."

Oscar asked, "Where in the US do you teach?"

"I am originally from Minnesota but I teach at a university in Portland, Oregon and I belong to a group there who share the same Ideology as the folks here at the camp, the Aryan race is currently obsequious to their masters the Jews, we must do everything in our power to change this presumption."

Oscar took a big sigh. "I know what you mean Mr. Woodruff. Germany lost two wars because of them and the German people have had enough, we must unite all the Aryan people and explain the dangers these bastards are planning for us, they are using America's power and prestige to their end and the poor white man is toiling for their benefits.

Gordon Murphy, the affable Real Estate man was at LAX, Los Angeles' main airport when Helmut and Erika came through customs. "How was your flight, Mr. and Mrs. Spiegel?"

"A little bumpy when we crossed over the equator, but fairly smooth the rest of the way," Helmut answered in a tired voice.

"Well, I made you reservations at a nice hotel in Bel Air. You must need a rest after your long flight. I will drop you off now and pick you up first thing tomorrow morning. I have already researched your property in Orange County and let me tell you something, this piece is a beauty and close to Disneyland, in Anaheim."

The following day when Helmut arrived at the property, he didn't realize how big it was. "This is a huge parcel of land, and it is out in the middle of nowhere! I don't think we would want to live here," he complained. "I didn't realize it is an hour drive from LA! We have to change plans and look for a property in the city instead."

The two returned to LA, and Gordon Murphy was charged with the task to find a brand new house on a golf course, preferably in Santa Monica or Bel Air, Erika's favorite areas in California. They signed the real estate documents to give authority to Gordon to search for the house that better fit his clients' criteria.

CHAPTER 32

David received several job offers but he turned them all down. His family expected him to continue with his studies and become a lawyer, or at least that was the impression David had cultivated over the years and that was what he has been telling everybody over the past several months. However, he decided to defer his career in law for the time being. He told his family, "The United States must win the war in Vietnam and stop the spread of communism! I have therefore decided to do my patriotic duty and join the marines next week fighting the enemy in South East Asia." His family was stunned, and they pleaded with him to change his mind, but David was determined. Like many of the enlistees before him, David was sent to Fort Benning, in Georgia for his basic military training before going to Vietnam. The first week was not easy but after eight weeks of exhausting training he was ready and eager to join the fight. Ingrid was so happy to see him when he returned from Fort Benning; he looked so smart in military uniform. Greg sat with David in the evening to discuss his deployment.

"Do you know where you will be stationed, son?"

"No dad, I don't. I was told they will assign us to the front line, but where exactly is still unclear."

"How long will your deployment there last?"

"I am not so sure of that either, but I do hope I will come face to face with those little Vietcong! I want to show them who is in charge, this is the United States Army you are fighting and we will wipe you all out!"

Greg however, wanted the conversation to focus on something else. "Ever since you announced your intention to go to Vietnam, your mother and I have been watching the news. There isn't a day passes without reports on casualties and it is quite clear we are losing our young men by the hundreds every month."

"You do exaggerate dad. There are just few hundred casualties every month. Hey, this is war and people die in wars!"

"But we don't want to lose you, son, you have so much going for you.

You are very bright and I am sure you can serve your country better doing something else."

"Dad, I am not the only one who is bright. All the guys in my regiment are very bright and motivated. Please wait and see, we will win at the end, and there is no possible outcome except total victory for the United States and the total capitulation of the enemy, period."

Ingrid and Sonia cried when David left the house in the morning. "Be careful son, please look after yourself and remember you will be in our thoughts day and night!"

"I love you and God be with you all the way," Ingrid told her son as he walked out the door."

Ingrid nearly fainted when David originally told her he was going to Vietnam; she knew her son was headstrong and naturally she tried to dissuade him, but her effort was futile. Eventually she came to terms with the fact he was going and her life turned upside down worrying about him. Sonia noticed her mother became addicted to watching the news on TV every night; she was so keen to garner information from the war zone, and she panicked when her son was deployed to an area which has experienced a spike in military engagement. Ingrid never left the house in the morning until the mail was delivered. The letters stamped with the Armed Forces were opened first and read many times over, normally with tears streaming down her cheeks.

Sonia, in the meanwhile, was doing well in school and happy to be living with her family. However, her relationship went through a strained phase with her mother when she quit going to the synagogue altogether.

Ingrid was deeply upset but Sonia explained her position. "Ever since Rabbi Lieberman retired, I didn't care too much for the new rabbi and I genuinely feel more comfortable going to church. Sometimes I go on my own, but often times I go to bible classes with my friend Veronica at her church. I really enjoy going, mom, I feel this is where I belong. It doesn't mean I don't care for the Jewish religion, quite the contrary, I feel the Jewish faith is part of me and it will remain so forever.

CHAPTER 33

Oscar and Gretchen took Karl to Los Angeles to celebrate his ninth birthday with his grandparents. The trip was now an annual pilgrimage for the family, and Karl looked forward to spending the summer there, and to visit Disneyland, his most favorite place in the world. The family always brought Elsa when they came to the US. She and Karl were inseparable and the young boy was much attached to her. She taught him to speak Spanish with encouragement from his parents; they believed it was necessary the boy to speak the preeminent language in South America.

Ricardo came with them this time but for a different reason. He and Oscar made plans to do two things in America before returning to Brazil. Helmut had been prodding his son-in-law to check out the ever expanding real estate opportunities on the Pacific coast, He told Oscar the house he purchased in Santa Monica has doubled in value in the last five years, and the state is experiencing phenomenal population growth, and will surpass New York to become the largest in the nation in short order. Helmut wanted to gauge Oscar's level of interest to develop the piece of land he inherited from his father and he arranged for a surveyor and realtor Gordon Murphy to meet with Oscar and Ricardo at the property.

"Mr. Spiegel," Gordon began," you are sitting on a goldmine! This property was zoned agriculture when your father purchased it, but since Walt Disney built his theme park in the vicinity, property values in the area have gone through the roof after the zoning changed. The demand for housing in this area forced the city planners to change it to residential and commercial usage, I have not reached an exact figure for the value of this property, but I assure you, for this raw land, it runs in the millions of dollars. I cannot begin to think how much it will be worth once you develop it."

After Gordon left, the three men were deep in their thoughts trying to digest the numbers the real estate broker came up with. "This is unbelievable," Ricardo said with enthusiasm, "if Murphy is correct, we don't have to think twice about developing this land."

Oscar agreed. "This tract is very well positioned on two intersections, with endless possibilities, but we must first verify the facts presented to us by Mr. Murphy, and I recommend we hire an independent engineering firm to look into the details and the cost associated with developments."

Helmut jumped into the fray and suggested to do a thorough feasibility study before proceeding with anything. "Our due diligence is very important when it comes to high dollar projects," he insisted.

Ricardo and Oscar took a side trip to see their professor friend in Portland, Oregon. The guys became good friends with Richard Woodruff before he departed from Brazil. The elderly professor was waiting for them at Portland's airport when they arrived. He drove east in the direction of the Cascade Range where the American chapter of the Aryan Group have established a home base. The camp was eerily similar to the one in Brazil but unlike the group there, Ricardo noticed the men were carrying big semi-automatic guns like the ones used by the military. The professor explained many of the members are ex-service men with military training. "They are fed up with the federal government in Washington DC, for curtailing our freedom!" Oscar gave a big donation to the group, who made fuss of him and Ricardo when they became aware of their Nazi past. "One day we will restore the Aryan rule across this land and restore America to its rightful masters!" the professor proclaimed, to the cheers and applause of all the men at the camp.

Before the trip to Los Angeles, Oscar and Gretchen decided to enroll Karl in a prestigious private school on the east coast, and after a long search they settled on Milton Academy in Boston, Massachusetts, a school renowned for high quality education and excellent curriculum. They took both Karl and Elsa to Boston to enroll him in third grade; Karl was initially hesitant to stay in a foreign country on his own but gradually relented after they assured him he wasn't going to be there on his own.

"Elsa also will be staying here with you son," Oscar told him, "we will be buying a house for you here in Boston and Elsa will look after the house and you, too." Their rationale was not only to assuage the boy's fears but also to provide him with a family atmosphere and adult supervision. After he purchased a house in a nice neighborhood close to the school, Oscar took the family for a tour around Boston, then they drove down the coast to see New York City and everybody had a wonderful time before he and Gretchen had to return to Brazil

CHAPTER 34

Ingrid was both intrigued and concerned for her daughter when Sonia turned fourteen; she noticed the girl's interest in religion has become more intense, and she related her concern to Greg. "You know, all Sonia talks about nowadays is her bible class; she goes to church several times a week and to Sunday mass as well."

Greg attributed the interest to growing up. "This is just a fad and she will grow out of it, just give her time."

"No Greg," Ingrid answered with concern, "I don't mind my daughter's decision to make religion an important part of her life, but this is all she talks about and I find it strange for a young girl her age to occupy her mind with one single issue. She has her whole life to look forward to and she should develop other interests as well."

"I agree with you darling, but what are our choices? Sonia is not doing anything bad like taking drugs or skipping school. She has an interest in God and that is something admirable, but I will have a word with her when she gets home this evening, if you want."

Sonia was indeed at the church again. She did not tell her parents she was no longer interested in the Presbyterian Church and now goes to the Catholic church her best friend Veronica convinced her to attend. Veronica explained the Catholic Church is considered the mother church, and was founded by Jesus Christ himself who established the Ministry two thousand years ago. The Pope, who resides in the Vatican is considered the leader of the church at the present. In contrast, the Presbyterian Church was established approximately five hundred years ago and is deemed an offshoot of the original Ministry of God. After few visits to the Catholic Church, Sonia quickly concluded there were hardly any doctrinal differences between the two,, however, she found the Catholic Church steeped in traditions and more appealing to her sensibilities.

When she arrived home in the late afternoon, her father gently inquired if she had a nice day at school.

"Yes dad, I had wonderful time and guess what? I managed to get a B+ in my history exam!"

"Great, Sonia! I see you are doing well in school, but your mother and I noticed your keen interest to go to church and bible class. Is there a particular reason for your elevated interest?"

"Yes, dad, when you and I went to church together it was fun and I really enjoyed it, but my best friend asked me to go to bible class with her at the Catholic Church and I agreed. Oh dad, you should come with me one day, I am sure you will love the church! And the bible classes are so interesting and so is father O'Malley; he is great, a very interesting man."

"Honey, we just noticed you're a lot more interested in it now, and wonder why the sudden change?"

"I just love Jesus, dad. I appreciate the message of love he brought to humanity and he sacrificed himself on the cross for us, and the bible stories are so enjoyable. I would really like you to come to mass with us next Sunday to see for yourself."

On Ingrid's behest, Greg decided to visit father O'Malley at the Catholic Church where Sonia has been going for the last few weeks, and after his talk with the genteel priest, he came to the conclusion there is no harm for his daughter to continue with her bible classes, and there is no good reason to deter her from going. Quite the contrary it was a spiritual awakening that will guide her for the rest of her life, and he told his wife, "Sonia is fine, and we shouldn't worry about her. Sooner or later, her interest will fade away."

David arrived in Vietnam in the middle of September after a long and tiring flight. Strong wind and driving rain was pouring down over Saigon airport. David and the rest of the infantry troops were briefed by the officers in charge.

"The enemy is everywhere and you guys must be on the alert and look out for each other. Make sure you look down at the ground before you take a single step. These slant-eyed bastards use punji traps to inflict real and psychological wounds and they appear from nowhere. They dig underground tunnels and use them to launch surprise attacks against us. Their favorite method to engage us is to hit and run, so be careful of booby traps and mines, avoid anything that looks suspicious. You guys will be assigned under First Lieutenant Hughes, his word is final. Any questions?"

"Yes sir," one of the soldiers raised his hand, "What is a punji trap sir, and how can we avoid it?"

"Punji traps are sharp spikes laced with poison. The spikes are made with bamboo and placed in the bottom of a pit then covered over with leafs to provide camouflage. If any one of the guys in your platoon falls in these pits, you must be careful when you dig them out."

David was assigned first to the offense operation Cedar Falls; his unit was sent to Tay Ninh province, north of Saigon, and from the first day the unit was deployed it came under heavy attack. One soldier died instantly when he stepped on a hidden landmine and several others were injured, one of those was Officer Hughes himself, the gallant leader of the unit. When David rushed over to help he came under intense fire, but he managed to drag the injured leader behind a tree until reinforcements arrived.

He wrote a letter on the weekend to his family:

> Dear Mom, Dad and Sonia
>
> Well I have been in Vietnam for just few days and it has been wet and humid. The rain never stopped and the heat is oppressive. Fighting with the enemy started as soon as we arrived at the front. I am currently assigned to second battalion, 3rd regiment. My first combat mission didn't go as planned; we were ambushed and attacked from all directions and sadly we lost two of our comrades, two young men from Alabama. This morning again we came under intense fire and we lost one more guy and the platoon leader was injured. I jumped behind him and dragged him to safety until assistance arrived. It was absolutely horrific and we were soaked in blood, it was a miracle he survived. I think our high command should work harder to improve the morale among the troops here, but I assure you we will come out on top at the end. My love and kisses to all of you,
>
> Your loving son, David.

When he finished writing, he placed the letter in the military mailbag.

The fighting continued and David's platoon was out looking for enemy units every day but the fight against this determined enemy was brutal. One day while walking in a field of tall thick grass a GI fell in a punji trap; he stepped on a piece of wood covered with dead leaves. The soldier screamed with pain, all his body was torn from his feet to his waist by the side spikes in the trap, and the Vietcong had laced the bamboo with deadly decomposed body parts and excrement. It was worse than biological poison. A chopper was sent to evacuate him but he died of his wounds several days later. David was so sad to see his comrade in arms die this horrible way.

The war continued unabated, and in 1968, Richard Nixon, the Republican Party candidate for president, campaigned on a platform to bring peace with honor to end the war in Vietnam. David didn't believe this was the best course for America, but he was in a minority among the troops, who were tired of fighting this horrendous war in terrible weather and unfamiliar surroundings. The majority wanted to go back home and be with their families, and the prevailing morale among the troops was low and getting worse with casualties mounting every passing day. David had to be careful not to express his strong opinion in favor of the war.

His unit was designated to lead other units in the area and confront the enemy day and night in order to prevent them gaining the opportunity to launch surprise attacks. David was always on the lookout for the cunning and determined enemy; he got used to their tactics and anticipated their moves well, and he built a reputation for audacity in the battlefield. He later was assigned to the Special Forces in charge of search and rescue, and the scope of action took him all over the country. On one of those missions in the spring of 1969, the chopper he was in hovered over soggy ground to rescue a platoon surrounded by the enemy. David jumped out ready for battle and the fighting lasted more than fifty minutes. He took a direct hit to his upper pelvis when a mortar exploded close by, and he fell down screaming with pain. The tall grass provided cover and prevented certain death until additional troops reached the battle area and tipped the scale in favor of the Americans. David was flown to a military hospital in Saigon and he lost consciousness on route. The shrapnel shattered his pelvis beyond local medical abilities, and he had to be flown back home for treatment. He was sedated for the duration of the journey because he was in such agony, and when he awoke the following day, he found himself in a bedroom at Walter Reed hospital near Washington, D.C.

CHAPTER 35

The independent engineering and real estate reports exceeded the assessment Gordon Murphy had originally furnished for the parcel of land Helmut owned in California. All the data indicated the land was ideal for commercial and residential development and in their estimate the banks will most likely agree to underwrite a loan for its development. Oscar asked Ricardo to remain in California to follow up and prepare for the large scale construction. His assistant René Luna was assigned to replace him in Brazil. They figured the high return this project will generate justifies the collective effort of all the principles. Helmut, who became a US citizen a few weeks earlier, told both Oscar and Ricardo that the success of this project will pave the way for both to become US citizens and has the potential to generate more profits than what is typical in Brazil, since the US economy is much greater and the demand for housing in California remains very strong.

Ricardo was especially happy to remain behind in the US. His relationship with Bridget was getting more serious by the day and he decided it was time for him to tie the knot with the girl he truly loved and bring her to the US so they can start a family right away. He booked a flight to Sao Paulo and proposed to her at a romantic dinner at one of the city's elegant restaurants. She cried with happiness as she accepted, but the thought of leaving her beloved country was a little unsettling to her. Nevertheless she agreed to give it a try.

Meanwhile, Karl suffered in his first term at the Milton Academy in Boston. He missed his school friends from back home terribly, his command of the English language was still poor, and he was utterly unprepared when the weather turned cold in December. No one forewarned him about winters on the east coast of the United States. Elsa wasn't much of a help either, she had never experienced this cold before, either, but when Oscar and Gretchen came to visit for Christmas, they bought the right winter clothes for them and reassured them they will get used to it. As a diversion, Oscar took his family to celebrate Christmas and New Year in New York City. Both

Gretchen and Karl enjoyed the trip and danced with the crowd in Times Square at the stroke of midnight.

While in Boston, Oscar met school officials who advised him Karl wasn't doing well and spends most of the time playing sports and not engaging new friends. The principal recommended a special tutor to improve his English language and Oscar agreed to fully cooperate. Elsa was trying her best to cope with the new circumstances. She even enrolled in a language school to improve her conversational English and overall she was happy to be in Boston; Karl's parents had no doubts about her sincerity and devotion to their son.

Helmut, Oscar and their families were present at Ricardo's lavish wedding in Sao Paulo. The wedding, held at a Lutheran Church in the city, was attended by lots of friends. Many came down from the mountain camp for the auspicious occasion, and although the wedding was very elegant, it did become rowdy at times before the newlyweds were off to Hawaii for their honeymoon.

CHAPTER 36

Ingrid nearly fainted when she opened the front door to her house and two uniformed army officers were standing there with serious looks on their faces.

"My son, my son! Oh my God!" she shouted, "Is he okay, is there anything wrong with David?"

"Ma'am, we are here to inform you about David. May we come in?"

Trembling with fear, Ingrid led them to the living room, where they continued. "Your brave son has been injured in line of duty in Vietnam and he has been transported to Walter Reed Hospital in Washington DC." They went on to give her details about the injury and the hospital where he was receiving treatment before they somberly returned to the military vehicle waiting for them.

Ingrid was hysterical when Greg answered the phone at the nursery. "Please calm down honey, you are not making much sense, now tell me again what is wrong with David?"

"My boy is hurt, he is lying in the hospital in Washington, please come home right away!" Greg rushed out and drove first to pick up Sonia from school; the principal and other teachers came out to express their sympathy and support for the family during this trying time.

Sonia found her mother in a terrible state when they arrived home. She was all curled up on the kitchen floor crying and shouting, "Oh God why me! What have I done to deserve all of this? These God damn politicians start wars all over the world and our children are the ones who get hurt, not them! Please God, save my boy! He is a good man."

Once they were able to calm her down, the family immediately drove south to Washington to be with David. The attending doctor explained David's injury was typical of what he is used to see coming from the battlefield; he sustained two shrapnel fragments that caused moderately severe damage to the groin area. Had the injury been an inch above where he was hit, he would have been paralyzed from the waist down. The doctor further explained the injuries are not life threatening and David will have to go through reconstructive surgery before he fully recovers.

"How long will it take before he is back to normal, doctor?" Greg asked.

"I think he stands a very good chance to fully recover all his normal functions within several months. He is young, strong and with intensive physiotherapy I predict he should be just fine, it is just a matter of time."

When they were allowed to go in the room Ingrid ran to the side of her son and gently held his hand in hers, "How are you David? You gave us the scare of our life, my baby, how are you feeling now?" David couldn't speak; he stroked his mom's hand and raised his thumb up.

A high ranking army officer came to see David the following day. He took the family to the side and informed them David will be awarded the Purple Heart for military merit and valor, as he risked his life to save others. The president of the United States will award him the medal at a special ceremony in the White House upon his release. "Your son, I must add, is among the finest in our military. He is disciplined, motivated and daring, he showed no fear in battle and upon his arrival in Vietnam requested to be at the forefront fighting the enemy, and you should be proud of him. We certainly are very proud of him in the United States Armed Forces."

A few days after they arrived in Washington, David's condition improved and he started to talk and eat on his own. He recounted to his family the events that led to his injury. "I was dispatched with fellow troops to support one of our platoons entrapped by the enemy, and as soon as the chopper pilot found a suitable spot, we jumped off under a hail of fire. The gunners on the choppers flying overhead gave us enough cover to reach our injured comrades and drag them to safety, but as we retreated back to the chopper a mortar shell exploded and I fell down with half a dozen of my fellow soldiers. The next thing I remember I was in a hospital bed. It was a horrific scene and my wounds are really painful, but I would do it all over again if I had to."

Greg had to leave to Detroit to take Sonia back to school. Ingrid insisted she stay with David. "I am not coming back home unless David is with me. I will stay with my son until he recovers completely," she told her husband. "He is a piece of me, Honey, and I will stay with him for as long as it takes. This is what mothers do when their children are hurt."

Greg just kissed his wife and whispered, "I love you," in her ear before he and Sonia waved goodbye.

A few months after David was admitted to hospital, his condition improved significantly and the first reconstructive surgery was scheduled. The doctors explained his recovery was going better than expected and he is now able to walk on his own aided by a cane. Ingrid, who has been at David's bedside from the morning to the evening every single day of the week was very attentive to her son's needs. She talked to him about events from her childhood and the time when she first arrived in America, and how Greg courted her for a few years before he eventually proposed. She also listened to David about his experience in Vietnam, but deliberately avoided the subject about his future plans until one day David himself brought up the subject.

"Mother, what do you think the future holds for me when I get out of the hospital?"

"I don't know, son. That is entirely your option; your family will back you up no matter what you choose to do."

"This subject has been in the back of my mind for a while and I believe it is time I make a decision. The doctor dropped in last night after you left. He and I had a long chat about my future and where I should go after my release from hospital. It was nice he took the time to talk to me, you know how busy they get during their shift, but he went out of his way to listen and to give advice."

"What did he tell you, David?"

"He first talked about my injuries and the progress I made from the time I was admitted in hospital, essentially he said I can go home to recuperate in two to three weeks. He expects me to recover completely and without complications. I asked his opinion if I should continue my education and get a law degree first or opt to work for the private sector for a while before I pursue a law career. So what do you think, Mom?"

"You didn't finish your story David, what was the doctor's opinion, what did he advise you to do?"

"I thought I'd ask you first, I didn't want to influence you!"

"Son, I think working for the private sector will provide firsthand experience and will teach you how to interact with people and gain invaluable knowledge and training. This is important in life because it will build up your confidence and increase your sense of responsibility. Above all it will give you a lesson about the value of money, this experience will come to play in the future when you become a lawyer. Now tell me what the doctor had to say about it."

David moved over to the side of the bed where his mother sat and gave her a big hug. "Mother, the doctor gave the exact same advice!"

David was soon released from hospital so he could travel home to recuperate for the next two months. He was still sore and sluggish but full of hope and determination. His family was relieved to see him back on his feet and they had no doubt he will mend quickly. David contacted some of the employers who were interested to hire him before he went to Vietnam, and was surprised to receive two lucrative offers right away. The first came from JP Morgan and the other was from Merrill Lynch, both world renowned investment and wealth management institutions with a large number of clients and employees. JP Morgan's offer contained a package of incentives that was more appealing and he therefore decided to sign up with them.

When David recovered entirely from his injuries he received a phone call from the office of the President of the United States inviting him to attend the Purple Heart Ceremonial Award. He and other recipients were invited to the White House where President Nixon was slated to bestow the honor on these brave Americans for their service to the country and fellow troops. David was against Nixon before he was elected but changed his mind after he recognized the merit of what the President was trying to achieve in reaching a settlement for this protracted and unpopular war. He fundamentally didn't change his mind about fighting the communists but the tide against the war was gaining so much momentum at home and it was imprudent to ignore the collective well of the majority of American people.

Greg took the family to Washington DC for the award ceremony. It was a beautiful fall day when they arrived and the family was proud when David shook the hand of the President after he fastened the medal around his neck. Ingrid cried with joy at the sight of her son receiving one of the highest military honors. She remembered her brave mother dying on the battlefield for her country and what she believed in. Although this was a somber thought, Ingrid was so thrilled and proud of her son.

CHAPTER 37

Karl's mother and grandparents spent most of the summer on the east coast with him. They drove up from Boston to Maine and the youth loved the Bar Harbor area so much he asked his grandfather if he could go on board one of the many lobster boats operating in the area. He was impressed with the night adventure and stayed up with the fishermen until their return to shore in the early hours of the morning with a good harvest from the bottom of the ocean. Karl's first year in junior high started well, he took a great interest in seventh grade world History and Geography and became very fluent in English. Now thirteen, he showed much promise as a swimmer but ice hockey was his passion and he caught the eye of the coach who invited him to join the school team.

Elsa took Karl to a different church every Sunday before they settled on the Catholic Church in the Milton area. The Priest, Edwin Mooney, was a popular middle aged man who had spent time in South America as a missionary before he settled down in his hometown of Boston. He spoke Spanish well and loved the people and the cuisine of South America. He initially observed the lady and the young man coming to church every once in a while but the last few months he noticed them regularly at Sunday mass. He also noticed the large contribution they give to the church on every visit despite their young ages. The woman didn't appear old enough to be the mother of the young man with her, and they also looked remarkably different; Karl's golden hair and fair complexion stood in contrast to Elsa's distinctly Latin appearance. After mass one Sunday he finally had the opportunity to approach them before they went home.

"Pardon me, welcome! Allow me to formally introduce myself. I'm Edwin Mooney. I'm so sorry I've been unable to speak with you until now. What is your name young man?" he asked.

"My name is Karl Silva."

"How about you, young lady?"

"My name is Elsa Montez."

174

"I detect a little accent; may I ask where you folks are from?"

"Karl is from Brazil, but I am originally from Paraguay."

"That is so interesting, are you just visiting here in Massachusetts?"

"No, we live here, Karl goes to Milton Academy and I am here to look after him."

"Are you two related to one another?"

"No, I was hired to work for Karl's family in Brazil and when Karl came to Milton I came too, as per the wishes of his family to have an adult with him."

"You are like a governess for Karl then?" Father Mooney chuckled.

"Well you can call it that, but I consider him my little brother!" They all laughed.

"Well, this is very interesting. I hope your stay here in Milton will be memorable and you will excel in school! You look like a smart young man; do you speak Portuguese as well?"

Yes, Father, I speak three languages now, English, Portuguese and Elsa taught me to speak Spanish too."

"That is very clever indeed! I also speak Spanish and I visited Brazil many times in the past."

Edwin Mooney told them about his missionary work in South America and spoke with them in Spanish, much to the delight of Elsa. He told them it was his honor to have them as part of the congregation and he looked forward to seeing them at mass on future Sundays.

Soon after Ricardo returned from his honeymoon in Hawaii, he and Bridget bought a house in Anaheim, California. The property was not far from the parcel of land where the upscale residential project was slated to begin soon. Oscar and Helmut took part in the ceremonial breaking of the ground to mark the first phase of construction after H&O became a corporation in the state of California, a subsidiary of the original company in Brazil. Oscar was successful in obtaining a large bank loan so the construction began in earnest. He was assigned the title of chairman and Ricardo was the general manager of the company. They both retained the services of an immigration lawyer to help them with their legal status in the United States.

Gretchen suggested they travel to Germany after the ceremony was over. She always had wanted to see the country, but circumstances prevented her from going. Her father and husband were dedicated to their work, and it seems this is all they do. This time however, she was hoping to spend some time with her husband alone on the trip. Oscar was reluctant to go, and he told her to wait until the beginning of the summer when Karl was out of school, but she wasn't swayed.

"No darling, I want to go before you get busy with your new project, just the two of us this time. Karl can come with us again in the future." Oscar relented and agreed after his wife pleaded her case, but they decided to stop in Boston to check on Karl on the way.

When Oscar and Gretchen stopped to see the school principal before their trip to Europe they were pleased to learn their son was doing well and his performance improved considerably over the last year. He seems to be enjoying school and made many new friends and the principal also believed Elsa was doing a great job looking after him.

"That young lady is on top of things and she is constantly in touch with the school administration to follow up on Karl's progress," reported the principal.

Elsa told Gretchen she and Karl never miss Sunday mass at the church, he was deeply religious and differentiates between right and wrong. She told them about Karl's reaction upon hearing of Martin Luther King's assassination. "Your boy was very upset about the injustice the Negro community is facing, and he didn't care when other boys in school made fun of him for siding with the black people. I can tell you with confidence madam, your son's heart is in the right place, he is such a nice little gentleman and a pleasure to look after!"

Both Oscar and Gretchen were pleased Karl was going to church on Sundays and didn't mind him going to a Catholic church either. They inquired from Elsa the name of the church she and Karl attend and decided to pay Father Edwin Mooney a visit. To their delight the priest was also full of praise for their son.

"Your boy is a mature young man and his love and devotion for Jesus Christ our Lord is beyond doubt. He is a good and honest boy."

Düsseldorf on the Rhine was the first city Oscar and Gretchen visited; she was enchanted with the city where her father had been born. From there they drove to the more familiar territory in the south. They stopped in the town of Offenburg where Oscar spent many days during his youth, and took a detour to his grandfather's house. They found out George the farmer had died many years earlier and his son Fritz took over the business after his father's death. Fritz gave them a tour of the property and the farm with great enthusiasm; the house looked a little different from when Oscar sold it and the room attached to the back was still there but used for storage now.

He couldn't believe the city of Munich when they arrived there; it was rebuilt from the ground up after the war. He hardly remembered the city as it existed when he was young; nevertheless he took his wife all over and even made time for a side trip to the mountains nearby where they skied at his favorite Alpine resort. It was for Oscar an exhausting but nostalgic trip, and they both slept all the way back to Los Angeles.

CHAPTER 38

T he first week at JP Morgan was very hectic for David; this was his first experience with the corporate culture and the fast pace of New York's financial world. Many of his colleagues didn't share his views about the Vietnam War and they weren't impressed he was awarded the Purple Heart for bravery. His immediate boss, a middle aged Jewish man called "The Bull" by his colleagues was in favor of the war, however, and though he and David shared the same views they distinctly lacked personal chemistry. David started his banking career as an analyst; he was good with numbers and had the right analytical mind for it. He was also a hardworking man who arrived early and never left his office until late so he quickly made a name for himself and earned the respect of his fellow workers.

He found an apartment in Brooklyn, a short metro ride from his work and quickly adapted to the fast pace in the city. His favorite place to spend leisure time was around Greenwich Village; he loved both the culinary and the arts scene common in this rowdy part of New York. One of his colleagues at work invited him to attend a debate about the war in Vietnam and when he joined the debate he was met with a hostile crowd who opposed the war unlike his position in favor of it. He explained his views about communism and the failed efforts of the President to end the war with pride and dignity for the American people. "So far the President has been in office for two years and Henry Kissinger, his National Security chief has had several meetings with the North Vietnamese with hardly any progress to show for it. It is quite apparent the enemy wants us to leave defeated, and this outcome will not resonate well with the proud people of this country!"

One of the participants in the debate was a young lady by the name of Nancy Avilov. She was two years younger than David and recently moved from Merrill Lynch to JP Morgan. A Jewish girl from Manhattan, to David's surprise she too argued passionately in favor of the war. Vietnam, she stressed, was just a proxy war with the USSR. "We must fight them on every front and everywhere they try to spread communism; those people will not rest until they achieve world dominance!" Her defense of the war, like David's didn't sit well with the other people present who argued in favor of the US withdrawing with no preconditions. They simply want the war to end soon, and emphasized the human cost and the tragedy inflicted on both sides.

"You were awesome back there," David told Nancy when the debate was over. "You really hammered them, they simply fail to look at the wider picture and the sacrifices we must make in order to preserve our freedom."

"You weren't so bad yourself," Nancy responded gleefully to his kind words. "I am so glad somebody agrees with me! My grandparents came to the US because they lost everything they worked for in Russia. The communists claimed they did it for the common good of society but evidence suggests they did it to enrich themselves and their communist ilk at the expense of the hard working people."

"You really are passionate about the communists. How about we finish our discussion at Gene's pizza?" David suggested, "It is not too far from here, we can actually walk to it."

"I don't know Gene's pizza, but why not, I could go for a pizza and a cold pitcher of beer," she answered.

"I'm sorry Nancy, but I am not much of a drinker. I'll be happy with a cup of coffee though."

The two walked leisurely to the pizzeria, and Nancy ordered a small pizza with Canadian bacon and extra cheese while David ordered a vegetarian pizza. He was a little puzzled when Nancy ordered bacon. "I don't know, but I was under the impression you were Jewish?"

"Yes I am; I come from a mixed religion. My mother is a Russian Jew and my father is Orthodox Christian. You can call my father a dove, he contemplated going to priesthood before my mother seduced him," she explained with a broad smile. David laughed at the quip but he admired her style. "You are Jewish yourself, aren't you?"

"Yes I am," David answered. "My mother is a concentration camp survivor. She was pregnant when she arrived in this country. Sadly I lost my father at the concentration camp where he was incarcerated; my mother never saw him again after the Nazis arrested them toward the end of the war. But against all odds my mother survived and so did the baby she was carrying. That baby was me.

David and Nancy spent almost two hours chatting about the war and Nixon, then Nancy said, "I better get going, I told my mother I am going for a debate with my work colleagues and I am already an hour late, she will be panicking now."

"Do you live far from here?"

"No, I used to, but we live in Manhattan now."

Half of the bonus he received David sent to his mother as a gift. He put a check in an envelope and sent her a small note to tell her how much he loved her and to thank her for giving him all the support, standing by him all of those years especially when he was hospitalized. Ingrid was overcome with joy when she received the letter. She called David in the evening to tell him how much she loved him.

"You are everything in the world to me son, you are so thoughtful and I love you dearly! I also want to discuss something that has been bothering me for a while and the more I think about it the worse it gets. I am at a loss how to resolve it."

"You've got me worried mother, what is bothering you?"

"Well, it's about Sonia. Your sister is getting opinionated and she likes to get her own way. I don't deny she is doing very well at school, but she recently became a fanatic about religion."

"Stop there, mother. What do you mean fanatic about religion? What is she doing to arouse your concern?"

"It began few months back when she started going to bible class at the Catholic Church with her best friend Veronica, but now she goes there at least twice a week in addition to Sunday mass. The other day she signed up for a crash course to learn Latin. She believes it will make her understand the Bible better. All her talk is about Jesus and the other day she even mentioned becoming a nun!"

David wasn't at all surprised, he knew his sister had a strong personality, but she has a soft heart and would give the shirt off her back to the needy. She has always been like that, fiercely on the side of the underdog, the poor, and the disenfranchised so David was not confounded at her devotion to Jesus and his message of love and peace. What baffled him however, is the disavowal of her mother's Jewish faith and her father's Protestant faith in favor of the Catholic Church, and he failed to understand her desire not to follow in their footsteps like most people her age are expected to do. But he attributed it to growing up and the desire to chart her own path without influence from traditional sources like her parents. Nevertheless he loved her so much and he knew in his heart she loved him even more.

The following week David ran into Nancy when she was taking a group of people on a tour of the offices. She waved to him and he waved back.

"Come see me when you finish!" he shouted.

"I might," she said with a smile, but when she came to his office an hour later David was on the phone in the middle of a heated argument.

When he finished talking he turned towards her and said, "I don't know what this guy is doing, but he defies logic."

"Who are you talking about?"

"Ernie Adelman, my boss. I don't know how on earth he reached the position he is in, the man doesn't know diddly about finance!"

"I know him well," she answered. "He is an old acquaintance of my father. JP Morgan brought him here to run your department but he used to work for the Treasury Department. I think his contacts at the Treasury is what made JP Morgan interested in him. I agree, it certainly was not his credentials, and he is a dull person. Even Mr. Elliot, my boss doesn't care for him that much."

"Neither do I," David said emphatically, "But hey, never mind that. Would you like to go out for lunch today?"

"I wish I could, but my boss wants me present at a meeting with an important client at lunchtime. I'm not doing anything this weekend if you want to go out for dinner," she answered invitingly.

"This will work for me too; I know a great restaurant called Toggles in Greenwich Village, if that's alright with you?"

"Yes, I know it well, I ate there before, and they make fabulous martinis!"

"What time is good for you?"

"How about 9 pm, I don't like to go early, is that okay?"

"Sure," answered David, "it actually works out great, I can have an extra hour to prepare for my exam on Monday."

Nancy came dressed up in a very elegant red dress with a nice string of pearls round her neck; David was already inside, worried, when she arrived twenty minutes late. "Sorry about that, the traffic was so bad!"

"Oh, you don't take the metro?"

"No, Byron, my dad's chauffer dropped me off. I don't like to walk to the metro when it's raining. It messes up my hair!"

"Well, you look very nice, Nancy," he said as he pulled out her chair.

"Thank you so much, David, but please tell me what exam are you taking? The girls in the office told me you have a degree already from the University of Chicago."

David gave her a broad smile, "What else did the girls in the office tell you about me?"

"They told me a lot," she answered laughing, "You know girls like to talk, and I just sat there and listened...but seriously, what are you studying?"

"I am doing an advance study in computational programs, it will help accelerate my career, and you know how employers are bent up on qualifications."

"Yes I understand, but didn't you do this in college?"

"Of course, but not in great detail. Besides, it has been few years since I graduated and I need to brush up a little."

"Does the program involve a lot of math?"

"Yes it does, but math has always been one of my strong subjects. How about yourself, what is it you exactly do at JP Morgan?" David asked, "I see you often with Mr. Elliot."

"Mr. Elliot is a close family friend, he used to work with dad at Solomon Sachs before he moved to JP Morgan, and I work in sales and promotion."

"How interesting, do you like what you do?"

"It's okay I guess, at least I don't have the same pressure brokers and associates have, and I also get to be out most of the time, but I wish the pay was better."

Nancy suggested they go for a drink when they finished their dinner, but David resisted, reminding her he didn't drink.

"No problem, you can order a juice," she answered with encouragement. They went to a fancy bar and she had few martinis on top of the two she had at the restaurant, and he noticed she was tipsy when he dropped her off at her parents' apartment.

David went to bed thinking about Nancy; he found her attractive and light hearted and she comes from good pedigree, but he didn't endorse her drinking habit. Still, he felt the chemistry between them was good; in fact it was very good.

President Nixon was ahead in the polls in the summer of 1972. He ran his re-election campaign with a promise to end the war in Vietnam with determination and honor for America. This resonated well with the American public and both David and Nancy took personal interest in the President's bid for re-election. They attended rallies and spoke in favor of ending the war if in fact the outcome will bring honor for the United States. On election night, David was at home watching the results on TV, and when California was declared Republican and sealed the election for the President, David was thrilled, he didn't like the weak Democratic candidate.

The following morning he ran into Nancy in the office. "Hey, congratulations," she said, "our man won!"

"He sure did, I stayed up till the networks proclaimed him the winner."

"So did I," she answered, laughing.

Nancy and David continued to see each other regularly. They made it a habit to meet for dinner every Saturday evening. On one of these dates Nancy was interested to hear about the time he spent in Vietnam.

"What do you want to know?" he asked her.

"What was your motive to volunteer to fight in Vietnam? The war was so unpopular and public sentiment was resolutely against it, so, what prompted you?"

"To tell you the truth, part of it is due to my mother's experience under the Nazis. When Hitler came to power, people underestimated this evil man and the world powers let him build his military unchecked. He consolidated his power and spread his evil ideology and before we knew it, Germany became too powerful, and the West didn't have the stomach for a military encounter to stop him when his troops marched into Czechoslovakia. Appeasement was their strategy and the United States sat on the sidelines believing the war was a European affair that didn't have anything to do with us. And the rest is history; America was attacked when we were unprepared and we lost more than quarter of a million of our brave men as a result. It is deja vu now; the communists are on the march and we must remain steadfast in our opposition and fight them everywhere before they reach our shores and take our freedom."

Nancy was impressed by his political conviction, "You need to meet my mother, she will love you so much! Her parents lost everything they had under the communists."

Nancy told her parents about David. "He is such a mature man, and he risked his life for something he believed in." She told them about his enrollment to fight in Vietnam and the medal he received for bravery, "He is a true hero!" she added with passion in her voice.

"What does he do at JP Morgan?" her father asked.

"He is the assistant manager in the securities department and everybody speaks very highly of him. I predict he will rise fast and may reach top management one day."

"You seem to like him, don't you Nancy?" her mother asked craftily.

"Yes mother, I find him very honest and not into playing games. He seems to be focused and knows where he is going in life, and to top it all up, he is so good looking, and Jewish also!"

"Why don't you have him come over for dinner with us one evening, we would like to meet him. You make him sound so interesting the way you talk."

Sonia graduated from high school in the summer of 1974 among the top five in her class. David came home to Detroit to attend her graduation; he was proud of his sister, and was on his feet clapping when the principal handed her the diploma. Ingrid and Greg were crying with joy and pride. Sonia was a mature young lady, outspoken about issues close to her heart. She argued with David about the need to bring justice and equality to all citizens of the world, advocating that wars don't achieve anything except hate and bigotry and more hate, it is a vicious cycle that must be broken. David admired his sister's idealism and sense of justice; he too wants to see justice all over the world too, but he had no qualms that evil must be stamped out before justice can be established.

He asked Sonia about her plans now she had graduated from high school. "I have applied to several colleges and I am still waiting to see if I can get a scholarship."

"Which universities have you applied to?" David queried.

"I want to go to a top university on either the east or west coasts. I will not settle for any university, the one I will finally choose must be renowned and offer outstanding education."

"Okay," David said impatiently, "You neglected to tell me which university interests you the most?"

"It is a toss-up between Harvard and Stanford, but Harvard is where I'm really hoping to go; I want to study English literature and philosophy."

"This all sounds great, but what options will you have after graduation from college? The subjects you chose will qualify you for a career in teaching and not much else!"

"Yes, big brother, you hit the nail right on the head! That is exactly what I want to be, a teacher in a good school. I want to be able to influence the minds of my students just as Mr. Jeffries influenced mine."

"Who is Mr. Jeffries?"

"My English teacher. He is so brilliant, and against the war in Vietnam and strongly believes the cost of the war should have been spent on education, not on killing innocent Vietnamese people who have done nothing bad to our country."

CHAPTER 39

O scar and Helmut and their wives arrived in Boston to be with Karl at the end of his junior high school term. They were proud the boy had refocused on his studies after the rocky start in the first few years at Milton Academy. He passed all the exams successfully and was slated to return at the end of the summer to begin high school. The school administrator recommended Karl use the school boarding facilities in lieu of living at the house with his beloved Elsa. He felt the boy mature and old enough to look after himself. The school's residence is available only to students from grade nine to grade twelve. The family respected the recommendations and so did Karl; he felt it was the right moment to be independent and spend more time with friends at the residence.

Oscar and Gretchen thanked Elsa for staying with Karl during his junior years in Boston. "You have done a wonderful job, all of us are grateful to you and we sincerely appreciate your kindness and dedication to Karl," said Gretchen. Elsa was given two choices; either stay in the service of the family at their residence in Los Angeles or return to Brazil and continue to work at the family residence there. Without hesitation she chose to stay in California.

"After living in the US for the last few years, I became used to the country and speak English well, but I'm going to miss my boy so much!" She hugged him and wouldn't let go for several minutes. "You are part of me Karl, I feel you are the little brother I never had." The whole family was touched by her sincerity and devotion.

Karl started high school at Milton after he returned from vacation with his family. However, living on his own wasn't easy at the beginning and it took him time to adjust to the disciplined life at the school's boarding facilities. But after making friends there, he found the atmosphere pleasant and comfortable. Karl was an intermediate student in his academic studies but when it came to sports, he was a natural. Swimming, diving and ice hockey were his favorites sports and he often stayed for hours in the pool practicing until he perfected the double somersaults, his fellow students and the school staff found him pleasant and modest, he never bragged about his family's wealth since many of the students at the academy came from wealthy families also. School staff remained vigilant and prodded him to do better in his studies and homework, he was by all accounts an average student, he didn't lack intelligence or aptitude; he nevertheless failed to apply himself to the fullest to get higher grades. His disposition and mild manners attracted others to him and girls noticed how good looking he was: tall, athletic and trim, with wide and shiny eyes and straight blond hair cut short. But the only girl who interested him was Tracy Collins, a slender blonde from Florida. Karl liked her easy manner and unpretentious personality.

One day after class when they came face to face in the hallway, Karl finally mustered his courage. "Would you like to go out for a pizza and watch a movie with me on Friday evening?" Tracy flashed him a big smile and quickly accepted the invitation.

The first phase of construction of the upscale subdivision in Southern California was drawing to an end and the results were outstanding. Sales of the properties exceeded wildest expectations; plans to start the next phase were nearing completion and Oscar came to visit Helmut to report on the progress.

Helmut was not surprised almost all the properties were sold already. He confidently told his son-in-law, "I predict the second phase will be even better, people from all over the country are coming to California in droves. The climate here is a big plus but people are pouring in because of job opportunities and the varied scenery this state has to offer. You have the ocean, the mountains and the desert, what else do people want other than good accommodation, and we are building it for them! Well done, Oscar!"

Oscar and Ricardo were pleased when granted permanent residency status to live and work in the United States; however they were required to wait a few more years before they become citizens. Their interest with the nationalist group in Oregon was going steady, yet they kept the engagement to a minimum for fear it may interfere with their bid to become citizens. The last time they went to the hideout in the Cascade Mountains of Oregon to meet with Professor Woodruff, they were surprised to find out the true leader of the group was in fact not Woodruff, but Alfred Hanson, a medical doctor from the neighboring state of Washington. His identity was withheld from them until a thorough background check was conducted to ascertain their loyalty and allegiance to the group. The main topic of discussion every time they visited was how to rid the world of Jewish influence, especially in the United States and the western countries of Europe. They made reference to how dominant Jews were in many professions and in Hollywood.

Ricardo voiced his frustration bitterly. "It is absolutely ridiculous they have a monopoly on everything from entertainment to education in this world! They put themselves at an advantage to brainwash all the children and win them to their cause, and guess what? They are profiting every step of the way. It is not only Hollywood they control, they've got all the politicians to rally to their cause, and they fight tooth and nail with any politician who speaks against them!"

CHAPTER 40

Nancy came to David's office the day he returned from Detroit. She was annoyed. "I see you are back. Your assistant told me you went to Detroit to be with your family. How come you never told me?"

"I am sorry but I had my dates mixed up. My sister's graduation was on Thursday and I had assumed it was the following week. I came up to tell you, but you weren't in the office. I was really lucky to find an airline ticket at the last minute."

"Did your sister graduate alright?"

"She sure did, as a matter of fact she graduated with honors. She's a smart kid, but a little idealistic about life."

"It looks like intelligence runs in your family," Nancy said dryly, "and by the way, my parents would like to invite you over for dinner one day. How is your schedule this week?"

"I am free on Saturday, if that is alright with them."

"No, that is not alright with me! I like to be alone with you on Saturdays. You have not taken enough notice of me, David. I guess I am not good enough for you?"

He was taken aback by this. "Wait a minute, Nancy; I thought we are just friends. I didn't know you are serious about our relationship. I'm sorry if I gave you false indications, I didn't even know you were that interested in me."

Nancy, standing in front of his desk started to cry. He noticed people in the hallway slowing down to listen.

"Of course I am interested in you David, but maybe you have somebody else in mind, do you?"

"Nancy, my dear! I don't have anybody. You are a beautiful lady, and I was under the impression you wanted to have somebody from your own privileged background, not just a junior employee like me!"

Nancy sat down on the chair. She looked miserable, with tears trickling down her face. David came round and closed the office door, then pulled her up and gave her a big kiss.

"Don't let go David, I love you, you are the only one for me! Yes, I like my lifestyle, but in many ways you are richer than most people. I haven't come across anybody like you before, and I want to be your girl, David."

David took Nancy home with him that evening. They prepared a nice pasta dish, and after a few hours of talking snuggled on the couch, they went to the bedroom and closed the door behind them. Before she left for home in the wee hours, he whispered in her ear, "You are beautiful and I want to be your man."

David arrived at Nancy's parents' apartment on Friday evening. A maid opened the door and Nancy came running to meet him. She took him by the hand to the living room and introduced him to her parents.

Her father found him a very interesting and mature man but a little peculiar. "You don't smoke or drink?" he asked.

"No sir, I don't, I never developed a habit for either, and there are better ways to spend my money."

"Like what?" Nancy's mother asked.

"Well, I am saving all I can to go back to school for a law degree, maybe I'll join my sister at Harvard or Yale. She is planning to go to university to study Philosophy and English I think."

Both of Nancy's parents were stunned when David told them he was leaving a lucrative career in finance and management at JP Morgan to start all over in a new direction. Nancy, sipping on a glass of wine on her favorite rocking chair, was perturbed with David for not mentioning his future plans.

"You never told me any of this before," she said awkwardly.

"You never asked. To tell you the truth, when I finished from the University of Chicago, the original plan was for me to continue with my law degree, but the issue of Vietnam came first and I opted to serve my country. Fundamentally a career in finance has many advantages and I enjoy it so much, but it doesn't satisfy my ambitions. I want something more challenging and I like a little more drama in my life."

"You are going out with Nancy, isn't that enough drama for you?" Nancy's mother said slyly.

"Mother, I object to that remark, I am a good girlfriend!"

"What kind of lawyer are you hoping to be?" her father asked.

"I would like to be a corporate lawyer, very much like Russell Eaton, my mother's employer when she first arrived in this country. He was a terrific man, who made a fortune from his law firm and business interests in Detroit."

Dinner was served and Nancy's family enjoyed David's company, and the topic of conversation turned to his mother. "Nancy was telling us your mother was a concentration camp survivor; I bet her experience must have been horrific there," gently began Mrs. Avilov.

"Yes indeed, she suffered at the hands of the Nazis and she was left for dead after severe torture and beating. It was a miracle she was still alive. She had to eat crumbs dumped on the floor and witnessed terrible things committed against fellow prisoners, and when the French liberated the camp they found her in an appalling condition. She was unconscious and her ribcage was clearly visible through her flesh, but she made it, and her pregnancy survived."

"How on earth was she able to survive the pregnancy after the severe beating, and with no food and water?"

"From what I understand, my mother was just few days pregnant when she was caught by the Nazis, and she scarcely stayed in the camp two weeks before the prison was liberated. The doctors explained to my mother the embryo didn't have enough time to develop and therefore it wasn't affected by the trauma she suffered. I personally believe it was the will of God to bring me out alive."

"How about your dad, David?" inquired Nancy's father.

"My father and mother were hiding in a safe house during the war but in the final few weeks of the war they were captured after somebody informed on them. My mother never saw her husband again. She heard later he was tortured to death."

"I am sorry David; it must have been so awful for your mother," Nancy's mother said sympathetically.

David enjoyed the visit at Nancy's parents, he found the Avilovs easy-going and unostentatious, and they did not attempt to show off like many wealthy New Yorkers. He also noticed the whole family drank wine and liquor and the atmosphere was merry and joyful.

"Hello big brother!" David could sense joy and happiness in his sister's voice on the phone.

"Hello Sonia, good to hear from you baby, what you are up to?"

"I am not a baby anymore; I am eighteen and a proud freshman at Harvard University!"

"Well, well, well, that is excellent news, I am so happy for you Sonia. You deserve it, congratulations!"

"Thank you so much. I was offered a partial scholarship and Dad said he will make up the rest of the tuition and pay the living expenses as well, isn't that wonderful?"

"Sure it is wonderful; I guess we all have to pitch in to help, because you are so special. How did Mum take the news?"

"She was so happy, we were jumping up and down together and when Dad came home he nearly cried when he heard. How about I drop in to see you in NYC on my way to Boston?"

"Sure, I look forward to having you here. I must also tell you I have been thinking I will pursue a law career at either Harvard or at Yale, and it will be great if you and I end up at the same college."

"That is marvelous news, I am so excited for you big brother!"

Sonia was unable to make it to New York City; she had a busy schedule preparing for her first year of college, but David and Nancy took Friday off and drove to meet her when she arrived at Boston's Logan airport. Sonia thought David and Nancy made a great couple. She knew her mother would be pleased David was dating a Jewish girl. They stayed for the weekend and Nancy acted like a tour guide. She and her family visited Boston many times before and she knew all the places to visit and the good restaurants to eat at. Sonia confirmed she was going to study English literature and a minor in Philosophy; theology would have been her first choice but Harvard didn't offer it for an undergraduate program.

"Why is she so interested to study Christianity?" Nancy asked David after they left Boston.

"I really don't know, but my sister decided to attend a Catholic church instead of going to either of her parents' places of worship. We thought it was just a fad and she will grow out of it, but no, she had apparently joined the Catholic faith out of conviction."

"What did your mother say? It must have been hard to see her only daughter leaving the Jewish faith?"

"I am sure it was, she never said though. But you have to understand the background to this uncommon situation; my mother met a man in Detroit after she arrived in America. He was the gardener for the same family my mother worked for; they fell in love and were married after a few years of courtship. His name is Greg McKay. Greg, who became my father, wasn't Jewish; he belonged to the Presbyterian Church. He and my mother agreed before marriage to keep their own separate religions, but expose their children to both Judaism and Christianity, so my sister attended services at mother's synagogue one week and at my father's Presbyterian church the next. But typical of my maverick sister, she chose neither religion and decided the Catholic faith is where she belongs."

"Boy, you have a very unusual family. How about you David, why didn't you switch religions?"

"My mother insisted when my father proposed that I stay Jewish. She argued both my biological parents were Jewish and naturally I must remain one, and to tell you the truth I am eternally grateful she insisted to bring me up in that tradition. I cannot imagine being anything else."

Nancy was a little perplexed and asked David if religion was a vital part of his life. He stated emphatically, without a shred of doubt, the Jewish religion is perhaps the single most important aspect of who he is, and it defines him as a person. "I am passionate about it," he said "and I seldom miss congregation on Saturdays. How about you, Nancy?"

"Yes, it is important for me to be Jewish," she answered, "but I wouldn't say it's the single most important thing in my life. You are the most important part of my life David, and I love you from the bottom of my heart."

David continued to do well at his job and received a big bonus at the end of the year. He again sent his mother few thousand dollars as a gift. "This is for you, Mother, enjoy it! I am sure it feels a little empty at home after Sonia left; I suggest you and Dad take a vacation somewhere nice and warm."

"Where will we go David?" Ingrid told her son she cried for days after Sonia was gone. "Your sister made the house lively, and I miss her terribly. I have nobody to talk to and it feels so lonely without her."

"This is why I suggest you go on a vacation, mother, maybe Mexico or Hawaii? Or somewhere equally warm, get away from that miserable Detroit winter!"

David and Nancy's relationship was getting serious with every passing day, and Nancy suggested he rent a larger apartment.

"What for? You know how expensive apartment rentals are in the city," he answered with disinterest.

"But I would like to move in with you; I guess I suffer from separation anxiety when you are not with me."

"Don't be silly Nancy! You can visit any time you wish and stay overnight if you so desire. I don't need a bigger apartment for now, especially when I am planning to move out of New York soon. Chances are I will tender my resignation before the start of the winter semester at law school."

Nancy was irritated but couldn't resist the next question. "How about me when you leave to college? Will I become your ex-girlfriend? I love you David, and I don't want to lose you!"

"No, you won't lose me. I love you dearly Nancy, and I want you to remain part of my life."

David walked in his boss's office at the beginning of November, and before he even sat down, his boss started the conversation. "I liked the presentation you prepared for the Milligan Chemical Company, but I have minor details I would like to discuss with you."

"Sure," David answered, "but to tell you the truth, the reason I came to see you sir has nothing to do with Milligan Chemical, but rather to inform you of my intention to resign from JP Morgan at the end of the year. I have applied to Yale University for a Law degree and this morning I received a letter of acceptance."

The manager's face changed color when David finished talking. He tried to change David's mind. "You are young and smart and likely to become somebody big in this company! Why on earth do you want to leave this lucrative career for something unknown?"

David however was adamant; he thanked his boss for his confidence and explained the decision was final.

David called Nancy after he finished with the boss. "Guess what? I just tendered my resignation from JP Morgan, effective the end of December."

"What? You must be kidding me!" Nancy started to cry, "You might have told me first."

"I am sorry Nancy, but I have told you of my intention several times in the past, I just this morning received the good news from Yale. They gave me a full scholarship! This opportunity will not come knocking at my door again; therefore, I accepted the offer immediately and thought it was appropriate to give JP Morgan time to find somebody to replace my position."

"I am coming with you David; I can't imagine my life in New York without you."

"Well darling, I am not going to the end of the world, Yale is not far from here, and you are always welcome to visit."

David also called his family in Detroit with his great news. Ingrid was thrilled her boy will become a lawyer in the future, and maybe one day he will be as big as Mr. Eaton!

Greg however was a little concerned. "Are you sure this is the right move for you now? You seem to be doing very well at JP Morgan, and have a promising career ahead of you."

"Yes sir," David answered, "But 1 always wanted to become a lawyer. It's now or never! I am only trying to fulfill a lifetime ambition and this opportunity will not repeat itself. Dad, this is Yale University we are talking about! Do you know how fierce the competition for admission at the best Law school in the world?"

David's office colleagues at JP Morgan threw a farewell party for him; he was a little pensive about leaving, but he knew he had to.

The first thing he did when he arrived at Yale in mid-January was to buy a small house with his savings. He also leased a new car.

Nancy was determined to come with him. She even quit her job against his advice and that of her parents. Her reasoning was, "I want to provide you with a loving home while you do your studying. I promise not to stand in your way but rather give you love and devotion instead, and all I want is to be with you, David."

"I am very flattered, but why give up a good paying job to be with someone who just took the first step in a new direction. Have you discussed this with your parents?"

"I love you David. You are my career. I will not live in New York on my own, I want to be with you, and I told my family I was quitting my job to be with you."

"What did they say when you told them?"

"You are a big girl, they said, and you should know what is good for you. You are good for me David, please understand how much I love you and want to be with you!"

CHAPTER 41

Karl entered the twelfth grade at Milton Academy with a different attitude and determination. His teachers quickly noticed how mature and focused he had become at the beginning of the fall semester, the determination to excel in his studies was a solid transformation from the year before, his teachers observed, and they were all pleased and impressed to see this energetic young man going in the right direction after the lackluster performance of earlier years. The enthusiasm he had for sports didn't fizzle, quite the contrary, his interest in swimming and ice hockey increased significantly and it was striking to notice how masculine and older looking he turned during the last several months. Many fellow students were attracted to him because of his magnetic personality. He developed a great love for music and purchased a guitar to practice his favorite tunes. Elsa, when she was his nanny, planted the seeds for the love of music and had convinced Gretchen to buy him a piano and hire a music teacher to teach him the basics.

A girl he met at school, Tracy Collins, introduced him to jazz which he greatly loved. Karl and Tracy's friendship grew stronger and she was a positive influence, always encouraging him to do better. She was an over achiever in school since she was a little kid back home in southern Florida. She grew up in a family of over achievers; her father was a successful heart surgeon and her mother was a nurse before she quit her career to raise a family. Tracy had two older brothers, one was a medical doctor and the second was in medical school at their father's alma mater, Georgetown University. Tracy was committed to her studying right from the start at Milton. She found Karl an easy going and unpretentious young man and she developed an interest in him after he asked her out, but she impugned his commitment to studying after she noticed the mediocre grades he was getting; Tracy almost always scored A's while Karl struggled to get passing grades.

"Karl!" she used to admonish. "We are here for a purpose and the purpose is to make good grades and receive a diploma! You don't seem to be focused on your books and you will struggle in the future if you don't have the right qualifications to pursue a university career. Would you like to meet me at the library after school? We can study together and exchange notes." Karl liked the idea and went to the library for few hours with Tracy every day and his grades gradually improved.

Tracy and Karl were suited for each other, they both had similar temperaments and outlook on life and their friendship progressed into a strong relationship. They often sat together in the cafeteria and went to the movies on the weekends. It was a friendship purely rested on the gratification of being with one another and a mutual love for music, sports and religion. Tracy was a devout Catholic who never missed mass on Sundays. She replaced Elsa as Karl's companion when they went to church, and she loved the sermons and Father Mooney in particular.

H&O's first phase of construction of the upscale development in Orange County was a spectacular success, and all the finished units were completely sold in record time. The profits from the sales made Oscar a very rich man; he and Gretchen lived in a gilded mansion in Bel Air and had a retinue of household staff: domestic servants, gardeners, chauffeurs and cooks. Gretchen loved to entertain and often had scores of friends and acquaintances from hers and Oscar's circles come for dinner. She also liked to travel and regularly accompanied her husband during business trips. Oscar divided his time between Los Angeles and the head offices of H&O Construction in Porto Alegre. He relied heavily on his trusted deputies: René Luna running the construction company and Manuel Alvarado at the helm of the shipping company. Both were long time employees and doing a great job in Brazil. Elsa settled in with the family in Los Angeles and she made it a habit to speak to her beloved Karl almost daily to follow his progress at school. She even asked Oscar if she could go with them to Boston next year when Karl is expected to graduate from school.

"Of course you can come with us Elsa, you are one of the family my dear, and Karl would love to see you at the graduation ceremony!" Oscar replied affectionately.

Karl was studying hard for the midterm exams. He wanted to put in extra effort to attain good grades, and he wanted to prove to everybody that he is not just a mediocre student. His relationship with Tracy Collins had blossomed in the last few weeks. He found her attractive physically and intellectually, but the girl was dead set in her mind to follow in her father's and siblings' footsteps and become a doctor. She passed all the university entrance exams and all she needed to qualify for a spot at a top university is to obtain good school results. Her father did his internship at Johns Hopkins and he wanted her to follow in the same path after Georgetown. However, she did not like the Washington area and preferred to stay in New England.

Karl on the other hand, had not taken his university entrance exams yet but was scheduled to take them in the middle of February, so his teachers worked out a program to help him achieve good scores. He told his father he would like to go to Harvard but Oscar had serious doubts. "Harvard is a great university son, but you have no chance going there unless your grades improve substantially. You have got to double your effort if this is where you want to go. This is an elite school and admission is limited to the top students only."

Tracy also had an ambition to go to Harvard, and she told Karl, "Wouldn't it be great if we both end up at the same college? I really like you Karl and it will make me very happy if you and I will be admitted there at the same time."

Karl's parents and grandparents arrived in Boston on a snowy Christmas Eve. The atmosphere was happy and turned more joyful when Karl's school report came. Everybody in the room cheered his outstanding performance; not only did he do well but his grades were mainly A's and B's, which was a marked departure from earlier reports. Helmut praised the boy's achievement and encouraged him to get even better marks at the end of his final term, and he promised to give him a big present upon graduation.

It was a white Christmas in Boston during Karl's family's visit. Oscar booked a private banquet for them at an exclusive hotel and Karl asked if he could bring his best friend along. "Of course, son, you can bring whomever you wish, this dinner is in your honor for doing so well in school!" The family arrived at the hotel after they finished mass in the morning. Deep down Karl wanted to go to the Catholic Church with Tracy but chose not to; he knew this may upset his Lutheran family. Tracy was already waiting in the lobby when the family arrived and when Karl spotted her he ran over and gave her a big hug and immediately introduced her.

"Mom and Dad, this is Tracy, my friend."

"Hello ma'am, hello sir. Merry Christmas."

"And these are my grandparents," Karl continued with the introductions.

"Merry Christmas ma'am, Merry Christmas, sir." Tracy knew the family's eyes were on her and she felt nervous.

"Merry Christmas to you, Tracy," Gretchen replied, "Nice to meet you. Are you also a student at the Milton Academy?"

"Yes ma'am, I am, in fact Karl and I are classmates and study partners."

"Very good, are you from the Boston area originally?"

"No, I am not, but wish I were though. I am actually from Florida and now reside at the school's boarding facility for girls."

Tracy sat next to Karl at the table. She was not sure about the family at the beginning but soon warmed up to them. She thought Karl would have told them about their relationship, but apparently they didn't know about her, yet everyone felt comfortable after the introduction.

Karl's last term in school proved to be the most demanding, and he was determined to work hard in order to make the grades to qualify for Harvard. He and Tracy spent hours studying together; she has had a genuine impact on him. Though she was a bright and motivated student she nevertheless dreaded Harvard might reject her, and this inner insecurity made her double her efforts to pass the requisite subjects with top marks. Her desire to stay in the Boston area was a great motivation; she found the New England area steeped in culture and well suited to her lifestyle. Karl also shared her love for Boston and he studied equally hard to earn the grades necessary for admittance to Harvard. He was so pleased the day he received the test results for the university entrance exams, he passed them all with flying colors!

Karl's family came over to Boston again in the middle of June and Ricardo, Bridget and Elsa flew from Los Angeles to attend Karl's graduation. Karl knew he had done well in the finals but he was still nervous. Tracy wasn't worried whatsoever, she knew in her heart she did well and when the school report finally came, Karl was ebullient; for the first time in his life he achieved the goal he aimed for with splendid results, he got straight A's in all of his exams. So did Tracy, who scored the highest in her class and as a result she was offered a scholarship to Harvard. Karl wasn't offered a scholarship, however his school report and the letters of recommendation from teachers helped him get admitted there as well. His folks attended the graduation ceremony and they were all on their feet clapping and Ricardo even gave a huge whistle when the principal handed the high school diploma to a tearful Karl.

Gretchen, Erika and Elsa cried with joy. "My son is a man now! I cannot believe how fast the time passed by!" wailed Gretchen.

Oscar invited everyone in the class and their families for a bash to celebrate the kids' graduation and coming of age. All school staff attended the celebration also, and Oscar and Gretchen met Tracy's parents for the first time. So did Karl, who found her parents friendly but reserved as he shook their hands and accepted their congratulations.

Helmut handed his grandson a key to a car.

"What's this? What kind did you get me grandpa?"

"It is sitting in front of the hotel," Helmut answered lovingly, "why don't you go out and take a look!"

Karl and Tracy walked out to have a peek. Parked in front of the entrance was a brand new two seater silver Porsche! Karl was so overtaken with emotions, he put his arms around Tracy and the two had their first passionate kiss.

CHAPTER 42

David McKay's first year at Yale law school was not too eventful. He managed to find a house in New Haven, Connecticut. Nancy originally planned to move in with him after quitting her job but changed her mind and decided to work part time at JP Morgan. She was fortunate to be able to use her father's connections to get her job back, and now worked only three days a weeks. She stayed at her parents' while in New York and traveled to New Haven to be with David for the rest of the week. The arrangement worked very well for everybody; David was busy with his demanding law school, and Nancy's father was glad to see his daughter change her plans but nobody was as pleased as her mother.

"I am so glad you changed your mind, Nancy," her mother said, "We would have missed you darling had you gone, and you do make the home shine brighter when you are around."

"I would have missed you too, Mother. I wish David had stayed in NYC instead of going to New Haven. It is so dull up there!"

"I know what you mean, and I cannot comprehend the reasons behind his decision to leave a good paying job! Do you think his law degree will be as lucrative as his career at JP Morgan?"

"I don't know mother, but he is adamant it will satisfy his ambition in life. He is very stubborn when it comes to his law career, and it is a taboo to talk about the subject at home. He gets so upset at the mere mention of it."

"Oh, I didn't realize he had a bad temper; does he get nasty when he is mad?"

"No, he really doesn't, but his whole demeanor changes when he is upset. He never raises his voice or uses foul language. As a matter of fact I have never heard him use an expletive yet! He is very prim and proper, and I think his family brought him up well."

David worked long hours every day of the week; law courses were demanding and cases were normally susceptible to different meanings and interpretations. There was so much to learn, evaluate and interpret. This is how law courses were structured at Yale; the emphasis focused on reasoning rather than memorizing. There were many cases to go over and investigate as there were many reports and assignments to prepare and present almost daily, but David was a gifted student. He trained himself to speed read and he had great propensity to articulate well in English, and at the end of the first term he wasn't only the top student in his class, he was one of the best first year students to ever have attended the law school.

Right from the beginning David decided to go into law practice with a reputable firm specializing in cooperate law; he therefore placed much emphasis on commercial law as well as legal contracts. He had to attend seminars and round table discussions with other students and this is where he showed his best attributes in deliberation; he won other students to his side by the power of his arguments and the appeal of his personality and people were naturally attracted to him; when it was his turn to speak everybody listened to what he had to say. David joined the *Yale Journal* as a contributing columnist; there, he showed his mastery in writing creative and often provocative articles. The second term at Yale was more demanding than the first; he had to study constitutional and comparative law. Both subjects were hard work and required hours of study and research, but he loved the subjects so much and envisaged himself an effective legislator debating a bill inside congressional halls. To his credit, debate had always been one of his strongest assets since high school days.

Nancy hardly saw him the first two terms when he was at Yale, he was either in class or doing an assignment at the library or someplace else, but she enjoyed Saturday mornings when they went to the synagogue together. David took her for lunch at a nice restaurant after the service, and on Sunday afternoon they drove along the New England coast. She loved to be alone with him; he was great company, always intense and serious when engaged in conversation. There were many issues close to his heart, especially his law career and fellow Jews.

He repeatedly told Nancy how proud he was of his mother. "Look at her, she arrived with just the shirt on her back, and didn't succumb to the terrible and horrific treatment at the hands of the Nazis. She survived all the horrible things they did to her and became a better person as a result. The Jews have suffered throughout history simply because they were Jews. Look what the Spanish did during the inquisition, and look at legislation made in Britain to bar them entering the country. The English even enacted legislation to disallow them living there! Look at the programs the czar created in Russia when he needed a scapegoat, and look what Hitler did to the millions who were gassed and burned--I want to make sure in this time and age nothing of this sort will ever happen again."

David felt strongly about the universal rights of all human beings, especially the poor and the Negro in the United States. "Some stupid people deny black people their equal and rightful place in our society. They don't give them the same opportunity to work and advance like everybody else, but when you deny people their divine right to earn a legitimate living, you will create a monster. Hungry people have no alternative but to steal to satisfy their hunger, they deal drugs to generate the means to live, they join gangs instead of going to schools. This is why our society is tearing apart, because our representatives pander to their constituents, putting the good of a few above the good of all. No system will endure much injustice; the whole thing will eventually come tumbling down."

Sonia decided to join the feminist movement soon after enrolling at Harvard. She called her brother David to tell him of her decision.

"This is great," he told her, "but what interests you so much?"

"Respect and equality for women," she responded, "we have lived in the shadow of men for so long, and we need emancipation from the cruel treatment subjected by men."

"I am sorry Sonia, but what cruel treatment you are talking about?"

"Just look around big brother, there isn't a day goes by without scores of women getting raped, battered, beaten or treated like a second class citizen just because they are women. How many women do you see in congress? And not a single woman elected to the presidency of this country. Women still have to have the permission of their husbands to do the simplest things in life. It was only in the 20th century women were given the right to vote, and again, who gave them the right to vote? It was men! God has created us equal and I want to be part of a movement that will bring women their much deserved equality and empowerment."

David listened to his sister passion in defense of women. He acknowledged some of her grievances and he knew joining a movement like this one would have benefits for his sister and women in general. "Well, did you call to ask my opinion on joining the feminist movement? I can tell you without reservation to go for it. I think it is good and will give you fulfillment that you have contributed to society, but I want to caution you: please do not to be drawn into radical left elements in the movement, some of these women don't want equality, they want socialism."

David completed the second year at Yale without encountering any problems, and he started the third and final year after he and Nancy had a romantic vacation in Nova Scotia.

"I am very much looking forward to finishing my degree and start practicing law," he told her.

"So am I darling," she quickly responded, "and I hope this time you will settle in one place and don't ask me to move again!"

"I object to that remark! I never asked you to move in the first place, it was your idea to come with me to New Haven."

"That is true darling, because I love you and want to be with you. Don't misunderstand me, I will go wherever you want to go, but I am hoping you will make New York home. I love the city, my family and friends are there, and this is where I grew up. To tell you the truth, I haven't been anywhere that can match New York, it has everything I want."

"I love you too darling," he answered affectionately, "I love New York as well, and I will make you a promise right now to make New York my top choice when I start my career in law, but I cannot commit exclusively to one city. This is simply too narrow minded."

His final year proved to be the most demanding; he was constantly involved in round table discussions and debates with other students over common law precedents and the merits of codified laws, and he spent most of the time preparing the thesis required for the doctorate in jurisprudence. Many of the professors recommended he practice law at one of the governments departments, but he was set in his mind to start in a private firm.

David's relationship with Nancy was going very well after living with each other for close to four years. He wasn't sure in the beginning, Nancy could be demanding and somewhat overbearing, but fundamentally she was sincere and good hearted and physically attractive, and after living together for a while they understood one another well. He missed her when she was in NYC working at JP Morgan, and longed for the quiet evenings at home with her. Deep down in his heart he knew it was Nancy who he would like to settle down with and he now appreciates how much he loves her. She was educated, brought up in a good family, and good looking, and she also shared his views about life and the world around them. But being Jewish was the most fundamental issue, as marrying a girl from outside the faith wasn't something he would ever contemplate. Because problems may arise by virtue of religious differences, he thought about his mother and he understood the happiness of him marrying a Jewish woman would bring to her heart. It was important her grandchildren belong firmly in the Jewish faith, and he was confidant of that. Nancy was indeed the right woman for him.

David graduated from Yale law school with honors. His family came from Detroit for the celebration, and Nancy and her parents drove to New Haven also, where they met David's family for the first time.

"I am so proud of David," Nancy's mother told Ingrid and Greg. "He is a fine young man and knows where he's going in life. You must be very proud of him!"

"Of course I am proud of my boy," Ingrid answered in her German accented English, "he has been the love of my life from the day he was born." I had nothing but problems from the day I conceived him, and it was a miracle he survived. I was in the concentration camp, and the boy in my belly withstood the torture and the beatings I endured, and because he survived, he gave me the will to survive, and fortunately the miracle continued throughout his life, he was at the top of his class when he was seven years old and at the top again when he is almost thirty, I am the proudest mother on this planet."

Ingrid, Greg, and Sonia were invited over to a big party in honor of David. Nancy's father was particularly fond of him and reserved a place at a high end restaurant in New York to celebrate his graduation from the prestigious law school. It was a fun evening and everybody had great time.

Ingrid and Nancy hit it off the minute the two met, and Ingrid confided in Sonia how much she liked Nancy. "She is a nice Jewish woman and I am sure she will make a good wife for David!" Before the evening was over, she sat next to Nancy, held her hand and told her how much she approved of the relationship with her son. "I hope you two will get married and give me lots of grandchildren! I love David more than life itself, he gives me so much joy and pride and I want him to be happy for the rest of his life. I hope you will share the same future with him."

David took the New York bar exam and was thrilled two weeks later when the license to practice law in that state came in the mail; he immediately called his mother to share the good news. He also called Nancy to invite her out to dinner.

"What is the occasion?" she asked.

"I have passed my bar exam," he said excitedly, "and I want to share the evening with you. I reserved a table at Toggles; I know how much you like it there. Is it okay with you, Hon?"

"Of course it is okay with me, I love you David."

"And I love you too Nancy," he told her before he hung up.

David was at the restaurant when Nancy arrived twenty minutes late as usual. She looked smart in a blue top and short white skirt and her signature string of pearls dangling down her plunging neck line. The restaurant was packed and cigarette smoke filled the air but the ambiance was nice and jovial. The waiter escorted them to a candle lit corner table at David's request, and as soon as they sat down she ordered a glass of wine and he ordered his usual apple juice. Nancy had cut down substantially on alcohol consumption; she acknowledged David didn't like to see her drink too much and therefore she limited herself to just a glass or two at the most, but when the waiter came again something unusual happened. David ordered a bottle of very expensive champagne. Nancy was mildly surprised.

"Are we expecting other people to join us?"

"No dear, we are here, just the two of us, to celebrate the beginning of a new career and a new phase in our relationship and I want you to enjoy the evening. He reached both his arms across the table, and Nancy impulsively put both her hands on top of his. He brought them to his face to kiss them, just as the waiter uncorked the champagne. David raised up his glass with a soft voice he began to tell her. "I want to celebrate with you this moment, Nancy, darling. I want to tell you how much I love you and how much joy you bring into my life. I cannot imagine spending my life with anybody other than you. You mean the world to me and from the bottom of my heart I love you and want you to be my wife." He kneeled at the side of the table and with quiet but loving voice he asked her, "Will you marry me?"

Nancy was in emotional meltdown; she couldn't believe what she was hearing, but with sheer joy she screamed, "Yes, yes, yes! I will!" She was crying when the restaurant proprietor and many guests stopped what they were doing and gathered round to share the couple's happiness and to offer congratulations.

Nancy was overjoyed and raised her champagne glass and repeated, "I love you David, I love you with every fiber in my body!" The couple stood up and kissed to the wild applause of the people in the restaurant.

David and his family were seated in the front row at the Synagogue in Brooklyn, the same Synagogue he has been attending since he came to New York. He stood up and moved to under the huppah where the Rabbi was standing when the music started to play to announce the arrival of the bride. Nancy, escorted by her father walked down the aisle. She was wearing a magnificent white gown and she looked glowing and beautiful. When they reached the huppah, her father kissed her on the cheek and David took her by the hand, and the Rabbi began the wedding ceremony to the cheers of all the people present. When David finally put the wedding ring in her finger and the rabbi announced them husband and wife, all the people stood up cheering and shouting as he stepped on the traditional wine glass wrapped in cloth. Ingrid nearly collapsed, she was so emotionally charged and happy her only son married the girl of his dreams, with the prospects for many grandchildren. David and Nancy and the rest of the guests attended a lavish reception in honor of the newlyweds.

He started his first day of work at the law offices of Stanly, Hanks, Elliot and Simmons, a highly reputable cooperate law firm soon after he passed the bar exam. He was recommended for the position by one of his law professors at Yale who was a personal friend of Mr. Stanly, the senior partner in the firm. Stanly was very impressed with David when he came in for the interview. David answered many of the questions thrown at him and he also had several questions of his own to ask, but at the end of the discussion both parties were very satisfied. He started as a junior lawyer under Mr. Stanly and he was assigned to the position of contract interpretations and preparations and to help Mr. Stanly with court documents and litigation files. However, the first assignment he dealt witch involved an acquisition deal for one of Mr. Stanly's important maritime clients. David enjoyed the non-adversarial facet of his job, cooperate law is team oriented and councils on both sides of the transaction are not in competition but work with each other to seek common ground to advance the interests of their respective clients. David was a natural at researching the intricate details of the draft agreements he prepared to ensure the transaction is not in conflict with the local, state or federal regulations. His flexible nature and excellent communication skills as well as his legal knowledge proved a potent asset for the firm and he quickly earned the respect of his peers and superiors.

Sonia joined the swim team on her first semester at Harvard; she had been an excellent swimmer all of her life and she liked the competition and the traveling to compete with other teams. Life at Harvard was so exciting. She found the English program challenging but thoroughly interesting, and she spent hours writing and researching essays in the library. She and her roommate seldom saw each other except when they retired late in the evening. Soon after she joined the swim team, she became friendly with another member who was studying at the Harvard school of dentistry. Her name was Tracy Collins. The two girls were similar in many ways; they shared a love for water sports; academically, they were at the top of their class and graduated from high school with honors; and their distinct physical resemblance was striking. Sonia had a shiny reddish blonde hair while Tracy's was sandy blonde, both of medium height and slender frame. The two girls quickly became friends during a swim meet against Boston University where they started chatting.

"What are you majoring in here at Harvard?" Sonia asked.

"I am doing dentistry. Originally I wanted to major in medicine, but the competition was stiff and the availability was limited so I picked the next best thing. How about you Sonia?"

"I am majoring in English Literature with a minor in Philosophy. I hope to become a teacher when I'm finished."

"I like that; teaching is a great and satisfying career and I believe only certain people can do it well, especially the ones who like to invest in the future of their students, and I sincerely feel this is an honorable profession."

"I agree with you entirely. I always tell people about the influence Mr. Jefferies, my high school English teacher had on me. I couldn't wait for his class to begin, he made it so interesting and he engaged the entire class in meaningful discussion. I will never forget him, he was the best and I am hoping to have the same impact on my students in the future."

"Was it your teacher who recommended you study English at Harvard?"

"No, it was not, at first I wanted to study theology, but the course at Harvard was only available at a graduate level, to students who already have an undergrad degree in the subject. So my brother kind of talked me out of it for now."

"How interesting!" Tracy answered, "What denomination are you, and is that why you wanted to get into theology?"

"Well, I have an unusual background. My father is Presbyterian and my mother is Jewish, and my parents decided to bring me up in both faiths.

But as I grew older neither faith appealed to me anymore, instead, I found Catholicism is where I belong. Jesus Christ is an important part of my life, I even contemplated becoming a nun when I was younger, but didn't. Sometimes I wish I had. But how about you, Tracy? Do you go to church?"

"I am also Catholic, and I am very much like you Sonia. Jesus is a big part of my life. My boyfriend and I go to church together every Sunday."

"I can't make out your accent Tracy, but I detect a tinge of southern twang when you speak. What part of the country are you from?"

"You're right, I was brought up in Florida but I lost most of my accent when I moved to the Boston area. I was a student at the Milton Academy in south Boston. I have been there since the ninth grade and many of the boys used to tease me when I first arrived, but after living in this part of the country I have lost most of my southern accent."

"You shouldn't have," Sonia remarked, "it sounds beautiful!"

"How about you Sonia, where do you come from?"

"I was born and brought up in Detroit. My father was born in Detroit also, but my mother was originally from Germany and she has been living in Detroit ever since she arrived in this country. You should hear her speak; she hasn't lost her German accent at all!"

"Wow! My boyfriend's parents are from Germany also! He and I met at Milton but he started there when he was young and now sounds like you and I. But his father when he speaks English, oh my God! You can really tell!"

"Did your boyfriend go back to Germany after he graduated from Milton?"

"No, he didn't, as a matter of fact he never lived in Germany. His father immigrated to Brazil where Karl, my boyfriend, was born. We met first at Milton Academy but he is doing a degree in business here at Harvard now. He's a great guy, very much typical of any American kid. Do you have any brothers and sisters, Sonia?"

"Yes I do, I have just one brother. He's a lawyer working in New York City. He got married last month to a nice lady from New York. How about you?"

"Two brothers, one is married but Phil the youngest boy is in his final year at Georgetown."

David and Nancy bought an apartment in Brooklyn; it was just a one bedroom but this is all they could afford at the beginning. He sold the house in New Haven and most of the revenue went either for a down payment or to cover the cost of the wedding. Money was tight and Nancy had to go back full time at JP Morgan. David's salary was not enough to meet all their expenses, but with her income they could manage. Nancy grumbled at the beginning, it was a step down from what she was used to, and she complained to her mother. However, her mother didn't mince words.

"You have more than I had when I was your age! Your father couldn't afford an apartment when we first married; I lived with my in-laws for a year and a half before we could afford a cheap apartment."

Nancy barely saw her husband during the first year of their marriage; he was out before 7 am and rarely returned home before 8 o'clock in the evening. Mr. Stanly found him a very dedicated and confident lawyer; he depended on him to prepare the legal files for court and often times asked David to aid in litigation or involve him in arbitration between the feuding parties.

Mr. Stanly summoned him to his office for an assessment on the first anniversary of his employment. "David, I had a call from Mr. Melville today. He wanted to know how did you do in your first year with us and I said to him 'this man beat my wildest expectations!' He wasn't surprised, he predicted you will make an excellent lawyer. Your old professor from Yale and I have been friends for more than thirty years. I don't always see eye to eye on legal matters with him, but I have to agree his assessment of you is spot on, you are one hell of a lawyer, and I am recommending you for a 20% increase in your salary, effective immediately."

"Mr. Stanly, thank you so much from the bottom of my heart! The money will certainly help at this stage in my life but to get this kind of compliment from your peers is absolutely priceless. I can only enrich my career working with people of your caliber; you have been a source of knowledge and inspiration, sir."

When the session with his boss was over, David picked up the phone and called Mr. Melville, his professor at Yale, to thank him for his kind words. "I am so grateful for recommending this job to me. Mr. Stanly is one of the finest lawyers I have come across. He passed a lot of his knowledge and expertise down to me, and I am eternally grateful to both of you."

Sonia and Tracy continued to see each other regularly during training; other than that, the two didn't socialize or run into one another, they were in different faculties on opposite corners of the campus. Sonia went home to spend the holiday with her family at the end of the first year. She liked Detroit's summers and loved to go with her parents to Belle Isle Park for a swim in the river. Greg, who enjoyed swimming as well, often took the afternoons off work to meet with his wife and daughter. He changed work clothes and put on Bermuda shorts and his customary straw hat and stopped on the way for a six pack of beer and meat for the BBQ at the park. Business was good and he was happy with life and enjoyed the time with his family very much.

The girls were delighted to see each other when they met at the gym at the start of the fall semester. "What a gorgeous tan!" Tracy told Sonia.

"Thank you so much. I guess I had enough sun just hanging out on the beach at Belle Isle."

"Oh? Where's that? I didn't know you were taking a trip?"

"Oh, no, Belle Isle is a popular place in Detroit. It's a beautiful island park in the Detroit River, not far from home, and my father loves to BBQ there. How about you Tracy? Did you go anywhere?"

"I wish I had a sunny holiday. I went to Europe with my family and it was a wash this year, we didn't see the sun in London for the whole seven days. It was either cloudy or raining and Paris wasn't much better, but Barcelona was great! We stayed for three days only, and I wish we had stopped there first instead. I loved the city and I got to practice my Spanish."

"Didn't you spend any of your summer at home? I recall you saying before the end of last term you were going home to Florida."

"Yes I did, and you know it was cloudy down there too, and I don't enjoy the stifling humid weather anymore. I guess I have been living in New England for a long time. I wish I went with my boyfriend to Los Angeles instead, he said the weather was beautiful. He came back tanned like you are."

After they finished their training Sonia and Tracy hit the locker room, changed their clothes and went outside to go home. Tracy usually just waved before heading off in the opposite direction, but this evening apparently she had other plans. "Oh, great, he's here! See you later, Sonia!"

As her friend jumped into the passenger seat of an expensive looking sports car, Sonia couldn't help but notice the very good looking blond guy driving the car.

CHAPTER 43

Oscar decided to go to Los Angeles ahead of schedule at the behest of Gretchen in order to celebrate Helmut's 80th birthday. Both he and Ricardo are now citizens of the United States and they can come and go from the country at their leisure, but ever since Karl was admitted to Harvard, Oscar had a tremendous upsurge in business activities at the shipping company head office in Brazil. Business almost increased by a third over the last two years and the traffic between North and South America multiplied to the extent the company was turning clients away for lack of ocean vessels to accommodate the extra tonnage, and Oscar had been devoting his time to purchasing additional ships to increase the capacity of the shipping line. He was dealing with two alternatives options; either order brand new ships from the shipping yard or else find used ships available for sale, but he eventually decided to look for used ones since building a new one from scratch takes on the average more than a year to complete. He brought up the subject with his father-in-law who was firmly on the side of buying used ships and Helmut directed him to contact several well-known shipping lines in Scandinavia and the Far East to find out if any were available for sale. The ones offered in the Far were unworthy, having outlived their usefulness, they looked old and unreliable. He declined to purchase them and decided to visit Scandinavia instead to try his luck there.

But first he had to go back to California to attend Helmut's birthday party. It was such an important occasion and Oscar owes it to Helmut to be there, after all he wouldn't be where he is now had it not been for the help and guidance from the old man. The visit will provide the opportunity to meet with Ricardo and Karl, who is expected to fly from Boston to attend his grandfather's birthday as well. Oscar wasn't worried about H&O in California; the company was doing extremely well under Ricardo's stewardship. The construction company in Orange County is generating more than 50% of the revenue of all the companies under the H&O umbrella, and the margin of profit produced in real estate transactions in California was definitely higher than the Brazilian real estate market. Oscar could not understand the logic behind it, but after he sat with Ricardo and Gordon Murphy he realized properties in California are sold at a higher profit margin than comparable properties in the Porto Alegre area, consequently he made the decision to concentrate more on the American market and let things continue as always in Brazil under the management of René Luna.

Karl brought Tracy with him to LA. Ricardo and Bridget were at the house as well as many of their friends and senior employees from H&O. Helmut was convinced to come to the house on the belief Karl came to visit on his school break, but he was overtaken with emotions and was nearly in tears when he walked in to the tune of "Happy Birthday" and "For he's a jolly good fellow!"

As he hugged his daughter and his grandson, he told them, "There is nobody in this world I love more than you two!"

Karl's first year at Harvard was not as hard as he had feared. He surprised himself by how committed and dedicated to his studies he became. It was a welcome transformation from the playful years when he was in junior high; he loved the challenge Harvard offered. He and Tracy saw each other at least once a week except when he or she had exams or had to prepare a paper, but he made it a point to go to mass with her on Sundays and they spoke on the phone most nights. They were good friends, and she liked to introduce him as her boyfriend but he called her his best friend. Deep down he liked Tracy, she was very intelligent and dedicated to her career and she fundamentally was a decent and honest girl, but he found her a bit on the dull side. He always bought her a present when he traveled away from Boston and she loved this about him, money never seemed to be an issue; she learned why when she visited his family's house in southern California. His folks lived in a big mansion with a huge household staff, and they looked extremely rich, but Tracy too was born to an affluent family. Her father was a successful surgeon in the affluent Boca Raton area of Southern Florida; he was very comfortable and afforded his family many luxuries, sent his children to top schools and took them on holidays to many places in the world, but his fortune was no match to the net worth of Karl's father. She speculated that everybody in the development where Karl's parents lived must be multimillionaires and of course since Karl was their only son, he stands to inherit all this wealth. She saw how much his grandparents doted on him and how much they showered him with gifts, but despite all of this wealth, she found Karl humble and down to earth and he never once flaunted his wealth or acted in a splashy manner. She really cared for him and was jealous when other girls looked at him, Karl after all had an athletic built and was extremely good looking. Tracy believed Karl liked and cared for her also and she wanted their relationship to be more serious; she even fantasized about moving in with him at his house, the same one his father purchased when Karl enrolled at the Milton Academy a few years earlier, but he resisted her request when she asked.

"I'm afraid we will end up failing our courses at Harvard if we move in together," he told her. "I would prefer just to keep our friendship the way it is, if you don't mind." She did mind, very much, but decided to drop the subject for now.

Karl joined the ice hockey team at Harvard and quickly won the respect of his coach and teammates. Tracy came over to cheer him whenever she had a chance, and the two normally went for something to eat after the game. One evening as she and Sonia were in the locker room after they finished their training at the gym, Tracy asked her friend, "Would you like to go to a hockey game? Harvard is playing Penn State, and my boyfriend, Karl is playing."

"Sure, that sounds like fun!" Sonia answered eagerly. By the time the two girls arrived the second period was already underway. Unfortunately Harvard lost and a dejected Karl came over to talk to Tracy after he changed his clothes.

Tracy greeted him with, "Karl, you disappointed me today!"

"Hello Tracy," he answered sarcastically, "it wasn't entirely my fault. The coach put up a game plan for us but it didn't work out. Penn State figured us all out this time, but we'll get them next time," he answered ruefully.

"Oh, by the way Karl, this is my friend Sonia."

"Hello Sonia, nice to meet you."

"Hi there, nice to meet you too. You were awesome out there, you guys played better than Penn State. I'm surprised they beat you."

"Yes, we tried to pile it on at the end but we couldn't catch up, they were up by three goals right from the first period. Anyway, I'm going for a coffee at the cafeteria would you like to join me ladies?"

Tracy was first to answer, "No, I have a quiz to work on tonight, I better get going."

"How about you, Sonia?"

"Why not, only if we can have a quick one, I too need to go and work on some papers."

Karl and Sonia walked to the cafeteria. Sonia sat on the bench while Karl went to the counter and brought two coffees back with him.

"Tracy told me your family is from Germany," she began.

Karl smiled broadly, "Yes, they are. My father was born in Germany. He immigrated to Brazil where he met and married my mother who was born in Brazil, but she too comes from German descent, so you can say I am 100 % German."

"Is your family in Brazil or are they back in Germany now?"

"My father is a businessman. He owns a construction company in Brazil and there's a branch office in southern California. My family split their time between the two countries. How about you Sonia? Where's your family from?"

"My mother is like your father; she immigrated to the US after WW2. She and my father got married here. My father's background is a mixture, but he is mainly Scottish. So, what are you taking here at Harvard, Karl?"

"I'm majoring in Business Administration; chances are I will work for the family business when I am done here."

Sonia originally wanted to stay for a quick cup of coffee and then leave to the residence to study in her room, but for some reason she enjoyed talking to Karl. She found him very fascinating and charming. Neither noticed the time but after an hour Karl got up. "I better get going; I have an appointment in downtown Boston. I enjoyed talking to you Sonia; maybe we will get together one day?"

"Yes, I enjoyed your company too, I look forward to meeting you again."

Sonia arrived at her residence having spent more time than she had planned with Karl. Now she couldn't concentrate on the paper she was working on; her mind was somewhere else. She thought about Karl and felt the electricity between them. He is so appealing, she thought. Like nobody else before. Dear God, he is so handsome, and that smile of his is just captivating! Sonia had to shake herself out of the trance she was in; she attempted to do some homework that evening but couldn't. Eventually she gave up and went to bed early.

Karl too enjoyed his time with Sonia. He found her very pretty, bubbling with charisma and personality, and she was in his thoughts for the rest of the evening.

Sonia met with Tracy at the gym again the following week for a scheduled training. She didn't mention Karl or how long they stayed at the cafeteria but Tracy brought up the subject. "Karl liked you; he was very impressed by your personality."

Sonia did not detect any ill feeling emanating from Tracy and she answered her friend nonchalantly. "Yes, he's a nice guy."

Sonia didn't want to think about him. She knew he was attached and probably happy with Tracy. She didn't want to spoil their relationship and decided to move him out of her mind; however, it was easier said than done. She couldn't help it, deep down she wished he was available. The guy was so good looking and charming and she distinctly remembers when she met him for the first time at the cafeteria how other girls were eyeing him.

Karl too liked Sonia, he found her spontaneous and easy to talk to, and when he compared her in his mind to Tracy, he concluded it was Sonia he felt more comfortable with. Both girls were nice to look at, but Tracy can be a little too straight-laced for his taste, all she wants to talk about is her books, assignments and studies, and ever since he and Sonia met, his feelings for Tracy became rather ambivalent. Impulsively he decided to go over to the dorm where Sonia was staying. He asked the dorm warden if she would allow him to come in to see Sonia.

"I am sorry," the warden responded, "but Sonia is not here right now. Besides, boys are not permitted in the girls' dorms. You can leave her a message if you wish and I will pass it on to her when she gets back." She gave him a piece of paper to write on.

Sonia, he wrote on the piece of paper. Hi, this is Karl, I would like to see you, please call me at the number below, Thanks.

Sonia got the shock of her life when the warden handed her Karl's note. Her entire body started to shake, and she raced up to her room to read the note again. Then she sat up in her bed and started to cry, she couldn't help it, she really wanted to call him but she wasn't comfortable doing that. She went down on her knees, "Oh Lord, I hope you will forgive me if I betray my friend, I didn't ask for any of this! Oh, Lord, I hope you guide me to do the right thing." Sonia opened her purse, found some coins and went out to the hallway to the pay phone.

Karl's cheerful voice warmed the line at her end. "This is Karl," he answered, "who am I speaking to?"

"Hello Karl, this is Sonia" Her voice was trembling, and she couldn't gather the courage to say anything else.

"Hellooo Sonia, it's so good to hear your voice. I have been thinking about you since the day we met. I wonder if you'd like to go out for dinner this coming Friday?" He paused to give Sonia time to respond, but she was shaking like a leaf, she couldn't even speak. "Are you still there Sonia?"

He could barely hear her response, "Yes I am," she said in a faint voice, "What time on Friday?"

"How about 8 pm? I'll pick you up in front of your dorm entrance."

"Okay, I will be there," she said before hanging up, actually relieved when she put the receiver down.

Sonia agonized after she finished talking to Karl over the phone, his voice was so warm and inviting as if he were pleading with her to go out with him. But something in her heart was bothering her about going out to dinner with him and she questioned herself if it was the right thing to do. Would the Lord sanction my behavior if I went out with him behind his girl-friend's back? How would Tracy react if she found out about the call? Tracy will be mad, chances are she will break up with Karl for this flirty behavior and Tracy would blame me for the debacle and probably point the finger at me and call me names. 'You bitch, you must have given him the come on, or worse you told him outright you were interested in him' she will say. I don't blame her if she does call me names, I would probably do the same thing if the situation was reversed. Sonia's mind was in turmoil. She didn't know what to do, but it dawned on her Tracy isn't exactly her best friend, but a little more than an acquaintance. She was her sports teammate and this is as far as their relationship goes. The two never socialized and hardly see each other outside the gym, they're at different faculties and chances are they will never meet again after they graduate from Harvard. She told herself, I am damned if I go out with him and I am damned if I don't, so I might as well go.

CHAPTER 44

Ricardo was impressed with Dr. Alfred Hanson. He told Oscar while driving from the group's hideaway in the Cascade Mountains to Portland's airport to catch a flight back to L.A, after they made the unscheduled visit to Oregon on the invitation of Professor Robert Woodruff.

The call from Mr. Woodruff came two days before Oscar arrived in LA for his father-in-law's 80th birthday. Erika answered the phone and told the caller her husband was expected home in two days. Mr. Woodruff indicated it was urgent to make the invitation in time to give them the opportunity to meet an important person, so she passed along Ricardo's phone number. Ricardo didn't hesitate for a second before he accepted the invitation.

"How about Oscar?" asked the Professor.

"He will be there as well," Ricardo answered affirmatively. Ricardo knew how important it is for him and Oscar to be part of this group and hopefully turn it into a nucleus to get rid of the Jews and their hegemony on the world, and to avenge the defeat of Germany. He therefore took it upon himself to speak on behalf of his friend, but when Oscar arrived in LA, and Ricardo informed him about the invitation to go to Oregon, Oscar at first objected. He explained to Ricardo he was pressed for time due to the urgent need to find cargo ships to satisfy future contract obligations, and failure to achieve this will put the shipping company in an awkward position. But Ricardo explained who Dr. Hanson was, and Oscar relented on condition they do it all in one day.

Oscar agreed with Ricardo's assessment the man was not only charismatic but rather a strong and effective leader. "He reminded me of Hitler, our great Fuehrer," he added.

"You are right," responded Ricardo, "this man is a no nonsense leader, and I have strong feelings he might be able to deliver this country out of the Jewish vise, and we may even save Germany in the future and eliminate the control of the Jewish collaborators running the country now. I think you and I should recruit everybody we know and feel safe in our just cause."

"No, Ricardo," Oscar cut him off forcefully, "we cannot recruit anyone working for us. This would be a big mistake and a conflict of interest, and if the performance of one employee declines, you won't be able to terminate his employment for fear he will expose us. This is a dangerous situation and I must insist nothing of this sort will ever transpire. The only people we can safely recruit are people from the outside and with whom we have a long standing relationship. I for instance, don't want Karl to be involved until he is finished with college. He doesn't need any distraction for now, but I have to agree with you Dr. Hanson does look like a man of steel, and I feel safe being a member of this group. Look at the security screening we had to go through before they allowed us to join."

"You're right Oscar; this group is organized and follows a systematic approach. Members' names appear nowhere and everybody is identified with just a number. I admire the security protocol they follow, but most importantly, they share our core belief the Jews are the mortal enemy of the Aryan people."

Ricardo was intrigued why his best friend wouldn't let his own son join, so he asked. "I am a little puzzled why won't you bring Karl and introduce him to the group when Dr. Hanson brought his own son with him? I'd say the boy is as old as Karl."

"You mean Brandon, the tall boy standing in the corner?"

"Yes, that's the one."

"I ran into him in the lounge, and we had a quick chat. He is just few months younger than Karl. He came down from Seattle to meet his Dad, and he's studying at the university there to become a land surveyor."

Dr. Alfred Hanson was born in Aalborg, Denmark. His father, Knut, was an instructor at the university who collaborated with the Nazis during their occupation of the country in WWII. After the war ended, he fled to neutral Sweden with his family under the cover of darkness disguised as a fisherman fearful of arrest and prosecution for collaborating with the enemy. From Sweden he immigrated to the United States and used his academic credentials to find a well-paying job at the University of Purdue in northwest Indiana, there he taught Biology and other applied sciences. Alfred was only 17 years old when his family made it to the US. Knut held strong racial views and fostered intense hatred for the Jews and the Negroes in particular, and he drummed those views into his son. Alfred was an excellent student all of his life and chose to study medicine at the same university where his father taught, and when he graduated with a degree in medicine, he worked at a hospital in Indianapolis. Alfred, after the death of his parents resettled with his new bride in Spokane, Washington, where his first son Brandon was born in the mid-fifties. Dr. Hanson became disenchanted with President Kennedy and his successor President Johnson for their civil rights policies and for allowing the Jews to take over the government from the Aryan people, whom he believed founded the country and therefore are its rightful leaders. He preached his views among friends and even patients with similar prejudices, and over the last twelve years he managed to have a substantial number of followers in several western states, but mainly in the northwest of the country.

Among his followers were rich benefactors who spared no effort to advance the cause of the movement. Dr. Alfred was a charismatic and outspoken leader who exuded knowledge and confidence. The group strongly advocated the repatriation of all the Jews and the Negroes out of the country and the restoration of the United States as the leader of the entire world. To that end he demanded total secrecy and devotion from his followers, and new members were given the choice to either contribute financially to the cause or volunteer in a militia training modeled after the Nazi's Brown Shirts.

When professor Woodruff recommended the two guys from Brazil to join the movement, Dr. Hanson conceded, and gave orders to have them vetted to ensure they don't pose any security risk and their views are compatible with the group goals. After strong assurances, Ricardo and Oscar were permitted to visit their camp location in Oregon, but more information about the organization was withheld until their background investigations were complete. They were viewed as beneficial to the cause since they have the wherewithal to provide financial largesse to the movement, and due to their Nazi past and strong views about the Jews. They also were members of a group in Brazil which to a large extent shares the same ideology.

Oscar stopped by to consult with Helmut regarding the purchase of the cargo ships, and to seek his advice about a new lead he received from a friend who works in the industry about a shipping company located in Halifax, Nova Scotia. The company is facing bankruptcy; they have a small fleet of eleven medium size cargo ships, and currently service the Great Lakes ports during the warm season and call on other ports along the eastern seaboard of the US in the winter shipping season. The company suffered great financial loss during the Arab oil embargo in 1974, and couldn't recover; they defaulted on their bank loans and were now looking for a partner to bail them out.

Helmut shook his head. "No, Oscar, I had a partner when I started in this business, and had I kept the partnership going, the company would not be what it is today. I recommend you take a look at their financial statements and see if it makes any sense and if it does, take a hard look at the ships to determine if they are even worth buying. My experience makes me think the company has poor management rather than suffers from the price of oil. Cargo rates are the product of operational cost; when the costs increase, the shipping rates increase as well, it is as simple as that."

Oscar listened to the old man and concluded the advice made sense. He thanked Helmut and expressed his appreciation. "I am grateful to have you here Helmut. You are my ultimate reference and a source of wisdom and inspiration!"

The shipping company's CEO was pleased when he received the call from Oscar to express desire to purchase the fleet of ships they offered for sale. He indicated the fate of the company now rests in the hands of a district judge in New York City and invited Oscar to come to Halifax to examine the ships first hand. Oscar thanked him for the invitation and expressed willingness to visit the company once the judge makes his ruling, and asked the CEO to send him profile for each ship.

Karl was particularly happy when Sonia accepted the invitation to go to dinner with him; he got undressed, picked up his guitar and sat in bed strumming familiar tunes until the phone rang, interrupting his train of thought.

"Hello Karl, how are you doing son? I have been thinking about you all day long. Your father is in Oregon today and I felt like talking to the other man in my life!"

"I love you too, Mother."

"How sweet of you darling, how are things going at Harvard?"

"Things are going just fine. I was a little disappointed we lost the game to Penn State the other day, they scored early and we were unable to catch up."

"That is alright son, you win some and sometimes you lose one. How is Tracy doing?"

"I don't know, mother. Tracy is really nice and she's motivated, and she was an inspiration for me when I was in high school, but I don't feel the same way about her anymore."

"Has something happened, son?"

"No, not really. I just don't have it for her in my heart. I don't know why, I don't think I know the answer myself."

When Gretchen finished the call, she too was searching for an answer. She knew Karl was loyal and sincere; he wouldn't drop Tracy unless there was a compelling reason, and her gut feeling told her Tracy was not the reason. It must be something else, but she hated to speculate.

Sonia was glad to get to her room on Friday afternoon after a long and hard week. She was exhausted, her hair was a mess and she looked sad and a tad overwhelmed. She threw her books on the desk and decided to have a nap, after all she had a date planned for the evening and she felt in desperate need for a rest. It was close to seven o'clock when she got up. Oh my God! she told herself, I only have one hour to get ready before Karl picks me up! She quickly showered, dried her hair and dressed in the outfit she had prepared the night before, making it down to the front of the building just in time to meet her date.

Karl was excited on Friday morning. After studying intently the night before for an important exam, he felt he did well after it was over. He grabbed lunch at the cafeteria then made a quick stop at the florist and lastly at the barber shop for a haircut before he went home. It was raining gently and his car was splashed on the way after he spent time cleaning and polishing it the day before. The first thing he did when he arrived home was to re-polish the car and keep it safe from rain in the garage, and when he finished he went to bed for a much needed rest. He woke up half an hour before he was supposed to pick up Sonia; he showered quickly, put on his blue jeans, a shirt and a jacket and sped off in his shiny Porsche.

Sonia spotted him through the glass entrance door when he pulled up in front of the dorm and she walked down to meet him. The rain had stopped and the moon was rising between the clouds; her beautiful hair was blowing gently in the light breeze, and she was wearing a red mini skirt with a white blouse. Karl was entranced as she walked down the few steps toward him. He went to the other side and opened the car door, then gently closed it behind her, walked round to his side and jumped in.

"Hello there! You look absolutely beautiful!" he said with a big smile while handing her a single stem red rose.

Sonia was up early the morning after she went to dinner with Karl, she had never felt happier in her life, it was Saturday morning and she didn't have to go to class, but she had to study, in fact she had a lot of catching up to do, last week had been traumatizing and her concentration was not up to par. She didn't fare any better this morning, Karl was on her mind and so was Tracy. She didn't want to betray her friend, but she didn't initiate the contact with Karl, quite the contrary, it was Karl who did the invitation. She didn't know why she accepted but was glad she did, what a wonderful man he turned out to be. He treated her like a princess, the chemistry was great and she thoroughly enjoyed the evening with him. She originally thought about calling him to cancel, she even went to the pay phone, but didn't have the courage to cancel at the last minute. However, when she woke up from her nap that evening, she had a tremendous urge to dress up and make herself pretty. When she looked in the mirror the blouse showed too much curve but she didn't mind, it made her feel feminine and happy with her decision.

Stealing side glances as he drove, Karl took her to a popular Mexican restaurant. It was very busy when they arrived and they had to wait before they were seated, at which point he asked her if she would like a Margarita.

"I am still under age to drink," she said demurely.

"Don't worry," he responded, "the waiter knows me and he is not going to ask for your ID."

"Okay then, you can get me one, but please don't make it too strong. I've never tried one before." She enjoyed it very much as they talked about Harvard and life in Boston and at the dorms. He listened eagerly to what she had to say and ordered another round of drinks when hers was almost empty. A Mariachi Band was making the rounds between the tables and when they came to the table where he and Sonia sat asked if they can play a song.

"Yes, please," he quickly answered. They played a nice tune in Spanish and Sonia had never heard this kind of music before, but she loved the rhythms. Karl asked them to play another song when they finished.

"What would you like us to play?" they asked.

He looked at Sonia and said, "It's your choice!"

"Oh no," she responded, "I don't know any Mexican songs."

"Okay, may I pick a nice Brazilian tune for you?"

"Yes please."

He turned to the band leader, spoke to him in Spanish and the band played The Girl from Ipanema much to Sonia's delight. She did recognize it, after all!

A sizzling plate of meat and vegetables with different kinds of dips and small plates came as per Karl's order; Sonia was impressed with the aroma and the taste of the exotic food. When they finished, Karl asked if she cared for a dessert.

"I have never eaten so much in my life; I don't think I have room for a dessert!"

The band stepped outside to an open courtyard and started to play music again. "Would you like to sit outside?" he asked.

"Yes, why not, it's a lovely evening." There was an open hearth and the flames were dancing in the dimly lit area. Karl ordered another round of Margaritas for both of them. The dance floor was filling up with patrons, "Would you like to dance?" he asked her.

"I'd love to," she answered joyfully. They joined the crowd and when the band played one of his favorite songs, he drew her closer to him. Sonia felt a current of electricity run through her body.

"You look like an angel," he said to her. She blushed and put her arms round him and danced to the tune of the slow music.

When he dropped her off at the end of their evening, he opened the car door and kissed her on both cheeks. "I enjoyed the night with you, Sonia," he whispered to her.

"I did too."

Tracy didn't know about the date Sonia had with Karl and Sonia decided not to discuss it with her when the two girls met for training at the gym. She did, however, bring up the subject. "I don't know why Karl is ignoring me. He hasn't been his usual self and he rebuffed all my attempts to see him. I'll admit I'm often busy with homework assignments, but he's never told anybody I was his girlfriend, like he was ashamed of me."

Sonia didn't know what to say. Karl didn't even mention Tracy's name when they were out to dinner. But Sonia genuinely felt sorry for her, it was clear Tracy still cares for Karl, but the feeling was not mutual. There was nothing wrong with Tracy, she is pretty, decent and intelligent but desperately lacks in personality. Maybe Karl found her a little stale and set in her ways, her education and studying was all she talks about, and it gets boring after a while. No wonder why Karl wasn't interested in her anymore.

Sonia was very attracted to him, not for his physical looks but for his great personality, easy demeanor and nonchalant attitude. Nothing seems to faze him, and of course he was very rich, though Sonia didn't care about that. He actually came to dinner like any American guy dressed in jeans and casual jacket. But now Tracy is crying on her shoulder and bemoaning her relationship with him. What can I possibly tell her at this stage, she asked herself. Should I be cruel and tell her the problem is not him, please look in the mirror? Or should I say, hey girl, you need to lighten up! You're a little old fashioned. Sonia however, decided to keep quiet; she didn't want to offend her friend.

Karl himself didn't get up early after their night out for dinner. As a matter of fact the insistent ringing of the phone is what made him get up.

"Good morning Karl," Tracy softly started.

"Good morning," he answered in a sleepy voice.

"I am sorry, did I wake you up?"

"Yes, you did, what do you need?" he answered bluntly.

"I was worried about you, I called you all night long but there was no answer."

"I guess I wasn't at home."

"I guess not, where did you go?" Gentle, trying not to be obtrusive.

"Please don't give me the third degree first thing in the morning. I just woke up, I'll call you later." He abruptly hung up the phone.

Tracy did call again in the evening, but he didn't answer. He knew it was her, and she called again a few times until she seemed to give up. Karl decided to spend the weekend at home to catch up on his studying; midterm exams are only three weeks away. But he felt lonely; he thought about Sonia and the fantastic time they spent together at the restaurant. She was so natural and spontaneous and easy going, very much like his own personality. I wish she had a phone in her room, he thought. I'd really like to talk to her. Suddenly he remembered Sonia did give him the number for her dorm.

"You can call me at this number," she told him, "my mother calls and leave messages all the time,"

So he dialed the number and a stern voice answered, "How can I help you?"

"I would like to leave a message for Sonia..."

Sonia was thrilled when she received the message. She immediately headed to the pay phone in the hallway. On his end, Karl didn't want to answer for fear it was Tracy, but he held his breath and crossed his fingers. He was so relieved when he heard Sonia's voice!

"I have been thinking about you, and I want to tell you how much I enjoyed my evening with you; you are truly a remarkable girl!"

"Me too Karl, I have been thinking about you. I wanted to call to thank you for the lovely dinner last night; I enjoyed the evening and your company so much."

"So, maybe we can go out for dinner again next Saturday? I know this steak house, and it's out of this world!"

"Yes, I would love to go, but we can't stay too late if you don't mind. I normally go to mass on Sunday morning."

"Hey, that's great, I go to mass in the morning as well. Maybe we can go together?"

"Oh, I didn't know you are Catholic. I don't know why but I assumed you were Protestant, I guess most people from Germany are."

"You're right, Sonia, I'm Lutheran and so are most Germans. But I have been going to Catholic Church ever since I arrived in this country when I was nine years old."

"How interesting, why would you go to church on your own when you were so little?"

"I hope I don't sound pompous, but my family decided to enroll me at the Milton Academy when I was young, and the school didn't offer boarding facilities for boys my age. So my family got me a house and brought Elsa, my nanny, to stay with me as an adult guardian. Elsa is Catholic and she took me with her to a Catholic church. I grew to like it and preferred it to my own."

"Wow, this is amazing Karl, you mean to tell me your parents didn't mind?"

"Elsa was totally honest; she told them what she was doing and my parents never questioned her intentions. All they cared about is I grow to believe and to love our Lord Jesus Christ; it was as simple as that. How about you Sonia, did you go to Catholic Church with your parents when you were young?"

"I am a unique case when it comes to religion. My family is very unusual. You see, my mother is Jewish and a concentration camp survivor. She was pregnant with my brother when she arrived in the US and she married my dad who is Presbyterian. But in Jewish canon I am considered Jewish because my mother is one herself. However as I grew older, I developed a strong penchant to the original tenet of Christianity and became a Catholic on my own."

A bit taken by surprise by this revelation, Karl was almost grateful for the interruption. "May I put you on hold Sonia? Somebody's knocking at my door." He put the phone receiver on the table and as he opened the door, he was completely caught off guard by the figure in front of him. "What are you doing here, Tracy?" he asked nervously.

"Aren't you going to let me in?" Tracy asked in a dismayed voice.

Karl moved to the side to make room. "Come on in," he beckoned.

"I have been calling you all day and you are ignoring me. What is this all about Karl? What have I done to deserve all of this?"

"I am sorry Tracy, but I am on the phone." He turned his back and walked to the table where the phone receiver was, with Tracy following.

"I don't know why you have been acting strangely."

But before she could finish her sentence Karl interrupted, he picked up the phone and said, "I am sorry Sonia, I have to finish this call, I have somebody with me right now."

Sonia could hear the conversation Karl was having with Tracy and she softly said, "No problem, I'll catch you later."

Tracy's face dropped when she heard Sonia's name. Karl didn't care however, he decided it was now or never.

She started to cry, her face ashen. "You never told me you have a relationship with Sonia!" she said, her voice hoarse. "Now I get it! You have been unfaithful with me Karl! Did that bitch seduce you or did you pursue her, which one is it Karl?"

"Well, I guess you know now. I don't want to upset you Tracy, but I have wanted to break off our relationship. It's not you, you are a beautiful girl and you deserve somebody better than me."

"But I love you Karl, and it is you who I want! I don't want anybody else, what have I done to deserve your rejection?"

"You haven't done anything at all; um, I feel you and I are not compatible, we just don't suit each other, and don't blame it on Sonia; she has not done anything wrong. I've been thinking about this for a long time. It was me who pursued her and not the other way around."

Tracy was heartbroken; she stormed out of the house and walked down the street in the rain. Karl made no attempt to follow her, and when she reached the main road, she hailed a taxi. She had the driver drop her off at Sonia's residence. She went up and knocked several times at her door but there was no answer. The girl next door came out of her room.

"Sonia isn't here, I saw her leaving fifteen minutes ago. Do you want to leave her a message?"

"Just tell her Tracy came over to see her." She left in a huff.

Karl felt relieved to have Tracy finally out of his life and immediately turned his attention to Sonia. She said something about being Jewish? Oh my God, my father will have a fit if he knew I was going out with a Jewish girl! But she said she was Catholic and goes to mass every Sunday; therefore I should believe her when she professed Jesus Christ is the son of God and our Lord. She definitely believes in the same thing I believe in, so that is the end of it, I'm not going to give it any more thought.

On Saturday evening, Karl picked up Sonia and drove to an exclusive restaurant overlooking the bay. His eyes were fixated on her, she truly looked stunning. Though she lived on a meager student income, Sonia decided to splurge. Earlier in the day she'd gone to the hairdresser. Her reddish blond hair was now styled with curls over the side and her unblemished skin looked shiny and soft. Then she stopped at a nice boutique and purchased a beautiful black dress with shoulder straps and plunging neckline. In black high heels, she looked remarkably suave and fashionable.

Karl too was smartly dressed in matching black pants and tweed jacket as he pulled up in front of the restaurant and handed the car keys to the parking valet. The maître d' opened the door and greeted the couple. "Good evening Mr. Silva, good evening mademoiselle," and he escorted them to the corner booth marked 'reserved'. "Your waiter will be with you shortly, please enjoy your meal."

When the wine steward came and presented the wine list to Karl, he immediately ordered a bottle of an expensive Rothschild Boudreaux wine without even looking at the list. Sonia was enjoying the candlelit evening; her eyes twinkled with happiness and enjoyment.

But there was something on her mind. "You never told me you broke off with Tracy."

"Who wants to talk about Tracy when you are in the company of someone like you?" he said with a slight grin. He held her hands in his. "You are so beautiful, Sonia, but this is not the only reason I am attracted to you. I just love your personality and feel you and I have something in common. Tracy is a nice and decent girl but her personality and mine simply don't jive. It worked when we were younger, but we both changed and I just don't have many things in common with her. Yet I feel you and I have similar personalities and share many things equally."

"I am very flattered, I also feel the same way about you Karl and feel you and I suit each other. We have lots to talk about. To tell you the truth, my heart beats faster when we're together. But I do empathize with Tracy. She came over to my room after you finished with her; the girl next door told me Tracy was in such a state and looked very upset. Her hair was soaked and she was drenched from head to toe. So I went down to the store and bought a box of chocolates and went over to her place. She was still crying when I arrived. I hugged her and told her how sorry I feel for her and told her the truth about what happened between you and I. At first she didn't accept it, but she relented in the end after she resigned herself to the fact you weren't interested in her. She accepted my gift, she even took a piece of chocolate out of the box and gave it to me. I guess that was her way of saying thank you."

"You are an amazing girl Sonia. I am attracted to you because of your charitable and humane character, and I have nothing but deep respect for you."

When they finished their lovely dinner, Karl asked Sonia if she would like to go dancing at the night club next door.

"You forgot already Karl, I have to go to mass tomorrow morning."

"Yes of course, what time do you want me to pick you up?"

"I normally walk; it's only a couple of blocks down the road from the dorm."

"I know which church you talking about. I drive passed it almost every day, but I hoped to introduce you to the church in Milton where I normally go. Would you like to try it?"

"Why not?" she responded affectionately. "What time does mass start?"

"It starts at 11 am."

"Very well, pick me up at 10:30."

CHAPTER 45

D avid moved up the ladder at the law firm and became in charge of a small staff. Mr. Stanly assigned him two cases to look after; one of the cases involved a group of sailors who filed a law suit in the federal court against a shipping company for violating their rights and their employments contracts. They claim to have become sick during their service on board one of the ships the company owned. It was alleged the shipping company didn't provide the sailors with the proper care to alleviate their sickness and they sought compensation from the company for violating their rights under the admiralty law for maintenance and cure provision. A seaman can sue the ship owner for breach of its obligation if evidence points to failure on the part of the company to provide the necessary medical treatment and therefore subject to punitive damages.

David, who represented the shipping company, questioned the veracity of their claim and over intense examination of the plaintiffs and key witnesses he was able to prove the allegations were bogus and contrived to embezzle a ransom from the ship owner. The court ruled in favor of the defendant and the lien placed by the sailors against the company was discharged. It was a difficult case to prove but David acted on a hunch and proved to the court that the plaintiff's story was full of contradiction and ambiguity, therefore solidifying his professional reputation.

David and Nancy were in love and people often commented on how much they suited one another. Their finances improved considerably after Nancy received a promotion and David had several pay increases and bonuses at the end of each successful trial. Nancy was happy and content with her life but she wanted to have children and move to a bigger apartment. David, though, was dead set against both propositions.

"This is not the right time, Nancy, darling. We need to save a large down payment to purchase an apartment in Manhattan close to our offices. We spend considerable time commuting from Brooklyn every day and I would rather put this wasted time to a better use, and we can wait a year or two before having a baby. Why are you in a rush now?"

"I am in a rush because my biological clock is ticking! The older I get the less chance I will conceive, and besides that, my mother is bugging me to have grandchildren."

"For God's sake Nancy, you are not thirty yet! I'm sure waiting a year or two wouldn't affect your ability to have children, and your mother can wait a little longer. We don't exist just for her convenience."

"My mother really wants to see our children before she is too old, can't you understand?"

"No, I cannot. Your mother is only 57 years old, and she will just have to wait until it is the right time for us to have children."

Ingrid was feeling lonely after all the children left the nest--David married living his own life in New York, and Sonia in college. Ingrid enjoyed last summer when her daughter came for a vacation in Detroit, and Greg noticed how sad his wife felt after Sonia went back to Boston.

He came home early one day and found his wife in the kitchen busy preparing dinner. "I have a little present for you," he announced. She looked at him with anticipation, and then he took her by the hand to the garage where his truck was parked. There, on the front seat was a small cage and a little furry creature was sitting inside anxious to get out. Ingrid ran to the driver's side and opened the cage, and a happy Golden Retriever wagging her tail jumped to the floor and ran in between her feet, licking her toes.

She picked up the puppy, while crying with delight. "Oh my God, he is so adorable!" The little beast was excited and fidgety in her arms. Greg just stood at the side door with a wide smile on his face.

"Does he have a name?" she asked.

"It is a she, and it is your dog, so you can have the honor of naming her!"

"I love her color, she is so beautiful! How about we call her Goldie?"

"Why not, it is a nice name. I will have new tags made. She had all the necessary shots done at the kennel so you don't have to worry about taking her to the vet for a while."

Ingrid called David right away to tell him about the puppy. "Hello son, are you busy?"

David normally doesn't like to be interrupted at work with personal calls but his mother was an exception; he too sensed her melancholy the last few times she called, but this time it was different, his mother sounded chirpy.

"Hello Mother," he answered in a loving voice, "No, I'm never too busy for you. How are you?"

"I have big news! I am so excited. Your father bought me a little present today, an adorable little puppy!"

"What kind did he get?"

"He bought a little Golden Retriever, she is not 10 pounds yet and I called her Goldie, do you think the name sounds silly?"

"No, Mother, it is a very nice and a fitting name considering her color. I hope you will have fun with her. Love you, Mother."

"Don't hang up yet! Your father and I are thinking we want to spend Christmas in Boston with Sonia, and I'd love to have you there with us. You know your dad and Sonia celebrate Christmas and it will be nice for the whole family to get together."

"Mother, I am so busy, but let me see what I can do. Maybe we can ask Nancy's parents to come with us to Boston; I will let you know tonight after I have a word with Nancy."

Sonia called her brother in New York. "I called you last Saturday big brother, but there was no answer."

"It's Saturday Sonia; I go to the Synagogue with Nancy as you already know."

"Silly me, I should have remembered, but my mind was not functioning well I guess."

"How is Harvard, sis?"

"Harvard is great and your sister is the happiest girl on this planet! I met this guy, Karl his name. He's such a great person, and a real gentleman, he is so much fun. And he's almost as good looking as you are!"

"And where did you meet Mr. Prince Charming?"

"We met at the gym. He plays hockey for Harvard. He really reminds me of you, David, he actually looks a little like you, except his hair is blond."

"You sound very happy, I am so glad for you Sonia. By the way, did mother call you about coming to Boston for Christmas and tell you about the puppy dad bought for her?"

"No, she didn't, but I will call her right away. I want to tell her about Karl, and no doubt she will tell me about the holiday."

Karl looked very smart in a suit and a tie when he picked up Sonia on Sunday morning. Sonia herself was dressed conservatively but she looked elegant. "You seem very happy this morning," he told her.

"Yes I am. My family will be coming to Boston for Christmas. Mother and father are coming from Detroit and my brother David and his wife are coming from New York. I hope you will be in Boston when they arrive for the holiday."

"No, I'm sorry, but I won't. I'm flying to LA to be with my family and I actually was going to ask if you were interested to come with me."

"I would have loved to go to LA, but I already told my mother I'll be in Boston. Is there any chance you can change your plans, Karl? I'd really like you to meet my family."

"Okay, let me see what I can do, but I am not promising anything for now."

Sonia expected the church to be a big one, but was surprised how small it was when she arrived with Karl. Father Mooney knew everybody by name.

"Good morning, Father," Karl addressed the priest.

"Good morning to you young man. We missed you the last couple of weeks. I thought you must have traveled far and away!"

"No Father, I haven't gone away, I have been in Boston all this time and please forgive me for failing my duty."

"You are here now, and that's what matters. Bless you son. May I ask who I have the pleasure of meeting here with you?"

"Oh, I am sorry Father; this is Sonia, my girlfriend."

"I am pleased to meet you Sonia; I hope you will enjoy mass with us today."

Sonia did enjoy mass immensely, and she thanked Father Mooney. "I loved it here Father, I hope to see you every Sunday from now on."

Karl called his mother that afternoon after he dropped Sonia at her residence. "Hello Mother, how are you?"

"I am doing very well son, what's new with you?"

Everything here is going really great. As a matter of fact I am a very happy man!"

"Glad to hear it son. You must have made up with Tracy?"

"No, Mother, I am happy because I love you and Dad more than anything in life!"

"How sweet, I love you too, my darling. But what's going on? It sounds like you're trying to butter me up!"

"Well, Mother, there is a slight change in plans. I'll be coming to LA later Christmas Eve; I want to stay here to meet some people coming from out of town."

"That's alright son, as long as you are here on Christmas morning to open your presents. So who is coming to see you from out of town?"

"I have a new girlfriend, Mother. Sonia is her name; she is amazing, wait till you meet her! She is beautiful, and much more fun than Tracy. Her family is traveling from Detroit to spend Christmas in Boston and she wanted me to meet them. Her mother is originally from Germany, I mean she was born in Germany just like dad."

"That's so nice, Karl. I hope one day we get to meet Sonia and her family."

Sonia and Karl's relation blossomed quickly; they continued to see each other several times a week if only for a cup of coffee at the cafeteria. They also made it a routine to go out every Friday night for something to eat but the last Friday before midterm recess it was snowing lightly in Boston.

Karl called Sonia and suggested, "Why don't you come over to my place instead of going out? We can order a pizza and watch a movie together."

"That sounds good to me," Sonia answered quickly. Karl picked her up in the early evening. She was dressed in jeans and a sweater just like he was; they looked forward to a comfortable time. When they arrived at his house, Sonia who never been there before was amazed how big it was. It had a grand piano and a huge stereo system with hundreds of LP's lying around.

"Who else lives here, Karl?"

"Nobody. My father bought the house when I first arrived in Boston with my 'nanny'. Elsa and I lived in it until I reached high school. She went to LA when I signed up at Milton's boarding residence for boys. The house was used when my family came to visit, otherwise it remained vacant until I enrolled at Harvard."

"Why did your father buy such a big house for just two people?"

"Well, he figured they needed a place to stay when they visited and he wanted the house to be large enough to accommodate all the family, in-cluding my grandparents. You see, my father is a real estate developer and he saw the benefit to invest in a property here in Boston knowing the value will go up in the future. After I am done here he will sell the property and make a decent profit."

"So your family live in LA permanently now!"

"My mother spends most of her time in LA but my dad splits his time between California and Brazil. He also runs another business for my grandfather who is now retired and lives in LA. He's a great guy; you will love him when he comes to Boston to visit. How about your family?"

"Well, I think I told you my mother was born in Germany, and she was a war refugee. She was married in Germany before she came to the US, but her husband was killed during the war. David is actually my half brother; he's a lawyer living with his wife in NYC.

"What kind of a lawyer is your brother?"

"He's a corporate lawyer, he graduated from Yale. You will meet him in few days, he is very sweet."

Karl put one of the Beatles LP's on. "Do you like the Beatles?"

"Yes I do. I like John Lennon best; I share his opposition to the war in Vietnam and his drive to spread peace in the world. There is absolutely no need for human beings to kill each other, and there are better ways to settle our differences and disputes. My brother on the other hand hates John Lennon; he thinks he is just a loudmouth communist. David joined the army after he finished college to fight in Vietnam, and he hates the communists with a passion."

"I think your brother and my dad will get along very well, he too hates the communists with a passion!"

After Karl ordered a pizza, he made a pitcher of margaritas for them, but before he sat down to watch the movie he went to his bedroom and brought back a huge box wrapped in gift paper.

"This is for you Sonia."

"What is it, Karl?"

"Just open it please."

Sonia removed the wrap and opened the box. She pulled out a beautiful fur jacket.

"Oh, my God!"

"Try it on."

She stood up and put the jacket on. "It feels so soft, I love it Karl!"

"It's mink. It's my Christmas present for you."

Sonia woke up in the morning a little sad. She curled up next to him and she started to cry softly.

"What is it?" Karl inquired.

She turned around and kissed him. "That was my first time."

"Mine, too."

She was madly in love with him and she sensed he was in love with her as they prepared breakfast together. Later that morning Karl dropped her at her residence to prepare for her family's visit.

Sonia called her mother in Detroit in the evening. "I finished the midterm exams Mother, and I feel very happy. To tell you the truth I have never felt happier in my life!"

"I am so glad to hear it Sonia. You must have done well in your exams!"

"Yes, of course I did. But there's something else. Someone else. Oh, Mother, I have fallen in love for the first time in my life! I am so in love with Karl, he is a wonderful guy and I love him with all my heart!"

"Well, that is so nice Sonia, but who is Karl?"

"Remember? I called you about this guy a few weeks ago! We've been going out with each other ever since and I am madly in love with him. He is from Brazil originally, but he has been living in this country since he was a child. He's a business student at Harvard; oh, and he gave me the most gorgeous mink jacket you will ever see! I bet it cost him a fortune!"

Ingrid was taken aback and immediately became concerned. "Wait a minute, Honey, how could a student afford to buy such an expensive present? I didn't know students had that kind of money, Sonia!"

"Don't worry Mother; this guy is as clean as a whistle. He comes from a very rich Brazilian family. His father is a developer over there and the company he owns has a branch office in California. You'll get to meet Karl in Boston when you get here. I have convinced him to stay, but he is leaving for LA on Christmas Eve to be with his family over the holidays."

Ingrid felt very uneasy when she finished the conversation with Sonia and when Greg arrived home from work in the evening she told him about it.

"I am not worried about Sonia," he reasoned. "She is smart and grown up, she can make her own decisions in life."

Ingrid was not convinced. "Honey, aren't you concerned about the present he gave her? People work all their lives and can't afford a mink jacket. Where does a student get that kind of money? Maybe it was illegally obtained, did this cross your mind?"

"I see it certainly crossed yours, but Sonia said her boyfriend comes from a rich family, and the boy is studying at Harvard which is hardly the place to do illicit things. Don't be over protective Ingrid, your daughter is a responsible girl."

Ingrid was still not convinced after her talk with Greg. She called David and told him the same thing about Sonia and her new boyfriend.

"I don't know, Mother, I certainly see your point, but let's not rock the boat for now. We will meet the boy in a few days, and we will be in a better position to evaluate the facts rather than worry ourselves with speculations."

Karl drove an ebullient Sonia to the airport to meet her family. She dashed over to hug her mother and father as soon as she spotted them entering the terminal building.

"Look at you Sonia! You look so nice!"

"And you too, Mother. How is Goldie doing?'

"Oh she is adorable. But she cried when we left her in the kennels."

Sonia pulled both her parents by the hands, "I cannot wait to introduce you to my boyfriend!" she said with glee as she nearly dragged them towards Karl, who was standing nervously away from the crowd.

"Karl, this is my mom and dad!"

Ingrid's jaw dropped the moment she saw him, and her knees began to shake. She could see him on top of her; she was gasping for air; she pictured him choking her. Her entire body started to tremble and she could not stand on her feet anymore; she had to lean over and grasp Greg's arm for support. Ingrid closed her eyes and started to shout, "Stop! Stop!"

Sonia, too, panicked. "What is wrong mother? What is it?"

Ingrid began to cry and continued to shout. "Stop! Stop!" but her cries faded as it soon dawned on her, it was all a mistake. The boy in front of her is from Brazil, and he couldn't possibly have anything to do with Hans. She regained her composure a little, but of course Karl was bewildered.

"What happened?" he asked.

"I am so sorry, I just felt dizzy. Flying doesn't agree with me. I was a little dazed and I pictured the airplane was going to crash."

Karl went to the bar and brought back a glass of water. "There you are ma'am, please have a drink."

Ingrid regained most of her composure by now, and she drank the water in one gulp. "I feel much better, thank you. I'm so sorry about that. Pleased to meet you, Karl."

"Very nice to meet you too, ma'am." Karl was obviously concerned for Ingrid. "Please sit down, let me ask if they have a doctor on duty to check you out, you don't look well at all."

Sonia was stroking her mother's hand and Greg was wiping the sweat beads on her forehead. "No, don't call the doctor, it won't be necessary. I feel fine now."

"Are you sure?" Greg asked.

"Yes, yes, I am very sure." Ingrid was utterly mesmerized, the boy looked like Hans at that age, the way he stood and his physical looks bear so much resemblance, and many memories from the past came flooding in her head. But she soon realized it was all a mistake and the whole thing must have been pure coincidence. She told herself it couldn't possibly have anything to do with that monster Hans; that bastard must be dead by now. He must have died when the allied forces invaded Germany. This boy is from Brazil, he didn't have anything to do with the evil Nazis.

Because of his flight later, Karl only had a few minutes to visit there in the airport before he had to finish up some business. He helped Ingrid with her suitcase and to climb in the waiting cab. He said goodbye and drove off on his own, leaving Sonia alone with her parents for the time being.

Ingrid was quiet during the drive to the hotel from the airport. "Are you alright, Mother?"

"Yes I am, I don't know what happened to me. Maybe the airline food did not agree with me, but I am perfectly alright now." Even so, Ingrid was still fidgeting.

Sonia decided to leave her mother and father to rest at the hotel, thinking maybe it was just fatigue; she always works herself up before she sets out on a trip. "I'll come over to the hotel tonight and we will have dinner together," she told her parents before she left.

Ingrid sat in bed, her mind torn with images from the past. It has been thirty years since she left Germany but images of Hans and the Nazis and the torture she encountered at their hands were still crisp in her mind. She recalled the time when she first arrived in Detroit and images from the concentration camp, the torture in the interrogation room and of course the rape, gave her many sleepless nights. She agonized for months and her pregnancy made matters worse, after all she was carrying the child of her tormentor and she couldn't get rid of it no matter how she tried. She remembered the awful times when she woke up in the middle of the night screaming at the top of her voice, her body drenched in sweat because of images of that monster raping and choking her. She was frightened and unable to fall back to sleep and often sat up in bed crying until the morning.

Rita used to ask when she came to the kitchen with her eyes puffed up and swollen, "What is wrong Ingrid? Your eyes are so red."

"Nothing," she used to answer, "I just have a condition with my tear glands."

Rita knew better but she didn't push the subject any further. Ingrid's memory of past events started to fade with time. She trained herself not to think about it anymore and the pain gradually dissipated. Over the years, she couldn't discuss her past with anybody; she locked her personal thoughts in her heart and didn't allow them to creep out, mainly because she couldn't stand the thought of revealing to David who his father actually was, and that he was born as the result of rape.

But it all came flooding back when she saw Karl standing in front of her at the airport; the uncanny resemblance he had to Hans made her sick to the stomach and shook her body and mind to the core. After resting at the hotel for a while, Ingrid finally realized the incident at the airport was all a silly mix up and decided to expel the evil thoughts out of her mind.

David arrived with Nancy just as Sonia and Karl were getting there. Ingrid and Greg were very happy to see their children, and for the chance to all get together at the hotel's restaurant. David sat for a chat with Karl but soon it was time for Karl to leave; he still had to pick up his stuff from home and drive to the airport to catch his flight to LA.

David found Karl a responsible and mature young man. He told his mother, "You don't have to worry about him; he is genuinely a good guy. He just happens to come from a fabulously wealthy family! I am not worried about him in any way, shape or form. I don't think Karl is engaged in illegal activities, quite the contrary, his level of knowledge in business is indicative of how focused he is on his career."

Greg also reached the same conclusion, and they both commended Sonia for her choice. "I think he is a good man for you, little sister," David told her.

Ingrid too found Karl very charming and a well-meaning young man. The first thing he did when he arrived at the hotel was to enquire about her wellbeing, he was genuinely concerned. She can tell her daughter was in love with the boy and now after she met him she can see why.

Karl stayed with his family over the holiday season; it was nice and warm in southern California and for him it was a welcome change from Boston's cold winter. Oscar had to go to Las Vegas with Ricardo to close on a land deal. He asked Karl to come along, and he decided to have a little conversation with him.

"One day son, I hope you will be taking over the business from me. But

I wonder if you have any other plans for the future when you finish from Harvard in a few years?"

"No, I haven't really given it to much thought, Father, but I enjoy Harvard. Maybe it would be in my best interest to continue there and get a master's degree in business administration."

"I will leave this up to you son. I know you are a responsible man, and I am impressed with your determination to do well in college. Your mother is telling me about your girlfriend, Sonia. It is your choice who you go out with as long as it doesn't interfere with your school and as long as the girl is nice and decent."

"Yes Dad, I was very careful with my choice. I wanted to bring Sonia with me to LA to meet you and Mother, but her family came from Detroit to stay with her over Christmas. I assure you Sonia comes from a very nice family. They are ordinary working people, and her father is one of the nicest men I have ever come across. Her brother is a successful attorney in NYC, and her mother is originally from Germany. She told me the name of the city where she came from but I did not recognize the name."

"You seem to be very happy and in love with her. That is fine, son, and from what you telling me the girl sounds very respectable. But you must be careful; there are girls out there who will do anything to hook up with a rich kid like you!"

"Yes Dad, I am totally aware of what you're saying, but in Sonia's case, I was the one to pursue her, not the other way around."

"There is one more thing I'd like to discuss with you. It is about the enemies working to enslave the Aryan people. You my boy represent the epitome of the Aryan race, and some people are working day and night behind the scenes to undermine your race and put us to work for their pleasure and benefits. Do you know what I am talking about?"

"I have not given this much thought. There was a group of students at Harvard talking trash about black people, but I don't like this group. All they are interested in is to foment hatred and discourse in our society. The black people have not done anything wrong to me and I am not going to engage in this racial hatred against them. They were made to come to this country against their will, and they suffered inhumane and cruel treatment when they arrived. I believe we should be cognizant and appreciative of the sufferings they endured, and we must commit not to repeat this barbaric and hateful episode."

"The group of people I alluded to is far more dangerous than Negroes.

These people are snakes and you will not recover from their bites. They spew their venom everywhere they go. This group is the mortal enemy of the Germanic people and the Aryan race, but sadly they are growing in power and influence. They now have a country of their own and they dominate the western world and the United States in particular. I speak of the Jewish people, of course. You are my only son Karl, the most precious and important thing I have on this earth and I want you to know the Jews are your enemy! They are the enemy of your father and they were the enemy of your grandfather and your forebears. I also want to tell you something important and I want you to keep it in strict confidence; not even your mother should know about it. Is that understood, Karl?"

"Yes sir, you are my father, and I would give up my body and soul for you Dad, and I promise in the name of our lord Jesus Christ, I will not reveal anything you tell me in confidence."

"That's my boy. I want you to know, Ricardo and I belong to a secret society. Our aim is to deal with this dangerous group of people and purge them out of western societies. Maybe when the time is right, after you finish your education, you will join our group and be at the forefront in the battle with these evil and ugly people. Our German patron, Martin Luther, warned us about them. He told us the Jews are alien to our society and must not be trusted, and so did our great leaders Bismarck and Adolf Hitler who dedicated their lives to get them out of our fatherland. But they didn't get the job done, and it is now our duty as Germans to continue the struggle to the end. They killed our Lord Jesus Christ 2000 years ago, they killed Adolf Hitler, the greatest leader Germany ever had, and we must do everything in our power to exact revenge and banish them out of our societies for good! Do you understand son?"

CHAPTER 46

David had been very busy on another maritime court case. It involved a claim by the owner of a ship who came to the rescue of a stricken ship caught in stormy weather in international waters carrying 100 tons of gold bullion worth millions of dollars; the owners of the rescue ship claimed interest under maritime salvage laws. They alleged had it not been for their heroic effort, the damaged ship would be at the bottom of the ocean by now and its cargo would have been lost to all. David spent countless hours preparing the lawsuit on behalf of his client, the salvor; court proceedings were scheduled to begin in the middle of January after attempts at mediation failed. The case was a top priority for David; the stakes were high and so was the reward.

Oscar and Helmut came to NYC to meet with the shipping company officials after H&O representatives had the chance to inspect the ships in Halifax and determined they were worth the asking price. The shipping company board of trustees met in the presence of a court appointed representative overseeing the interests of the two banks who hold the liens. The general manager informed Oscar the board unanimously approved the transaction as per the provisions in the conditional offer presented by H&O, and asked that he come to New York to work out the details. Oscar and Helmut were extremely pleased with the deal and decided to go through with it.

They also arranged with their wives to fly to Boston so the whole family can be with Karl for the spring break, although initially Karl was going to LA. Erika was behind the change; she wanted to visit Martha's Vineyard during early spring when the area wasn't too busy with throngs of tourists.

Karl and Sonia's relationship grew stronger; the two were madly in love. They talked on the phone every night and they went out together for dinner or to watch a movie on the weekends. Karl now wanted Sonia to move in with him.

"No Karl, you and I are here for a purpose. If we move in together we will not concentrate on our studies and we will fail in our mission."

"Okay, how about if you stay the weekends?"

"Yes, I can agree to that. We can have fun together and go to mass on Sundays. I happen to like father Mooney, he is welcoming and sincere. You can pick me up Friday and drop me off Sunday after lunch."

"That's one thing I love about you Sonia, you know how to compromise."

"And I love that you don't insist; you always meet me halfway."

The arrangement worked well for both of them, and it didn't affect their performance at Harvard. Quite the contrary, both were doing very well. Karl took Sonia out to dinner every Friday, and Sonia prepared a home meal for him on Saturday. Sometimes they ordered food and stayed in to watch a movie together.

After mass on the Sunday before his family were due to visit, Karl took Sonia out to brunch. He pulled her close to him and put his arms round her. "I have never loved anybody as much as I love you Sonia, you are part of me and you are my soul mate. And I promise, no matter what happens between you and I, I will always remain loyal and my love for you will be eternal."

She looked at him with her big adoring eyes and told him, "Me too Karl. There isn't a word sufficient enough to describe how much I adore you!"

Karl took Sonia to the airport to meet his family. Gretchen and Erika were out first and Karl walked over and hugged them both. His father and grandfather were very happy to see him. When he introduced Sonia to the family, it appeared their first impression was very positive.

"Tell us about out yourself, Sonia," Gretchen softly asked.

"Well, I am originally from Detroit, and my parents still live there. I have just one brother; he is a lawyer in New York. I am English Literature major at Harvard and I have an ambition to carry on and obtain a post graduate degree, then I hope to become a teacher."

"That is a very honorable career!" Gretchen lovingly commented.

While Oscar drove the family around Boston after they dropped Sonia at her residence, the whole family praised Karl for his choice of lady friend, especially Erika who was effusive with her praise. "She is a very pretty lady; I see why you are in love with her!"

Karl picked up Sonia the next day and the whole family drove to Martha's Vineyard. It was early spring, the air was still crisp and the roads weren't too busy, and they stopped for lunch at one of Karl's favorite seafood restaurants in the area.

Oscar asked Sonia about David. "You mentioned your brother is a lawyer in NYC?"

"Yes he is. Ever since he graduated from Yale, he's been working at one of NYC's most prestigious law firms. He told me he has not lost a single case in all the time he is been there!"

"What does he do exactly, what I mean to say is, what branch of law does he practice?"

"David is a corporate lawyer. I guess he represents companies when they have a dispute. I know he just won a big case for a ship owner whose employees tried to defraud him."

"I would like to contact your brother; I need some legal consultation in NYC."

"I would be delighted to give you his number, I am sure you will like David; he is a very brainy guy."

Sonia called her brother when she returned to Boston. "What's up Sonia?" David asked in his lawyerly voice.

"Guess what big brother? Karl's family is here in Boston visiting. We went to Martha's Vineyard and during the course of conversation Karl's father asked if I knew a lawyer in NYC, so I gave him your name."

"That's fine; I'll look out for him when he calls."

Karl's family were very pleased with the progress he had made at Harvard, they were very impressed with the university when Karl and Sonia took them on a tour of the historical institution which has been one of the leading centers for learning in the western world for almost five centuries. They met with one of Karl's professors who assured them Karl is a fine young man with a brilliant career ahead of him.

David picked up the phone when his secretary buzzed him.

"Mr. Silva is on the line; he said he is a referral from your sister."

"Yes, please put him through." David instantly recognized the German accented English he is so familiar with. "My name is Oscar Silva. I met your sister the other day in Boston. She gave me your name and phone number."

"Hello Mr. Silva, my sister gave me a heads up about your conversation with her. How may I be of service to you?"

"We own a marine shipping company in Brazil with an affiliated branch here in NYC. We presented an offer to purchase a fleet of cargo ships from a company based in NYC and Halifax, and our offer has been accepted by the company's management and the banks involved. We therefore would like to set up an appointment to discuss the transaction and to see if this legal matter lies within your scope of work and expertise."

"Yes, Mr. Silva, it is indeed the kind of work I do and my law firm specializes in. But I must caution you, my time is limited if you need this contract in a rush. How much time do you have to complete the deal?"

"We are in a bit of a hurry. We need to put these ships in service as soon as possible, but we can work with you if the wait is not too long."

"Very well, when would you like to come to my office?"

"How about tomorrow?" Oscar answered.

"I am sorry, but tomorrow I am in court all day long. Let me see, would the day after, say at 8 am work for you?"

"It sure does, we will see you then."

When Oscar and Helmut arrived at David's office, David himself came out of his office to greet them.

"This is my father-in-law, Helmut Spiegel."

"Nice to meet you sir." David ushered them to the conference room.

Oscar picked a file from his attaché case. "I have prepared this duplicate file for you with all the pertinent information. I placed the draft proposal right on top; it will give you a clear synopsis of the whole deal. I must draw your attention to the two important facts; our company is privately owned and registered in Brazil, and the seller has recently undergone restructuring with the court. I also included our company's portfolio at the end of the file. I would like to stress our intention to go ahead with the purchase in accordance with the offer provisions we presented."

David wrote some notes and slowly flipped through the pages. He was extremely impressed with how organized the file looked; the cover page, the photographs, the headings and the labeling between the pages, he even noticed each segment of the file was color coded for easy identification. "I wish all my clients were as organized as you Mr. Silva!"

Oscar laughed, "I have a good teacher here!" as he pointed at Helmut.

"Very well gentlemen, let me have a proper look at the information and when you come in next week, I will discuss the procedures to complete the sale, as well as my fees."

Helmut has been around business lawyers all his life and was impressed with David. "This lawyer looks very smart, and I think he will do a fine job for us, Oscar."

Sonia couldn't help but notice the physical resemblance and the mannerisms Karl has in common with his dad. "Your father is greying now, but I bet he looked the double of you when he was your age!"

"Yes everybody says that. My mother and my grandparents, even some of my dad's old friends tell me how much we look alike."

"He is so handsome, of course, just like you Karl," she teased. "How old is your dad?"

"Almost 54. How about your father?"

"Oh, he is older than your dad, he's over sixty already."

"I wish I would look half as good as he does when I make it to 60; he looks well for his age," Karl commented.

"My father takes life so easy, he has a relaxed personality and I think that had a profound effect on David and me."

"I thought your mother is very nice and easy going."

"Yes, she is to a certain extent, but with one big difference; she worries too much."

David was incredibly busy with the marine salvage suit and wouldn't have entertained taking another case if it weren't for his opinion that Oscar could become an important client in the future. He reached this conclusion after speaking to Karl back when the two met in Boston at Christmas time. Karl was forthcoming with information about his family, albeit in broad terms, and David came away with the impression Karl's family was fabulously rich. But when Oscar left the law office after the brief initial meeting, David realized this gentleman with his multiple business interests has the potential to generate major revenue for the firm. And of course this cargo ship transaction is worth upwards of $85 million, and though he was busy with another major case, he decided it would be imprudent not to take Oscar's case as well. David picked up the phone and called his boss. The two discussed the transaction and the possible amount the firm should charge for the service rendered, and also agreed on the split between the office and David. Mr. Stanly was particularly generous with David since Oscar was his own client.

By five o'clock Friday David was utterly exhausted. He had been working over 70 hours a week for the last several months with no end in sight, but he knew the reward for his time will be substantial and will make him financially comfortable and secure. He decided to take his wife out to dinner when he got home.

"Hello, honey," Nancy greeted him when he walked in.

"Hello darling, you look so nice and fresh!"

"Oh thank you, I was bored today, so I decided to go out and have a makeover," Nancy answered joyfully. "How has your day been?"

"It could not get any better! Let's go out and have dinner at the bistro in Greenwich Village."

Nancy got up quickly. "You don't have to ask me twice, I'll be ready in five!"

Though David was exhausted, he didn't feel the pain. The sweet scent of success was close; as a matter of fact he knew it was coming very soon. He and Nancy had a wonderful dinner that evening, and when he returned home, he confessed to her his desire to have a baby. Nancy was in tears, she couldn't be happier and when they finally went to bed, she made sure to lock the bedroom door behind her.

David called Oscar in LA two weeks later. He already had all the closing documents ready and he was surprised yet relieved when Oscar didn't seem to question the invoice.

"No problem," responded Oscar, "I have a feeling you will do a good job for us. I'll wire you the retainer immediately, and we will pay the balance at closing if this okay with you."

"Of course, sir," David replied. He was thrilled with the outcome of his conversation with Oscar; what a gentleman, he thought. I love clients like this man!

Sonia and Karl decided to visit NYC on Memorial Day weekend. It was the last opportunity for them to have a break before finals and Karl wanted to treat Sonia to a lavish holiday. He booked a suite in an exclusive Manhattan hotel; the two drove there in his Porsche, singing all the way down. Sonia didn't want anyone to be with them during their mini holiday; she didn't even tell David she was coming to town.

Sonia couldn't believe the luxury and she told him, "I would be just as content in a small hotel, Karl. It is you I love and want to be with. She gave him a silver cross on a chain, "This is a symbol of my love for you, I want you to promise me that every time you wear this cross you will think of me."

He brought her close to him and assured her, "I want you to know my love for you will last until the day I die. Sonia, you're all I think about from the moment I wake up to the moment I go to sleep." He put the cross around his neck and brought it over to his face and kissed it. "I love you, darling, with all of my heart."

David had been engaged in pretrial discovery and depositions with the defendants and their lawyers in the marine salvage case, but it had not been easy; a motion was filed in court to compel the other party to produce documents and provide answers and witnesses, the defendant's evasive tactics and the failure to produce a settlement during mediation were behind the motion filing. He and the defendant's lawyer finally agreed on a jury trial.

After eight weeks of intense court procedure, both lawyers presented their closing statements and the judge ordered the jury to deliberate and come back with a unanimous decision, first to determine if the salvor is entitled for a reward and second how much of a reward in terms of percentage of the value of the ship and its cargo.

Despite the extensive effort and time allotted to the salvage case, David worked just as diligently to prepare the pertinent documents to complete the sale of the eleven cargo ships for Oscar, he in fact proposed to prepare eleven separate contracts with specific details pertaining to each individual ship rather than lump the whole deal in one master contract. He also asked for an extension of the closing date due to the many documents involved which ultimately have to be filed with the court and appropriate agencies.

Finally, when everything was ready, David called Oscar to tell him, "Mr. Silva, I have sent the documents for you to review and approve, please let me know when you are ready."

A week later, Oscar informed David he had indeed reviewed the documents and everything looked fine. The banks are also satisfied with the deal and they are willing to wire the money as soon as they get their original copies of all the signed and notarized papers. The two gentlemen therefore agreed on a date for Oscar to come to NYC for the signing.

David escorted Oscar to the conference room when he arrived for the ceremonial signing. A notary public was also present, and the purchase was completed when Oscar placed his signature at the bottom of each contract.

Oscar was glad that all went through as planned; he knew the purchase was a great deal and he could turn around and sell the eleven ships at great profit if he wanted to, but the intention was to put the ships in immediate service to meet the backlog in the demand for cargo shipment.

David invited Oscar out for lunch afterwards. Once they arrived at the restaurant, he mentioned, "I had a chance to meet your son Karl in Boston last Christmas. He is a fine young man, I found him ambitious and motivated. Many kids his age pick up bad habits, but Karl seems much focused on his studies."

Oscar was pleased to hear David's assessment of his son. "Sure, he is focused. He needs to get the right qualifications to run our business in the future. I missed the chance to continue my own education when I was his age. Both my parents were college graduates, but war broke out in Europe when I reached college age and I was called to serve, and at the end of the war there was no prospect for education. As a matter of fact there was no work available in Germany so I was left with no choice but to seek another opportunity somewhere else, so I immigrated to Brazil."

David told him his mother, too, lost all her family during the war and her husband was killed. "She was penniless when she arrived in the US. She and my father worked very hard to put my sister and me though school."

"So, what did you do when you finished school, did you go to college for your law degree?" Oscar asked.

"No, I actually started very much like your son. I enrolled in college in Chicago to study business and finance and when I graduated I enlisted in the army. I was sent to Vietnam where I was injured during active duty and was hospitalized for a while. After my release from hospital, I was briefly employed at Merrill Lynch before I finally obtained a law degree from Yale."

"This is so interesting. The war in Vietnam was very unpopular, and we watched images of people demonstrating against the war on Brazilian TV. I am curious to know why you enlisted in the first place."

"You see Mr. Silva, ordinary people don't appreciate the freedom we have in this country and the menace of communism. The US had no choice but to fight the communists, otherwise they will devour our nation and take our freedom away."

"You know David, I have a lot of respect for you, and I also believe communism is a menace and it must be kept in check or defeated altogether. Those communists are trying to establish a foothold in South America; look what happened in Chile! I am glad the US engineered the ouster of the communist president, Salvador Allende."

Oscar was very careful not to mention his Nazi past; he wanted to present an image of neutrality and support for the US. Likewise, David didn't want to discuss his mother's past hardships with a total stranger.

CHAPTER 47

Karl called Sonia from LA with a surprise. "Hello love, I'm going with my family to Brazil for few weeks, I'd like it if you could come with me! I miss you so much, my beautiful girl."

"I miss you too, Karl, I wish I could be with you, maybe next time. But the other day my mother fell and broke her arm and she was taken to hospital."

"Why, what happened to her?" Karl asked anxiously.

"Oh, it wasn't a big deal, but she fractured her arm when she took Goldie, our golden retriever for a little trot round the block. Goldie spotted a squirrel and made a run for it. She pulled Mother hard and she fell on her arm at the edge of the curb. Some neighbors heard her scream and called the paramedics. The doctor informed us she had a breakage in her upper arm just below the shoulder, and he gave her two choices, but my stubborn mother refused to have any medical procedure and opted for natural healing instead. She is wearing a sling for support and has temporarily lost the use of her arm. So I'm staying here to nurse her and help with the cooking and housework.

"I am so sorry to hear this Sonia. Please pass my love to your mother and wish her well from me."

"I will do that, thank you so much."

"What happened to the dog, did she run away?"

"No, she was curled up on the front porch when we returned from hospital, and my father was so mad with her! But I told him she is only following her instincts, dogs love to chase squirrels, and he shouldn't blame her."

David received a call from the court saying the jury reached a decision on the marine salvage case. He and Mr. Stanly rushed over to the courthouse. Several newspaper reporters were already there as well as the lawyers representing the defendants. The large court room was packed to capacity with people; they all stood up as the judge entered the chamber. When the foreman announced the verdict in favor of the plaintiff, David pumped his fist and tapped the shoulder of his client. Mr. Stanly pushed his bifocals to the back of his nose and relaxed in his seat. David and the rest of the team threw their arms in the air and there were hugs all over. This verdict was a huge reward for all the hard work and long hours David and his team spent working on the case, but as expected their celebration was short lived as the defendant's lawyers announced their intention to appeal. David and his team however, were basking in the glow of camera flashes and newspaper reporters scrambling around, all wanting to interview David about this landmark trial. The following day his picture appeared in several newspapers and the *New York Times* ran an interview with him under the title *Jury Awards Unprecedented Compensation for Landmark Marine Salvage Case.* In the photo his arms were raised in jubilation. Nancy's father called to congratulate him and so did several of his law professors and former Yale colleagues. He became somewhat a celebrity at the office and he also received a request for an interview from the legal correspondent of the CBS News network.

Three months pregnant with her first child, Nancy was in tears when David called to tell her about the verdict. "Darling, you deserve to win! I haven't seen anybody work as hard as you do, and of course, you are the smartest man in the world! I love you so much and I hope little David will be as smart as his father!"

David laughed and asked her, "How do you know it's a boy?"

"Oh, I don't know for sure but I want my firstborn to be a boy," she answered affably.

David decided to take a mini break from work. He wanted to go back home to see his family and to check on his mother after her fall. He and Nancy flew to Detroit on Friday evening after work. Greg, Ingrid and Sonia were all there to greet them at the airport. He hugged his mother first, being careful not to hurt her arm.

"I miss you son, so much," she cried. "There isn't a day I don't think about you."

"I miss you and love you too mom, and you will be proud to know we won the big case I told you about! We have been so busy working on it for the last several months."

"I prayed for you son, you wouldn't know how much. You are so smart and I had no doubt you will win." She turned to Nancy, "Good to see you my dear, you look wonderful, how is the little baby?"

"He is growing, for sure. And I hope he will be as good looking as his father, with that beautiful dark hair and his handsome chiseled face!" Nancy said, tousling her husband's hair lovingly.

"Of course he will, he has a beautiful mother, doesn't he?" Ingrid said.

When David returned to New York, he was very relaxed. His reputation as a good lawyer was now firmly established, but he wasn't expecting what happened next. Mr. Stanly summoned him to his office, and when David arrived, he was surprised to see the three other partners there as well. They all sat around the conference table with a gorgeous view of the New York skyline. The meeting was called to discuss some important issues; the first item on the agenda is David's strategy for the marine salvage appeal case.

David answered forcefully and explained his approach to resolving the appeal. "I have given this case a lot of thought, I even discussed it briefly with one of my Yale professors, and my strategy is to get my client to understand it's in his best interest to give the defendants an incentive to drop the case, as there is no guarantee we will win the appeal. I also plan to make the defendant's council understand the appellate court will review the lower court decision only if they were convinced the proceedings weren't followed properly. We followed the court procedures to the letter, and therefore, they don't have a leg to stand on if they wish to have the verdict overturned. Having said that, I will also offer them an incentive and inform them of my client's decision to forfeit part of the court award which pertain to the loss of income for the days it took my client to accomplish the rescue mission in exchange for the defendants' dropping their appeal. It is a win, win situation for everybody; our client doesn't have to wait years for the award and the defendants will mitigate their losses and save the massive cost of the appeal."

The partners were satisfied with David's strategy and immediately jumped to the other important issue for which the meeting was called. Mr. Stanly started by telling David how happy they have been with his performance and in consideration for his exemplary service, they decided to make David an offer to become a full partner in the law firm. David was not expecting this at all; he was overjoyed with the announcement.

"I am absolutely thrilled you even considered me, it is my privilege and distinct honor to be associated with a group of distinguished councils! Words cannot even describe how I feel. The acknowledgement of my peers is priceless and I will treasure it for the rest of my life. Thank you so much and of course I am honored to become your partner."

Karl and Sonia started their junior year at Harvard at the same time. Sonia came back all tanned from days she spent on the beach with her family. Even after her injury, Ingrid loved to go to the beach with her daughter, Sonia lying in the sun and Ingrid sitting under an umbrella. She liked to bring a book with her, and she often dozed off laying on the lounger until Greg arrived in the afternoon with sandwiches and refreshments or meat to BBQ. He loved to jump in the water after a long day working in the office or meeting clients. He was a good swimmer but no match for his daughter, she was young and swimming was always her thing; she spent hours training with the swim team at Harvard. Ingrid loved to watch them racing and playing silly splash games. She only wished David was with them.

Ingrid discussed Karl with Sonia; she knew Karl and her daughter were madly in love, it was very evident. They spoke on the phone every single night; Karl even called her from Brazil. "Sonia!" she would shout, "Karl is on the phone!" and Ingrid watched Sonia rush in from the yard with a big smile on her face.

Deep down Ingrid felt comfortable her daughter was going out with a nice man like Karl, yet there was a tinge of uneasiness about the boy, like something was shrouded in mystery. She can't put her finger on it though. However, the assurances David and Greg accorded Karl alleviated her concerns to a large extent.

The subject about Karl came up one day during casual conversation on the beach; Ingrid asked her daughter how she and Karl first met. Sonia was proud of her relationship with Karl and she proceeded to tell her mother about their first encounter and how it developed from there.

"Tracy, a girl on my swim team asked me to go to a hockey game to see her boyfriend playing for Harvard against Penn State, so I went with her and Tracy introduced him to me after the game was over. He flashed me the most beautiful smile you can imagine. We went for coffee in the cafeteria and the next time I heard from him he asked me out. I felt comfortable with him from the start and our relationship blossomed, and now I love him more than life itself."

Ingrid then asked about Karl's family. "David said his father is a businessman in Brazil, what does he do exactly?"

"According to Karl, his father immigrated to Brazil from Germany when he was young. There he worked odd jobs in construction to make a living and to learn the trade, then built his company from scratch and became a very successful real estate developer. He also owns a marine shipping company with Karl's granddad."

"What is his father's name?"

"Ah, you should meet his father; he is the nicest man in the world! His name is Oscar Silva, he looks like his son but his hair is graying now, and he walks with slight limp."

"How about Karl's mother?"

"His mother is so nice; his father must have picked her from a beauty pageant! She is a very beautiful lady and she hasn't lost her looks. She must be in her late forties or early fifties, I don't know exactly."

Ingrid felt reassured after the conversation with her daughter. Karl couldn't possibly have anything to do with that awful person Hans, and that awkward episode she had at the airport when she met Karl for the first time was totally unfounded. Many German people have similar looks to one another anyway.

Gretchen and the rest of Karl's family expressed high regard for Sonia. He told them, "You know, Sonia is a very conservative girl and deeply religious, despite her outward bubbly character."

Gretchen asked, "What do you mean she is religious?"

He was happy to tell them more about her. "Sonia," he began, "loves our Lord Jesus and she devotes considerable time studying and learning about the message He brought to this world. She never fails to go to mass on Sundays, and she basically is a decent, honest and moral girl and loyal to her family and friends," he added.

Gretchen recalled Sonia saying her mother was a war refugee, who came to America after WWII. She therefore assumed Sonia's mother was Christian and had no reason to suspect anything else since Sonia was Catholic Christian herself. Karl, who was madly in love, knew better than to say anything about Sonia's mother's background. He felt it was not the right time, but when the appropriate moment comes he will tell his family the truth. After all, his relationship is with Sonia and not with her mother.

Karl and Sonia's relationship grew steadily stronger and their love for one another was intense. Both families knew they were destined to be together, without reservations. These two suited one another perfectly.

Karl finally got the chance to take Sonia to LA after the midterm exams. She agreed to go for few days only as she promised to be with her family over

Christmas. Sonia loved California, she had a wonderful time at Disneyland and Universal Studios, and they enjoyed strolling down Sunset Boulevard.

She didn't realize how wealthy Karl's family until she saw their house. She wasn't used to seeing such a large domestic staff, with chauffeured limousines and gardeners, even though her own father started out his career doing that. As Karl never bragged or even told her about all these privileges, her admiration for him multiplied because of his modesty. A highlight of her visit was getting to meet Elsa as well, and hearing stories about Karl's childhood adventures from his nanny.

CHAPTER 48

David was now busy with the negotiations for the marine salvage appeal case. It was much harder than he initially visualized; he encountered a tough patch convincing his client to accept the deal and take a cut in the reward the court awarded. Eventually and after a long discussion the client relented and accepted David's recommendation, but no sooner had he finished with the first hurdle than he came across a tougher problem with the defendant's new lawyers. The defendant himself was totally upset with the original defense team and had them replaced, and at the beginning, the new team wasn't in the mood to compromise, but after lengthy negotiations they too relented. This case ultimately brought a large financial reward for David and made him well known in the legal circles in New York and beyond.

Friday evening after he finished with the last file in his hand, David called it a day and went home. He had been so overwhelmed the last three weeks and he looked forward to a relaxing weekend with his wife.

He asked Nancy if she wanted to go downstairs for dinner in the bistro to celebrate this latest victory.

"You must be kidding me," she caustically replied, "I'm three days overdue! This baby is very stubborn like his dad; he is not in a hurry to come out." So they ordered food in and planned on spending the evening watching TV.

David was fast asleep on the couch soon after they finished eating when Nancy frantically tried to wake him up. "Get up David! My water broke!"

David answered her still half asleep. "What water?"

She nudged him again. "The baby is coming! Wake up!" David jumped up at the mention of the baby and he called for the ambulance.

Their baby boy was born almost 28 hours later. When the nurse handed the baby to Nancy after the necessary procedures, her heart leapt out of place, she was crying with happiness. David, who never thought he would cry, the moment he looked at his firstborn his heart melted with joy and happiness.

The nurse asked if they have a name, and David without hesitation told her, "Daniel Adam."

"What a pretty name," the nurse responded. She disappeared for a minute and when she returned she had the identification band with her and she put it round the baby's wrist. David and Nancy chose two names, one for a boy, Daniel Adam and Sara May in case the baby was a girl. Nancy was so pleased it was a boy; after all she got what she hoped for. David called his mother to tell her the good news about the baby. Ingrid nearly fainted with joy the moment he told her it was a boy. She shouted to Greg to come to the phone and the whole family was jubilant. Ingrid expressed great desire to come to New York to see her first grandson and David told her he will arrange airline tickets for her and Greg. He then called his sister at Karl's home number where she had been staying and she too cried with happiness at the news and promised to drive down to see the baby.

The following day, David made a side trip to Tiffany's, and bought two presents, an expensive diamond ring for his wife and a beautiful gold Star of David on a gold chain for his mother.

On the eighth day after the birth of Daniel Adam, the whole family went to the synagogue for the *brit milah*. The Rabbi welcomed the baby to the congregation. "*May God bless the tender circumcised Daniel Adam, son of David and send him complete recovery because he entered the covenant.*" Ingrid was so pleased her grandchild was accorded the proper Jewish traditional ceremony. David invited the whole family to a kosher restaurant in Brooklyn for seudat mitzvah, the traditional celebratory meal performed after the circumcision ceremony.

David had a message from Oscar waiting on his desk when he returned to his office from court. He picked up the phone and dialed the number in Los Angeles. "Hello Mr. Silva, I see you called, how can I help you?"

"David, we own a vacant land on the Las Vegas Strip and we are planning to build a resort hotel with a casino on it, and the reason I am calling is to find out if you were interested to represent us in negotiating a deal with a hotel operator experienced in running this kind of business. I wonder if this sort of thing is within the scope of your expertise."

There was a slight pause while David was trying to digest the request. "I'm afraid not; I personally don't have this kind of experience but I will ask my partners and let you know in due time if they have any previous experience with casino operators, or if they can recommend somebody who has."

"Very well, I would also appreciate if you can help with the loan negotiations to finance the construction of our Las Vegas deal with the banks; you
probably can negotiate a better deal than we can."

"Sure, I can help with the banks; this definitely lies within my scope of
work."

"Thank you so much David, I look forward to hearing from you soon."

David had a broad smile when he finished the call; he loved the way
Oscar spoke with his typical German accent and manners, always to the
point with no frills attached, always with serious tone void of real humor.
But he recognized the value of the property in Vegas and the cost associated
with building a casino. This is not your typical project but one that requires
expertise and an infusion of capital. David picked up the phone and called
his partner Mr. Stanly to ask if he knew anything about casino operators.
To his surprise, Mr. Stanly gave him a narrative of past experience he had in
Atlantic City putting deals together between owners and operators.

Oscar and Ricardo have been planning this project for a while since
the purchase of the vacant land on the Strip. They figured the casino will
generate steady income for the company with minimum effort if they were
successful in their attempt to partner with a well known brand name. They
summoned all the key staff and construction managers to a meeting to
chart the path for an expedited construction schedule, beginning as soon as
possible. Ricardo was assigned the task to obtain all the necessary permits
from the city of Las Vegas and from the gaming commission for the state
of Nevada.

Oscar soon received the call he was waiting for from David to tell him
about the new developments with the casino operator.

"I am glad to advise you, Mr. Stanly, the senior partner in our office has
had much experience putting together casino deals in Atlantic City, New
Jersey, and he will be delighted to represent you in the negotiations with operators like MGM and Harrah's. And I have also more exciting information
for you Mr. Silva. I have spoken to several financial institutions regarding the
construction loan; I came across two banks that are willing to put together
the necessary funds to finance the cost of your project at a favorable rate
and excellent terms. I don't know what your schedule is like in the next few
days but I urge you to come to New York so we can discuss your options."

Oscar immediately went to New York to meet with David. He brought
with him the feasibility report prepared by an independent consulting firm
with a specialty in the entertainment and hospitality business. The report

points to the high value of the project and the incredible rate of return on investment over a short period. David was very pleased when he read it and he sat with Oscar to lay out the loan details and the requirements the banks will demand from him in order to facilitate the loan. Oscar thanked David for his efforts to secure the loan with such excellent terms.

Mr. Stanly joined in the meeting and explained in great detail how he could structure the deal with a highly reputable company to manage and operate the hotel and casino on behalf of Oscar. They all shook hands at the end of the meeting and the lawyers were given the green light to proceed with their allotted tasks.

CHAPTER 49

Karl and Sonia were very happy at the end of their third year at Harvard; she was at first concerned living together may affect their performance at the university, but Karl gave her assurances it will not, and true to his word things worked out very well, and both passed all their courses with high marks. Karl made plans to go to California to learn the trade from his father and Sonia as usual went home to enjoy the summer in Detroit with her family.

Soon after Karl arrived in California, Oscar announced he was going to Brazil and asked his son to come with him for several weeks to learn more about the shipping business. Karl made it a habit to call Sonia from there every single night, and Oscar noticed how attached his son was to her. He blessed the relationship because Sonia suited his son and she would make an ideal wife for him in the future. He recalled how he felt about Gretchen when he was Karl's age, and he appreciated his son's devotion to the girl. He was also proud of his son for choosing a beautiful and well brought up girl and he hoped the relationship will grow stronger in the future.

On their return to LA, Oscar had another conversation with him. "Son, do you recall last summer the discussion we had about the secret group Ricardo and I belong to?"

"Yes Dad, I do."

"Well, I have changed my mind and decided to introduce you to the group and see if you can become a member. It will please me immensely if you belong to this group of like-minded people. They dedicate their lives in the defense of the Aryan race and the defeat of our mortal enemy, the Jewish people. I want you to come with us next week to attend the meeting and listen to our group leader deliver a speech to lay the plans for the future. I want you to be present so you get to meet the right people and build relationships with them. Don't worry, this trip will just serve as an introduction; you will not be required to do anything until you are finished with Harvard."

Karl's heart was not into joining ultra-nationalist groups, let alone a group which by all accounts was considered white supremacist. What they stand for and the teachings of Jesus, by his estimation are in profound conflict with one another. However, he didn't want to turn his father down and therefore agreed to go.

Karl had the impression before he arrived at the group's location in Oregon he would be listening to fiery speeches extolling the virtues of the Aryan race and denigrating the Jews and the Negroes. This image he had in his mind was the result of seeing clips of past speeches delivered by Hitler with excitement and fervor and he expected to see much the same in Oregon. But he was mildly surprised--the majority of the people present at the meeting were calm and collected and the speech was delivered by the group leader, Dr. Alfred Hanson, who laid out his vision for the future in a very articulate and effective manner and without the use of theatrics or rais- ing his voice. The message to the members was simple; get united and work in small groups in secrecy and train on the use of firearms to prepare for a showdown with the Jews and their supporters in the future, once the group reaches the critical mass in numbers and financial capability. At the top of the list marked for elimination are Jewish politicians, bankers and community leaders in the position to influence future generations. But Jewish money is by far the number one target since the Jews, according to Dr. Hanson, use their money to control everything.

The front seats in the hall where the speech was delivered were re- served for long-time members and big contributors like Oscar and Ricardo. Younger members were seated at the rear, where Karl sat next to Brandon, Dr. Hanson's son. The two had a lengthy conversation; Karl learned he and Brandon were born in the same year and they were both in their final year in college. Brandon was majoring in surveying at the University of Washington. Karl asked him, "Why did you choose surveying?"

With a small laugh Brandon told him his father wanted him to follow in his footsteps and become a medical doctor, but the sight of blood made his stomach turn, and therefore a career in medicine didn't agree with him! He loved the outdoors; camping, skiing and boating are some of the things he enjoyed most, and surveying involves being out in nature most of the time where he can earn a living and be outside at the same time.

"It sounds so exciting," Karl responded, "I do love nature and skiing is one of my favorite sports, too. I started skiing at resorts on the Andean sum- mits in Argentina when I was a little boy. How about you Brandon, where do you go skiing?"

"My favorite place is in Idaho not too far from Spokane, Washington. There are several resorts with excellent facilities in winter and beautiful lakes for boating in the summer. You should come for a visit in the future."

"Maybe I will one of these days," Karl replied eagerly. "So, what do you think of the speech Dr. Hanson just gave?" he asked.

"I don't know if I told you, Dr. Hanson is my father. I also strongly feel this country is slipping out of the hands of the Aryan people. The Jews are taking over, and the Negroes are no longer confined to the South, they are creeping up to the North to take our jobs and cavort with our women. I seriously believe we need to preserve our race and expel all the impurities out of our system. The Negroes were brought here to help on the farms but they outlived their usefulness and should be expelled back to Africa where they came from, otherwise the white people will end up a minority in this country."

Despite Karl's growing skepticism, the two guys liked each other's company and exchanged contact information and promised to keep in touch with one another.

The trip was an eye opener for Karl; he watched Dr. Hanson spell out the reasons why the Jews are the enemy of the Aryan people and why they plan to take over the world, using white people as indentured servants to achieve their goal. But he came away with the distinct feeling the approach the group advocated didn't serve their best interest and was not the appropriate path to follow. He recalled the time when he sat with his grandfather to discuss the Jews and Helmut gave him a brief lecture about how best to deal with them. When he compared his grandfather's approach to that of the group, he concluded Helmut has far more wisdom and his approach is more suited to the present.

His father's constant repetition of the same mantra about the Jews and their evil deeds prompted Karl to ask his granddad what he thought. The old man took a deep breath and told him, "Look son, Jews don't have a religion, the only thing they worship is money and Satan. They exploited every nation they lived in. Their aim and dream is to establish a one world government where they place themselves at the top and become masters of the world, and in order to beat them you must outsmart them. Successive leaders throughout history have tried to get rid of them but didn't succeed, and the reason they didn't succeed was because they used the same methods which had failed in the past. The last man to try this method was our great leader Adolf Hitler. The Jews were smarter than he was; they aligned themselves with world powers which proved too powerful for Germany to beat on its own. But now, it is not in your best interest to align yourself against them, they are too powerful. You should never reveal yourself to them, and never show your true feelings. Quite the contrary, what you need to do is learn from them, but don't emulate their bad traits, just see how they do things and learn their methods and crafts. You will never defeat your enemy unless you first know how they think and what they have in their arsenal. When you engage them, find out their strong and weak points, don't disclose how you feel and don't give them reason to suspect you. You need to enamor them and win their affection until they drop their guard. You also need to understand, the Jews are smart; they will smell a ruse a mile away, and they don't let anybody who is not Jewish in their inner circles."

Karl didn't think the Jews were bad people at all. They live in the same world like everybody else and therefore they have the same opportunity like everybody else. Good luck to those who use their chances to serve their best interest; anybody with the same opportunity would be stupid not to.

Karl was assigned to accompany Ricardo when he returned to California after the meeting with the group in Oregon. Oscar wanted his son to learn more about the business, and nobody in the company can be trusted more than Ricardo to pass years of experience on. Ricardo had known Karl since the day he was born and loved him as if he was his own. Now he is a grown man and will someday likely replace his father at the head of the company, so Ricardo was pleased to mentor him.

Ricardo loved to go hunting and camping in the Sierra Nevada Mountains in central California, just few hours ride from LA. Karl expressed a great desire to go with him.

"Sure, you can come with us," Ricardo invited, "I'm going with two other men who work for us. We camp in a tent and it's great fun to be out in the wilderness. But you need to learn how to use a gun first; you also need to get the proper gear to wear in the mountains. I know it is summer, but the weather can turn very suddenly. I have a few extra knives I can give you; you need to learn how to skin your catch and cut it up to eat or for storage, do you understand?"

"Yes sir," Karl answered with enthusiasm, "but where exactly are you planning to go?"

"I like it up in Sequoia National Park, a three hour drive north of LA. The park rangers know us. They are very friendly and helpful, we have to register with them first and let them know where we plan to go and for how long." Karl was excited; he signed up at a shooting range and Ricardo taught him how to use a hunting rifle equipped with a telescopic lens.

One week after Karl signed up for practice shooting, he was so thrilled to be dressed in camouflage and ready to go with Ricardo and the other guys. Ricardo handed him a hunting rifle and gave him ammunition and a knife, but kept the Jack Daniels whisky to himself. Karl felt like a real man in the company of accomplished hunters. The four guys drove north in Ricardo's double cabin truck, with their rifles and guns on a rack attached to the rear window. The scenery was breathtaking as they started their ascent to the mountains. The dusty San Joaquin valley lay behind, and the trees grew larger as they approached the park. Karl has never seen trees this size in his life. The three men took pleasure watching Karl expressing his love of nature and eagerness to start hunting.

After three days in the wilderness, each of the men was able to shoot down a deer, but Karl couldn't stomach killing defenseless animals, and when he spotted one, he pretended to take aim but deliberately missed. Despite the lack of a trophy to show for, he immensely enjoyed the camaraderie, the campfire at night and the early morning twittering of the birds filling the air.

Karl returned to Boston at the end of the summer to start his senior year at Harvard, arriving one day before Sonia. He missed her so much and couldn't wait to go to the airport to pick her up when she arrived from Detroit. He ran to hug her when she emerged through the door and the two lovebirds hugged and kissed in the terminal for several minutes. They stopped for something to eat on the way home and went to bed early that evening, and they didn't emerge from the room till sunrise the following day.

CHAPTER 50

David's interest in politics grew. He was now actively campaigning to raise funds for Ronald Reagan, the ex-governor of California who was running against the incumbent, President Jimmy Carter. David identified more with the Republican party and thought Carter's term in office was disappointing, especially his handling of the Iran hostage crisis.

David told a crowd, "The mullahs in Iran are the enemies of the United States and its allies. They vowed to wipe out Israel and we need a strong president to stand up to those bullies! Carter is a weak president who wants to work with our enemies. We need someone who will not appease our foes but stand up to them and fight with all our might!"

His performance at the rallies drew the attention of the Republican Party senior officials; they invited him to speak at several other gatherings because of his skills and eloquence. David spent much of the year working at the law firm and traveled several times to Iowa to drum up support for his favorite candidate to win the first primary.

Karl and Sonia's senior year at Harvard proved to be the toughest, particularly for Karl. Though the two lived together in the same house they seldom spoke and studying seemed to be all they did. But they wanted to finish their education and get on with their lives. Karl's grandfather and parents called him several times a week to give him support and encouragement and as midterm exams were drawing closer, Helmut called to promise him a brand new Porsche when he graduates from Harvard. The whole family promised to come to the graduation ceremony; so did Sonia's family.

For a brief getaway, Karl asked Sonia if she wanted to go on a ski trip with him during the Christmas break.

"I don't know Karl, I'm not an experienced skier, besides, it is Christmas and we need to be with our families."

"And so we should, but we still can go skiing over the New Year if you wish. To tell you the truth, I met this guy from Spokane last summer and he invited us to go for a vacation there. He talked endlessly about the many ski resorts in the area, especially in Idaho. I think it sounds like fun, what do you think?"

"Okay, why not," she answered cheerfully.

Karl called his friend to confirm he was coming with Sonia, and Brandon was thrilled at the prospect and promised them a memorable vacation.

He was at the airport to meet the couple when they arrived in Spokane, and he drove them to the town of Coeur d'Alene, 40 miles to the east in Idaho. They checked in a hotel overlooking the lake and the following morning, Penny, Brandon's girlfriend, joined them when they drove to the ski resort. Brandon who skied all of his life watched Karl going down the slope with amazement, impressed how skillfully his friend did the run in just a matter of seconds. Over the few days together, the two couples enjoyed the amenities of the resort and cemented their friendship. Brandon and Karl of course didn't talk about the group in Oregon; they knew better not to violate the oath of secrecy they swore to uphold when they joined.

The final semester for Karl and Sonia began in earnest when they returned from Idaho. They came back full of vigor and determination to continue to the finish line, and both had a solid idea where to go and what to do after graduation. Sonia originally thought about continuing her education to get a post graduate degree from Harvard, but changed her mind and opted instead to pursue a career in education. She had to enroll in college first to get the pertinent teaching credentials, and she chose the University of Michigan in Dearborn because of its reputation and proximity to home. She told Karl the love of teaching runs in her blood and nothing in this world gives her more satisfaction than to pass on knowledge to students in a class.

Karl on the other hand decided to go back to LA and join the family's construction business. He told Sonia he has been groomed for this position since a young age and he devoted many years to train on the business fundamentals. "I spent the last few summers shuttling between California and Brazil to train with many staff in our company. I know I have my work cut out for me and must live up to this responsibility and meet the expectations of my family. It will never be easy, their expectations are very high! But I also must tell you, Sonia; I promise when our mega resort project in Las Vegas winds down and I get settled in one location, that I'll come to Detroit and ask for your hand in marriage." He pulled her towards him and gave her a passionate kiss.

Sonia looked at him adoringly. "You're so sweet. I'll be waiting for you Karl. There is nobody else for me; you're the only one I have ever loved. I'm so looking forward to our wedding, and spending the rest of our lives together! I love you so much!"

"Well, we still have awhile to make plans. But in the meantime, are your parents looking forward to have you back in Detroit?"

"Oh my God, yes! My mother is feeling lonely and cannot wait to have me back, and the whole family will be at my graduation too. It will be great for our families to finally meet, won't it? I mean, my brother and your father met for business, but my parents never met yours and I have a distinct feeling my mother wants to meet your parents. I guess she hasn't spoken German in so many years and deep in her heart she loves her own people, and naturally she wants to speak to your dad in their native language."

On the last day of the finals, Karl was the happiest man in the world. He had no illusion the exams would be easy, but he was completely prepared as was Sonia. Both of them thought they did well and expected the results in few days; this is the culmination of their academic careers and soon they will be awarded a diploma from Harvard.

Karl was so happy, he called his family and told them, "I'm done at Harvard, I am now the proud graduate from the best university in the world and I cannot wait to begin my career!"

Helmut was nearly in tears. "I am so proud of you son and I am looking forward to being in Boston for your graduation ceremony. All of us will be there cheering. You are the best, my boy, and we will see you in a few of days!"

Three days before the ceremony, Ingrid and Greg checked into a hotel in Boston. They were thrilled at the chance for the whole family to be together to cheer Sonia when she receives her diploma. Karl's family was also excited he finished his education and promised to take him and Sonia to Europe for a two week vacation after the ceremony. Sonia was full of joy at the prospect; she hadn't been to Europe since she was a child when her parents stopped in London on the way to Israel.

She took her family on a tour of Boston and the surrounding areas and Greg took many photographs. The one Sonia loved most was the one of her wearing her graduation gown, flanked on each side by her mother and Karl.

The picture was taken on a beautiful sunny day in front of the administration building at Harvard; the sun was shining softly on their beaming faces, and it was such a beautiful photo Sonia promised to send a copy to Karl when she returned home.

The night before his family was scheduled to arrive, Karl asked a bunch of friends over to the house in order to bid farewell and swap contact information. Before they got there, Oscar called to advise him they were taking an early morning flight so they have time to relax and maybe get together with Sonia's parents in the evening. "No, problem Dad, Sonia and I will be at the airport when you arrive from LA. Her parents are already here and her brother is coming up from New York tomorrow as well. I think her mother will be excited to meet you and Mom. She probably wants to reminisce about the good old days back in Germany when you two were still young!"

"That is great son; tell her I too look forward to meeting her soon."

Friends arrived at the party and as expected they were in a great mood. They all attended Harvard and had developed great friendships with one another. Karl invited his ice hockey team and Sonia invited her swimming team. Sonia even invited Tracy but she was already gone for the summer to be with her family but she wished Sonia all the best. The guys were in good spirits when they arrived with liquor and beer in hand. Music was blaring all night long, the atmosphere was joyful and convivial and it was after 3 am before the last guest went home. Karl and Sonia also had few drinks. When they'd finished cleaning up, they went to bed feeling very happy. Since Karl's family was not expected until later in the afternoon, they decided they could sleep in as they turned off the lights and snuggled in each other's arms.

Karl looked at the clock; it was approaching 9 a.m. "The God damn phone won't stop ringing! This is the third time in a row!" He wanted to ignore it; nobody calls him at this time. He cursed and struggled to get out of bed. "I bet somebody dialed our number by mistake," he told Sonia as he finally got up to answer it, fully prepared to give the rude person on the other end of the line a piece of his mind. But before he spoke, he could hear his mother and grandmother crying in the background. His heart sank and Sonia noticed how his face turned white. It was Karl's father on the phone; Oscar had been crying.

He choked before he said to his son, "I am sorry. Granddad died this morning. You better come home immediately."

Karl started shaking and screaming. Sonia jumped out of bed, "What is the matter Karl?" On the other end, Oscar was trying to console his son, but Karl lost it. Sonia had never seen him cry before, obviously he was dev-astated, and she didn't know what to do. Unable to speak, he handed Sonia the phone. Oscar told her what had happened and she too, started crying.

"I am very sorry Mr. Silva. Please accept my sincere condolences and sympathy. Yes, whatever you need, whatever Karl needs..."

Helmut and Erika went to sleep early the night before. They asked their driver to be at the house at 4 o'clock in the morning; they lived approxi-mately 25 minutes by car from LAX, so Helmut figured getting up an hour before the chauffer arrives will give them ample time to get ready and make the 6 am flight to Boston. When Scotty Wood, the chauffeur, approached the house in the morning, he could see the lights of emergency vehicles flashing in the dark; the house was perched at the top of a knoll at the end of a long driveway with tall hedges adorning the sides and obscuring it from the street. He felt a little uneasy when he approached and the gate was wide open. Maria the housemaid was standing frantically waving her arms in the middle of the driveway.

"What is wrong, Maria?"

"Oh! Mr. Helmut is sick!"

"Mr. Helmut is very sick!" she repeated. Scotty sped up the driveway and when the house came into view, he could see an ambulance and a police car parked in front. The back doors of the ambulance were swung open, the entrance door to the house was wide open and lights were on everywhere. As Scotty emerged from the car he could see two paramedics carrying what appeared to be Helmut. Erika was walking behind them still in her bathrobe weeping softly.

Scotty dashed towards the ambulance. "What is going on?" he asked frantically.

One of the men wearing a white coat told him, "We need to take Mr. Spiegel to the hospital."

Helmut was already dead when Erika tried to wake him up in the morn-ing, his body didn't move and his face looked unusual. She panicked, she shook him again, but he didn't move. Thinking he had passed out, she called her daughter's house and Oscar immediately called for an ambulance. Gretchen and Oscar stayed on the phone with Erika until the emergency crew arrived but it was too late.

Scotty waited until Erika changed and he got her to the hospital; then 45 minutes later Oscar and his wife arrived. Helmut passed away peacefully in the early hours of the morning the doctor informed them. He had congestive heart failure; he was already dead when he arrived at the hospital, and the doctors could not do anything to help the 84 year old man.

Karl arrived at his grandparents' home that same evening, still in a state of shock. He was particularly close to the old man and what made it worse it happened just one day before his graduation ceremony; he was really looking forward to seeing his grandfather standing up and clapping for him. There wasn't anything wrong with Helmut before he died and he didn't even complain of a headache or pain or anything else, it just happened so suddenly!

Helmut was buried a few days later. Hundreds of people were at his funeral and more than two dozen people flew from Brazil. David and Sonia sent condolence telegrams. Erika could not face going to the house again so she moved in with her daughter. It was such a tragic loss for the family to lose the much loved and admired Helmut.

Sonia was awarded her degree, and her family was there to cheer her on, but she was in a subdued mood. Her mind was with Karl, how much she was looking forward to this day when the two of them would stand on the stage together, their finest moment, receiving the reward for the toil and hard work they had put in. But regretfully the love of her life wasn't there to share her happiness and celebrate the day with her.

Karl stayed a week in LA before he flew back to Boston on his own to receive the degree. Sonia who waited there for him to get back had never seen him so sad in her life. Of course, his family cancelled their trip to Europe, so for the young couple it was time to say goodbye. It was an extremely sad and emotional evening. They lay in bed in each other's arms; she cried on his shoulder and whispered how much she loved him, he stroked her hair and kissed her endearingly. She squeezed him closer to her and held him for several minutes and wouldn't let go.

The following day they were holding hands at the airport. She was crying softly when they finally announced her flight. He held her close and they embraced for a while, then he pulled a small box from his pocket and when he opened it, her eyes widened with amazement. It was a gold ring with beautiful ruby solitaire encircled with diamonds. He took her hand and slipped it on her finger, saying, "This is an affirmation of my love to you my beautiful Sonia. The next one will be the wedding ring." They kissed and kissed again, and she was crying when she waved him goodbye.

Helmut had of course prepared a will before he died: he left fifty percent of everything to his beloved Erika and the other fifty percent to Karl. All his assets are to remain under the guardianship of Oscar and Gretchen until Karl reaches the age of thirty. Erika's assets left to her by her husband will also pass to Karl on her death, so Karl stands to inherit all of his grandparents' wealth at the age of thirty.

True to his word, Karl remained in touch with Sonia, as no other girl interested him. But his focus now was his family's business. The inheritance his grandfather left for him did not go to his head. He continued to get up early with his dad, and he saw no reason to change his car. He had his Porsche shipped from Boston and drove it to work himself in the morning. Oscar on the other hand liked to be driven in his black limo by his personal chauffeur. Karl also stayed at the family's palatial residence. He loved the family atmosphere at home, and soon settled into a routine of working five days a week and spending the weekends at home or going on hunting trips with Ricardo. Sometimes they went to the Sierras and sometimes to the bushy mountains east of LA. He still hated to kill animals, but he enjoyed nature and loved to be in the company of his fun loving Uncle Ricardo.

CHAPTER 51

David received several letters from Republican officials urging him to run for the seat to be vacated by a retiring congressman from NY. David had shown he is an effective campaigner and eloquent speaker; his good looks gave him an advantage especially with female voters, and his religion was a big asset since the district the retiring congressman represented is predominantly Jewish. He read the letters with incredulity; he liked the campaigning part but he has been doing it for the benefit of other politicians whose messages resonated with him. He was neither a politician nor did he have political ambitions of his own, and being a partner in a busy and successful law firm was already gratifying. Doing very well, Nancy and David now lived in a spacious high-rise unit with a spectacular view of the Manhattan skyline. Nancy was happy and proud her husband provided the standard of living to which she was accustomed and they had the material possessions to show for their elevated financial status. The vacation property they purchased in Long Island was another testimony of their wealth. Life was good and comfortable and David was well respected among the lawyers of NY. The marine salvage lawsuit had given him national exposure, so now the phone calls and letters kept coming in to urge him to run for political office. Two officials from the Republican Party were head over heels when they came in for a chat.

"We have observed how skillfully you speak and how well you deliver the message, and we are happy to advise you of the great opportunity available to you to win a congressional seat. Should you decide to run for election to represent Brooklyn and New York in Congress, we strongly believe you will make a good legislator in Washington where you will have direct influence on the course of this nation. You can try it for one term, and if you don't like it, you can always go back to practicing law. And of course, should you decide to run, we will provide you all the help you need--money and volunteers, etc. We can also engage prominent Republicans to campaign on your behalf or appear with you at campaign rallies, including the president himself!"

When David came home in the evening he looked unusually haggard. He didn't go to play with little Daniel as usual, but instead he lay on the couch and turned the TV on to one of the news channels. This in itself was not out of the ordinary; David had always been interested in the news and he followed US politics diligently. Nancy who was busy in the kitchen came to see what the matter was with her husband.

"Hello darling," she sat next to him on the couch, "are you alright?"

"Yes I'm alright, I am just tired, and to tell you the truth I'm exhausted mentally."

"You said you wanted to be a lawyer, this law business will stress you out honey! Can I get you anything?"

"No, I don't need anything. The law business doesn't tire me, its people who stress me out. I have been getting phone calls and letters and visits from Republican Party officials urging me to run for office."

"What office are you talking about, David?"

"They want me to run for a seat in the US Congress to represent the district in Brooklyn; the incumbent representative is retiring at the end of his term."

"Brooklyn, is it not traditionally Democrat?" Nancy commented with curiosity.

"You are right darling, it is." David answered, "But the officials who came to see me believe I stand a good chance to win the seat from the Democrats if I were to run on the Republican ticket."

"How do you feel about it yourself?"

"I don't know...I enjoy being a lawyer, it is what I have wanted to do since I was little. But on the other hand I feel I could be an effective legislator and help frame the policy and the destiny of this country."

"Well, why don't you run then? I fancy being married to a congressman; I'll get to see you on TV!" Nancy said jokingly.

"I don't know if I should or not, maybe I should seek the advice of my partners and gauge how they feel."

David spoke to each of his partners the following day and explained the encouragement he has been receiving and the Republican representatives' visit. He was utterly taken aback by their response; they were unanimous in their support and encouraged him to run. "We don't want to lose you David, but maybe this is your calling! Perhaps the country needs people of your caliber in congress. You will be a brilliant legislator and we are certain you will be the better representative in your district, and don't worry, your position in the firm will be yours when you want it back."

So David picked up the phone and called Al Gossamer, the Republican official who came to his office. "Okay Al," David started, "I'm in and glad to give it my best shot!"

"I am very delighted to hear it, David. I think your chances to extricate the Democrats from Brooklyn are pretty good, and with a candidate like you, the Democrats won't know what is coming their way."

It was the landmark marine salvage case that brought David to Al Gossamer's attention. He followed his legal career with interest and was impressed when he heard him speak in favor of Ronald Reagan. Al was a lawyer himself; he could easily spot talent and he recognized David's ability to deliver a good and effective speech. His oral prose was beyond question and he had the magical talent to communicate his message to a crowd with charm and panache, and though David has the right personality and the essential qualifications, Al had no illusion the hotly contested congressional seat in Brooklyn would be difficult to win and the odds were against the Republicans.

Al Gossamer arrived at David's office in a jovial mood and the two men sat to discuss options and strategies. Al drew David's attention to the basic requirements needed for a successful campaign. "You must first announce in public your intention to run, and file a petition with the NY secretary of state in Albany. Then you have to arrange for a campaign manager and work on getting staff and volunteers..."

David appreciated the visit. He already knew most of the stuff Al told him but was most appreciative of the names he suggested to manage the campaign, and decided to interview a few in the coming days.

The following day, Al filed the necessary forms with the Secretary of State, and David spent most of the day working and strategizing to move the fledgling campaign forward. The last thing he did before he went home was to call his family in Detroit, waiting until Greg got home from work before he made the call. Ingrid answered the phone.

"Hello Mother, how are you doing?"

"I'm cooking up a storm. Sonia wants all kinds of goodies for dinner, but it is great to hear your voice son. Are Nancy and Daniel doing alright?"

"Yes, Mother they are doing just fine. I wanted to give you a call to break some important news. Is Dad there?"

"He's in the other room. Sonia is right here."

"Well, your son is running for a seat in the house of representatives of the United States!"

"What is the House of Representatives, David? You're not changing your job again, are you?"

"Mother, I am running for Congress in Washington, I would like to be a congressman for the district of Brooklyn in NY."

"Oh, my God, David is going to be a politician!" She shouted loud enough for Greg to hear. "I am so excited for you son, but when will you become a congressman?"

"Oh Mother, I have to be elected first, it will be approximately eleven more months before the election. I have to campaign and convince the voters that I am their best choice to represent them in Washington."

"This is wonderful news, David, here, tell your sister about it, she can explain it to me later."

Ingrid was excited as the family gathered round her and each had a turn listening to David spell his intention to become a politician. The whole family was very supportive of his efforts to run for political office Sonia even volunteered to put her studies on hold and come to NY to help him. "I don't believe in the Republican Party," she told him, "but for you, big brother, I'll do anything!"

"Thanks Sonia, but that won't be necessary. You need to concentrate on your studies."

Sonia stayed in Detroit with her family after she signed up for a two year master's degree in education at U of M, Dearborn, and once the program is completed, she will have the necessary qualifications for a teaching position in the school district.

Life was good in Detroit for Sonia. Her father and brother pitched in together and bought her a small car as a graduation present. She kept in touch with Karl, in fact they spoke on the phone every single night and took mini vacations to Hawaii and Idaho, and so they remained passionately in love and firmly attached to each other.

Sonia was pleased to be back at her church, and Father O'Malley welcomed her with open arms. "Glad to see you are with us again and congratulations for the Harvard achievement! We really missed you when you were away in college, and we hope you will be staying here for a while."

"Me too, Father. I missed mass and bible studies so much and cannot wait to start again." Sonia volunteered for all the church activities, she even helped with the weekly cleaning of the church grounds and attended mass every Sunday on her own. She tried to talk her father into going but Greg confessed he was not too much into church.

Indignant, Sonia cautioned him about the consequences of not going to church. "How could you say that, Dad? We all have to face our Creator one day. You need to be close to our Lord, Jesus Christ," and she quoted, "Blessed are those who believe in Lord Jesus and follow his commands."

She called Karl after David announced he was running for political office.

"This is incredible news Sonia, you must be proud of your brother!"

"Sure I am, but not half as proud as my mother. She is over the moon with excitement. She even asked David if he was eligible to run for Congress when his mother was a Holocaust survivor."

Karl laughed out loud at the incongruous comment. "I think David will do well, even my own father thinks he is brilliant." Karl told Sonia how much he missed her and how much he loved her and expressed a great desire to see her. "Can I invite you out to LA for few days' vacation, all expenses paid?"

"I wish I could, Karl. I have less than two months before I finish college and I am planning to spend the rest of the summer looking for a job in different school districts."

"But you have been working so hard in college the past two years; a little break wouldn't hurt, would it?"

"No, it wouldn't, but I already worked on my planner and this summer will be rather impossible. I need to find an inspiring work atmosphere before I take a vacation."

"How about I come there instead? We can take a long weekend, maybe sometime in the middle of summer?"

"That's a great idea Karl, I'd love to see you, and we can even drive to the Upper Peninsula."

"What is the Upper Peninsula?" Karl asked. Sonia laughed as she explained Michigan geography to him, and described some places they might visit.

A week later, he couldn't wait for the plane to touch down at Detroit Metro airport. Sonia was there waiting, and as soon as he walked out in the passenger lobby, the two lovers embraced; he was so excited to see her he lifted her off her feet and with hands clasped round her back he squeezed tight, telling her how much he loved and missed her. "You look so beautiful! I just can't take my eyes off you!"

"You too look so handsome and I love you and miss you more than anything in this world!" she said once he gave her room to breathe. Sonia then drove him around town and showed him the many attractions the city has to offer. They arranged to travel to the Upper Peninsula the following day and Karl suggested, "Why don't you ask your folks if they wish to come with us tomorrow?"

"Sure I can, my mother would love to come, she hasn't seen the UP before."

Sonia's parents accepted the invitation to go for a small vacation to the north part of the state, and were pleased to see Karl in the morning when they picked him up. He was now considered a member of the family and everybody simply loved him and firmly expected he and Sonia will be married in the future.

Greg headed up I-75 out of Detroit. Their first stop was at the little town of Frankenmuth, where they had lunch and visited Bavarian Village, the largest Christmas store in the world. Ingrid was so taken with the small town, and everywhere she looked something reminded her of pleasant times with her parents when she was a little girl. Karl was mesmerized by the display of lights and Christmas decorations from all over and he purchased gifts for his mother to brighten the atmosphere over the holidays. They continued the drive north and when they reached the Mackinac Bridge, the famous suspension bridge connecting the lower and the Upper peninsulas, they pulled over at the welcome center vista and walked around admiring the beautiful scene before them. Both Ingrid and Karl were impressed by the long bridge and the cascading landscape straddling the lakes. Camera in hand, Greg asked Karl to stand with his wife and daughter, and then another tourist offered to take the picture for all of them with the bridge soaring above the water in the background. They walked all the way around the visitors' center and stopped for ice cream before they reached the town of Sault Ste. Marie at the northern tip of the UP peninsula on the Canadian border. Right on the waterway they sat in the observation deck to watch cargo ships go through the lock system that adjoins Lake Superior and Lake Huron. It was informative to see the locks fill up with water in order to allow ships to float up and down from lower to higher elevation. Over the following two days they toured the rest of the Upper Peninsula before they drove back to Detroit, very tired but happy with the memorable time they spent together.

Sonia took Karl to meet Father O'Malley at her Catholic Church and the gentle priest stood up to greet them. "Hello Sonia," Father O'Malley put his hand out to shake her hand, "and who do I have the pleasure to meet with you today?"

"Sorry Father, this is my boyfriend Karl, he and I studied at Harvard together."

"Welcome my son; I hope you will be joining our congregation."

"I wish I could Father. I am in Detroit for a brief visit to see Sonia, but I promise to come to mass next time I am in town."

"Bless you my son, we will be glad to have you."

Sonia graduated from University of Michigan with a Master's degree in education and was quickly recruited by the Detroit school board to teach English at a high school near Dearborn. She settled into a routine and loved to stimulate her students to excel in school; she often took them on trips to visit places of interest or to listen to motivational speakers in different parts of the city.

Ingrid too was happy with her life. She liked having Sonia around; mother and daughter were very close and often sat in the backyard to rest and to chat with one another. During one of these conversations, Ingrid brought up the subject of marriage with Sonia.

"I see you are not interested to go out and enjoy yourself, how on earth you expect to make friends or meet a future husband?"

"You know, Mother, there is only one man for me. I intend to marry Karl and there will be nobody else. He is the love of my life and I know in my heart he will marry me in the future and I want to wait for him."

"How long are you planning to wait Sonia? What if Karl doesn't come knocking at your door?" You are a pretty girl and many men dream to have somebody like you."

Mother, I will not marry another man but Karl. I am prepared to stay single for the rest of my life if he doesn't propose. That is my final decision and I am not going to change my mind, period."

Ingrid knew better not to challenge her daughter, but she couldn't fathom her unwillingness to explore different opportunities just in case Karl's option doesn't materialize at the end. But she dropped the subject; Sonia can be stubborn.

CHAPTER 52

After interviewing several potential candidates for the job of campaign manager, David picked Norman Wolf, a veteran of the Republican Party machine with wide experience managing political campaigns. He was an elderly gentleman from Newark, New Jersey, who began his career as an electrical engineer for Bell Labs. At the age of 30 he joined a consulting firm in NY to be part of the team which rendered services to commercial broadcasting networks in the eastern United States. There he developed a lifelong love for journalism and broadcasting and became intensely interested in politics. He volunteered to help Richard Nixon in his 1960 presidential bid, but Nixon lost the election by a very thin margin. In 1968, Nixon prevailed; Wolf continued in this line of work and successfully helped several other state and federal representatives get elected to office. He and David shared a strong anticommunist views, and both believed in the special place America must have amongst the nations of the world. Norman was bullheaded and knew his business well and had a broad range of important contacts. His biggest asset however, was his relationship with the media bosses and news journalists.

Norman assembled an impressive campaign staff and prepared a list of fundraisers to call and solicitations letters to mail. He also arranged for David to speak before many volunteers and well-wishers to announce his candidacy for the United States House of Representatives. All major TV stations in NYC carried it live and so did most newspapers covering the story. *The New Yorker* magazine ran an interview with David, where he pledged to fight for the interests of New York, maintain peace and prosperity for all Americans and promised to do all he could to reduce the national debt which had reached unprecedented levels. He also talked about America's dangerous enemies, especially the Soviet Union.

"Communism is a grave danger to our way of life, not only for us here in the US, but for all our allies. We must not ignore this threat but take a firm stand and fight it wherever it attempts to creep into our hemisphere."

But after two months on the trail, polls still showed David behind the other candidates in the field; in fact he was dead last. Marven Crystal, the Democratic rival firmly believed the election fight will be a cakewalk against a novice politician like David, and recent polls suggested he was many percentage points ahead, but to David's credit the people of Brooklyn warmed up to him and numbers slowly began to improve in David's favor.

Oscar called David to congratulate him on his political ambitions; he was full of praise and pledged to send a campaign contribution. David thanked him, and when the check arrived in the mail from Oscar, it was one of the largest single contributions he received from any individual. Money however, wasn't a problem. As a matter of fact he was puzzled by the amounts pouring in from so many different sources; all the law firm partners gave hefty amounts, his father-in-law and some of his old professors and even fellow students from Yale sent contributions. Norman was able to use this money deftly; he ran ads in the newspapers and on TV, organized rallies and sent letters to all the people on the state voters' list and arranged for David to appear on TV talk shows and conduct interviews with newspaper and magazines.

David's good looks worked greatly to his advantage since the Democratic opponent was a balding man of little stature and marginal appearance. This was evident when the two debated for the first time before a live audience. The Democratic opponent was no match for David and appeared rather awkward and pathetic in comparison. The poll numbers start to improve steadily after the second debate when David's power of argument was on full display; he spoke with discipline and a lawyerly tone and came across as a man of authority and leadership. His coming from behind was truly Herculean after some newspapers had written him off at the beginning of the race. The debates however, made the newspaper editors look again at this formidable candidate, and on the eve of the election, David was neck and neck with his opponent and most pundits gave him and his rival equal chance to win the race.

Sonia and her parents came to NY to be with David on election night. Early returns were not good and showed him behind and he had a lot of catching up to do, but by late afternoon things started to improve. David and his party checked in at a hotel in the early evening to watch the election updates on TV. The room was tense, but nobody was as taut as Ingrid. She sat in one corner and prayed for her son; she wanted him to win, she wanted to be proud and wanted him to make a name for himself.

Results were still coming in and both candidates were within hundreds of votes of each other, and just before midnight one of the local TV stations put a bulletin out: "We are ready to declare a winner in just few minutes, please stay tuned; we will be back after this short break for the national results." It was very tense inside the room. Ingrid covered her face with her hands and peeked between her fingers, but she didn't have to cover her face too long. The room erupted in deafening applause when David was declared the winner!

David and Nancy moved to Washington and settled in an apartment not too far from Capitol Hill. When David assumed his duty as a freshman representative from NY he and other new members were sworn in by Tip O'Neal, the House Speaker. He spent the first few weeks in office meeting with constituents and discussing different issues ranging from increased funding for Medicaid to the financial woes plaguing New York City; there was need for continued funding from the Department of Housing to meet the growing demand for affordable dwellings. The Democrats proposed budget cuts in the department which according to city officials would have a devastating effect on people with low incomes. David pledged to work hard with other Republican members to block the cuts from being implemented. He was a passionate advocate to keep America strong; he backed the president's strategic defense initiative and supported a massive budget to strengthen the Defense Department.

Oscar, Karl and Ricardo were in Las Vegas for the ribbon cutting ceremony of the new hotel casino they had just finished building. After carefully interviewing more than a dozen casino and resort operators, they eventually settled on Monarch International LLG, a multinational hospitality and casino operator with experience in North America and the Far East. The newly finished casino will be called Monarch Resort, a five star hotel with a large gaming area adjoined to outlet stores and restaurants in a beautiful tropical setting, with waterfalls and dazzling lights. The opening day saw throngs of people lining up to see the new addition to the famous Las Vegas Strip; it didn't take long before the massive floor was filled to capacity. People's first impression of the casino was genuinely commendable and praiseworthy. The atmosphere was happy and festive, and Oscar and his entourage mingled with the crowd and gave an interview with the local newspaper which hailed the project a huge success.

Karl called Sonia and told her about the great grand opening they had in Las Vegas. "The last few months were hectic trying to meet the deadline. I am utterly exhausted but happy it's over. I can't wait to see you soon, sweetheart," he said to her before finishing the call.

PART 3

CHAPTER 53

David's first term in office went smoother than expected, he was by now a seasoned politician with good track record and the voters of New York were satisfied with his performance to serve them. He had many supporters and was comfortably re-elected for a second and third term. Ingrid couldn't hide her pride in her son when she visited him in Washington. She and Greg stayed with Nancy and little Daniel at their apartment, and it was a much happier occasion than her first visit when she came to care for David while recuperating at Walter Reed Hospital. David was now an important politician who earned the respect of his peers and foes alike. He was a popular member of the judiciary committee, and many colleagues sought his advice on legal issues. He represented his district with honor and vigor, and never compromised on his core values when it came to the benefit of his constituency or the security of the United States where many considered him a hawk.

"I will never drop my guard against the Communists and the enemies of this great nation," he declared, "our armed forces are the solid foundation upon which this country is built and prospered, they are our defense against foreign enemies and a great comfort when we go to sleep at night knowing they are watching over us."

A few months after his mother returned home, David received a phone call from Sonia. She sounded very upset.

"What is wrong Sonia?" he asked with a soothing voice.

"It's mother," she answered in a panic.

"Why, what's the problem?"

"A few weeks back, Mother showed me a little swelling under her arm. I urged her to see the doctor immediately, but she refused, and dad begged her to go but you know your mother, she said no, I will be fine, don't you worry about me, the swelling will go away."

"So what's happening now?" David asked impatiently.

"Mother is losing weight rapidly and she is not eating well. I made her a little plate of vegetables in the afternoon and she won't even finish it. She is breaking out in a sweat at night and constantly itching on her feet and legs. I took a day off from school to take her to the hospital, but she won't go. Will you please talk to her?"

"Put her on the phone," David ordered.

"Hello David, good to hear your voice, son."

"Hello Mother, how you doing, are you feeling okay?"

"Well, I guess so, it is this sweating at night and the damn itch won't go away."

David could hear Sonia's voice in the background. "No mother, you don't look well to me!"

"Mother, why don't you listen to the people who love you and go for a checkup at the hospital, there is no harm in that, is there?"

"I guess not, David, but I don't like hospitals; I'll call my doctor and make an appointment, if it pleases you."

"Yes Mother, please do that. We love you so much, we don't want to see you sick."

Sonia called and made an appointment with the family doctor. Ingrid was losing weight at an alarming rate and didn't look well or seem to have any appetite and her face looked drawn and pale. Greg took his wife to see doctor Stanley Rogers, who had been the family doctor for more than twenty years; his practice was only minutes' drive from their house.

"Good morning Mrs. McKay, how are you?" The doctor greeted when she walked in.

"I am a little tired doctor, and my husband and children insisted I come see you."

"What seems to be the problem?"

Ingrid showed him the swelling under her arm and on her neck. The doctor put his hand on the swelling and applied a little pressure, "Does it hurt you?"

"Just a little," she softly answered, "the problem is my sweat. I am drenched when I wake up and sometimes I get a little fever."

"How is your appetite?" the doctor asked.

"It's not the best, I don't know why; I just don't feel hungry anymore."

"You look like you have lost some weight since the last time you were here."

"Yes, I have doctor, but I don't know how much."

The doctor wrote her a prescription, and gave her a requisition to do some tests at the lab. "I would like you to make an appointment to see me again in ten days."

Ingrid went to the lab to do the tests the following day. David called in the evening to check on his mother. "How did your visit to the doctor go?" he asked.

"It went alright son, he didn't say much, he just asked some questions and had me do lab tests and gave me medicine. I will be fine David, don't worry about me."

When Ingrid went to see Dr. Rogers for a follow up visit, the doctor told her the test results showed some abnormalities and ordered her to go home and rest. Somebody from Dr. Morgan's office will be calling you," he told her.

"Who is Doctor Morgan?" she asked.

"Dr. Morgan is an oncologist. He will be examining you further; we need to find the reason for your swelling. It has not responded well to the medicine I gave you. Dr. Morgan is a very nice and competent doctor; you don't have to fear anything."

David received another call from Sonia, two weeks before Christmas. She was crying this time. "What is the problem, little sister, are you alright?"

"Mother is not well at all, you better come home, David."

"Calm down Sonia, what seems to be the problem this time? I spoke with her last night and she said she was alright," David answered.

"No, David, Dr. Morgan has diagnosed mother with lymphoma. He ordered a biopsy and an MRI scan." David was listening intently to his sister, who was trying very hard to control her emotions. He was very concerned about both of them.

"Okay Sonia, let me speak with mother, please."

"I am here in Dad's office; I didn't call you from home. I didn't want mother to hear my conversation with you."

"Then let me speak to Dad, please."

Greg came on the phone; he was very emotional and he too sounded like he had been crying. "Hello David," he said, barely audible.

"Hello Dad, what is going on?"

"You heard it from Sonia, your mother has stage two lymphoma and her fevers are getting worse already."

"Alright Dad, I am coming home to Detroit tonight."

He arrived at nearly midnight. Ingrid still didn't know the details and seriousness of her illness, but she was so happy to see her son. "I am glad you are here David, but you didn't have to leave your work for my sake! I will be just fine, your dad and sister are making it sound worse than it actually is."

David fought back tears; she always placed her feelings behind everybody else. "She is the strong one in the family, I don't know what I will do if I lose my mother, I worship the ground she walks on," he told his sister.

Dr. Morgan's secretary came into his office the moment he walked in. "There is a gentleman on the phone who wants to speak to you, Doctor. He said he was a congressman from NY; his name is David McKay."

Dr. Morgan didn't even know Ingrid's son was a congressman, but the name sounded familiar. He picked up the phone. "This is Dr. Morgan, how may I help you?"

David introduced himself and asked the doctor about his mother's condition. "I am sorry Mr. McKay, but your mother has a serious issue. She has been diagnosed with a rare form of cancer which affects her immune system. But the good news is we caught it early and she stands a good chance to beat the disease with a combination of chemotherapy and immunotherapy. Our last resort will be radiation to target the infected area if all else fails. Her family doctor indicated your mother is a tough lady, and I am optimistic the odds to treat her successfully are good."

"Yes doctor, my mother is very tough lady indeed. After all, she is a holocaust survivor." David stated.

He set out to change the solemn mood in the house; everybody expressed too much concern and sadness over Ingrid's situation, so he insisted they change direction. "What we need to do from now on is to provide mother with a happy atmosphere, and be cheerful and positive around her. We need to give her all the support we possibly can and stand with her until she is well again."

CHAPTER 54

David gathered with his advisors the week after he made his announcement to run for the Governor of New York. During the meeting he set the agenda to focus on three things and make them the core of his campaign; prominent issues New Yorkers felt strongly about were the struggling economy, the financial stagnation and the record unemployment. The candidate who offers the best solution to get out of this economic mess is the one who stands the biggest chance with the voters. One way to achieve this goal is to petition the US Congress to allocate more funds for the construction of mega projects for the people of New York, and to use his connections in the house to make this goal a reality. His ratings in the polls steadily increased after he stumped in various cities in the state, and people where pleased to gather in great numbers to hear him deliver his message. Big donors gave large checks as did major financial institutions; they believed in one of their own to lead the state through this difficult time. Several knew him personally when he worked for JP Morgan and were assured by his ability after they witnessed his performance in Congress.

Oscar arrived in NY with Gretchen on their way to the Caribbean, and he dropped by to see Mr. Stanly for another legal consultation before their departure. As their meeting was wrapping up, Mr. Stanly asked, "Why don't you join us, Mr. Silva; we are throwing a big surprise party for David's 40th birthday. It will also be an opportunity to raise money for his campaign, I am sure he will be delighted to see you!"

"I wish I could Mr. Stanly, but I am already booked on a flight to Puerto Rico. Please wish him a happy birthday from me. By the way, I cannot believe he is forty! He has such a youthful face. I am sure his family must be proud of his achievements, he certainly has done well for himself."

Oscar and Karl arrived home in Los Angeles after the scheduled meeting with the group in Oregon, where Dr. Hanson delivered a lecture and showed a movie to the audience highlighting the treachery of the Jews and the need to accelerate the recruiting drive to increase membership in the group. The

Doctor explained their finances are getting stronger by the day thanks to the many big donors who joined lately. "However," he cautioned, "we must embark on a concerted drive to get young men and women join our group and begin combat and guerrilla warfare training. We need to establish a little army to serve as the nucleus for the Aryan Race to march behind and deal with the Jewish problem once and for all. We need to establish our own little fighting force to eradicate these cockroaches and get rid of them one by one until they all disappear and forever vanish from our beloved country!"

Karl was listening with little enthusiasm but Brandon Hanson, the doctor's son, was listening to his father with great interest and determination, and when his dad finished he was the first on his feet cheering with arms raised up in a show of strength and solidarity with the message.

After the lecture finished, Karl and Brandon went out for lunch. Karl didn't have the courage to reveal how he felt about the group to his friend and wished Brandon didn't have that much hate in his heart, but obviously he did, and Karl saw no point to trying to change his mind for fear he will be exposed and expelled from the group. He knew how important the group was to his father and he didn't want to let him down, but despite this outward show of rancor he found Brandon a really nice person and he considered him a good friend. He thought the time not right to say anything. Perhaps in the future he will ask Brandon what the Jews did to him personally to earn this much hate. David believed that after all, they are humans like us, and given the opportunity we probably would do no different than what they do. They happen to be more organized and work in tandem, and we would be better off to emulate their good deeds instead of hating them altogether.

As the two of them sat in a little restaurant talking and reminiscing about the good time they had together on the ski slopes in Idaho, Brandon told Karl he and Penny were getting married in few weeks and invited him and Sonia to come to Chicago for the wedding, as Penny was originally from the Windy City and her family still live there. Karl accepted the invitation and promised to attend.

Karl sat at his office desk looking at Sonia's photos which he had framed. There was this beautiful one of him and her with their arms around each other's shoulders. He loved that one the most; it was taken just after they started dating. Another favorite photo was of him standing with Sonia and her parents with the Mackinac Bridge in the background, but the photo he treasured most was taken in front of the admin building at Harvard with him, Sonia and Ingrid. The picture was taken by Greg when the family came to Boston for the graduation ceremony. There were many other favorites of his grandparents and several others of him and his parents that Karl loved to look at; they reminded him of the people he loved and the happy times he spent with them. He was particularly proud of one photo on the wall of him and Uncle Ricardo dressed in hunting gear with rifles strapped to their shoulders. There was yet another photo of him and Elsa, hugging on his high school graduation.

It was Christmas and the holiday season was in full swing. He always loved this time of the year and he wished he was with his parents. They called the day before from Puerto Rico. "Wish you were with us son! It is even more beautiful this time than the last time we were here, and the weather reminds us of Porto Alegre in springtime, nice and warm and not too hot." He loved his parents and thought they are the best parents in the world.

When Karl received the wedding invitation from his friend Brandon, he immediately called Sonia. It was Saturday lunch time and he just caught her as she was preparing to go to bible class.

"Hello love," she said with a big smile when she heard his warm voice.

"Hello Sonia, how is your mother doing?"

"Mother is improving a little but the medicine is making her feel ill. The doctor warned her it might make her sick before she gets better."

"Oh, well please tell her I'm thinking about her. By the way, you and I have been invited to go to Brandon and Penny's wedding next month in Chicago. Would you like to come?"

"I would like to, but Chicago is a little over four hours' drive from Detroit, and I won't be able to make it on time after I finish on Friday afternoon."

"The wedding is on a Saturday evening," Karl responded, "and I can fly to Detroit on Friday to spend a night with you and the following day we can drive together to the wedding, then drive you back on Sunday."

"I don't want to miss mass on Sunday, Karl, I have been telling my students at school how important it is in the eyes of the Lord to attend church on Sundays and I shouldn't be a hypocrite and miss it myself."

"You don't have to miss it honey, we will leave Chicago first thing Sunday and we will be in Detroit in time for mass."

A few weeks later, Karl picked Sonia as planned and the two attended the beautiful wedding and reception in Chicago before driving back the following day to Detroit. Karl went to mass with her and on their way out Father O'Malley came to thank him for the large contribution he gave the church.

The priest took that opportunity to have a little chat with them. "You two really suit one another, I wonder if you have any plans for the future?"

Karl was quick to respond. "We do indeed father! Sonia is the love of my life and I cannot imagine life without her. We want to get married when the time is right, probably in the next few months, and I would like to ask if you would officiate our wedding at your beautiful church if you don't mind."

"Of course not, on the contrary it would be my honor and I look forward to the happy occasion soon."

Sonia was in tears after the conversation with the priest. "Did you mean that Karl? Are you really thinking we can get married soon?"

"Sonia, I love you so much. You are the most precious thing in my life and yes, of course I want to marry you soon! You and I have been waiting more than seven years, it is definitely the right time for both us and I cannot wait for you and I to be together forever. I hate this separation."

"So, when are you thinking, Karl?"

"Well, my parents are globetrotting at the moment; they were in Puerto Rico last week, and they stopped in Martinique for few days before they head to Brazil. I understand my father has important issues at our marine shipping company and is likely to stay there for the next two months and when they return I intend to talk to my folks about my wedding plans. The whole family will come to Detroit so we can officially ask for your hand from your family."

"Oh, that sounds so nice! You are so thoughtful and I applaud you for doing things the traditional way; my mother will appreciate that. And by the way she is genuinely eager to meet your parents. She's heard so much about your father from David and I."

Karl had stopped at a jeweler in Beverly Hills before he came to Detroit and when he took her home from mass he presented her with a gorgeous string of pink pearls he specially ordered. As he fastened it round Sonia's neck, her heart melted. Looking in the mirror she exclaimed, "My God, they look amazingly beautiful! I love you Karl! I love you so much!"

David called Oscar after the New Year to thank him for the money contribution and the birthday present he received. "Hello Mr. Silva and happy New Year to you, sir!"

"Happy New Year to you, David! I wish you all the best in your bid to become the next Governor of New York. You deserve to be in high office, you are smart and have been very dedicated to your home district. Gretchen and I wish you all the best."

David responded in kind. "Well first of all, I thank you for the birthday present; I was touched, it really warmed my heart. I also want to express gratitude for the contribution to my campaign. We have tremendous support from the community and they are excited to see me run for Governor, but it is not going to be easy. On a personal note, my mother, who is only 65 years old, was recently diagnosed with cancer, and I must stand with her during this terrible time. She certainly sacrificed enough to bring me up and helped me be the man I am."

"I am sorry to hear about your mother, David. I wish her well and a speedy recovery; please convey my best wishes to her."

Oscar and Gretchen continued to Brazil after their holiday to tackle important issues which required decisions at the highest level of management. The tremendous increase in the volume of the marine cargo business was anticipated but the old calculations about the eleven cargo ships purchased a few years back was off the mark; back then they figured the purchase deal would satisfy the demand for the next dozen years, but they were wrong with their estimate. Business according to their manager, Manuel Alvarado, was booming, and the entire fleet was operating at full capacity. It reached the stage where additional cargo business was turned away just like it did before the last ship acquisition. Oscar decided to spend a few months in Porto Alegre to find alternate solutions to cope with this steep increase in business activity without having to make additional purchases. From what he was reading in specialty cargo magazines, the ship building industry was experiencing a backlog in the ship building yards, and used ships available for sale were scarce. In order to alleviate the problem and cope with the increased demand for cargo space, Oscar, as a first measure ordered the installation of newer and more efficient cargo handling equipment at the port facilities designated exclusively for their own fleet.

"The faster we load and unload the cargo the less time the ships have to stay at the port," he told Senor Alvarado, "this way you save time and speed up the entire operation." He decided to stay in Brazil to observe the outcome of the new installation.

Gretchen too was busy; she was invited to attend the wedding of Elena, Elsa's sister, who was getting married to the operator of a small motel in

Tucson, Arizona. Jose, the groom to be, was originally from Mexico. He started his career as a laborer in the construction business when he came to Tucson and over the years saved enough for a down payment to buy a dilapidated motel which he spent considerable time repairing in his spare time; in a matter of a few years he was able to turn the motel into a thriving business along a busy freeway. While on vacation in Brazil he met Elena where she was working as a receptionist in a hotel near the Iguazu Falls, and after two years of courtship the two decided to get married. Elsa was so excited her sister was coming to live nearby in Arizona.

Gretchen and the whole family loved Elsa, she had been in their employment since Karl was a baby, and they trusted her to be his guardian during his schooldays in Boston. Once he was in boarding school, she continued to work for the family at their California house, and became the unofficial head of the household staff. She was considered part of the family and Gretchen was obligated to attend the wedding and present the bride with a nice wedding gift as a token of appreciation to Elsa's many years of good service and devotion.

Karl was very excited when he returned to LA. With Sonia constantly on his mind, he decided to take the plunge and ask his father's permission to marry her. He believed strongly in tradition and though he was a mature adult and needed no permission from his family to marry, he nevertheless recognized the value in having the family bless the marriage. However Karl was entirely cognizant of the huge stumbling block facing him; how can he reconcile his father's visceral hate for the Jews when his bride to be was born to a Jewish mother? He was sure it will upset his father terribly; he may even condemn him as a traitor to his own race or disown him all together and banish him from the house. Karl agonized for a while on the best method to approach his father. He counted on the fact the family was fond of Sonia and on their belief she was the right girl for him. His family was also aware Sonia belonged to the Christian faith and she loves Jesus Christ just as much as they do, furthermore, Oscar has an ongoing relationship with Sonia's brother, David, whom he professed to like and admire. All those things when added tip the scale in Sonia's favor. As he pondered his chances to succeed he concluded they are poor at best, especially after seeing his father cheering at the group's meetings in Oregon, but he decided to give it a try when his parents return home from their extended trip to Brazil.

He determined his best chance to convince his dad is to approach him on a day when things are going well and tell him everything. He must urge him to at least take another look at Sonia's mother. This meek and gracious person who happened to have been born Jewish doesn't pose the slightest danger to anybody let alone the whole Aryan race. Besides, the intention is to marry Sonia and not her mother, and Sonia has consciously abandoned her Jewish faith to become a devout Christian on her own accord. More importantly, her core beliefs are no different to him or his dad, therefore, there is no harm in marrying a girl whose fundamental convictions are the same as your own, and there will be no complications in the future should they decide to have children since both parents are Christians.

Sonia was so happy after Karl left for LA, she returned home with a big smile, her face was beaming with happiness and contentment and her mother noticed her mood first then she spotted the beautiful string of pearls round her neck.

"Those pearls are really pretty Sonia, are they real?"

"Of course mother they are real, do you think Karl will buy me a fake present?"

"I didn't think he would, but you two have been going out for seven years and nothing serious has happened. Is it going to be just presents to compensate for the empty promises?"

"No mother, Karl told me he and his family are planning to come to Detroit to ask for my hand in marriage soon. He even repeated the same thing to Father O'Malley when we went to mass this afternoon."

"Well, that's something, but when is 'soon'?"

"I don't know exactly, but his family is away on extended business trip and Karl promised when they return he will organize a trip to Detroit in just few months, and I'll be waiting for him. I cannot tell you how much I want to be married, Mother. I love him so much!"

"I know you do, Sonia, and I hope the wait is worth it. I just want you to be happy, my girl, and give me lots of children! Please promise you will."

"Well, of course. I love children myself and I want to have as many as I possibly can," Sonia answered self-consciously.

Oscar decided to drop by at his son's office when he returned from Brazil to update him about the marine shipping company and the positive measures he introduced to cope with the increased business. He was feeling great after a successful trip and he cheerfully went in to see his son. Oscar had only visited his son's office once when Karl first joined the company, he normally invited his son to his own office if he needed to discuss something with him, but today he decided to chat a little about the business, and ask about Sonia as well.

"Hello Dad," Karl rose to his feet to greet his father.

"Hello Karl." Oscar gave his son a big hug and sat on the chair in front of his son's desk.

"How was your trip to Brazil? Were you able to resolve the problems at the shipping company?"

"I have indeed, but we must keep an eye on cargo ships for sale. The measures I introduced will help reduce but not solve the problem. With the markets currently in the upswing, I don't believe we are ready for a purchase; nevertheless we must look for opportunities in the future. But never mind that for now. Have you heard about Sonia's mother? She has been diagnosed with cancer; I spoke with David before we went to Brazil and he told me about his mother's ailment."

"Yes Dad, Sonia called me when it first happened, she was absolutely devastated. She told me her mother had lost a lot of weight and she was having chemotherapy."

"David said she was only 65 years old but for some strange reason I thought she was younger; she must have had Sonia when she was older."

"I don't think you have met her mother, have you Dad?"

"No, I don't think I met Sonia's father or mother; we were planning to meet before grandpa died, of course you know what happened and we couldn't go to Boston."

"That is right, I remember now, Sonia's parents came to Boston for our graduation and of course grandpa died that morning and you couldn't come. But here, take a look; this is a photo of all of us. We took it at Harvard when they came for the graduation ceremony."

Karl picked up the photo of him and Sonia standing with her mother in front of the administration building and handed it to his father, Oscar took one look and his face turned beet red. Then he fumbled for the glasses in his jacket pocket and peered at the photo again with great concentration. His whole demeanor changed, and sweat started to bead on his forehead.

"What is the matter, Dad, are you alright?"

"What is her name?"

"Who's name, Father?"

"Sonia's mother," Oscar said, his face contorted, and eyes glistening red.

"Ingrid. She is originally from Germany." Karl noticed his father's neck start to swell and his breathing getting heavier, and it was worrisome. Oscar stood up, took off his jacket and walked round to the other side of the desk where Karl was seated. He picked up all the photos sitting on the desk of Sonia and her family; instantly recognizing Ingrid, he was trembling with anger. Rage was building up inside his chest and he looked ready to pounce on his prey; there was no doubt in his mind, Ingrid is the same Ingrid he knew, that fucking bitch is still alive! How could this have possibly happened!

Karl was very concerned about his dad by now. "Dad, you look very upset, please tell me what seems to be the problem. Have I done anything wrong?"

Oscar's mind was racing; he was deliberating how to deal with this unraveling situation in his mind. He held two photos in his hand, obviously one was taken several years earlier than the other but there was no mistake in his mind who he was looking at. He didn't know or expect the bitch to be alive still, how can he explain to his son what happened? Of course he cannot, events in the past must remain in the past and never ever be revealed. But he knew the time was not right to do or say anything now, it would serve his purpose best if he waited for his head to clear then determine what to do and how to react to this unexpected development. He turned his face towards his son and asked again. "What did you say her name was, son?"

"Ingrid, her name is Ingrid. Dad, do you know her?"

"No, I don't, but she sure looks like somebody with whom I had a very unpleasant encounter in Porto Alegre. She definitely reminded me of that woman who tried to steal my wallet many years ago, but the more I look at the photo the more I realize it wasn't her. The woman in Brazil had darker skin, yet surprisingly, both women have similar facial features. I'm sorry, I was just angry when I looked at the photo before I realized it was all a silly mix up. The photos brought back some bad memories."

"Can I get you anything to drink, Dad?"

Oscar had recovered a little by now; he picked up his jacket and walked out without uttering a word, and left Karl totally bewildered by this experience. What exactly happened? Why did his father react to Ingrid's photo the way he did? What made his father change so rapidly, his bright red face, his demeanor and the sweat pouring down; it was scary to witness this instant change and the compulsive interest to inquire more about Ingrid. Could he have known her before or had a previous encounter with her? Karl's mind was racing, trying to find an explanation to this bizarre behavior, but his father also said Ingrid reminded him of someone in Brazil with whom he had a bad encounter. Karl couldn't fathom how an incident like the one his father described could have triggered such a reaction; was his father really so traumatized with this woman who tried to steal from him? This doesn't sound too plausible unless he had very little money when he first arrived in Brazil. Maybe the incident left an indelible mark on his psyche with deep emotional scars; after all, had the robbery been successful he would have been left penniless with nothing to survive on in a foreign country and no-where to turn. It must have been traumatic back then. Karl wasn't perfectly happy with the explanation he worked out; however it partially satisfied the intrigue. Yet his mind wasn't completely settled.

Oscar returned to his office shaken to the core. He locked the door behind him and called the secretary to have her cancel all the appointments. "I am not available for the rest of the day." he told her, "and don't buzz my office, do you understand?"

"Yes sir," the secretary answered. He threw his jacket on the chair, removed his necktie, undid his belt and laid down on one of the two couches facing each other in the middle of the spacious office. Eyes wide open, fixated on Ingrid, and with piercing eyes full of anger and despair he bewailed his luck. So much time has lapsed yet it has come back to haunt him. Photo frames of the past started to move slowly in his mind; he could see the Jewish bitch in the nude when the towel wrapped on her body dropped on the floor as she stepped out of the bathroom. He never saw a naked woman before and the scene aroused him at the time. Another frame rolled in when he looked in her duffle bag and realized she was a Jew hiding in plain sight. He remembered when Ingrid walked in the room and saw him standing there; he pounced at her like a raging bull with a desire to kill her with his bare hands. He was never fond of her when she came to work for his grandparents and he couldn't understand why; everybody else seemed to like her just fine. But he didn't feel the same, there was something about her that didn't agree with him, and he couldn't explain why. It was like a sixth sense the girl was hiding something: maybe she didn't look German enough, even though she had light complexion and blue eyes, it simply didn't make her a bona fide girl born to the bosom of a German mother. Her friendliness was just a fake front to hide her true filthy identity. The frames continued to roll in his mind; he remembered how aroused he became when he exposed her breasts. He could see her trembling like a leaf, she was very scared and that excited him more.

He threw her violently on bed and was delirious with excitement when she was totally naked and he began to take her.

The final frame came crashing in his mind as he remembered the flash of the gun. He closed his eyes and attempted to sleep.

CHAPTER 55

O scar's body was stiff when he woke up in the darkened room. The quiet was eerie and frightening; a sinking feeling of dread and foreboding swept through his body. When he pulled himself together enough to get up and go look in the bathroom mirror, he couldn't believe the state he was in. His eyes were swollen and glazed, his body drenched in sweat and his hair was disheveled. He hunched over the sink and tried to be sick, but was unable to; pushed his finger back and down his throat and tried again but with little success, the little yellowy liquid that came up nearly choked him. He quickly abandoned the attempt, turned the tap on and splashed some cold water on his face, wetting the sweat soaked shirt even more. He staggered back to his office and turned the lights on. It was close to 7 pm, so he had been sleeping for several hours. He remembered somebody knocking on the office door earlier but he didn't bother to answer it. He felt worse than before and decided not to go home for the evening for fear Gretchen and Karl might think something was wrong, so he picked up the phone and dialed. Karl answered the phone on the first ring.

"Hi Dad, how are you?"

Oscar tried to put on a normal voice to conceal how he felt. "I'm doing great, son."

"I was worried about you, Dad. You didn't look very well when you left my office; I even came to check on you, but your door was locked,"

"Yes, I had a bad headache and decided to lie down, but I feel fine now. Let me speak to your mom."

Oscar explained to Gretchen that something important had come up and he was going to San Francisco later in the evening for a short trip and will be back the following day. He tried to sound cheerful over the phone.

"Have a safe trip Honey, see you tomorrow, I love you!" Gretchen chirped.

Next he picked up the phone and called Ricardo. "Meet me at the Bel

Air hotel right now, Ricardo; I am leaving the office right this minute, I'll probably be there in less than 40 minutes."

"I have an appointment with a client this evening; do you want me to come after the appointment?"

"Cancel it Ricardo, and come see me right away!"

Ricardo didn't ask further questions, he's known his friend long enough, something important must have happened. He put his jacket on and walked out.

Oscar hurried out of the office; his chauffeur had parked the limousine right in front of the building and when he saw his boss coming down, rushed towards the limo and opened the back door.

"Good evening Mr. Silva."

"Good evening Thurman. Take me to the hotel. I want you to go home after you drop me off; I will call you in the morning if I need you."

Oscar arrived at the hotel before Ricardo, he went straight to the desk and checked into one of the ground floor suites and left a note with the concierge to send Ricardo directly to the room when he arrives.

"Yes sir, I will do that Mr. Silva."

"Would you also send a bottle of Jack Daniels Black Label with a bucket of ice and a tray of sandwiches to my room?"

"Of course Mr. Silva," the concierge genially answered; he knew Oscar well.

Oscar opened the room door when his friend arrived. "Care for a glass of whisky?" he asked Ricardo.

"Yes, just two ice and no water," Ricardo sat on the chair and realized Oscar was wearing his white undershirt and pants only and looked unusually solemn, like something was bothering him. It was a cool but pleasant evening in LA and the patio door was wide open. Oscar returned with two full glasses of the dark spirit. His was straight with no ice; he took a big slug and started the conversation.

"We have a big problem, I mean serious problem." Ricardo didn't show any emotions, he sat down with the glass in hand not saying a word. "You remember that fucking Jew bitch Ingrid?"

"Who are you talking about, Oscar?"

"You know that fucking Jewish girl who used to work for my grandparents at their home near Offenburg, the girl who shot me in the leg and ran away and you later captured?"

"Yes, I remember her, she's been long dead, I handed her to one of my

Gestapo colleagues. They had her shipped to Dautmergen concentration camp for incineration, and they assured me she will not see the light of day ever again. What brings up the subject anew?"

"She's not fucking dead, Ricardo! She is alive and well, she lives in Detroit with her family. We have a serious situation on our hands, can't you see it?"

Ricardo put his drink on the table, "I am sorry Oscar, but you are not making much sense at all."

Oscar's eyes looked like they were going to pop out of their sockets, and he wasn't behaving rationally. He picked up his whisky glass and poured it all down in one gulp, then poured himself another one, and turned towards Ricardo.

"Well done, Ricardo! I trusted you to finish that fucking Jew off, but you did not. She is very much alive and now poses the greatest threat to our existence."

"Wait a minute Oscar, please sit down and explain what is going on. You are apparently upset and you are not making yourself clear. Please start at the beginning and tell me, how did you find out she was alive and why is she a threat to us? As far as I am concerned the woman is dead; did you see her? Maybe you are confusing her with somebody else?"

"No, Ricardo, I am not confusing her with anybody. I am confident it is her. Have you seen the photos sitting on Karl's desk?"

"Yes, I've seen them sitting there on the desk, but I really didn't pay much attention to them. I am normally seeing the back of them from my seat across from Karl."

"Well, I looked at them for the first time earlier today."

"Are you talking about the photos of the chick Karl is going out with?"

"Yes, I am. And get this: that chick you are talking about is Ingrid's daughter! The fucking slut who used to work for my grandparents back in Germany during the war, the bitch who shot me! Do you understand who I am talking about now??

"You must be kidding me, Oscar, how could this be possible? I don't understand-- how did you figure out it was her from a small picture?"

"No Ricardo, the photos are not that small. Karl has two of them sitting on his desk and they looked like they were taken on two different occasions. I picked them both up and looked at them carefully. I thought I was seeing things at the beginning but when I looked again, there was no doubt in my mind it was her. I recognized Ingrid right away, even the scar on her neck from the cigarette burn is still visible in one of the pictures. Then I asked Karl if he knew Sonia's mother name? Guess what his answer was?"

"What was his answer, Oscar?"

"Ingrid! He told me her name was Ingrid! The fucking bitch didn't even change her name, and of all the fucking girls in the world my son had to choose her daughter. This is unbelievable; I am in shock, Ricardo!"

"I am in shock too, I don't know how on earth she survived all the beatings we gave her. Oscar, you cannot even imagine what we did to her; we stripped her naked and kicked the fuck out of her with our boots and batons, we dragged her by the hair then tied her hands and used the leather whip to beat the shit out of her. She was bleeding all over and lost consciousness, so we ran electric shock and her body twitched and convulsed until it turned blue. And this is before you arrived to give her more. The girl was practically dead when they picked her up for transfer to Dautmergen; the Gestapo officer assured me she was going in the oven as soon as she gets there, there was no way she'd come out of there alive."

Oscar thought about this as he stared at his drink. "You know we have a business relationship with her son David, that lawyer turned politician from New York?"

"Yes, I know who you mean."

"A few months ago, Gretchen and I were in New York and David's law partner, Mr. Stanly, invited us to attend a surprise 40th birthday party for David, but we didn't go. Gretchen and I were on our way to the Caribbean on that day. Apparently the event was also an occasion to raise money for David's campaign; I sent him a political contribution as a birthday present after we arrived in Puerto Rico. He called to thank me and said he was looking forward to begin his campaign but was very sad that his mother was diagnosed with cancer at the age of sixty-five."

Ricardo was still thinking about how Ingrid came to be in Oscar's life in the first place. "Hmmmm. Strange how this all came about. I'm wondering, back when she was first brought to Offenburg, how did your grandparents like her? Do you think they suspected anything?"

"Oh, she had them fooled! They liked her very much; they thought she was a great housekeeper."

"But for some reason you hated her from the start?"

"No, I wouldn't say I hated her back then, I just really didn't care for her, as if something inside told me the bitch was not for real and was hiding something. And all those years as a kid I couldn't figure it out. But my curiosity got the better of me and I decided to look in her room after I saw her going through her duffel bag a few times. What raised my interest was her spontaneous reaction to put things back in the bag when she spotted me walking by her room. I had to find out what was she hiding in there, I actually tried a couple of times, but she started to lock the door whenever she went out for a walk with the dog. Grandma sent me there one time to fetch her and the door accidentally opened when I knocked. She was coming out of the bathroom and the towel she had round her body accidentally dropped on the floor and she stood there naked. I'll tell you, the fucking bitch was beautiful when she was young. Then came the day when she shot me; initially, I snuck in her room after I saw her leaving with the dog, and when I found the bag, guess what I found inside it?"

"What did you find, Oscar?"

"I found a chain with a Star of David on it. That and a Jewish prayer book with a letter stuffed inside. It was not addressed to Ingrid but to somebody called Rachel if I am not mistaken. I suspect that was her original name and she had it changed to a more German sounding name."

"Yes, that is very possible," responded Ricardo, "I know from experience the Jews did change their names to hide their identity and to escape detection."

"Do you believe Ingrid changed her religion when she arrived in the US?" Oscar asked with disgust.

"I asked Karl on one of our hunting trips if he attended church while at Harvard. He said he did indeed go to a Catholic Church in Boston with his girlfriend. I was intrigued as to why he went there when he was born Lutheran, and Karl explained that it all started with Elsa. She went to mass at a Catholic Church and he used to accompany her, and when Elsa returned to California he continued to go to the same church with his girlfriend who also happened to be Catholic. So I asked him if his girlfriend was the religious type, and he told me Sonia is very religious."

"I know all of this Ricardo, and I naturally assumed she must have come from a Catholic family, why would I think differently? We realized Sonia was Catholic when she and Karl attended the same church, and we assumed her brother David must be Catholic like his sister. It never crossed our mind they are anything but Christian, and funny enough David never talked about religion. I bet Ingrid must have married a man of Christian faith, and this explains why the children are Catholic."

"You are probably right," Ricardo answered, "but it is unusual, because in the Jewish tradition, children normally follow their mother's faith. As a matter of fact, one is not considered Jewish unless born to a Jewish mother."

"Is that so, how do you know all of this, Ricardo?"

"I have always known that, my father told me when I was a child. A Jewish person must be born from a Jewish womb; it is so unlike other religions where children traditionally follow their father's faith."

"So, where do you recommend we go from here, Ricardo, or more to the point, what do we do about the fucking bitch, Ingrid?" Oscar was staggering when he got up to refill his whiskey glass. His speech began to slur, and he asked Ricardo if he wanted another shot.

"No, Oscar, I don't want to drink anymore, I need to have a clear head."

Oscar drank the glass quickly and went to get another. He was mumbling to himself, "I don't want to have a fucking clear head; I am pissed off with the whole fucking world."

Oscar didn't make it back to the table where they sat; he just collapsed on the bed. Ricardo got up and tucked him in, turned off the lights, closed the door behind him and went home.

When Karl arrived at work at his usual time the following morning, he was surprised to see his father's limo parked in the front. He was under the impression his father went to San Francisco the night before. He went up to his father's office. "Good morning, Dad, I didn't expect to see you here this morning."

"Good morning son. My meeting was short and I took an early flight back to LA. I didn't feel like staying another day. I have a lot to do this morning, and I asked Janice to book a flight for you and I to go to Brazil."

"What's going on, Dad? Why do we have to go when you just came back from there? I thought you and I were going to Las Vegas next week."

"No, Karl, I put Las Vegas on hold for now. There are more important things we need to do in Porto Alegre."

Oscar's mind was in turmoil debating what to do next ever since he found out Ingrid was alive and well. He has been evaluating his options and the first thing to cross his mind was Karl. The boy is so attached to Sonia and it seems his mind was dead set on marrying her. Oscar knew all of that since Karl often told his mother and grandmother how much he loved Sonia and how much he was looking forward to the day he marries her. The big question is how to break up this relationship? It was easier said than done and there was no simple answer to this thorny problem. He was perfectly aware how futile and impractical it would be to give orders to his son to break up the relationship when Karl is so infatuated with Sonia, naturally he would want to know why? What did Sonia do, he would ask, and if Oscar insists without giving convincing reasons it would make Karl rebel against his family. This is totally expected when things are considered matters of the heart. It may even aggravate the situation and make it worse, and it has the potential to expose him and Ricardo's true identity and past misdeeds. Oscar knew damn well if their Nazi past is uncovered, it will spell the end for both of them, especially if their involvement in atrocities and other criminal acts against a defenseless woman is discovered. It would signal the beginning of the end for them in the US, and possibly elsewhere. This woman's son is a Congressman, for God's sake, which means the case will be given more attention and the repercussions will be even more acute.

Oscar felt life closing in on him. After all these years of toil and hard work, he reached the pinnacle of his career and now stands to lose it all if the situation isn't handled wisely. He picked up the phone and dialed Ricardo's number.

Ricardo answered the phone and immediately noticed the anguish in Oscar's voice, yet he remained calm, mindful not to burden his friend further.

"Are you alright, Oscar?" he gently asked.

"No, I am not fucking alright! I am going to the Beverly Hills Hotel right now. Please drop everything and meet me there."

"Alright Oscar, I'm on my way."

Ricardo, too, has been thinking about this totally unexpected development. His focus was to find a solution and find it fast; he also realized how serious the situation was and how severe the consequences if their past identities were revealed.

When he arrived at the hotel Oscar was in total state of agitation and dread, pacing inside the room with glass of whiskey in his hand. He didn't spare a second and started as soon as Ricardo entered. "I am glad you are here Ricardo. I feel absolutely terrible. Do you understand how grave the situation we are in is?"

"Relax Oscar, the first thing we need to have is a clear head, the glass in your hand isn't going to do you any good. Please listen to me and let us analyze the situation and figure out what we need to do."

"You're right. But I haven't been able to sleep and I just need a glass or two to calm my nerves. I have been thinking about this from the moment I saw the photo of the fucking whore."

"Likewise, I have been thinking about it, but please sit down. I will tell you how we can avoid this problem."

Oscar sat down, he was anxious to hear what Ricardo had to say; he always appreciated how clever his friend was, especially when dealing with bad and demanding situations.

"Look Oscar, the first thing we must do is remove Karl from the scene. We need to create a situation where his services are no longer required here but are needed somewhere outside of the US."

Oscar interrupted him with a snap of his fingers. "Yes! The first thing that crossed my mind is to do what you just recommended! As a matter of fact I have already booked tickets for Karl and myself to travel to Brazil next week."

"Wow, that's great Oscar, great minds think alike."

"Yes, they sure do, but what do we do next?"

Ricardo took a deep draw on his cigarette. "We must first hire a private detective to collect information so we can establish who is this woman who calls herself Ingrid is. What does she do living in Detroit and how did she end up there? We need to also determine where she comes from, who is her family, her habits, her likes and dislikes, every God damn thing about her and her children. Once we get our facts then we can respond to the situation properly. But I don't want Karl to be back in the US, period. We must create the right conditions for Karl to find an alternative romantic relationship and get him to drop Sonia. If we can get him to fall into that trap, then Sonia and her mother will be out of the picture and all communications with her will be severed."

"That is all very well, Ricardo, but I want to warn you, it won't be easy. My son is very attached to Sonia and I am not sure if the bond between them is breakable at the moment."

"I am not so sure what you are saying is true and I strongly believe what I suggested is worth trying. How about if you hire a bunch of pretty girls at the office in Brazil where Karl is going to work and maybe entice them to flirt with the boss's son? You never know what might transpire; he may be tempted by one if we are lucky and our problem will therefore vanish!"

Ricardo had also been considering another side of the problem--David, Ingrid's son. He asked Oscar, "Okay, but I thought of something else. You said David celebrated his 40th birthday the last time you visited NY?"

"That's right, I was invited to his birthday party but couldn't go. David's partner Mr. Stanly told me he was 40 years old at the beginning of last January."

"Yes, this is exactly what I thought," Ricardo answered, and his face completely changed when he continued. "You are not going to like what I have to tell you Oscar, but if David is 40 years old, it means his mother must had him at the beginning of 1946, which means she must have conceived him in late March or the beginning of April 1945. This jives with the date when you raped the bitch, do you still remember the day?"

"Yes, I do," Oscar said with a puzzled look on his face.

"I am sorry, Oscar but that could make you David's father."

Oscar's face was as white as a sheet as the realization took over. He felt completely drained, his head slumped down, his body shook and he gagged trying to fight tears. "You could be right Ricardo, but I don't think so. It is highly unlikely a woman carrying a child and subjected to torture and starvation for more than two weeks can survive her pregnancy?" He was desperately seeking an alternative scenario.

"I am not a doctor, Oscar, but remember, we caught her just a few days after she shot you. Maybe the Lord decided to let the pregnancy survive? I don't know for sure but my common sense is telling me you are the most likely father."

"Well, have you thought if David was born prematurely, what I mean to say, Ingrid could have been made pregnant in May, 1945, and carried her child for seven months instead of a full term. If that is the case, it would exclude me as David's father. I have not seen or touched the bitch after she was sent to the concentration camp."

"Possibly, but not probably. I speculate when the French army found her at Dautmergen she was clinging to life by a thread before she was taken to hospital for treatment. I cannot see her getting pregnant inside the hospital ward. First, her medical condition must have been grave, and second there must have been many people inside the ward watching over her."

"But do you think David and I have any resemblance?"

"I am not so sure, Oscar, I haven't met the man. But I was in Karl's office this morning and I took a really good look at David's only photo on Karl's desk. I would say he certainly has more of his mother's looks than yours, but I wouldn't exclude the possibility he is your son based on looks only. I personally don't look anything like my father. This is why we need to hire a private detective and have him report back to us about her--from the day she was born all the way to the present time, including the period when the French army took possession of the camp at Dautmergen, her subsequent treatment and the eventual immigration to this country. It will be an expensive investigation but it is very necessary and it will help us determine our next move."

"I don't care how much this thing costs Ricardo, I want you to take care of the situation and devote your time exclusively to it."

Oscar flew to Brazil two days after he had the discussion with Ricardo. He had already prepared a plan in his mind that involved the engagement of Karl in every facet of the business in Brazil and the complete disengagement of his involvements in all the businesses located within the US. In order to achieve this outcome he decided to start with the acting manager of the marine shipping company in Porto Alegre. As soon as he arrived in Brazil, he summoned Manuel Alvarado to his office to offer him a very attractive retirement package. Mr. Alvarado, the ever competent and cheerful manager walked in expecting Oscar to discuss future business plans and the possible purchase of additional cargo ships to cope with the increased demand in shipping, but he was in for a jolt.

Oscar didn't waste time and began his scripted conversation as soon as Manuel sat down. "Mr. Alvarado, you have been with this company close to thirty years and I must admit you have been doing a wonderful job and we value your service greatly. But our company needs younger blood to take over from you at the helm. We therefore decided to offer you a very attractive retirement package, with additional benefits as a token of appreciation for your loyalty and good service to our company and to us." Oscar proceeded to give him the full details of this generous retirement award.

Manuel sat silently listening to what seemed a rehearsed speech. He was in a total state of indignation when Oscar finished, and in a deliberate tone he proceeded to tell Oscar, "Mr. Silva, I have worked in this company since I was 22 years old, fresh out of college. Helmut recognized my capability, competence and loyalty and made me his right hand man. I served under you when you took over from Helmut and I executed my duty with the same competence and dedication, and all the profit we have been making is a testimony to my leadership and diligence. I appreciate you want to bring Karl in, but why do you have to get rid of me? This company is my life, to throw me out is akin to giving me the death sentence. Is there any chance I could remain in my capacity as acting manager? Surely Karl can be assigned another title and I don't mind to be subordinate in rank to him. I am pleading with you sir to save my job!"

Oscar, whose face was now red with anger and frustration at Mr. Alvarado's response swiftly advised him, "The retirement package I offered, Mr. Alvarado, is very generous indeed, and you must have recognized your-self how generous I have been. Nobody would ever contemplate making an offer like the one I made to you; you will be a rich and comfortable man! You can easily retire and travel the world with your family and spend your afternoons at the golf course, what more do you want? Life will be good! I advise you to accept this offer because my decision is final and effective immediately. This meeting is over, thank you."

Manuel was furious. He slammed the door behind him and walked back to launch a quick cleanup of the office he cherished so much. His body was throbbing, hands shaking and mind spinning trying to comprehend the reasons for this abrupt and undignified termination of his employment. He neither understood nor accepted what was happening, what did he do to deserve this kind of treatment? After all, he has served the company he loved with great honor and dedication, why does it have to come to this? An hour later he walked out of the building still quivering with anger and frustration. He never harbored as much dislike for a person in his life as the dislike he now has for Oscar, and he vowed revenge.

Karl arrived in Porto Alegre four days after his dad, accompanied by his mother and grandmother. The two ladies were quite happy to come back home, after all, they made this journey between PA and LA quite regularly, and they fully enjoyed the travel and the constant change in scenery and cultures. Karl on the other hand was very confused when he met with his father at the marine cargo office the following day. He got the impression he was not going back to the US. His father explained Mr. Alvarado the acting manager had resigned unexpectedly, and now the shipping company is in dire need for a new manager; who could possibly be a better choice to manage the shipping company more than Karl!

But Karl was distinctly anxious and rather distressed about the startling development, and he communicated his displeasure forcefully to his father. "Dad, you told me you had big plans for me in LA, and you want me to take over from you. We have many projects on the drawing board, not to mention the ongoing investments in California and Las Vegas. You also wanted me to get involved more with the group in Oregon, what happened? And why did you change your mind? I feel you are punishing me for something I haven't done or even know about..."

Oscar was getting frustrated with his son and broke in, "I already explained. Manuel has resigned his position as acting manager, and you need to stay here to look after your interest and your family's interests, it is as simple as that. I have been thinking to reduce the scope of our business interests in the US and concentrate again on the market here; I see dark clouds gathering over the US economy."

"But Dad, you recently told me about your great plans for new ventures in the US, and twice you mentioned your ambition to double our building footprint in five years! You even told me of your desire to build another casino in Las Vegas; surely you will need me more in LA than here in Brazil. And come to think of it, I am not the right person to replace Manuel at the helm of this business which I know little about. You could very easily find somebody with the proper qualifications to run the shipping company. I hate to say it, but I am the wrong man for this job. All the experience I have down here amounts to two brief stints during summer breaks; this doesn't qualify me to run the company."

Oscar was getting angry with his son. He banged on the table then stood up. "This is it, Karl, the decision is final, you better get used to it. You are not going back to California and I don't want to hear any more about it, do you understand!"

"Whatever you say, Dad. I'll do what you ordered, but don't expect me to be too happy about it."

CHAPTER 56

Ricardo spent all his time researching private investigators and detective agencies in Detroit and in Germany in order to find someone with the experience and stamina to conduct an extensive investigation on Ingrid and members of her family. The aim was to carry out a thorough probe to establish what happened to Ingrid from the moment she was born till the present and to produce a detailed report that chronicles her journey from the concentration camp in Germany to her present whereabouts in Detroit. He decided to call Dr. Hanson in Spokane to set up an appointment and learned the first possible date to meet him was two weeks away. In the meantime, he booked a ticket to fly to Germany to see what he could find out there.

Ricardo's calculation to involve the group in Oregon was typical of his long term planning and attention to detail. He figured his best option is to involve a third party to contact the detective in Detroit instead of carrying the task on his own. Doing it himself entails unnecessary risk in the future should he and Oscar decide to get rid of Ingrid, as may very well be the case. Then the detective who was charged with the task to surveil Ingrid would naturally alert the police; if Ricardo himself initiated the contact with the detective then the police would want to know why. It would not take them long to establish a connection between Ingrid and Oscar through Karl's relationship with Sonia. But if a third party is the one to make the contact, it will be impossible for the police to tie either him or Oscar to the murder providing the third person remains anonymous.

Ricardo arrived in Frankfurt after a long overnight flight from LA and immediately took a taxi to the train station, then continued to Stuttgart to meet some people. He brought with him a list of three private investigators he intended to interview the following day. He also brought with him photos of Ingrid, her children and all the relevant information about the family and had the information neatly organized inside a folder.

He determined Andreas Winkle was the right man for the job after conducting interviews with the three detectives. The seventy-year-old no nonsense man was in excellent shape and looked conspicuously fit for his age, but most importantly he came with an impressive resumé and law enforcement background. Andreas lived in the little town of Obertarkhiem, a short distance from Stuttgart. He started his career working on the assembly line of a major car manufacturing company, but later quit to join the police department in Stuttgart, and after three years on the job he signed up for a night course in criminal justice at the local college and successfully obtained a degree. After graduation, he was quickly elevated in rank and became a detective in the police department and stayed in the same job until his retirement.

Herr Winkle established a private investigation agency in the city, and after a few years in business he was able to make a name for himself with a good reputation for competent and thorough work. Many clients were satisfied with the service he provided including insurance companies who used him to investigate fraudulent claims to recover stolen assets, particularly expensive art works. Ricardo liked the earnest detective and found him trustworthy; he described a systematic approach to solving problems and finding information, so Ricardo assigned him the case.

As a back story, he explained his client has been blackmailed by a woman from Detroit by the name of Ingrid McKay. This lady who immigrated to the US after WWII from her native Germany is Jewish and used to work under false pretense for his client's grandparents in Offenburg during the war. Her Jewish identity was later uncovered and she subsequently was arrested and sent to Dautmergen concentration camp but survived. After settling in the US she found out his client was alive and lives in California. She discovered his whereabouts through her daughter, who happens to be in a relationship with his client's son. Once she found out, she started to make blackmail threats. She claimed he sired a son with her when the two lived in Germany. The purpose of the investigation is to gather as much information about this woman as possible; where she came from and what happened to her after she was admitted at Dautmergen and the circumstances that led to her immigration to the US. He handed Andreas the folder when he finished with the introduction and the background details and asked him if he had any questions.

"Yes, I do," Andreas quickly answered, "would you happen to know her maiden name before she emigrated?"

"Her name was Ingrid Schroeder, at least this was what she led all of us to believe her name was, but we strongly suspect it was an assumed name. My client discovered evidence that her original first name was Rachel, but we don't know her family name or where she was originally from," Ricardo told him.

"How old is she now?"

"Her son, David, informed my client his mother was 65 years old."

"Do you know when she was captured in Germany?"

"Yes I do, it was roughly close to the end of March, 1945, just four weeks before the war ended and less than twenty days from the time Dautmergen fell in the hands of the French army."

"What is your client's name?"

"His name is Hans Schmidt; you also need to know his grandfather was General Karl Schneider, and the General's address near the town of Offenburg where Ingrid used to work is included in the file as well as other information about people we know she was in contact with."

"Very well, I will start on this right away, and I will let you know my findings as soon as I am able to gather the necessary information. I must warn you, many of the documents we need may have been destroyed during the war, but let me see what I can do."

Oscar decided to stay in Brazil for a few more weeks to give his son additional training on how to manage the two companies they own. He began by telling Karl, "Your granddad built this company over many years and made sure to leave it all for you, son, before he passed away. I therefore want to give you important advice on running our businesses. Your prime responsibility is to find good and trustworthy staff you can depend on to do the work for you, and your job is to delegate authority to these subordinates to carry out their duties as the circumstances require. Let them do their assignments with your consultation and direction and make sure to follow up on their work and give them encouragement and assistance when they need it, but don't fall in the trap to micro manage your employees. You need to set your short and long term goals and monitor the progress and make the necessary alignment when things stray off course."

Oscar escorted his son to work every day and introduced him to all his important contacts and helped him hire a new experienced assistant to replace Manuel Alvarado. He also set up a new sales and public relations office on the same floor where Karl's office was located and hired four young, pretty girls to staff it. Karl asked his dad why he created another sales office when they already have one on the lower floor, and Oscar assured him it was good for the company's image. He encouraged his son to interact with the girls and take them along whenever he is out on business. Karl, the ever obliging son went with the flow and reluctantly agreed to stay in Brazil for the foreseeable time, but deep down he resented getting transferred from California against his will and desire.

He picked up the phone and called Sonia in Detroit. "Hello love, how are you doing and how is your mom?"

"I am doing fine and so is mother. She's improving slowly; the medicine she is on doesn't agree with her stomach, but at least her health is getting better. Other than that, it's the usual routine at school and the church, but I cannot tell you how much I miss you Honey! I just want to hold you in my arms and not let go. I love you so much and I still don't quite understand why you had to leave for Brazil so abruptly."

"I wish I had a reasonable answer, Sonia. My dad has been telling me about his big dream to double the size of our company in the US over the next five years but unexpectedly and without warning decided to bring me here to Porto Alegre. He suddenly believes I can serve our business better here, and though I disagreed with him, he still is the boss and I have to accept his decision. But I decided to work on him and see if I can get him to change his mind. I'm not quite sure of my chances yet, but I promise to let you know. Time will tell."

"But how about your plans to come to Detroit and ask for my hand in marriage, has this gone out of the window, Karl?" she asked sheepishly.

"Absolutely not, I'll be coming to get you my beautiful girl! You are the one I love and there is nobody I wish to spend my life with other than you, I love you so much Sonia!"

"But when will you come? It's embarrassing; I told my family you were coming to marry me soon and lo and behold you don't show up. Even father O'Malley asked the other day when you and I are getting married; don't you understand my frustration, Karl?"

"I do indeed, darling. Things have been put off a little, but I promise you with all of my being to come in a short period of time. Let me figure out the situation I am in, and I will be there knocking at your door soon. I have a little question for you though. Do you mind living with me here in Brazil after we get married and until the time is right for us to return to the US?"

"Well, I prefer to live in the US if it's possible, but I will live wherever my husband wants me to go. I love you Karl and all I ask for is to be with you. Please don't make me wait too much longer!"

"I will not Sonia, I promise."

CHAPTER 57

It had been two months and Ricardo had not yet received a report from the detective. Oscar was antsy and getting fidgety and irritable; he drank heavily and ate very little, he lost weight and his famous work stamina as well. Gretchen noticed the sudden changes in her husband and thought he must be too busy with work problems and didn't want to burden him further; therefore she didn't ask what was bothering him. But the situation persisted and Oscar became unbearable; one evening he came home drunk and Gretchen got up in a huff and went upstairs to her room crying. She didn't want to create a scene in front of her mother.

Oscar followed her up. "I am sorry Honey if I upset you; please bear with me, I am a little strained and under pressure." He sat down next to her and put his arms round her, "I promise you things will get better soon."

Ingrid had been going through chemotherapy for the last several months and the drugs she was taking agitated her stomach and made her feel sick. She suffered a great deal; there were times when she couldn't do anything but lie in bed staring at the ceiling half dazed. The pain was so severe and caused such havoc to her internal organs, she even considered giving up the cancer treatment. Greg showered his wife with love and attention and decided to reduce his work schedule to give her the time she deserved, and Sonia called several times a day from work to check on her. When she returned home she had to perform household duties on behalf of her sick mother; she kept the house clean and prepared food and the special meals recommended by her doctor. Greg too helped with household duties, did grocery shopping and took Goldie, the golden retriever for her regular walks. Both Greg and Sonia tried hard to give Ingrid a semblance of normalcy during this horrible ordeal and luckily the medicine was working well, and after many months of treatment the cancer finally began to ebb.

The task Andreas Winkle took upon himself was not an easy one. The woman he was asked to collect information on was a German citizen of Jewish ancestry and that posed a serious problem as there were few known records available for search. The Nazis did all they could to destroy records of the civilians they annihilated during the war in order to conceal their crimes against the Jews and others. And to complicate matters further, Ingrid was known to have changed her name; that in itself was confusing and offered the most challenging facet of the investigation. According to Ricardo, the girl may have been born Rachael. Yet her last name was the most puzzling; she is currently called McKay, but was Schroeder before she married Greg and her original maiden name remains a mystery yet. To make matters worse, he found the name Ingrid Schroeder is very common in Germany. But on the bright side being Jewish helped a little, since the target of the search was a Jewish woman; it therefore eliminates many girls with a similar name who were not Jewish. Further still there was no known information on Ingrid's exact date and location of her birth, and it seems no one knows anything about her parents, grandparents or relatives. To trace genealogy in a fragmented country posed the toughest problem for Andreas since Germany was ripped apart after WWII, with some parts of the country ceded to Czechoslovakia and Poland in the east and the other parts were given to Belgium and Denmark in the west. Winkle decided to commence the search by trying to locate people who may have met or known Ingrid while she was in the employment of Oscar's grandparents near Offenburg. Ricardo gave him the exact address of the General's house where Ingrid used to work and he decided to begin there in the hope somebody at the house still remembers who she was and where she came from. Herr Winkle drove down the Autobahn to Offenburg and then turned south and headed in the direction of Gengenbach. He spotted the wooden plank on the main road and turned into the long unpaved driveway to the meadow where the General's house was located. He parked the car in the front and put his favorite hat on and walked towards the house. The door opened before he even reached it and a middle aged man appeared. He looked like a typical farmer from the region.

"How can I help you?" he asked.

Herr Winkle introduced himself. "I am a private investigator, and my client's grandfather, General Karl Schneider used to own this house many years ago. I am looking for the girl who was in their employment during the war, I wonder if you have any information about her?"

"Yes, my father purchased this property from General Schneider's grandson Hans, and before he died he told me what happened to the girl who used to work there. I cannot recall her name, I was in the army at the time but I remember meeting her few times when I came to visit my family. They lived on the property over there." He stepped out of the house and pointed in the direction of the farm house where his father George used to live. The girl stayed in the room at the back of the house, but we use that room for storage now. Would you please tell me why are you looking for this girl?"

"I am afraid I won't be able to share this information with you, it is a confidential matter. You didn't finish telling me what did your father say happened to the girl?"

"My father before he passed away repeated this story in front of me many times whenever people came to visit and asked questions about the General. He said he was sitting with my mother in the living room when he heard a noise that sounded like a gun coming from the General's property. Then he heard the same sound again and ran over to investigate. When he got there, he found Hans, the General's grandson, lying naked on the floor with bullet wounds and blood all over. He thought Hans was dead at first, but then he heard a faint murmur. He rushed to town and alerted the authorities. Hans was taken to the infirmary, and thank God he survived."

"Did your father see the girl in the room when he arrived?"

"I don't believe he did, but my father told us Hans was up to something no good, because when he found him he was lying on the floor naked, and he suspected the girl shot him because he was trying to do something bad."

"Do you think he was trying to rape her?"

"Without doubt, my father even used the same word. It was very shocking at the time."

"Do you know what happened to the girl?"

"I really don't know, but I understand she ran away and was never seen again."

"Do you know where Hans could be living?"

"Hans sold the property to my father, and I believe he went to South America. He stopped to see us many years ago, I guess he wanted to show his wife where he lived in Germany before he emigrated, but that was the last time I saw him."

Andreas thanked the farmer for the valuable information he graciously gave, but he was perplexed from what he learned; the information confirms Hans may have had an encounter with Ingrid, he could not however ascertain with degree of certainty if Oscar's encounter with her was an ongoing relationship that went awry and culminated in the shooting, or was it a one time incident where Hans forced himself on Ingrid and that too ended with her shooting him? It was still early in the investigation to conclude if Oscar's brush with Ingrid resulted in her pregnancy. His hunch however tells him it probably was.

Ricardo provided Herr Winkle the address of Colonel Alexander Hendrix's house, where he believed Ingrid ran for help after she shot Hans. He portrayed the relationship Ingrid had with Yvonne, the colonel's live-in maid as close and friendly. Winkle decided to stop for lunch in town then head to the house to see if anybody there still remembers events from more than forty years ago. He had no trouble finding it with the distinctive orange gabled roof with a chimney at each end. He put on his hat, stepped out of his car and walked straight to the front door and knocked.

A young girl answered. "How can I help you, sir?" she asked.

"I am looking for the owner of the house please."

A woman wearing a kitchen apron came to the door. "Hello, how may I be of assistance?"

Herr Winkle introduced himself and explained he was looking for a lady called Yvonne who used to work at the house for a retired army colonel during the war.

"Yes, I have heard of this lady, my father met her years ago after the war ended when he purchased the house from the colonel's heirs."

"May I speak to your father?"

"I'm afraid you won't be able to, my father has Alzheimers, and he would not be of any benefit to you. But I believe the lady you are talking about moved to Strasbourg, France."

"Do you happen to know her last name, or her address in Strasbourg?"

"I am sorry, but I have no idea."

Herr Winkle was not too disappointed, he has two people independently connecting Yvonne to the French city; he remembered Ricardo also mentioning Yvonne had some connection to Strasbourg, and that she spoke French and likely lived there still. The challenge now is to search for this person based on a general description of how she looked forty years ago, using her first name only. There was no known last name and to make the search even more difficult, the name Yvonne is very common in France.

It was getting late, and Andreas decided to drive to Strasbourg half an hour away and stay overnight there, hoping to get a good night's sleep and start afresh in the morning. He always liked Strasbourg for its history, bearing the imprint of German and French cultures and known for its magnificent wine and cuisine.

He started his morning early, and after a quick breakfast he made his first stop the city's registrar for birth, death and marriage records. He determined after reading the file, Yvonne was married to a German man and her age was around 36 at the end of the war, this would make her roughly 77 years old at present if she was still alive. He got this information from Ricardo who determined her age after reading the Gestapo report on the aftermath of Hans's shooting. At the time of her interrogation Yvonne indicated she was born five years before the beginning of WWI in Strasbourg, France, and that her deceased husband was originally from Germany. Ricardo somehow remembered this information but couldn't recall Yvonne's last name, which was ironic since her last name would've been the more pertinent piece of information. He chose the city's registrar to check the possibility the lady he is looking for matched entries of other women that fit Yvonne's general details. The death records produced no results, and the birth records produced way too many, but when he looked at the marriage certificates he was able to find six entries which possibly could lead him to Yvonne based on the bride's date of birth and first name and the groom's German last name. He decided to look into all possible leads so he wrote down the addresses as they appeared in the marriage certificates; the first four searches produced no results but the fifth one aroused his interest.

He couldn't believe his luck when a middle-aged man answered the door. "I am sorry to bother you, monsieur, but I am looking for a lady called Yvonne. She used to live at this address back in the nineteen thirties. Do you have anybody with this name still living at the house or is there anyone else here who might help me?"

"I don't know anybody by this name. We purchased the house twenty years ago from a gentleman and there were no ladies involved in the sale or living in the house at the time of the purchase. But monsieur Jacque across the road has been living on this street all of his life, he probably can tell you who lived here back then."

Andreas thanked the man and walked across the street and introduced himself to the elderly gentleman when he opened the door.

"Would you happen to know if one of the occupants of the house facing yours was called Yvonne back in the nineteen thirties?"

"Yes," the elderly man responded, "the Bouchard family lived at the house for many years, and their daughter was called Yvonne. She was married to a German man I believe. I think she moved to Germany after she was married."

"Where would I be able to locate her?"

"I don't know where she lives, her brother Simon sold the house after his parents passed away, but I have lost contact with him. Sorry I cannot help you there."

Herr Winkle thanked the man for the information he offered; it confirmed to him he was on the right track and it provided the full name of the man who may provide the best chance to locate Yvonne. She might be the only one who can shed light on what happened on that dreadful day when Hans was shot and what happened to Ingrid thereafter. It may even provide a treasure trove of other important information, but in order to find Yvonne he needs to find her brother Simon Bouchard first.

Herr Winkle stopped at a restaurant in the city's historic downtown for something to eat and asked the waiter to bring him the local phone directory. He couldn't believe his luck when he had two possible matches right away. There they were, two entry listings for the name Simon Bouchard, one with initial J and the other with the initial M. He picked up the phone and dialed the number with the J middle initial first.

"*Bonjour Monsieur*, my name is Andreas Winkle, and I am looking for a lady who goes by the name Yvonne. Do you happen to know where I can find her?"

There was a pause on the other line, and when the person spoke, Andreas sensed an uncomfortable tone in his voice. "Are you looking for Yvonne Fischer?" he asked.

Andreas thought for a second before he answered; the name Fischer sounds a definite possibility for the person he was looking for and was also on the list he found at the city's registry, and he intuitively answered. "Yes, that is her."

Simon, with a tinge of hostility in his voice asked, "Why are you looking for Yvonne?"

Andreas explained who he was and the reason for the investigation, and asked again if he knew Yvonne.

"Yes, Yvonne is my sister; she lives in a nursing home at the moment."

"Would I be able to speak to her, please?"

"I am afraid she would not be much help; she is in poor health and confined to a wheelchair. You see she had a heart attack many years ago and is paralyzed from the waist down and cannot speak."

"Oh dear, I am sorry to hear that, but it is not Yvonne I am actually trying to find information on, it is in fact another woman whose name is Ingrid Schroeder. She used to work near Offenburg during the war."

Andreas was head over heels when he heard Simon exclaim, "Yes! I knew Ingrid very well!" Andreas's ears perked up and immediately arranged to meet with Simon face to face.

Over a long chat the old Frenchman told the story of how they met with Ingrid for the first time in the Black Forest when Yvonne, his sister brought her up there. How, they all promised to help her escape from Germany to join her mother in the Holy Land, but then the war broke out and the poor girl was trapped and not able to get out. He told how towards the end of the war the girl was captured, as well as the gory details of Ingrid's rape and her shooting of Hans in self-defense, and about hiding in the barn before her eventual capture by the Gestapo. Simon didn't know what happened to her thereafter, but he strongly suspects she was tortured and killed. However, he shed some light on her background: he told Andreas she came from the city of Stettin, in Pomerania, in what used to be Germany before WWII, but now is part of Poland.

Herr Winkle spent the next few weeks preparing a file full of information on Ingrid. He made several trips to Stettin, or Szczecin as it is now called in Poland and discovered the name Ingrid Schroeder used to belong to a dead German girl. He immediately figured out the unfortunate Jewish girl had to assume somebody else's identity, a common practice used by Jews to avoid capture by the Nazis. Further research led him to discover Rachel's birth certificate which fits Ingrid's description and age. He was now satisfied that the woman who calls herself Ingrid was originally born Rachel Lieberman in 1921, and records indicate her father committed suicide by taking rat poison. Herr Winkle continued his search and found records of Ingrid being incarcerated at Dautmergen concentration camp. He found the information after researching the French unit which liberated the camp and the field hospital where she was taken. The records also showed Ingrid was transferred to a hospital in Strasbourg after the liberation of the camp and she was sent to the US after her release from hospital with the help of the Quaker organization, which was known to have helped Jews re-settle in the US back then. And he learned that she was six months pregnant at the time of her release. Herr Winkle concluded that Ingrid most likely delivered her baby in the last week of December 1945 or the first week of 1946, and the most likely father of the child is Hans, who was confirmed to have raped Ingrid around the end of March 1945.

CHAPTER 58

D r. Hanson apologized for arriving late for the meeting at the hotel in
Spokane where Ricardo checked in earlier. He disclosed that Brandon,
his son was having marital problems and the reconciliation session he me-
diated took longer than planned. But he wasted no time to get on with
business and find out the purpose for this important meeting. He sat on the
chair across from Ricardo listening to him tell about this congressman from
New York whose sister has seduced Karl into a relationship. The boy is now
totally smitten with the girl and wants to marry her, but Oscar is dead set
against it because he suspects her mother is Jewish. Oscar, he added, wants
to find out if the group is able to send somebody to Detroit to contact a local
detective from there to collect information on this congressman and his
family, especially the mother and the daughter. He opened his attaché case
and produced a file and handed it to the doctor along with a check written
out to the group. The doctor was flabbergasted how substantial the amount,
however, two things intrigued him after he went through the file, as well as
a photo of the detective Ricardo suggested they use.

"Have you done any dealings with this detective, Marvin Cline before?"

"No, we haven't. To tell you the truth we never met the guy before."

"I don't understand why a man of your background would choose a
black man to do the job? You know these people have no intelligence; there
are hundreds of white detectives in the Detroit area who will be much more
beneficial to your investigation."

"You are absolutely correct doctor, but this man runs the detective business on his own, which makes it easier should we decide to get rid of him
in the future. And believe me, I won't lose much sleep if it comes to that."

The doctor gave a big chuckle, "You are right about those bastards, all
of them on food stamps depleting our country's treasury. But I want you
to understand this organization is not set up to do petty things like killing
somebody as trivial as this detective."

"Neither would we ask you to be involved, doctor. You asked me and I honestly answered you. Our main target is not this black person but rather the Jewish people who are snatching Karl into their fold. You know this boy is the apple of his father's eye and among the best the Aryan Race has to offer. Detective Cline is superfluous to what we trying to accomplish and will amount to nothing if he is eliminated as residue."

"But I still don't understand why you want us to contact the detective when you can easily do it yourself?"

"Very good question indeed, Doctor, but the whole purpose to involve you is for us to remain anonymous and things cannot be traced back to us or to the organization. If you send somebody from the ranks of your trusted people in Oregon, he wouldn't find out if a murder was supposed to take place in Michigan more than two thousand miles away, plus he wouldn't even give a damn if the murdered was a black man. My only request you instruct this person to act casually and under a false name."

"Very well, Ricardo, we will be happy to cooperate. Please tell me when you need us to start."

Ricardo was happy with the meeting after he convinced the group's leader to recruit somebody to travel to Detroit and hire the detective to prepare a file on Ingrid and her family, with instructions to keep his identity secret and the whole thing discrete.

Dr. Hanson recommended Maurice Ferguson for the job. "Maurice is a very unassuming man and he will not draw attention to himself or to us. I am confident he will do a good job for you."

Marvin Klein, the private investigator in Detroit, like Andreas Winkle in Germany was a police veteran, and he too built a reputation as one of the best in the business. Acting on behalf of Ricardo, Maurice Ferguson used a false name when he came to meet with the good natured investigator. He didn't explain to Marvin who his client was and the reason for the investigation, he just gave him the file containing all the information they had on Ingrid and her family and asked him to compile a dossier on her, from the day she arrived in the US and up to today's date. The investigation must also include her children, David and Sonia.

"Please don't spare any cost in your effort to find the information we requested. We will, of course, take care of all your expenses." Marvin was impressed with his new client and wished all of them were the same.

Detective Kline's job was much easier than Andreas Winkle's job; he prepared his report rather quickly after his search led him to discover records of Ingrid's arrival in the US and her subsequent placement with the Eaton family in Detroit with the help of the Quaker charitable organization. A copy of David's birth certificate indicated he was born on New Year's Day, 1946 at a Detroit Hospital. The certificate also showed David's mother was Ingrid Schroeder, and the father was listed as David Schroeder and marked deceased. A copy of Ingrid's marriage certificate to Greg and additional information about Sonia, from the day she was born until her current employment at Wayne County School District in Detroit, were also included in the file. Other related information like phone numbers, house address, social security numbers, places of worship and even photos of Jacob Levine, the new Rabbi at Ingrid's synagogue and father O'Malley at the Catholic Church were included.

Ricardo's heart was pounding when he finished reading the detectives' reports. It provided solid evidence Oscar was indeed David's father and Ingrid was the mother. There was no doubt in Ricardo's mind who Ingrid was and the potential damage she would cause if Oscar's identity is uncovered. Obviously, the only way Ingrid could ever find Oscar's true identity is through Karl, and Ricardo felt a great sense of unease in his stomach. To him it was glaringly obvious banishing Karl from the scene will only reduce the chances of Ingrid finding out but will not completely eliminate them. Just as Oscar accidentally found out whom she was, Ingrid too is bound to uncover his identity sometime soon. She is likely to come across a photo of Oscar; surely Sonia must have taken photos during her trip to LA, or during visits Oscar made to Boston when Karl and Sonia were at Harvard. And if Ingrid found out as common sense suggests she may, then the shit will hit the fan and there is no telling what will happen next. The best case scenario is her cancer takes a turn for the worse and she dies soon, or maybe she will get too sick and her condition worsens to the extent she is too mentally and physically sick to give a damn about Oscar. But all of that is wishful thinking, and the most likely scenario when she finds out who Oscar truly was, is to immediately run to that lawyer son of hers and tell him. 'Guess what son? That bastard who tormented and tortured me and sent me to die in the concentration camp is alive and kicking. His name is Oscar Silva, you know, your esteemed client and the father of Karl, Sonia's future husband?'

And of course the fucking vindictive Jew will take great umbrage and will use his position in congress to pull all the strings at his disposal to inflict maximum damage on Oscar in order to avenge what happened to his mother. We are all screwed and stand to lose everything we worked for all of our lives! Ricardo had a bad intuition and it swept over his body; he knew in his heart this is the most likely outcome once Oscar's identity is revealed.

He stood up and paced back and forth in his office cursing the day they made the decision to come to the US, and cursing the Jews for causing him so much pain. Even if they escape to South America and never return to the US, he knew damn well the long arm of the law will reach them, even in Brazil. There are many dedicated Nazi hunters who will be on their trail once they get a whiff of their shadowy past and the atrocities they committed against Ingrid and other Jews. There are many Jewish and Zionist organizations set up to track down ex-Nazi officers and in the prevailing political climate these organizations with the help of the US government will apply pressure on foreign governments to hand over ex-Nazis and put them on trial.

There is one way to solve this problem, and only one way to make this predicament disappear. Ricardo nervously stamped out his cigarette and picked up the phone to make an urgent call to Brazil.

Oscar's world was turned upside down by the discovery of Ingrid's identity. He abruptly moved his family from LA, but allowed his wife and mother-in-law to travel back and forth as they please. However when it came to Karl he invented excuses to discourage him from going back. He hoped Karl might develop an interest in one of the new girls in the sales office and encouraged him to always bring one or two with him on business, on the premise that it would boost the company's image. Yet after several months passed Karl showed no particular interest; on the contrary, he remained in contact with Sonia. Home and office phone records indicated several calls a week were made to Detroit. Oscar was further discouraged and perturbed when Karl confirmed the relationship with Sonia was still going steady and remained as strong as it had ever been. Oscar never felt so bad in his life and was at a loss as to what to do until he received the call from Ricardo.

CHAPTER 59

D avid's final few months before the November election were hectic, but he was relaxed as recent polls results gave him a big lead and almost assured him a win for the most coveted political office in the state. He was pleased when the call from Oscar came in to express his desire to visit him in Washington at the end of summer, but he had to apologize first for not able to meet him there. "I am sorry Mr. Silva but I'll be in my district in NY for the remaining days before the election."

"Very well, maybe I can come to New York instead, nothing important, just a little gesture of support!" Oscar said humorously. David anticipated a generous contribution from Oscar every time he comes to see him, and he liked and admired the man for his integrity and generosity. He never even asked for favors in return and always carried himself in professional and cordial manner when he comes to visit.

David had even more reason to be happy. His wife announced the other day her pregnancy test came back positive; their new baby would arrive in seven months. Nancy told David, "I'd love to have a little girl I can dress up and make her look nice and pretty! And Daniel too will be thrilled to have a sister to play with, won't he darling?"

"Yes, Honey, he and I both will be thrilled."

David also called Dr. Morgan in Detroit to enquire about his mother's cancer treatment. The last two tests Ingrid had at the clinic showed no abnormalities and her general health was gradually improving. The doctor was glad to pass along the good news. "I am confident your mother's cancer has entered a dormant phase. The last test results were encouraging and showed no abnormalities for nine weeks running. I think the intense treatment we administered on her helped, but I believe your mother's determination to beat the disease is what made things turn in her favor. She truly is a remarkable lady!"

"Thank you so much, Doctor! And I do share your assessment of my mother, she is indeed a strong lady, but does this mean she is cured and out of danger?"

"It all depends," the doctor answered, "but we believe the tumor cells are under control and no longer multiplying abnormally. In other words, her cancer is in remission and your mother is out of danger at the present and her life is no longer threatened. We will keep on monitoring her condition to ensure there are no flare ups in the future."

Nobody was more pleased with the news about the dramatic turn in Ingrid's health than her daughter. Sonia bore the brunt of the illness and was in agony watching her mother during the worst spells. Ingrid was afflicted with constant pain, vomiting, appetite loss and bad headaches. Sonia couldn't even comb her mother's hair for fear it came out in clumps, but luckily enough, Ingrid did not lose too much of it. Sonia also did most everything at home; she took care of the house cleaning, cooking, and laundry and drove her mother back and forth to the doctor and to do tests at the clinic. She dressed her when Ingrid didn't have the strength to dress herself and she did it all without uttering a complaint or missing a day at school. Teaching was not a job for Sonia, it was a passion. She gave a lot of love, knowledge and attention and even went to the homes of struggling students to give them private tutoring and encouragement to do better and she never asked for anything in return.

Sonia called Karl to tell him the good news about her mother, but Karl had been a little peculiar since he went to Brazil. He seemed quieter and a little distant, the vigor and intensity dropped out of his voice, but he was still loving and always concerned about Ingrid's wellbeing. Sonia couldn't determine the reasons for his mood change or why he had to leave the US. He initially told her he had to go to Brazil because of a surge in business which required him and his father to be there, but he didn't know how long he was likely to stay. It could be two months or even a year, he told her. There was always a current of unhappiness in his tone, but she attributed it to his work load and the pressure of being at the helm of a very demanding business.

Ricardo was waiting at the airport for the last four hours before Oscar's plane finally arrived. There was a weather related delay in Mexico City where the plane stopped on route to LA. Ricardo sat in the lounge nursing a single beer, and he had already burned more than fifteen cigarettes in the last few hours.

His lips were numb from the constant contact with nicotine, but his mind was alert and going at full speed. The damning reports he received from the investigators had confirmed his worst fears, and he spent the last few nights thinking what to do about the terrible situation. All the possible remedies he considered led to the same conclusion. If Ingrid disappeared, all their problems will too. But this is easier said than done. He was fully cognitive of the repercussions if a premeditated attempt to kill her fails to go as planned. Nevertheless a quick solution must be found before it is too late. He was mentally exhausted by the time Oscar's plane taxied to the terminal building.

Oscar too was seated in the airplane fidgeting and thinking what to do about everything. He was looking forward to what Ricardo might offer, but deep in his heart he too knew what the solution was; their problem will go away only when Ingrid goes away and vanishes off of the face of this earth.

The two friends drove to Oscar's house for a private talk without interference. Ricardo gave Oscar copies of the reports the investigators prepared, and systematically briefed him, item by item about the contents and the seriousness of the situation. He emphasized time was of the essence and plans must be made to eradicate the source of this potentially grave problem.

Oscar did not need any more bad news; he knew damn well what was in the reports before he was briefed by Ricardo. His mind was in a bedlam and burdened by the weight of it all. But for strange reasons and to Ricardo's surprise he decided to put off doing anything until he meets with his unwanted son, David. He felt an overwhelming desire to meet him again, and see this man up close. He wanted to understand what made his mind tick, was it money? After all, he inherited his mother's Jewish genes and all Jews are interested in is to accumulate money and wealth. Or was it pride? In this regard he definitely has German genes and nobody has more pride in themselves than German people. Put the pride aside; money and power are the only things the Jews relish and that son of a bitch, David, is a Jew alright, by virtue of his mother. There is no doubt money and power is his motivation in life as well, and he told himself he must meet with David face to face. I don't particularly hate him, he thought, as a matter of fact I feel utterly indifferent. He was useful in the past but a threat to my very existence now. I wish the God damn rape never happened and I never met the fucking Jew bitch, and I wish the whole Jewish race would disappear from the face of the earth. These conniving people caused so much havoc and turmoil in the world. Why did my son, my own flesh and blood have to be born a Jew? God has been good so far, ever since I left Germany, I was able to rebuild my life from scratch and I have been a force for good in the lives of so many people, I don't understand why God is punishing me now!

He woke up from his trance and went down on his knees and repeated, "Please God, I beg you to make this problem go away, please God give me the strength to overcome these ugly Jews! They took your son, our Lord and now they want to take my Karl as well. Please God help me avenge the murder of your son and help me save my own boy and my own wealth from these greedy bastards."

He turned towards Ricardo. "The question is: where do we go from here, my friend?"

"This bitch has to go, the longer she stays the more likely you and I will be exposed. She must vanish without a trace."

"But how do we achieve this without being implicated?"

Ricardo drew heavily on his cigarette and shrugged. "Maybe God will do it for us, the woman is terminally ill with cancer."

"No, Ricardo, the fucking whore has already recovered and her cancer is in remission," Oscar said impatiently.

"What do you mean she's recovered? The P.I. has been trailing her from one clinic to another, and the report clearly suggests she is frail and sick looking."

"I am telling you she has totally recovered. Sonia spoke to Karl a couple of days ago and she told him the news about her mother. I was in Karl's office when the call came in; she told him her mother's cancer was in remission and the doctor believes her life is not in any immediate danger, so you might as well scrap the notion God will do the job for us."

"I have been thinking, Oscar, what if we hire somebody who can get the job done on our behalf; call it a murder for hire, if you wish?"

"I don't know about all of this, Ricardo, I don't particularly feel comfortable with a murder for hire. Most likely you will be dealing with an unreliable and despicable breed of people who are notorious for bungling the job. And even if they were successful and carry out the hit, they still remain a great threat to our safety. How do you guarantee the hired assassins will remain silent once they discover we have money? They no doubt will blackmail us for the rest of our lives. The only way we can ensure the job is done right is if we are the ones who carry it out."

Ricardo recognized his friend was right, and there was indeed great risk inherent in using the services of paid assassins. He suggested using the group in Oregon as an alternative. "Maybe we need to enlist the organization to get rid of David first and his mother second. You know the police will give Ingrid's murder investigation more weight because her son is a politician, but if David goes first, then Ingrid's investigation will not be as robust. David's murder however will never be traced back to us because the organization is the one who will commit the act. The murder will be blamed on a right wing fringe group. You and I will not be in the picture; the same can be said if we make Ingrid's murder appear as an accident."

Karl was trying to adjust to life in Brazil, the country of his birth and a source of great pride, but things there were so different from the US, He left Brazil when he was very young, not even a teenager at the time, and though he made many trips back and forth to Porto Alegre, the trips were short and different when compared to permanent living, and since the day his father hastily made him return, living there has not been easy. He spent most of his life in the US and that made him more American than he was Brazilian; he found himself thinking like a foreigner in his own country. The first few weeks had been terribly hard. He missed his friends and many of the American products not readily available in Brazil; he missed speaking in English, the pace of life and southern California in particular. But the person he missed most was the love of his life, Sonia. Oh, how much he longs to be with her, hold her tight and look at her pretty face and experience the intensity of her personality and the softness of her heart. There are many beautiful women in Brazil, especially in his home town of Porto Alegre. Even his own office was full of them, and he enjoyed talking to the flirty girls, but he was not interested in anything more than a laugh or a friendly chat. Karl spent hours on his own walking on the beach and lying down on the sand gazing at the stars and listening to the sound of the waves breaking on the shore. He thought about work problems, office staff, Sonia, his kind mother and grandmother, but the one person who occupied his thoughts more than any other now was his father.

When Karl graduated from Harvard Oscar was very proud of his son; he had grand designs for Karl to be in charge of the company and bring it from one triumph to the next. Karl's thoughts always come back to how much he loved his father and always looked up to him and admired his determination to succeed and his will to climb up to the top of the ladder even in foreign lands. Oscar was the eternal optimist, the one never to consider any challenge insurmountable, but as of late, one cannot help but notice the profound and sudden change ever since that day he came to Karl's office in California. Something must have provoked him to undergo this radical transformation; his demeanor is not what it used to be, and as much as Oscar tries to mask it, the worries nevertheless are still visible and lingering on his face. Karl also couldn't escape the none too subtle changes in his habits; he drank more, spent more time on his own, became short tempered and liked to get his own way, and the lives of those around him were being affected. Initially, Karl tried to put it all out of his mind and after a few months living in Brazil, he nearly did, but several things happened and brought it all back crashing on his mind night after night.

Karl sat in his office chair to ponder and analyze what his dad told him before he came back to Brazil. Initially he believed his dad was sincere.

"Son I am going to Brazil next week. I have also booked you a flight to come down there with Ma and Grandma few days after me. Our shipping company general manager has tendered his resignation and the company needs someone like you to run it. This company needs somebody who is family to look after it; we simply cannot afford to hire an untested manager who may run our business into the ground. Your grandfather worked hard all his life to build this company, and until the day he died he wanted you, Karl, to be in charge. He told me and your mom nothing in the world would give him greater pleasure than to see you running the company and bring it higher and higher."

Karl loved his granddad so much and if that was his wish, he will no doubt work to make his wish come true. But then, something very unusual happened one morning which turned Oscar's argument about the company's manager on its head. He went to the office to discuss a work related issue with his father and before he even sat down the door was swung violently open. The old manager, Manuel Alvarado stormed in cursing and using foul language, making abusive remarks and threatening gestures with his hands. He even snarled at Karl when he walked past him. Manuel departed as suddenly as he entered, slamming the door shut behind him, leaving both men thunderstruck. This normally very placid and gentle natured man whom Helmut hired right out of university and who had remained in the service of the family for decades, did not now look like somebody who tendered his resignation peacefully. Karl was totally bewildered.

"What is going on Dad? Why is Mr. Alvarado acting so peculiar and why is he so angry? I understood he tendered in his resignation?"

Oscar was shaken up by the incident but remained calm. "Don't worry son, this son of bitch is not your concern, I will take care of him."

"But what just happened, Dad?"

"I want you to drop it, son, I told you I'll take care of him, and that's the end of it, do you understand?"

Karl did indeed drop it; he didn't mention it for the rest of the day, but the incident made him wonder about the veracity of his father's story. What he saw on that day was not the behavior of a man who resigned willingly and looked forward to retirement. If anything, it was the behavior of someone who was fired for unknown and clearly bogus reasons. Karl also noticed another weird thing happening with his father, especially when he was on the phone talking to Ricardo in LA. Oscar quickly changed the topic of conversation whenever Karl came in the office. He never thought much of it at the time, but now it looks obvious his father was attempting to hide something from him, and it became even more obvious when the two of them switched from English to German. Then, what about the pretty girls his father hired in the office? Clearly their service is not needed, and the reason Oscar hired them to work on the same floor where Karl's office was located was to tempt him to start a relationship with one of them and estrange him from Sonia.

Karl's family had always been keen on Sonia. Both his mother and grandmother regularly asked about her; his dad however, had been nonchalant and seldom inquired or showed enthusiasm. But his interest spiked dramatically when they returned to Brazil; he constantly wanted to know more about her family and her mother's late bout with cancer. It seemed rather odd he suddenly began asking questions and making inquiries when he only showed casual interest in the past. And there was the day he was talking to Sonia on the phone and his father walked in the office to discuss some issues; he overheard Sonia telling him the good news about her mother's cancer remission. Karl distinctly noticed his father's keen interest to tune in to the conversation and was anxious to ask questions about Sonia and her mother after the call ended. There was this inexplicable yet clear dismay on his face when he inferred Ingrid's health has improved substantially, and Karl felt troubled with his dad's unmistaken display of ill wish.

The week before his father's departure to LA, Karl went to see his dad's secretary in her office. She was on the phone discussing the company's phone bills with Oscar, and he noticed all the phone calls made to Sonia in Detroit were highlighted with yellow marker. He recognized the numbers right away because of the US international dial code. "That is odd!" he said to the secretary when she finished the call. "Why are you marking these numbers?"

"I am sorry sir," the secretary answered politely, "Mr. Silva senior requested I prepare this for him."

"And how long have you been doing this?"

"Mr. Silva asked me to highlight all the phone calls to the US made from the company phone," she replied.

Karl could not contain his anger but chose not to say anything; he just walked back to his office feeling betrayed and dumbfounded with the knowledge his father was spying on him. He didn't say anything to his dad, but decided from now on to use his new but cumbersome cellular phone to make all his personal calls. He was so glad this technology was now available in Brazil, and should his father ever ask him why he is no longer calling Sonia, he planned to tell him the truth.

"I am using my new cellular phone because I believe you are spying on me, Father!"

Karl's mind was in a state of angst from the day his father left for California. He buzzed his own secretary and had her cancel the remaining appointments for the day, left the office and drove his 4x4 truck to the beach. It was late afternoon, and as he stood at the edge of the water the sun was hanging low in the horizon and shining its red hues on the ocean. He walked along the sand and watched it slowly disappear behind the mountains. The sound of the water calmed his nerves, and he stretched out on the sand and watched the twinkling stars in the dark sky. Here, he usually felt at peace with himself; however, his mind was with his dad. He thought of that night in LA when his dad came into his office; that awful night that had so many ramifications in his life and the life of his family. He thought about his father's reaction when he looked at the photos sitting on his desk, that photo of him standing with Sonia and her mother in front of the admin building at Harvard, and the other one of him and her family with the Mackinac Bridge in the background. He remembered distinctly his father's weird reaction; it was the response of someone who has detected and identified a person in the photos, and it seems this person must have stirred up distant yet unpleasant memories from the past. His father has met Sonia many times and he never showed any weird reaction, so if Sonia was not the reason for this abnormal reaction, then who was responsible? It must be then one of the other two people in the picture that stirred his interest; it is either Sonia's father or her mother. Come to think of it, it must absolutely be her mother, because Oscar's demeanor began to turn when he first looked at the photo taken in front of the admin building and Greg was not in that photo. Further, his dad referred to that woman who brought back bad memories and didn't mention a man at all when provided explanation for his weird behavior. Back then Karl truly believed the account his father offered for his untoward behavior; of course Oscar had been traveling the day before and must have been jetlagged and tired and may have genuinely mistaken the woman in the photo for someone else. Nevertheless, this grotesque conduct continued unabated and even intensified when they arrived in Brazil. Oscar was not his usual self and was acting rather bizarre. It is plainly obvious he is spying on his own son and shutting him out of conversations with Ricardo, something he never did before. He was making up stories about the company's manager, Mr. Alvarado, and he was showing more interest in Sonia and her family. It is quite clear now there was never any need for him to come back to Brazil; he no longer believed or accepted his father's account about the manager's resignation. The whole thing must have been contrived to provide an excuse to bring him back to Brazil, and the only reason his father forced him to come was to remove him from California and distance him from the United States.

In the distance he could hear the foghorn of a ship announcing its imminent departure from the busy port of Porto Alegre. It sounded like his grandfather was calling him. Karl's eyes closed for few moments, and he could hear his grandfather's voice; "Karl you must pursue and find out what's bothering you till it is no more." He opened his eyes and remembered this great man and how much he missed him now, how much he wished he was still alive. Helmut instilled in his grandson the love and value of knowledge, but the pursuit of honesty and honor was the most important lesson he learned.

His mind then shifted from his father to Sonia's family. He remembered the strange look on Sonia's mother face that day at the airport in Boston when she saw him for the first time. This small, slender lady panicked and shook like a leaf, gasping for air; she had this weird and terrified look on her face, very much like that of his father when he looked at her photos. Karl knew how much he and his father resembled one another. He rolled over and now was lying on his stomach, elbows resting on the sand and his face cradled in the palms of his hands. He could see the city lights shining in the distance, but it was dark and serene where he was. His thoughts went back and forth between his father and Sonia's mother; Ingrid and his dad must have known each other or their paths must have crossed somehow!

But where could a Jewish woman from Germany have met his father? He turned over again, facing the water now; the reflection of the city lights, were churning with the frothy waves. He looked up at the sky and heard his grandfather's voice again; Karl my boy, you will not rest till you find the truth, and you must go after it with determination and rectitude until you reveal it for all to behold.

When he finally got up, he had never felt as good in his life. He strode with a steady pace to his truck, put the keys in the ignition and the sound of the engine came roaring to life. Karl felt alive and well when he drove off in the night.

CHAPTER 60

Oscar arrived in NY just a few weeks before the election. He expected David's busy schedule may not provide him the opportunity to meet but was surprised when he called to set up time for a meeting.

"Not at all Mr. Silva," David cheerfully responded, "it will be my pleasure to meet with you, how about you come to my old law office? You probably have something on your mind you want to discuss."

In fact Oscar didn't have any specific reason to see David that day, and he made sure to have with him a big contribution check made out to the campaign. The real reason however was to meet with his own son face to face to gauge how he felt and how his heart will prompt him to react. Oscar had met with David many times in the past, but this is the first encounter he will have with the knowledge David was in fact his own flesh and blood.

Oscar arrived on time, and David gave him the customary warm welcome. Oscar was so thoroughly consumed with emotions when he sat across the conference table from David. He felt extremely nervous, his legs beneath the table were trembling, but obviously he didn't want David to notice.

"How is your campaign going, David?" Oscar began.

"The campaign is going very well, thank you. We don't expect any surprises. As a matter of fact my Democratic opponent almost conceded when he realized the odds against him were so great. I owe it to people like you Mr. Silva, you have been generous with your contributions and I am very appreciative of your continued support."

"What are your plans for the future, David?"

"There are of course some legislations close to my heart and I will concentrate my efforts to push them through with the help of my cabinet colleagues. There are signs the economy is weakening in New York and we might end up in a big financial mess; we are hoping the next few years will usher in a new economic approach under my leadership."

Oscar's eyes were fixated on David, who then switched the subject to the cold war with the communists. He can see how this man, his own son was so very smart, so intelligent and articulate; it is the German genes and the blood that runs in his veins what makes him so intelligent. His dirty Jewish mother only tainted the purity of his blood! Oscar felt rage going through his body, how much he loathed Jewish people and how much he hated David's mother and David himself by extension. He hates this son of a bitch so much now, he is like his mother, a self-serving Jew, and this bastard will not spare any effort to place himself over and above everybody else! These Jews use their intelligence and charm to fleece the white people of their dignity and possessions. They are aligned with the devil, and behave like rodents creeping in the dark to chew on our assets one bite at a time! Oscar's mind was racing, he felt tremendous revulsion now for the man across the table from him; he regretted ever giving him money, he regretted ever dealing with him. He was not listening to David telling him about the Soviet Union now and the possible destruction of the Berlin Wall; after all, it was your ilk who put the wall up in the first place! It was the Jews who came up with the theory of Communism, it was the Jews who divided Germany in two, and it is time for revenge against all Jews!

Oscar suddenly stood up while David was in mid-sentence. He nervously looked at his watch. "I had better get going. I am going to be late for my next appointment." And with that he waved David goodbye and couldn't get out of the office fast enough. Oscar was gasping for air and felt the need to wash his hands after he touched that mongrel Jew. He stood on the side of the street and hailed a cab, and when he arrived at the hotel room he darted to the bathroom, hunched over the sink and threw up. He still felt very sick, his whole body was shaking and he got in bed and curled up under the covers.

He was awakened late in the evening to the sound of the phone ringing. It was Ricardo. "How did it go with David?"

Oscar mumbled few words but obviously wasn't in the mood to talk to anyone. "...and I'll see you tomorrow in LA," was all Ricardo understood from him.

Karl was feeling great when he arrived at his office the following morning. He was rested after he returned home from the beach the night before; in fact he never had a better sleep in his life. His mind was with Sonia; I wonder what she's doing, she is probably on her way to school right now, she is so diligent and dedicated to her job... Then his thoughts turned towards his father; he must be in bed now, it is still early morning in California. He loved his dad so very much but cannot understand him lately, but last night on the beach he made up his mind to find the true reasons behind the recent odd behavior and it was important to do it discreetly.

Nothing bothered him more than his father's reaction when he looked at Sonia's family photos. He picked up several pictures of his own family; in one of them he was standing with his father and mother, another was a portrait of him and his father standing alone. He put those two in an envelope and sent it by express courier to Sonia's address in Michigan, paying the extra charge for next day delivery.

When he finished, he called Sonia. "Hello sweetheart, how have you been?"

"Hello darling! I have been thinking about you from the moment I woke up this morning."

"Likewise," he said lovingly, "I have been thinking about you and I cannot begin to tell you how much I miss you and how much I love you sweetheart. By the way, I have put some photos of me and my family in an envelope and send it to you by express mail. You should receive them tomorrow. Please let me know what you think and please share them with your mom and dad and tell me what they think of my family."

"That is so sweet; I look forward to receiving them. I will definitely show them to Mom and Dad. I don't believe they have seen any photos of your family. How is it going for you in Brazil and when will you come to see me?"

"It is going fine here. I am planning to come up there when my dad returns from his business trip. I am counting the days before you and I get married. I promise, this is the last time you have to wait sweetie, it is a matter of just few more weeks now."

"I would love to be with you Karl, I miss you so very much darling, and I wish I could be with you right this minute. I want you to love me and cuddle me and I want to give you the biggest kiss in the world to show how much I love you and miss you!"

"Me too darling, I cannot wait for the moment you and I are married and live under the same roof. But I have to get to work now. Have a wonderful day and I will call you tomorrow evening to make sure you received the photos I sent. Love you, sweetheart!"

Sonia returned home from school in the late afternoon the day after she spoke to Karl. Ingrid was so pleased to see her daughter and had good news to share with her.

"Hello mother, how did your appointment with Dr. Morgan go?"

"I am very happy, he finally confirmed everything is going in the right direction and my cancer is in remission. All the tests came back negative, and he doesn't want to send me to do lab tests for another three months, isn't that terrific Sonia?"

"I am so happy for you mother, nothing makes me happier than to see a big smile on your face!" She gave her mother a big hug.

"Oh, my sweetheart, I love you so much. By the way, you received a letter; the FedEx man delivered it this afternoon just before you got home."

"Yes Mother, I know about it. Karl called yesterday to tell me about some photographs of him and his family. Where is it?"

"I put it on top of the dresser in your bedroom."

Sonia went to her bedroom, opened the envelope and brought it back to the living room where her mother was sitting. "Oh, Mother! Look how handsome Karl and his father are! Here, take a look!"

Ingrid put her glasses on and picked up the photo. She gazed at it for a minute, then took off her glasses, wiped her eyes and looked at it again, albeit with more concern. Then suddenly her hand started to shake and her entire body was trembling like a seismic wave had hit her with great ferocity.

She got up and ran to the kitchen screaming. "I know this man! He is an evil person!"

Sonia ran after her mother, "Are you alright, Mom? What is going on? Who are you talking about?"

"Let me see the rest of the photos!" Ingrid demanded.

Sonia handed her the photos and noticed her mother's face change dramatically and she was crying loudly now.

"Keep this man away from me; he is an evil and wicked person!"

"Who are you talking about, Mother?" Sonia herself was beginning to panic.

"Karl's father! Hans was his name; he did terrible things to me in the past!"

"I am so confused mother, are you talking about Oscar, Karl's dad? What possibly could he have done, you never met the man?"

"Yes, I have. I knew this man very well, and how could I forget him?" Ingrid jabbed her finger angrily at the picture. "He was the man who captured me when I tried to escape from Germany. He is the one who tortured me and sent me to die in the concentration camp. He is a nasty and cruel man, I don't want to see him or his son ever again!" Her whole body was shivering in terror.

"Wait a minute, Mother. Are you suggesting Karl's father was a Nazi and he was responsible for all the bad things that happened to you during your ordeal in the concentration camp?" Sonia couldn't believe her own questions.

Ingrid's mind was in utter turbulence and she looked genuinely frightened, yet she could not bring herself to mention the rape. She didn't want to grapple with this and how it would impact her family, nor could she contend with the thought her beloved son was born out of molestation. All she could think of was David, and how it might ruin his career.

"Please, Sonia, remove these photos from our home, I cannot bear to see this man again. Please, please get them out of my view right now! I don't want to relive the misery and pain he inflicted on me!" She reached to grab the photos. "I cannot stand it Sonia, this man is torturing me again. He is an evil Nazi and served in Hitler's army! I don't want to lay my eyes on him ever again!"

Sonia herself was crying in her own confusion. "Mother, no, please stop and tell me what happened! Let's show these pictures to Dad, later." She tucked them away in her pocket. "Look, how can you be so sure it was him? He could be a different person from the man who did all these terrible things to you in Germany! Are you sure it's the same person?"

"Yes, Sonia, I am so very sure it is him." They both calmed down a bit once the pictures were out of sight. "He is older now, but hasn't lost his looks. I have known him since he was a boy and I saw him grow up and become a man and finally join the army. I know this man very well, and he is a very bad person, and please don't ever doubt what I say."

Sonia was very confused now, how could her mother and Oscar know each other? How did their lives cross? How on earth could this man with such high moral values have committed all these terrible things to her mother? How did she meet him in the first place? Sonia wanted to find answers, but her mother was obviously so shaken and upset; maybe she must leave it for now until things cool down a little.

Ingrid was in no mood to talk about it either when Greg came home in the evening. "What is going on? Why are you crying? Are you alright?" he asked his wife.

"No, I am not alright! Please leave me alone. I need my nerves to cool down a little." Greg knew his wife well, and he left her alone.

Sonia stayed in bed that evening thinking about her mother. No doubt her mother was telling the truth, why would she make it all up? She must have gone through a horrible experience at the hands of Karl's father. Sonia picked up the phone and called Karl in Brazil; she couldn't wait for him to call her as he promised.

"Oh, hi Sonia, I was going to call you shortly."

"I couldn't wait, Karl, something very terrible happened here with my mother. She became absolutely hysterical when she looked at the photos you sent. She was crying so hard her whole body was trembling."

"Why, what upset her?" He would rather Sonia be the first one to say it.

"Oh, Karl, I don't think you are going to like this. But my mother says she knows your father very well, apparently. She knew him from when she was in Germany. I am so upset! She actually believes it was your father who arrested her when she was trying to flee from the Nazis!"

"Oh, wow! No, I can't imagine my father doing anything like that. Could she possibly be mixing him up with somebody else?"

"But, was your father in Hitler's army? Was he a Nazi?"

"I don't know for sure if my father was in the army during the war. He never talks about it to me. But he was 14 years old when the war started, he was too young. If he was drafted while the war was still going on, he probably had no choice in the matter. All men were drafted when they reached the enlistment age, I don't think it was optional at the time."

"So do you think it's possible?" Sonia paused, as something occurred to her. "Karl, is that why you sent those photos? Did you know? You said it was important; you sent them by express mail! Why, Karl? Is it true?" Sonia's voice began to break.

"There's no way to be sure, Sonia. Maybe a lot of young German men looked similar, and she's confused. Or maybe their paths did cross at some point. I don't know."

"This may very well be the case, but how does that explain her reaction to the pictures, and all the torture and pain my mother says she suffered at his hands?"

"I cannot explain anything Sonia; I am truly ashamed of my father if her allegations are true. Please express my sincere regret that she had to go through such a horrible experience, especially if she claims it was my father who did anything to her."

They talked for a while longer, and Sonia felt somewhat better after she hung up the phone. Karl sounded very sincere as usual, but she was in no doubt her relationship with him was in jeopardy if her mother's assertions turn out to be true. She lay awake in her bedroom trying to visualize her mother being tortured at the hands of the Nazis. The scar on her neck was a constant reminder of what happened to her more than forty years ago. Sonia cannot comprehend how human beings can be so cruel to one another, what could her mother have possibly done to make the Nazis hate her with such intensity? How could Karl's father be responsible? Was he acting in his capacity as an officer and therefore following orders to torture her from his superiors, or was he as how Ingrid portrayed, a man who inflicted so much pain on her out of pure evil? Sonia could not forget her mother's description of the lust and the pleasure the officer enjoyed with every lash or kick she received, and of course how she got the cigarette burn on her neck. There was more pleasure on his face with every scream from her.

Sonia was in a trance until the morning, when she finally slipped out of bed after a very long, miserable and sleepless night. She put on her clothes and went to school in an utterly confused state, full of anguish and trepidation. All day her mind was on her mother and what happened the night before; she called home a couple of times to check up on her, and Ingrid sounded much better. By midafternoon Sonia was mentally worn out, but on the way home from work her thoughts turned from her mother to Father O'Malley

Karl felt very depressed when he finished the call with Sonia. He never expected things to get as ugly as they did now. How could he possibly defend his father's actions if the torture and sufferings were as Ingrid described to her daughter? In his mind these were the actions of a very cruel and inhumane person, and now there was no doubt his father was responsible for all the horror and barbarity committed against this defenseless and sweet woman. He knows how much his father hated the Jews and how much he wanted to rid the world of them, but he didn't share nor understand his father's beliefs. Karl was pacing his office trying to evaluate his options. He has no illusion his father was somehow responsible for what happened to Ingrid in the past, judging by his father's erratic behavior and the complete change in his attitude after seeing and identifying Sonia's mother in the photo. The worried look on his face, the instant shift in his demeanor, the bizarre conduct and the subsequent transformation in his character, all point to a man trying to hide his shameful past, and it looks like the missing pieces of the puzzle are finally falling in place. Karl knows damn well why his father brought him back to Brazil, and why he invented the stories about the manager. His father wants him removed from the US to distance him from Sonia and therefore eliminate any chance of exposure!

He felt a little dizzy, his mind was reeling and he felt utterly powerless. He sat numbly in his chair, not knowing what to do or what his father was up to. What was he doing in the US now? Karl instinctively felt his father may be plotting something against Ingrid; he felt the whole world is crumbling on his head and he was powerless to affect the course of events. His first concern was for Sonia; his love for her has not diminished. Quite the contrary he felt an overwhelming affection for her, and need to protect her. She occupied his thoughts and heart all the time; he felt her hurt and agony when they spoke on the phone. Nothing in the world mattered more to him than her, not even his own father. Yes, he loved his parents dearly, but it was a different kind of love. He felt the burden and the responsibility to defend her and to stand with Sonia through this terrible time.

CHAPTER 61

Sonia parked in the church parking lot, walked to the rectory door around the back and knocked timidly. Father O'Malley was surprised to see her at this time and asked her in his warm voice to come in.

"What brings you here at this time, my child? You look like something is bothering you, like you have something on your mind."

"Yes Father, I have so many things on my mind, but this is not why I came to see you. To tell you the truth, I have made a decision. I have been thinking I must devote my life to the service of our Lord, Jesus Christ, because I believe God is calling on me to serve."

"But you are serving the Lord already my child, and you are doing it in so many different ways. Your duty at school is a laudable service to the Almighty. Your attending mass on Sundays is a service to the ministry of our Lord; what else do you wish to do Sonia?"

"I am here to confess my desire to become a nun. I think I want to join my Christian sisters and make my faith the essence of my life."

"This is all admirable, Sonia, but I was under the impression you and Karl are getting married in few months. I therefore strongly recommend your first priorities go to your husband. You are a young and intelligent girl and you have your life to live and you do not want to spend the rest of it in seclusion. At your age you should be celebrating life and planning to bring the next generation of good Christians to this world."

"No, Father, marriage is not on my mind. The service of the Lord is."

"This is no easy decision, Sonia. What came about to make you change your plans? Is everything alright with Karl?" He waited patiently as she seemed agitated, but unwilling to disclose something important. "Please share with me what happened and what motivated you to want to become a nun. You have to understand to become a Catholic sister is a commitment for life and you must absolutely comprehend what all of this means. I can tell you with certainty it will bring radical change into your life," he advised quietly.

"I take my duty to the Lord very seriously and deep down I feel a devout Christian. I have to be honest with you father, yes, something drastic indeed happened in my life, and here I am seeking to find comfort in Jesus and solace in my faith. I feel a strong impulse to become a Catholic sister and I have this great urge to spend the rest of my life in the service of Christ, our Lord."

"Please Sonia, take a deep breath and relax a little. I would like you to share the drastic thing that happened to you. I can perhaps help you overcome some of the pain, and I hope this is not too personal."

"Father, maybe in due time I will share the facts about my complicated life, but I sinned father when I was in college and I strongly believe what happened is the comeuppance I deserve. This is why I am looking for Jesus. I want to repent and ask the Lord for forgiveness; this is what I came here to talk about."

"Very well Sonia, let me think about it for a while. But I feel it is my duty to warn you again about the dire changes this will bring into your life and the lives of those you love. This is not a decision to be made in haste, it requires much nuance and deliberation and I trust you and your family will give the matter deep consideration."

"I am not ready to talk Father, but when I am ready, I'll be here to see you. All I am doing at the moment is exploring my options. I still have a few months before the school term finishes, and I still have a great responsibility for my students and I will never let them down. Nevertheless I feel the Lord is calling me and I feel a strong obligation to answer His call."

Father O'Malley sat down in his office after Sonia left. What a lovely young lady, he told himself. I have cared for this girl from the day she started to come to our church when she was just a teenager, full of life and zest. I followed her career through school and college. She always carried herself with poise, honor and dignity and her devotion to the Lord is beyond question. I saw how delighted she was when her boyfriend announced his desire to marry her at our church; I could see her eyes moisten with happiness and anticipation. Something very dire must have happened to make her abandon her marriage plans. I do care for Sonia with all of my heart, and I seek your guidance Oh, Lord.

Sonia found her mother in the kitchen preparing dinner. "Hello Mother, how are you feeling now?"

"I am fine. I am so sorry for what happened last night, Sonia. Apparently I lost my composure and I must have been intolerable, please forgive me?"

"You don't have to apologize to me, Mother; all I care about is that you are happy and content. I hope you are back to normal now, are you?"

"Well, I had all day to look back at my life and to appraise this new development coming so unexpectedly in our lives. I thought things will have quieted down after what happened in Germany and the cancer. Now, obviously things keep coming at me and I dread what will be next. I never thought I would again run into the man who caused me so much pain and anguish, and whose very son is now the love of the only daughter I have in this life. And as much as I don't want to be reminded of the past, the past came back knocking at my door so I guess it's here to stay."

"No mother, that is not necessarily true. This is your life and you can do what you want with it. I will always stand by you and support you and forever love you. You are my mother, you gave birth to me and I am your living extension. Whatever happened in the past must be erased from our thoughts; we need to concentrate on the future. As for Karl's father, you need to take him off of your mind. I do understand it is easier said than done, but you have to believe me mother, the more you think about this evil man the more it will hurt you. I hope you might find it in your heart to forgive him, I believe this will be the first step to healing your heart."

"Yes Sonia, it is easy to say, but you don't know how this evil and sadistic man tormented and treated me worse than a cockroach. He inflicted the kind of pain and anguish few people will ever experience, pain that still lingers to this day. Over the years I put this man out of my mind and almost forgot him, until the day I met Karl at the airport in Boston. It brought the memories flooding back; you wouldn't believe how much he reminded me of Oscar, or 'Hans' as he was called back then. The two looked so much alike, especially when Hans was as old as Karl is now. I know it's not Karl's fault his father is evil, in fact I like Karl and find him a nice and decent man, but I don't know how I would feel if you marry him. I know in my heart I will never speak to his father again; I don't even contemplate being in the same room with this awful man."

"You don't have to worry about this mother. I loved Karl with all of my heart and I always will, but at this stage in my life, I love you more than anything in the world, and I promise never to allow Karl or his father to bring you pain in the future."

"Bless your heart Sonia! I love you so much, I love you more than words can describe and I am so sorry I if came between you and Karl. This has never been my intension or the outcome I contemplated, all I want is to see you married and happy."

Greg came home from work and found his wife in a better mood than the night before. "Hi Honey, how are you doing today? I hope you are feeling better."

"Much better now, thank you. How was your day?"

"Pretty good." He looked at Sonia and realized she was in a reflective mood. " How about you, Sonia?"

"I guess it was alright. Mother and I had a little talk and we both feel better."

"Great, glad to hear it, but I would like to know what happened last night. I hate to come home and see everybody in a sour mood. Can we please sit down and get it all off of our chests?

Sonia let Ingrid over to the couch and they sat there, hand in hand. "It's pretty complicated, Dad. Something has come up; it's really upsetting for all of us."

Greg's face dropped, not knowing what to expect. "What, is it David...?"

"No, no, he's fine. Dad, we have found out Mom knew Karl's father from when she was in Germany. In fact, Karl's dad was the very evil man who perpetrated all the pain and torment on Mother."

"Oh my God, this is quite something." Greg was at a loss for words. "I don't quite understand why we didn't know about him before. What did this man actually do to you, Ingrid?"

"Dad, you don't want to know, but this man was a Nazi officer, and he is responsible for the torture and beatings mom suffered when she was in the concentration camp. But this is the past and we don't want to keep talking about it, it brings so much pain to mother."

"Wait a minute Sonia! This man's son is involved with you, and suddenly we discover his father was the SOB who tortured your mother? For God's sake, you are going to marry this boy and we need to talk about it! So where do you stand with Karl and his father? Can anyone please tell me?"

"Yes, Dad, I was involved with Karl, but I assure you mom is my first priority at the moment. I will have all the time in the world to think and reflect about him. But I also want you to recognize that Karl has not personally done anything bad to Mom. Please allow me time to think over my future."

"Very well sweetie, I trust you will make the right decision. I have great faith in you, you have always been wise and mature. But how about David?

I know Karl's father had some dealings with him, don't you think we ought to let him know?"

"No, please don't get David involved in this!" Ingrid shouted, "I don't want David to know about Karl's father for now. I will break the story to him when I feel more comfortable to talk about it. It is just, I am not ready now." She was nearly in tears again.

"Whatever you say, Honey. We are here to support you, but I still think David must be told soon."

Nancy was thrilled when David first announced his intention to become the next Governor of New York. Her immediate thought when he called to tell her was to ask about the extra perks.

"I am not running for the Governor's office because of the perks!" he admonished his wife. "You have to put things in perspective and act responsibly when you are married to a politician, dear. Can you imagine the consequences if you were heard in public saying what you just did! There will be scandalous reports in all the papers, so please drop this nonsense!"

"I am only joking dear; you don't have to be such a prude!"

CHAPTER 62

Ricardo drove his brand new sports car over to Oscar's home. He strongly recommended they hold all talks about Ingrid there, or in the car while driving but definitely not at the office where somebody may overhear their conversation. They sat down in the living room to watch David's interview on the news channel about his plans for upper New York's economically depressed region. The phone rang but Oscar didn't get up to answer. Elsa came in to tell him Gretchen was calling from Brazil.

"Tell her I am busy, I will call her back in few minutes," he instructed Elsa.

Ricardo stood up and gave a big sigh when David finished. "These fucking Jews will take over this country and become the effective rulers of the world," he said with pain in his voice. "They want to implement their agenda to form a one world government under their leadership and all they care about is to reap the benefit from the toils and hard work of ordinary white citizens in this country and beyond."

Oscar and Ricardo have been agonizing for the past few weeks over their options to get rid of both Ingrid and David. They had no inkling Karl contacted Sonia and now Ingrid herself knows who Oscar was. They weren't aware Karl knew about his father's colorful past and Ingrid's torture. This new development, David running for Governor, forced them to think and think hard how to get rid of Ingrid and her bastard son. Both men knew damn well they cannot remain idle and therefore had no choice now but to take matters into their own hands and plan for Ingrid and David's murder. Failure to accomplish this will increase the risk their identities will be exposed. Everything they worked for and acquired through their lives will be lost, they may even spend the rest of their lives in prison for the crimes committed against this defenseless Jewish woman and for not declaring their Nazi past when they became citizens of the United States. They thought about all the wealth they managed to accumulate over the last forty years and became concerned they may lose it all if they don't act in a hurry. Everything so dear to their hearts will go down the drain and they will be destitute in their old age with no means to survive. It was a sobering thought indeed.

Oscar returned his wife's call a little later. It turned out she was planning to come to California with her mother for a scheduled appointment with Erika's heart specialist. Oscar did instruct his wife to remain in Brazil while he was away in LA, but after she called he advised her to come long enough to see the doctor then return immediately to Porto Alegre after the appointment. He used Karl as an excuse, saying it was necessary to provide him a family atmosphere at home and not leave him all alone in Brazil. The real reason though was to get her out of the way as he feared having her at the house in LA may raise her suspicion and she may get wind if his plans to get rid of Ingrid.

Father O'Malley was preparing for mass on Sunday morning. He felt a current of uneasiness sweeping his body when Sonia came to his mind. This young and attractive lady is now looking to serve the lord and become a nun? He questioned her motives and wondered about the reasons that prompted her to speculate a life in seclusion. Something abominable must have happened in the last few weeks. He recalled how happy she was when Karl told him about his plans to marry her; the two of them looked so much in love and so suited for one another. What developed in Sonia's life to make her break up the relationship and announce her desire to become a nun? He knows from experience some of the women who join the sisterhood have done so as a result of something traumatic. Of course there are many women who solely believe in the sanctity of their choice and join in purely for the love of Jesus, but in Sonia's case however, Father O'Malley strongly suspects Karl was somehow behind her decision to join. Has he changed his mind and decided to marry someone else? And Sonia became the jilted woman who turn to religion to sooth and forget her pain? Sonia however, never said anything negative about him. Father O'Malley felt great sympathy and decided to have a chat with her after mass later today.

Patrick O'Malley was born in Dayton, Ohio to an immigrant Irish family, who escaped the economic depression and the rigor of the Catholic Church in their native Ireland. He recalled his mother talking about her own mother's experience with the Church back in the old country and the coercion she endured at the monastery after she was made a nun against her will. It was absolutely horrendous what happened to her and to other women who were forcefully made to join in order to make them repent for social infractions. Many of them had little or no education and they accepted their fate and the appalling conditions they lived in, and he vowed upon becoming a priest to help women who suffer with emotional distress. Of course the circumstances here are vastly different from the turn of the century Ireland. The monasteries in the United States treat women with respect and dignity and nobody is forced to join against their will, and those who willingly choose to join are subject to strict stipulations. Chief among the requirements is a stable emotional background.

When Father O'Malley finished his sermon, he stood like he always did at the front door shaking the hands of the congregants as they filed out of the church. When it was Sonia's turn he signaled her to wait until everyone was gone. "Good to see you again my child. I see a little more twinkle in your eyes today; I hope you worked out what was bothering you!"

"Yes, Father, I feel much better now, I am sorry if I was a nuisance."

"You are not a nuisance my child. The good Lord is watching over you because you are a good person and you deserve our love and attention."

"You are so kind, Father. I had such a bad day when I came the other time, but I feel much better after I had a talk with my mother."

"That is to your credit Sonia. You talk about your problems and work out solutions. I am ever so proud of you, and I hope you reconsidered the yearning for the Christian Sisterhood."

"No, Father, I have indeed made up my mind to join, and I want to begin my journey as soon as possible at the end of the school term."

"Oh, my! Perhaps we should go sit down inside for a few minutes." He led her down the hall to his office and resumed the discussion. "I don't quite understand, Sonia, I thought you worked out your problems and your mind is more settled now? I wish you would share with me what is bothering you? Perhaps I can guide you through before you make up your mind."

"Father, I wish I could, but it is very complicated; it seems everything in my life is."

"You are no different than me or the many people you see around you, Sonia. We all have problems, but what matters is how we deal with these problems, and I hate to see you make the wrong choices in life."

"I hope not, Father, but where do I begin when my problems are much intertwined, and I feel my emotions are a little too flaccid at the moment?"

"That is the point my child. To qualify to be a nun you are first required to purge the emotional stresses. The church wants people to join but they don't want them to join when they are so emotionally overwhelmed and the reason to join was the by-product of upheaval and instability in their mind."

Sonia was getting emotional and her eyes moistened a bit, but she mustered enough courage to continue. "I have decided to join because I sinned when I was in college. I came in between my girlfriend Tracy, and her boyfriend, and their relationship unraveled because of me. The devil tempted me to take her boyfriend away from her, and now the Lord is making me pay for my sin."

"I take it the boyfriend was Karl, was he?"

"Yes, Father, it was, and I am ashamed of what happened."

"You need not be ashamed, Sonia. We all make mistakes and our Lord is the more encompassing and forgiving. And don't forget, Jesus died on the cross for our sins. You need to express empathy and regret to your friend, but you need not punish yourself for the rest of your life for a single mistake during your youth."

"The problem is far more convoluted than you think, Father. I must break this relationship with the love of my life not because of anything he did, but because of what his father had done to my mother. I know this sounds rather silly, but I assure there is more to it than meet the eye."

"The choice to marry is a matter of the heart; if you love this man and this man wants to marry you then you must follow your heart and join him in holy matrimony. The Lord will bless and condone."

"I love Karl with all of my heart, Father, but if I follow my heart and marry him, this may cause great anguish or even death to my mother. I cannot allow it to happen and then have all of this on my conscience for the rest of my life. Please, Father, understand my predicament."

"Of course I do, my child, but there must be a way to reconcile your mother's emotional needs and your own?"

"My mother is a holocaust survivor. The torture and pain she suffered is beyond description. Father, we have learned that the man who perpetrated all this pain on her was Karl's father! He is an evil man and I don't have it in my heart to cause mother to re-live this pain if I married Karl." Sonia started to sob, and Father O'Malley was patting on her shoulder to soothe her pain, finally understanding the cause.

"Very well my child, I will have a word with Sister Anne. In the meantime, I shall say a verse for you and your mother as well."

A week after she had the talk with Father O'Malley Sonia received a phone call from Sister Anne.

"Hello Sonia, I am Sister Anne; I am the coordinator here at the St. Theresa monastery. I understand from Father O'Malley, you have expressed interest to join our sisterhood?"

"Thank you so much for calling me, Sister. Yes, I have in fact spoken to Father O'Malley about my desire to become a Catholic sister."

"Very well Sonia, would you like to come over for a little chat? Sister Annabelle Dean, our Mother Superior is available this coming Saturday." Sonia jotted down the address of the monastery in Clinton Township in the outskirts of the greater Detroit area; she was thrilled at the invitation.

She got up early on Saturday morning, had a hot, relaxing bath and put on a long skirt, a dark blouse and jacket. Through the kitchen window she could see it was sunny, a nice day. Her mother and father were at the table reading the morning paper and having coffee.

"Good morning!"

"Good morning, Sonia," Greg answered, "you are all dressed up, where are you planning to go so early?"

"I am going to see Sister Annabelle; she invited me to come for a prayer at their monastery."

"Oh, that's nice, but who is Sister Annabelle?"

"Oh Dad, you are so inquisitive. I will tell you about her later. I haven't even met her. I better get going or I will be late."

Sonia arrived at the monastery exactly on time. She couldn't help but notice the beautiful setting where the building was situated. She walked up to the front door and rang the bell; a middle-aged woman in a brown habit opened it.

"Good morning young lady, you must be Sonia. I am Sister Anne. Our Mother Superior, Sister Annabelle is expecting you. Please follow me; I will escort you to her office."

Sonia walked behind Sister Anne through a cloister and then to the office, where a bespectacled older lady was sitting behind the desk. She stood up to greet Sonia. "Hello Sonia, I am Sister Annabelle, the Mother Superior at St. Theresa. Welcome to our monastery, and please sit down." Sonia was a little nervous yet she felt serene inside. "I am glad you came here to see us, please relax and feel comfortable. But before we start let's say a prayer together.

O almighty and eternal God!
Who through Jesus Christ
hast revealed Your glory to all nations,
to preserve the works of Your mercy,
that Your Church,
being spread through the whole world,
may continue with unchanging faith
in the confession of your name.
Amen.

Now, please tell me my child, what brought you here to our monastery, what are your motivations?"

Sonia had prepared for this moment in her mind, debating it back and forth ever since she went to see Father O'Malley. She knew very well this topic would be brought up; the monastery would want to know if her decision to join was a rational one, one which is based on faith and not emotional trauma.

"To tell you the truth your benevolence, as a child growing up I had great affinity and love for Jesus. I was born here in Detroit, my father is a Lutheran Christian, and my mother is a devout Jewish lady, a holocaust survivor originally from Germany. She escaped to this country after she survived the most horrific experience at the hands of the evil Nazis. The nice doctor who treated my mother after she was found hanging to life by a thread in a concentration camp helped her move here, where she met and married my father. At first mother took me and my brother for prayer at the synagogue when we were little, but I grew to like my father's Lutheran church more and as I grew older I determined the Catholic Church is where my spiritual needs lay."

Sister Annabelle interrupted momentarily. "Well this is very interesting; you followed neither your father nor your mother's faith. You must have a strong attachment to the Catholic faith."

"Yes, your benevolence, faith is the essence of who I am. I often go to church on my own, and I do say a prayer before going to bed and when I get up in the morning. I don't eat a meal till I say grace; I am very attached to our Lord Jesus."

"I believe you are a teacher, can you tell me more about your background?"

"Of course, your benevolence. I wanted to study theology in college, but there was a conflict with the admission requirements at Harvard where I studied and I chose English instead. After four years I graduated with honors then continued my studies at the university here in Dearborn and became a teacher. I love the job and my students with passion, and it will be a sad day for me when I leave them, but I have great spiritual needs and even greater desire to pursue these needs. I hope my school colleagues and students will forgive me."

"This is all very well Sonia. But Father O'Malley did mention you are in a relationship with a man and there was talk of marriage even. Can you please tell us more about that?"

"His name is Karl Silva; he was my boyfriend. Our relationship started when we were in college and developed over the last several years. He and I were planning to get married and were counting the days to get married in a few weeks but a big problem came upon us from out of nowhere."

"Did this man break up with you?"

"No, your benevolence, he and I are still the best of friends. It pains me to talk about him, he is the love of my life and I am the love of his, and he adamantly still wants to marry me. But this problem we now face will make it impossible."

"What seems to be the problem? Sonia, if this man expressed his love to you and you to him, where is the harm if you two are wed?"

"There will be tremendous harm, your benevolence. My mother's very wellbeing and existence depends on me not marrying the man I love, but it isn't because of anything he did personally."

"I am a tad confused, Sonia; you love this man and your family has no objection you marrying him, so what seems to be the problem?"

"This is exactly what I told Father O'Malley; I have a complicated problem to say the least. Karl's father was the Nazi officer who tortured and tormented my mother and then threw her to die in the concentration camp. But this information about his father surfaced after Karl and I have been together for a long time. You can understand how my mother feels if her only daughter marries the son of the man who caused her so much harm and grief? You should have seen my mother's reaction when she saw his photo after forty years; she was a total wreck!" Sonia was trying very hard to hold back her tears as she confessed to Sister Annabelle. "How do you expect me to marry him, we cannot live in isolation without our families! But my mother cannot even stand to be in the same room with his father, the pain is too great for her to handle!"

"I am sorry to hear about your mother, Sonia. This is a very extraordinary

tragedy and I greatly sympathize with you my dear. It must have been traumatizing for you."

"Yes, your benevolence, it struck me like a thunderbolt, and I had many
sleepless nights when it happened. But things have eased off since my mother
and I had a serious conversation about the problem."

"And may I ask what you and your mother discussed?"

"My mother was diagnosed with lymphoma and suffered through
months of agonizing treatment, but thank the Lord she recovered not too
long ago. The doctor told us she was out of danger at present but he didn't
preclude the recurrence of this horrible disease. Because of her condition
I have to be careful and tread delicately when I speak to her. At the outset
of our conversation my mother said the thought of seeing Karl's father will
make her sick and nauseous. Unfortunately, Karl, my boyfriend and his dad
are almost the mirror image of each other; the resemblance is indeed uncanny. I fear if we get married my mother will suffer immeasurably like what
happened at Boston airport when she laid her eyes on Karl for the first time."

"Why, what happened at the airport?"

"You cannot believe it, your benevolence, but my mother was in a total
meltdown. She was gasping for air and her body shook like a leaf. She recalled the torture and the pain Karl's father inflicted on her because of the
physical similarity between them. It was agonizing for all of us to watch
when it happened back then."

"This will bring us now to your intentions for the future, Sonia. Where
do you plan to go from here?"

"I have spent countless hours thinking about this quagmire and recognized two options available to me now; I can go ahead and marry the man
I love with the knowledge such a marriage will bring quick death to my
mother and destroy our families, or the other option is to call off the marriage and leave Karl for good. He is a very eligible bachelor and can easily
find love and happiness with another woman, and chances are he will forget
me altogether in the future. I, on the other hand, will find love in Jesus our
Lord, and hope time will heal my heart. So I made my decision to prevent
tragedy to the people I love and preserve the unity of the families involved."

"I don't quite understand why marrying Karl will bring death and destruction to your family and his? Surely your mother doesn't have to see or
interact with his father?"

"I thought this may have a chance to succeed until you consider the consequences and the possible involvement of my brother. You see, my brother is

a politician with a lot of clout and I fear he will seek to avenge what happened to mother. David, my brother, worships the ground Mother walks on and there is no doubt in my mind he will retaliate somehow, and when he does it will destroy Karl's family and my own."

"How did you cope with all of this, Sonia? This could be very hard on you now and in the future, my child."

"Yes, your benevolence, but my faith kept me together; I prayed during these difficult days, and I cried for hours at end, but I hope to come through it with the help of Jesus."

"And what did Karl say, or more to the point, what did he do when you told him?"

"I haven't yet broken the news to him. But Karl is a very sweet person; he will not do anything to hurt me. He was deeply upset about his father's past and couldn't apologize to me enough, but the truth is neither he nor I can change the past. I love my mother and Karl equally, but how can I marry this man when he will be a constant reminder of her suffering?"

"Yes, I understand the depth of your feelings, Sonia. You are torn between your love for him and the love for your mother and you feel one comes at the expense of the other. But I would like to encourage you to see if you can reach an understanding with your mother about Karl. After all, as you've already realized, it wasn't his fault his father committed all those atrocities against your mother."

"My mother is a very sweet woman; she will do anything in this world to make me happy. As a matter of fact, she grew to like Karl so much before she realized who his father was. But her wounds run deep and Karl is the manifestation of the very man she hated and feared, the thought of me marrying Karl would be emotionally and psychologically devastating, and I'm truly afraid it will send her to her grave before her time. I love my mother so much and I will not do such a thing to hurt her."

Sister Annabelle explained to Sonia who they are and what their mission is at the cloistered community of Carmelite Nuns. She told her they are a happy group of nuns, who dedicate their lives in prayer for the Lord and the service of his ministry, and explained some of the rules and regulations. Then she informed Sonia they will contact her in few weeks after they conduct a background check and discuss her suitability.

Sonia was introspective on the drive home from the monastery. She was not angry or upset anymore; all she wanted to do now is to concentrate her feelings for the love and service of the Lord. She felt at peace with herself and when she arrived home she was very hungry. After having something to eat, she asked Ingrid, "Where is Dad, Mother?"

"Your dad is working in the backyard, tidying up putting things away in the shed. But what are you up to Sonia? You rushed out this morning without saying much."

"What do you mean, Mother?"

"Well, you were gone this morning for several hours; your dad and I were concerned about you."

"You don't have to worry yourself about me, Mother, I am a very happy girl today!"

"I am glad to hear it, but do you mind sharing the source of your happiness with me?" Ingrid asked with hope.

"I went over to see Sister Annabelle this morning and I had a little conversation with her at the monastery."

"Who is Sister Annabelle? And what church does she belong to, Sonia?"

"Sister Annabelle is a Carmelite nun. She is the Mother Superior at the Monastery of St. Theresa, and she is a lovely lady, Mother."

"What kind of church is St. Theresa? What do you mean Carmelite nun, what do they do at the church there?"

"Oh, Mother, St. Theresa is a different kind of church. It is a monastery where the nuns live in seclusion and spend most of their time in prayer and contemplation. They offer a simple life and I am attracted to join them."

"Sonia, what are you saying? You will leave your job and leave us to become a nun? Let me call your dad. Ingrid opened the back door and shouted her husband to come in.

Greg was a little perplexed when his wife delivered the news that Sonia is thinking of becoming a nun. "What is this all about?" he softly asked his daughter.

"Yes Dad, I am exploring my options at this stage. No decision has been made."

"I am always proud of you Sonia. I trust you will make the right decisions in life. I was very proud when you made the decision to go to Harvard and I was more proud when you received your teaching credentials, but I don't understand what or who is pushing you to give up everything you worked for all your life to live the life of a hermit?"

"Dad, this is rather a callous way to describe the kind, Catholic women who chose to give up everything material in this world for the love of Jesus."

"I am so sorry, Sonia, but you spent your entire life preparing to reach where you are now. I don't understand what is making you give it all up and become a nun?"

"There is one simple answer to all of this, Dad, and it is the same answer nuns the world over give when they choose this life and that is the love of Jesus and Mary his virgin mother."

"I admire you for the devotion you have for the Lord, but I think teaching will benefit society more than being a nun whose life is cut off from that society."

"No father, I am sure each has some merits and drawbacks, but we live in a free society where everybody can make their own rational decision. I have stated that I have not made a decision yet, all I am doing at this stage is exploring my options, and then I can determine which one best suit my needs."

"Is this all because of Karl and his father?" Ingrid interjected, with obvious frustration in her voice.

"Mother, there are many things influencing my mind at the moment. Karl, you, Dad, David, school kids, my friends, and it would be utterly simplistic to concentrate the issue around one person. I love you dearly mother and I also love Karl, I don't see anything wrong if I add Jesus to the mix. Loving Jesus doesn't mean I will stop loving you, and I hope neither of you will object if I share my love of you with Jesus."

"Of course not, Sonia," Greg answered impatiently, "all we'd like to see is you are happy and fulfilled in life, all we want is for you to get married and give us grandchildren to be proud of. Please don't think we are against you, quite the contrary, we are concerned parents and we are trying to help our daughter make the right decision and not squander her life."

"Dad, I appreciate what you saying, but it is my life you talking about. Please afford me the time to think and debate the issue in my mind. I promise to look at things carefully and prudently and I will be mindful of the consequences my decision will have on you and Mom. All I can ask at this stage is for your loving support. But I have one additional request to make; I don't want David or anyone else for that matter to know about this. The last thing I want for David is negative publicity for his campaign."

Karl was not upset with Sonia when the two spoke after the discovery of his father's past. He knew in his heart Sonia was vulnerable when it comes to her mother and the disclosure must have hit her like a ton of bricks. He recalled the hurt in her voice the day after her mother found out and he truly empathized with her over the terrible situation she is in. He realizes how torn she was because the same situation applies to him; he too was torn between his deep love for Sonia and his love and loyalty for his father. He was ashamed his father was responsible for such heinous crimes, but powerless to change what happened forty years earlier. He felt so sad and dejected and wished he could take Sonia under his wing and go somewhere desolate to live the rest of his life with her, just the two of them without anybody breathing over their shoulders. He yearned for the good times when the two were innocent lovers attending college with no worries in the world. Karl was tempted to call Sonia many times when he felt lonely, but resisted the temptation; his instincts pulled him back, he was aware of her need for space to think the problem through, and he reckoned it is best to give her the room to do just that.

David's campaign gave him the ideal opportunity to contact Sonia. He contrived a call to offer his support for her brother's run for Governor and stayed late in the evening until all the employees went home. He also felt this great urge to call his father first and castigate him for not telling the truth about his past identity or show remorse for his inhumane treatment of Ingrid, but he dropped the idea knowing how much his father hated the Jews and everything Jewish. Instead he dialed Sonia's number; he knew she would be at home at night after a long and tiring day at school.

Sonia was in the kitchen helping her mother with the dinner dishes when the phone rang.

"Hello Sonia, how are you darling? I miss you so much."

Sonia's mind was spinning a mile a minute when she heard the familiar voice. "I am doing fine, thank you. May I put you on hold for a minute please?" Karl overheard Sonia telling her mother she needed to take the call in her bedroom; he waited impatiently for Sonia to come back on the line.

"Hi Karl." She started the conversation with a rather serious tone different from her normal loving tenor. "I am fine, how about you?"

"I am not doing well at all. I miss you so much my darling and I've wanted so much to speak to you the last few days, but I thought you might wish to have some space for a while. But I wanted to know how David's election campaigning is going, and I thought to offer my congratulations, as well as a donation."

"Thank you Karl. Yes, my brother always thinks big; he's running for the biggest office in the state as you know."

Karl wasn't really interested in David's career. "I love you so much Sonia, my whole body is aching for you! I wish I could give you a big hug now; I know how difficult this all must have been for you."

"Yes, Karl, my days have been dark and terrible; I cannot tell you how much hurt the news about your father has caused my family."

"I am so sorry my father caused all of this; I wish in my heart this isn't the case, but we know it is and I have to deal with it now."

"You don't have to apologize, Karl, it was not your fault. Whatever your father did was way before you were born, and you cannot blame yourself for his actions."

"But I do, Sonia. Plus my father and I look so much alike and I understand how your mother feels when she sees me. It is like looking at my father, and of course that can only bring sad memories and perpetuate her pain."

"You are right Karl, my mother has mentioned the incident when she turned sick at Boston airport after she saw you for the first time; you definitely reminded her of your father. I am sorry to say it but it is a fact of life."

"Where do we go from here Sonia? I still love you more than anything in this world and I will do whatever necessary to have you with me, even if it alienates my family. My love for you is more than I can express in words."

"Karl, stop this right now, I think we have to be realistic about the situation we are in. It is simply not going to work out for you and I, no matter how much love we have for each other. The situation we are in is not of our creation. Nevertheless, we are part of it and cannot escape it. As much as we both love each other, this love will come crashing down on our heads in the future. And we cannot and should not live in a vacuum, forever separate from our families. It is especially unfair on our future children. When they grow up, they will ask us about their grandparents. What would we tell them? We cannot hide forever and withhold the truth from them. I am not going to consider a marriage which is not blessed and sanctioned by my family, it will destroy us and consume all those around us. I am sorry to put it like that; I know truth hurts, Karl, and nobody is more hurt than me, because I still love you with all of my heart. Deep down, I think God is punishing me for taking you away from Tracy. Maybe I should have resisted the temptation back then."

"This is absolute nonsense, Sonia! I don't understand how two people who love one another so intensely cannot get married. This is absolutely absurd! I am not asking you to give up your family, I am the one who suggested working on my own family and seeing if I can get them to rectify what happened in the past. Maybe I can convince my father to ask for your mother's forgiveness. Maybe if you and I get married our families will come to terms with the new situation and it may influence their minds to redress the animosity between them."

"This is all wishful thinking, Karl, it is not going to happen. The hurt is big and the wounds are very deep. I don't think my mother will survive even one day if you and I get married, and I would forever blame myself for her death. The best thing we can do at the moment is to drop the idea of marriage and let events play out the way our Lord intends them. I'm sorry, Karl, but I've been thinking. I am now contemplating a life devoted to the service of the Lord and my fellow human beings. Marriage is not on my agenda, not to you or anybody else. But I want you to know I will love you for the rest of my life."

Karl was very overtaken by emotions when Sonia hung up. Tears were pouring down his face, his body shook and his mind heaved with self-hatred for being the son of a Nazi criminal; he hated himself for being who he is. Head down on his desk he started crying, with images of Sonia flooding his mind. Why is it his fault he cannot marry the only person he ever loved in this world, the only one who occupies his heart and mind round the clock? But suddenly his focus changed, Sonia's images were replaced with his father's, and he felt a loathing like he never had before. His father was the one to blame for the loss of the only girl he ever loved. He sat straight up in his chair and through his tears he saw the letter opener. In pure anger he picked it up, aimed it at his father's portrait on the office wall and with all the power he could muster threw the metal piece.

CHAPTER 63

Oscar and Ricardo spent days and days meeting at the house to figure out a way to get rid of Ingrid until they finally settled on a plan for her and for Marvin Kline, the detective who gathered the report on her. They believed the detective still constitutes a threat and possible source of harmful information if he ran to the police after learning of Ingrid's murder. Of course he would inform them of the liaison he had with the man who requested surveillance on the murdered woman, and naturally he would be compelled to provide a description of the client. The only way to stop the progress in its tracks is to kill the private sleuth. Those investigating Ingrid's killing will have no reason to suspect her murder and Marvin Cline's murder are connected. And in order to ensure total secrecy, they also decided to rely on themselves to do the job

Karl was in his office when his secretary came on the phone intercom. "There is someone called Brandon, from Chicago on the phone for you, sir."

"Yes, I know Brandon, put him through, please. Good to hear your voice, Brandon, how have you been?"

"Hello, Karl, I am doing great and everybody is fine here. There have been many changes in my life and I will fill you in next time we meet. I am actually calling to ask you how far you live from Cusco, Peru? My companion and I are coming on vacation to South America to see Macho Picchu, and I wonder if you would like to meet us there?"

"I am not too close, Brandon. It's more than two hours flying time to Cusco, but why not, I'll meet you there. I will serve as your personal guide. I visited the city with my family many years ago, you will be impressed. The place is amazing but I hope it won't be raining like the last time we vacationed there. When are you planning to come and how long will you stay?"

"We booked the tickets today and we will be arriving in two weeks, first to Lima and then we take an internal flight to Cusco. I will fax you the itinerary."

"Please do that, I look forward to seeing you soon, have a safe flight."

Karl had been in a miserable mood ever since Sonia told him she was not interested in marriage anymore, and that she was planning to devote her life to the service of Jesus Christ instead. He didn't internalize what she meant back then, and he thought it was all just declarations pronounced at a time of anguish and uncertainty with no chance of implementation. He considered the devotion she has for her family and for him too important factors to ignore and believed she would ultimately change her mind and return to sanity. So when Brandon suggested meeting in Cusco he agreed to go because he was tired of feeling miserable and desperately needed a change in atmosphere.

After she and Father O'Malley had a long consultation, Sister Annabelle summoned Sister Anne to the office for a final discussion and to make a decision on whether to allow Sonia to join the monastery or not. The background report they gathered points to her good character and stable state of mind, Mother Superior began the debate the minute Sister Anne sat down.

"I had two conversations with Father O'Malley and he strongly believes Sonia is an excellent person and a good candidate for our monastery. What do you think Sister Anne?"

"I liked Sonia the first time she came to talk to us, and I do share Father O'Malley's assessment of her, but I am not so sure she will stay the course to the end with us."

"I agree with you Sister Anne. Even Father O'Malley has doubts, yet he put forward a strong argument in support of her joining us. He believes time will determine how far she will go and how long she is likely to stay, but he insisted she will in the meantime be an excellent nun and a great asset to the monastery."

"What reasons did Father O'Malley give in support of her joining us and what was the basis for his argument?"

"He knew her for many years, and he vouched for her integrity and devotion to the Lord. He also thinks her educational background is a credit to the monastery. But Father still has reservations about Karl. He said Sonia adored the boy with a passion and she was looking forward to getting married to him before all of this happened to her, and Father believes these forces could prove a strong pull away from us. Nevertheless he firmly believes we should give her a chance to serve the Lord, and see how things pan out in the future."

"If Father questions her long term commitments, why on earth does he believe she is a good candidate to join? You remember what happened to Sister Pauline many years ago; she reneged on her commitment in favor of getting married to her old boyfriend."

"Yes, I do remember her well, I even reminded Father O'Malley about our experience with Sister Pauline. He understood our concern yet he still argued in favor of letting Sonia join. What do we have to lose if we admit her? He argued the worst case scenario is she leaves us in the future. However, if we fail to admit her, this could bring intolerable impact on her life he fears. Father admitted to having a soft heart for the poor girl and that it would pain him enormously if something unpleasant happens to her."

"This is interesting, Sister Annabelle. I do sincerely believe Sonia is a nice and well-meaning girl and she also conforms to our ideals, and Father is right, what do we lose if she decided to leave in the future? I therefore recommend allowing her to join; she is bright and will be dedicated to the service of the Lord and his monastery."

"I feel the same way Sister Anne; you may contact her with our decision."

When Sonia broke the news to her parents she finally had made up her mind to join after receiving the official invitation from Sister Anne, Ingrid nearly fainted and Greg's mood turned sour. They sat with their daughter for hours trying to talk her out of it but to no avail, Sonia was steadfast in her decision. She was aware her decision to join will bring major discomfort and heartache to her family, but the pain she concealed in her own heart the moment she broke off her relationship with Karl was immense and she suffered for days on end. She picked up the bible and read for hours to soothe her agony and calm her nerves. She wanted to escape into her own sanctuary and lock herself in that cocoon forever; her heart was ripped apart and no force other than the Lord could ever repair it. She bawled her eyes out for hours, knowing how hard this will be on her family and on Karl, the love of her life.

Sonia couldn't leave before saying goodbye to him for the last time. "Hello Karl," she said with her voice trembling, heart pounding and tears cascading down her face.

Karl was so excited to hear from her. He wanted to tell her about his upcoming trip to meet with Brandon and to see if she was interested to join them, but he was taken by total surprise. "Hello my love," he answered with eagerness, "it's so good to hear your voice! I miss you so much and cannot wait to hold you in my arms again. I'm meeting up with Brandon in Peru and I was hoping you'd like to come with us to Machu Pichu!"

"Karl, I have something very serious to tell you."

"What is it, is it your mother? Is she okay?"

"No, it's about a decision I have made. I am going to be a nun. I will become a sister at the Carmelite Monastery next week. I wanted you to know."

Karl wasn't sure if she was joking, but her tone sounded ominous. "What are you talking about?" he asked in disbelief.

"You heard me Karl. I am joining the Carmelite Monastery next week. I will join my Catholic Sisters in devotion to the monastery and the service of our Lord."

Karl felt a baseball bat had hit him on the head. "You must be kidding me."

"No Karl," she interrupted before he could go further, "I am dead serious. I have already been accepted; there is no doubt about it in my mind."

Karl started to cry and his voice was rising in anger and protest. "So you've decided to run away from our problems, and leave the ones who love you to deal with your decision? What about your parents? And me! I love you Sonia and I don't know if I could continue to live without you! Please Sonia, don't do this to me, please, please, I love you!"

"I loved you too Karl, but my decision is final. Please don't waste your breath to change my mind, because I won't."

"Oh, my God, I cannot believe what I am hearing; I cannot believe the only woman I ever loved on this earth is doing this to me! Why are you taking it out on me Sonia! Please understand how much I love you, I will do anything to be with you, anything you want Sonia, please don't leave me!"

Sonia was crying too. She knew how much hurt her decision will cause but she was resolute. "Karl, I said I am joining my Christian Sisters so I can spend the rest of my life in prayer and contemplation. This is my therapy and away from the miseries of this life. I have loved you with all of my heart and you know that, but it is time we said goodbye. But before I go, I want to tell you it would make me happy if you find love with another woman. Please Karl, forget about me and try to find happiness with someone else, I shall pray for that, and I will forever love you."

After she hung up, Karl was lying stretched on his office floor crying like a baby, kicking at the floor and desk. He was so angry with the whole world, livid for losing his soul mate, the love of his life and the only one in the whole wide world who ever brought him joy. He blamed himself for not marrying her earlier, as they both desperately wanted and now his beloved Sonia is gone.

Ingrid and Greg tried very hard to dissuade their daughter from joining, but their effort didn't produce any results. Sonia had made up her mind and no amount of pressure could make her change, not even David. He recognized the seriousness of the situation and left the campaign trail to come to Detroit with his wife and son in an effort to change his sister's mind but Sonia was unwavering. But after the shocking disclosures about Karl's father, he finally understood the reason for the break-up. Naturally, he was furious, and vowed to her he would deal with that son of a bitch personally once he's sworn in as Governor.

"But Sonia, surely there has to be a better path for you to take. You love teaching so much! Maybe if you just move away, have a change of scenery; I'm sure I can help you find a position in New York."

"Thank you, David, but no. My decision is final. I'm sorry you wasted your time coming to Detroit to talk to me."

"Don't be silly Sonia," he responded, "nothing is more serious to me than the future of my little sister!" He pleaded with her for hours and at the end he concluded it was all over; she was dead set on this. He hugged his sister and told her how much he loved her and he too will always be there for her.

It was one of the darkest days in Ingrid's life when she and Greg drove Sonia to the monastery. Greg warned his wife the night before not to have her emotions on display, but Ingrid couldn't help it, she broke down in tears when Sonia emerged from her room that morning wearing her nun's habit. She ran into her daughter's arms and sobbed like a baby, she stood with her arms round her and she wouldn't let go. Sonia stroked her back and brought her hand to her face and kissed it in a show of love and respect for her mother, but Ingrid was heartbroken to see her baby leave.

The forty-five minute ride felt like an eternity. Ingrid sat in the front with her husband and Sonia sat quietly in the back of the car. The atmosphere was so sad and full of melancholy, and when they finally arrived, Ingrid didn't have enough strength to get out of the car to say goodbye. Greg came out and put his arms round his daughter, hugged her tight and with choking voice told her how much he loved her and he will be there if she ever needed anything. Sonia walked steadily to the gate and stood there for a moment facing her parents. She raised her arm and waved, and then she turned her back and went in and closed the gate behind her, tears rolling down her face. But she walked with poise and determination, knowing her decision to join in was the right one.

In the car, her parents were both crying. When they saw the gate close, Ingrid reached over to her dress sleeve and with all the power she could assemble ripped the sleeve off in a show of immeasurable grief at the loss of her only daughter.

Life at the Monastery was indeed a radical departure from what Sonia's life had been thus far. She now wears the brown Carmelite Nun's habit to consecrate her life to Jesus and his most sacred mother, Mary, and she withdrew from this world to pray to the Lord unceasingly, to lead a life of solitude and contemplation. It is indeed a life rooted in limitations and scarcity of the material world and the intensification of spirituality and prayer. It was difficult at the beginning but deep down she was happy and satisfied she joined, and she quickly blended in with the community of women who chose to live in isolation, silence and poverty.

Karl wanted to cancel the trip to Cusco to meet his friend, Brandon. After Sonia's call, he'd never felt as bad in his life and he was full remorse for not proposing to her earlier. He cursed himself for not revealing the truth about Sonia's family to his father. He would have objected but even if they got married without his approval Karl was sure his father would have come to terms with the facts and Sonia would have been accepted by everyone. But her mother's past relationship with his dad complicated matters to the breaking point. Karl now vowed to never marry anybody for the rest of his life. Nobody could possibly replace Sonia in his heart, nobody ever. He picked up the phone to call his friend to make a last minute apology and cancel the trip, but reconsidered his decision and decided to go in the end; Sonia would want me to do it, she always liked Brandon and felt so comfortable in his company, he told himself.

Karl was subdued when he arrived at the hotel in Cusco. He expected to see Penny in the room and thought she was the companion Brandon referred to in their phone conversation, but he was taken aback when another man opened the door. He thought it was the wrong room he went to before he heard Brandon's voice urging him to come in. He soon learned Brandon and Penny were divorcing, because of Mark. It was a shock at first to learn his friend was engaged in a homosexual relationship, but Karl, with his accepting, liberal outlook on life didn't care. He liked Brandon a lot and if this is his friend's choice, so be it. He hated to judge people and preferred to afford them the space to behave as they pleased and in the manner that best suits their needs.

The three men had great time and the weather cooperated well when they visited Macho Picchu. The train ride from Cusco was enjoyable and they were impressed with the proud people of the Andes and the outstanding ruins perched atop the mountain overlooking the sacred Urubamba River. They spent the remaining time in Cusco, the historic town nestled in the Andes Mountains that served as the capital of the Incas before the Spanish invaders destroyed their civilization.

Brandon finally admitted to Karl his loathing of the group in Oregon and everything they stood for. Karl too told him the same thing and both were surprised their affiliation with the group was commissioned to please their fathers. Brandon also mentioned that Ricardo came to Spokane recently to meet privately with his dad.

"What was he up to?" asked Karl.

"I have no idea; I was at my family's residence in Spokane with Penny and her folks. My dad arranged for the meeting as a last effort to get Penny and I to work out our differences and rekindle the faltering marriage but he got up in a hurry when he determined it wasn't possible. He said he was late for an appointment with Ricardo and I didn't ask him any further questions."

"I guess your father didn't know about Mark?"

"Are you kidding me? He would kill me if he knew about my sexual orientation; my dad is so caught up in his beliefs. I even kept Penny in the dark; I didn't want to hurt her any further. To tell you the truth nobody knows about Mark except you, Karl."

Among the first things Oscar did was to call Stewart Perkins, the makeup artist in Burbank, to discuss making a latex face mask. Mr. Perkins was a distant relative of one of Oscar's senior employees and the two met several months before the Las Vegas casino resort was opened to discuss dressing up figures in various outfits and horror faces for one of the theme attractions at the casino. The artist with the signature serious look on his face was a master; he started his career working at one of the major motion pictures studios in Hollywood and after he retired he opened a private studio and continued to do subcontract assignments for his old employer in addition to designing different themes for other clients including casinos and theater productions. He was a well-respected man in the industry. Stewart came to Oscar's mind when he remembered how well he did at the casino in Las Vegas, converting lifeless mannequins into different and distinct images vibrant enough to almost converse with the people looking at them. It was surreal to look at the horror scene he created in the casino; crowds of onlookers admired and praised his craftsmanship.

"Hello Stewart, this is Oscar Silva, do you still remember me?"

"How could I forget you Mr. Silva, you are a kind and generous man! How is business in Las Vegas?"

"We're doing great, thank you so much. The reason I called is to see if you can make a mask replica of a man's face by looking at just a small photo of this person?"

"The quick answer is yes, but it all depends on what you need the mask for."

"It all started as a joke; I want to bring you a photograph of my cousin in Brazil, I would like to have a mask made in his image."

"That is no problem, but who will wear the mask?"

"It will be me, my cousin is celebrating his sixtieth and we want to play a practical joke on his older sister at the family gathering."

"Yes, I can do it providing his head and yours are similar in size, and if they are not, I will have to make some modifications that may show minor detail defects to the trained eye."

"This wouldn't be a problem at all for as long as the image looks similar."

"Yes, Mr. Silva, they will be very close when I finish with them. I have to make an exact profile of your face then make a mask in the shape of your cousin's face to fit your face profile, I therefore need you to come to my studio for a session to make the prototype. Please allow several hours when you come; this takes time if you want the end product to be top quality. You will also need a wig to match your cousin's hair."

Karl was at a loss when he returned home after his brief visit to see his friend in Peru. It disturbed him immensely uncle Ricardo took the time to visit with Brandon's father, Dr. Hanson. He sat at home with his mother after her return from LA.

He asked her how his dad was doing in California on his own; this was an attempt to glean information about what Oscar was up to, and if his mother knew anything out of the ordinary. But from the mundane answers she gave, he established she wasn't aware of anything irregular. He was tempted to fly to LA in defiance of his father's orders to remain in Brazil and confront him face to face. He wanted to tell him about the pain and suffering he has caused and the new development with Sonia becoming a nun, however, he decided not to follow through for fear it may sour their relationship further and alienate him from the rest of the family. He therefore resisted the temptation to stir the pot for now, until out of the blue he received an unexpected call.

"Mr. Silva," said his secretary, "you have a long distance call from somebody in the United States. He says it is rather urgent but he refused to give his name."

"Put him through."

"Are you Karl Silva?" the caller inquired.

"Yes, I am. To whom am I speaking?"

"That's not important. I was asked to convey a message to you," the caller said with a slight quiver in his voice. "You better do something. Some people have found out your father is plotting to kill Sonia's mother."

Karl's blood boiled in his veins when he heard this. "I am sorry, but who are you and who told you to call me?"

"I am sorry sir, but the people who asked me don't want to disclose their identity, but I assure you the information I provided is credible."

"Listen, pal, you've got to give me more than that to go on. Tell me who those people are, and how did they find out?" But before he finished the question the phone went dead.

Karl was distraught after the call. He couldn't comprehend or acknowledge his father was about to commit any crime, let alone murder Sonia's dear mother. He believed his father was heartless during his youth for torturing and attempting to kill this woman by virtue of her being Jewish, but that was in the past. His father is a grown man and enjoys tremendous respect, and it defies logic he was plotting to kill her again. Why on earth...what possibly could she have done to him now! Dad, just move on with your life and let others live theirs! You are not the only one God put on this earth, he created her as well for a purpose and that purpose in the eyes of the Lord is equal in value to yours.

Karl was livid. He picked up the phone three times to call and confront him. However, he changed his mind when he concluded his father will vehemently deny such accusations and demand to know who in fact relayed this slanderous information. Karl spent the next few days reviewing in his mind the warning from the nameless man in order to narrow down the list of people who could be responsible. Could his mother have overheard his dad talking to an assassin about killing Ingrid? He dismissed that given the conversation he had with her upon returning from California. He concluded his mother didn't know anything, or else she could be the best actress in the world and feigned her answers to keep him in the dark. But deep down he didn't believe his mother would provide cover for murder. He also thought about Ricardo; could he have made the arrangements for the anonymous man to contact Karl to stir up his passion and get him involved in a counter effort to stop Oscar from perpetrating this crime? It is possible but knowing how staunch a friend Ricardo was to his father, he determined this too was hogwash and too absurd to pass serious examination. He considered the group in Oregon, maybe one of the people involved in the plot had a change of heart and decided to sound the alarm. How about Dr. Hanson, after all this is an intelligent person who may have a vendetta against the Jews, but his plans for them are grander than killing a single unimportant woman. Karl spent the rest of the day trying to work it out, but eventually it dawned on him the person who phoned couldn't possibly be credible, because if he were, he would have given more details and divulged his true identity.

CHAPTER 64

David's campaign was going strong and the last stretch before the election proved harder than initially predicted. It seemed there weren't enough hours in the day to travel from one city to another. The campaign bus with his name and campaign slogan, *"United for New York's Bright Future"* printed on all sides was making the rounds to rally support in the traditionally Democratic stronghold. A large contingent of reporters followed him wherever he traveled to report on his message of hope and determination to rid the state of the problems plaguing its progress. His Democratic opponent was a seasoned politician who was able to turn the campaign around and make a significant comeback, narrowing David's lead but David pressed on with his and many people in the hard hit north came to see him. He promised more investments for the crumbling infrastructure and urged the Defense Department to relocate military bases to the state to give a boost to the depressed areas. He was confident of his chances and recent polls put him slightly ahead of his opponent.

After fifteen hours campaigning on the road, the evening turned sour when he arrived home and Nancy told him Greg had called from Detroit about something urgent.

David instantly dialed his parents' number in Detroit. "Hello Dad, I'm told you called, what's up?"

"It is your mother, David. I hate to tell you but her cancer is back, and it's back with a vengeance."

"Oh, my God, what happened? And how do you know?"

"We tried to hide things from you son, because of your campaign, but the same lump your mother had before is back. She went to see the family doctor last month and he sent her for tests and referred her to Doctor Morgan, the same oncologist who treated her in the past. This afternoon Dr. Morgan called to discuss her condition and said it was serious and that her cancer is back stronger than before. I'm so upset I can barely stand on my feet."

"Alright, Dad. I don't care about anything more than I care about Mom, I will be there first thing tomorrow morning."

David arrived home to find his father in a depressed mood. His mother was out when he arrived but she soon returned from her regular morning walk with Goldie. Ingrid was surprised to see her son and she ran over and gave him a big hug.

"I didn't expect to see you here David! What a pleasant surprise!"

David fought back tears when he saw her; she didn't look well at all. Her face was drawn and she appeared fragile, her skin had turned yellowish and unhealthy looking. Ever since Sonia left home the after effects of her departure had been devastating for Ingrid. She refused to accept what happened to her daughter. Sonia was her life, she made the house full and lively and suddenly she was gone and the house turned empty and quiet. Greg did all he could to alleviate her pain and longings but Ingrid was hurt beyond rehabilitation. He often found her lying in bed crying, with photos of her daughter setting on her chest, and her visits to the Synagogue more than doubled in the hope prayers might deliver her daughter back. Then the lump started to appear again and the same symptoms recurred-- no appetite, constant itching and sweating. Greg suffered in his own silence for the loss of his daughter and now his beloved wife was withering away before his eyes.

"Hello mother," David answered after he kissed her on both cheeks, "how are you doing?"

"Well, this problem with itching and sweating is back, I hope it's not as serious as last time."

David's heart was pounding a mile a minute and he never felt so sad in his life. He put his arms round his mother and started to cry.

The routine at the monastery made Sonia happy and content and it seemed the other sisters liked and welcomed her. Although the sad images of her parents the day they dropped her off were still fresh in her mind, she got on with her life; she was determined to make a go of it.

Sonia was deeply hurt when all of this with Karl's father broke out. She spent many sleepless nights thinking about it, and no matter where her mind ventured it came back to the same conclusion; marriage to Karl was out of question because of his father. She even considered accepting her mother's recommendation to look somewhere else and find an alternative to him.

Perhaps she will be lucky and meet another man and find new love. That again was struck down in her mind; nobody in the whole world could make her eyes twinkle, her face shine or her heart tick more than Karl. It will be futile to look for a replacement when her heart is already occupied. She considered carrying on with her life the same way she had been doing since graduating from university; that too wouldn't have worked, she was able to carry on because she had something to look forward to; marriage was in the plans and her future with him was assured. Karl showered her with love, attention and gifts, and he was sincere about his intent to marry her. However circumstances beyond their control influenced events to their detriment, so what are her choices now? Can she continue to carry on the same way when she no longer has Karl to look forward to? This option wasn't going to work either, the spark is already extinguished and to carry on like she always had was equal to slow death.

Her mind strayed and then the image of Jesus appeared. She thought, the Lord came to rescue me and I am eternally grateful for the divine intervention. I always loved Jesus and his pure mother, I want to be like her and give myself to the Lord only. I cannot imagine another man touching me, the thought of it makes me sick, I know the decision to join my Christian Sisters will make my mother terribly unhappy, and it pains me to see her and father cry, but I had to go. I feel like a bird, I just want to fly up to the heavens to touch the face of the Lord and tell him how much I love him and how much I want to serve and be with him.

Father O'Malley called to check on her progress and was pleased when Sister Annabelle reported how well Sonia had settled at the monastery.

"Yes, Father, Sonia has been very much like the person you portrayed. She is honest, sincere and devoted to the lord. All the sisters get on well with her and she seems to have settled in happily here."

Election Day finally arrived for the people of New York. Their choice for governor was between two candidates with starkly different outlooks and a different destiny for the state. David promised to improve the prevailing economic conditions and eliminate the root cause for the downward spiral. He also pledged to work on the safety and security of the people and provide their children with a bright future. On the other hand, his opponent advocated the same failed policies of his predecessor, so at the end of the day,

David triumphed by a comfortable margin, much to the delight of his family and friends. His victory speech was eloquent and forceful yet magnanimous to the defeated candidate. He pledged to work on his campaign promises from the first day he is sworn in.

Though he was happy and delivered a good speech, his mind nevertheless was with his mother; it affected him terribly to see her cancer come back again. The phone conversation he had with the oncologist was not reassuring. The doctor explained the seriousness of his mother's condition and the need to start chemotherapy right away. David knew how much the treatment affected his mother last time, the poor woman was in pain and couldn't do any of her normal household chores, and she had to depend on Sonia back then. But Sonia is gone and Greg must look after her now, and he is so different from Sonia, who catered for all her mother's needs and did household duties as well. Greg on the other hand has to start late in life and learn how to do things at home and care for his wife at the same time then attend to his business on top of that. David recognized the situation was untenable and promised to hire a full time medical assistant to look after Ingrid while his dad was at work.

CHAPTER 65

Oscar and Ricardo sat in the house for yet one last session; their plan was taking shape and the missing pieces were steadily falling into place. They discussed which guns are best suited; Ricardo, who was an expert, recommended the Beretta 93, a semiautomatic hand gun small enough to fit in the pocket of a coat and capable of firing one shot at a time or a three round burst with deadly accuracy at a range up to 150 feet. As he owned one already, he stopped at the gun shop and purchased another one for Oscar and also ordered small size silencers to be fitted. Their plan was to get rid of Ingrid and Marvin Kline on the same day then get the group to aid in David's assassination in the future after the dust is settled down from Ingrid's murder. Dr. Hanson would be motivated to have the group involved in the killing of an important Jewish politician as it conforms to their fundamental goal of eliminating Jewish influence from the United States.

Ricardo was given the responsibility to plan and execute the murder of the private investigator. But Oscar, who has so much hate and personal vendetta against Ingrid decided to take it upon himself to murder her with his own hands. He told Ricardo, "I cannot wait to get rid of this whore once and for all. I want to satisfy my lust when I see her blood spill. I want her to suffer like she did in the concentration camp and I will be thrilled to see her squirm and plead for her life when I point the gun to her head. The fucking whore doesn't deserve to live after the havoc she's wrought on my life."

Oscar received a call from Stewart Perkins to tell him he was ready for the first dressing trial to examine the mask and see if it fits snugly on his face. When he arrived there to try it on, he was impressed how well it was made and how smoothly it fits, and he couldn't believe the resemblance to the person in the photo when he looked in the mirror, especially with the wig on. After happily paying for the product, Oscar stopped to pick up the piece of garment he had ordered at the tailor shop and there again he was pleased with the outcome when he tried it on. It too made him look unmistakably like the person in the photo. Oscar was finally finished with the preparation in LA and was ready to carry out the plan.

David came to Detroit over Christmas to be with his family. He brought Nancy and little Daniel to brighten the atmosphere at home and he bought a beautiful gift for his mother and one for his father. Ingrid was so happy to see him and sat in the living room to listen about him becoming the Governor of the second largest state in the Union and the awesome responsibility associated with the job. His father was enthusiastic about going to Albany, New York for the upcoming inauguration of his son. Earlier in the week David decided to have a private ceremony for the oath of office at the Governor's mansion at the stroke of midnight on New Year's Eve and another public ceremony in the assembly hall inside the State Capitol. Greg wanted to go to the public ceremony scheduled for the third week of January when all the legislators are back from vacation.

On Christmas Eve the whole family drove to the monastery to visit Sonia. David purchased a large bouquet of red and white roses for his sister. Ingrid cried when her angelic daughter entered the guest house designated for family members visiting their loved ones. Typically, nuns are not allowed to have vacations or visit family outside the monastery except in an emergency. Sonia expressed her deep love for all her family and soothed her mother upon learning of her cancer. "It will be alright mother, you are a tough fighter and a survivor and I have great confidence you are going to beat this awful illness. I will pray for you every day and I love you more than anything in this world." She wished them happy Christmas before she returned to the cloister.

Oscar and Ricardo determined it was necessary to put their targets under surveillance for at least a week prior to the day they planned to commit their murders. Ricardo was chosen to drive in his car from California all the way to Detroit to carry out the important task and to do the final last minute preparation. He was also supposed to bring the guns and ammunition in his suitcase as they may encounter problems if Oscar attempts to take the prohibited items on the plane.

The day Ricardo left for Detroit Karl received another call from the same man who called several weeks earlier.

"You better believe me now, Karl. Your dad's accomplice is on his way to Detroit as we speak to conclude Sonia's mother's murder, and you must do something to stop it before it's too late!"

"Look! Who the hell are you and how do you know any of this is true?"

"I am absolutely sure the information I am passing to you is true because the people who asked me to convey this message care about you and Sonia and they want to stop this crime before it happens. This is why we called the first time, but unfortunately you left it too late and the accomplice is already on his way to Detroit. Please understand if you don't act quickly you can be sure of a great tragedy falling on your family."

"What? I am sorry -- but who are you!"

"I am just a messenger, and I am not at liberty to reveal the identity of the people who asked to convey this message."

"Why didn't they call the police if that is the case and report this imminent crime?"

"The people don't want police involvement; preventing the crime altogether is what they would like to see happen. They explained it will be impossible to report a crime to the police before the crime takes place. The police, they say, will dismiss unsubstantiated accusations and innuendo and therefore will not act without solid evidence. Please realize how serious the situation is."

"I am here in Brazil. What am I supposed to do from here?"

"You better come to the USA right away and convince Sonia's mother to leave her house to a safe haven before the killer gets there first. This is their recommendation and they asked me to convey it to you."

"You mean to say my father personally will be the man who does the killing, or will he be hiring a hit person to perpetrate the crime?"

"That I am not sure of, but I advise you to act and act fast to convince the woman in Detroit to go to a safe house before it is too late."

The caller once again hung up before providing additional answers. Karl agonized on how to tackle this problem. He was trying to figure out who was behind the calls but judging from the events of the past months with his dad, he concluded there could be some merit to the message. For the first time he had a strong feeling the man was telling the truth and decided to take action before it's too late. The worst thing that could happen if the caller turned out to be a hoax is the inconvenience Ingrid will sustain as a result of leaving her house for few days. But the big challenge for him is how on earth will he be able to talk to her, let alone convince her to leave her house when he knows damn well she will slam the door in his face if he goes there and knocked on her door. He was sure she will accuse him of being the reason for her daughter becoming a nun, on top of reminding her of the man who had all but destroyed her. Karl was searching his head for other options; on a hunch he picked the phone and called Brandon in Chicago.

Brandon, who received his marriage annulment a few days prior, was in a jovial mood when he picked up the phone in his new office. "This is Brandon, how may I help you?"

"Hi, Brandon, I am so glad to find you so quickly. I wonder if I can count on you to help me. It's an emergency."

"Hi Karl, where are you calling from? Of course, what kind of emergency are you talking about?"

Karl was torn to tell him what his father was up to, so he invented a story about another man and claimed this person is out to kill Sonia's mother. He went on to tell him more details and the sort of help he needed. Brandon, who has tremendous respect for his friend, agreed to drive immediately to Detroit and meet him there.

Ricardo arrived in Detroit three days after leaving California and checked in at a cheap motel close to Metro Airport, in order not to attract attention to himself or to Oscar when he arrives the following week. He brought with him the two Beretta guns equipped with silencers and a high powered binoculars and tripod. After taking a much needed rest he ordered a taxi to come to the motel to take him to the car rental company to pick the long van with no side windows he reserved. He intended to use the van to tail his targets unobtrusively when they are out and about and get a sense of their daily routines.

After spending six days following the private investigator and Ingrid he established a strong sense of their everyday patterns. He also drove around the countryside on the outskirts of the city and settled on the murder site for the private investigator in a secluded area near Ypsilanti. When he returned to the hotel in the evening he picked up the phone and called Oscar to announce everything was in place.

Marvin Cline was born in Huntsville, Alabama. When his parents divorced his mother moved to Detroit to live with her folks. He decided his best option when he graduated from high school in 1951 was to join the army, to escape poverty and his grandparents' crowded house. He served in Vietnam for several years before he was honorably discharged, and when he returned to Detroit he joined the police force and became a successful detective. He stayed on the force for fifteen years and after retirement established a private investigator agency. Marvin was a tall and athletic man with few friends other than the guys he meets regularly at the gym. His business took off and became profitable just few months after he started. His main clients were law firms who used the services he offered to spy on people on behalf of their own clients. When Maurice Ferguson contacted him to spy and prepare a file on Ingrid, he didn't hesitate to do the job. The elderly man gave him a fabricated name and arranged to meet him in person to discuss the case and then again when the file was ready for pick up. Marvin didn't question Maurice for paying cash for his service; he knew from experience his client was operating under false pretense yet he acted as professionally as he would for any other client.

Ricardo worked out a plan in his mind to murder Marvin. It was essential to remove the link between the detective and Ingrid; otherwise there still remains a chance the murders will be traced to Oscar and him in the future.

He took Oscar when he arrived in Detroit for a drive around the neighborhood where Ingrid lives to familiarize him with the house and the area. He spent the entire time briefing his best friend about the information he collected on Ingrid and to point out important facts about her and the area where she lives. There were obviously unexplained and unaccounted aberrations in his findings: he had expected to account for Sonia's whereabouts and her daily routine but she was nowhere to be seen. Where could she have possibly gone, what was she possibly up to? The report Marvin Cline prepared earlier indicated she was a teacher at high school and it delves in great detail about her daily schedule, from the minute she leaves the house to the moment she returns. It even alludes to the regular visits she made with her mother to the hospital and to medical labs as well as the visits she regularly makes to church. But where is she now? Schools are back from Christmas break and he fully expected to see her going to work every morning.

The morning of Oscar's arrival, Ricardo drove past Ingrid's house for a few more hours of surveillance before he went to the airport. He saw Greg loading a small suitcase in the driver's seat of his truck. This is unusual, he told himself; Greg who parks his car on the driveway outside but let his wife park hers in the garage, usually jumps in his truck and drives to work. But this morning is different; he was intrigued and decided to follow him to find out what he was up to. Ricardo was relieved to observe Greg driving to the airport, where he followed him to the airline counter and saw him check in for a flight bound for New York. He correctly surmised Greg must be going to his son's inauguration and he was happy to eventually figure out what may have happened to Sonia as well. He drew the false conclusion Sonia must have already gone to New York before her dad to spend part of the holiday and to attend her brother's swearing in ceremony, and she will be returning to school when the festivities are over. Still, this doesn't explain why Ingrid was not going with Greg to the ceremony, after all, it was her son who will be sworn in as governor. Then he reasoned to himself after trailing Ingrid from one medical lab to the next she must be too sick to go; this is the only logical conclusion knowing that no proud mother would miss such an important and gratifying occasion. Ricardo was pleased with the turn of events since the new prevailing circumstances would to a large degree serve their purpose by removing the possibility of any unexpected visits to the house by either Greg or Sonia.

When they returned to the motel both he and Oscar were in a buoyant mood and were counting the hours until they could set their plan in motion. But there was one last thing he had to do; he picked up the phone and dialed Ingrid's house number.

Trying to disguise his accent, he said, "Hello, Mrs. McKay, I am John Woolsey, Father O'Malley's new assistant. Father asked if he could drop by to see you tomorrow morning, perhaps around noon. He said it is about a gentleman by the name Karl Silva, and he wants this meeting kept in confidence."

Ingrid was surprised by the call, what could Father O'Malley possibly want to talk about Karl and why does it have to be confidential? But Father O'Malley enjoyed great respect and she didn't see any harm talking to the priest, she was sure he will have valid reasons for the confidentiality which he will explain. "Sure," she answered the caller, "Please tell Father I look forward to his visit."

The day before, Ricardo called Marvin Kline. He introduced himself as Roger Clarke from Kalamazoo and asked if he was interested in meeting with him the day after tomorrow to discuss spying on his wife. He told the detective his wife ran off with another man who lives in a rural area off I-94, approximately 35 miles west of Detroit. Marvin asked for the time and agreed to meet with him in front of the vacant building at the top of the highway exit to Ypsilanti. The stage was set for Ricardo to eliminate the detective at the same time Oscar is with Ingrid.

On his way to the Porto Alegre airport to catch a flight to Detroit, Karl called his mother. He told her he was taking a business trip to Sao Paulo and would likely be gone for several days and he promised to call her when he was ready to come back. When he arrived at the airport he was able to find a flight to Detroit with a layover in Miami. He was very nervous and deep down hoped the caller was lying and he wasn't being impelled into a situation where he is perceived as going against his father's best interest. But he made up his mind to act and act fast after quick evaluation and understanding of the repercussions this crime may instigate should the anonymous information turned to be factually correct.

Karl was pacing at Miami airport after the announcement his flight to Detroit was delayed for a short while, he was tempted to call his father but quickly abandoned the idea and decided to continue in his effort to convince Ingrid to leave her house, his father would be appalled if he to find out his son was back in the US against his order to remain in Brazil, he was relieved when they finally announced his flight departure at 7:08 am, he reckoned he will be in Detroit before 10 am, and he will have enough time to make it to the church to see the pastor.

Brandon was there when Karl arrived at Detroit Metro and as per Karl's instructions he had already stopped at a gun shop earlier in the day and purchased two small revolvers just in case they need to defend themselves. The two friends jumped in the car and drove off to see Father O'Malley at the church; Karl had already devised a plan in his head to get Ingrid to leave the house peacefully. The plan was centered round convincing Father O'Malley to cooperate with them in their effort to ask Ingrid to vacate to a safe house until the threat on her life passes. After more than an hour of intense discussion the priest relented and agreed to help. But there was still another hurdle on the way. Father O'Malley didn't know Ingrid well and he was unsure she would listen to him when he goes to the house to advise her of the imminent danger to her life. He wanted to call the police instead, but Karl explained the police will not get involved once they determine the whole issue was based on unsubstantiated claims. And they simply don't have the time to wait for the police to conduct their tedious investigations. The priest was put in an uncomfortable position, unsure how to respond to this most unusual situation. He has never even met Ingrid before, all he knows is what Sonia told him about her mother and he was at a loss what to do. But he was also aware he couldn't stand idle and do nothing. It is his religious and civic duty to prevent a crime. In a moment of reflection he suggested they get Sonia involved and he told Karl, "She is the only person Ingrid trusts and will listen to."

Sonia was in her room when Sister Abigail came knocking at her door. "Please come with me, Sonia, Sister Annabelle wants to see you, it is rather important." Sonia was a little bemused. What could Mother Superior possibly want from me that is this important? Has anything happened to Mother or to David? She anxiously followed Sister Abigail through the cloister and into Sister Annabelle's office.

"Good morning Your Reverend," she addressed Mother Superior.

"Sit down Sonia. Father O'Malley is on his way to pick us up right now, we are going over to your mother's house," and the gentle elderly sister proceeded to tell her the reasons for this rather unusual situation. When she finished she led a prayer for the safety of Sonia's mother.

Oscar was up early. He went outside and got one cup of coffee from the coin operated machine and a bucket of ice from the ice dispenser. When he returned to the room Ricardo was just getting out of bed.

"How thoughtless" he told his friend, when he saw him with only one cup of coffee in his hand. "You didn't bring me a cup, mister?"

"I got this for you, Ricardo; I am not having one myself. I brought ice instead for a glass or two of whiskey to calm my nerves."

After his friend finished with the bathroom, Oscar went in there carrying with him the items he purchased to assist with the murder of Ingrid, he turned the hot water on and stood in the old tub thinking through his plan of action and when he finished the shower he was satisfied and elated he had an iron clad plan and was sure he can leave the scene of the crime unnoticed after he finishes off his enemy, he moved the cassock from the laundry wrap and slowly and methodically put the garment on, then he put the mask and the wig on and looked in the mirror, he made a final adjustment to the collar and looked again, this time he was satisfied with the outcome.

Ricardo was just walking in the front door after he went out for a second cup of coffee when Oscar came out of the bathroom wearing his new clergy costume, Ricardo thought he was in the wrong room, but soon realized what his friend was up to and the two of them broke out in laughter,

Damn Oscar, you gave me the fright of my life, but you are spot on, you really do look like his eminence, wait until you yank that mask off, I bet the fucking scumbag will crap in her pants

I cannot wait to see it Ricardo, I want this woman to suffer, I want to put my hands round her neck and squeeze as hard as I can, I want to see her begging for her life, I want to torture her again and again for all the headache and heartache she caused us, then finish her off with a bullet to the head.

This is all a load of bull, Oscar, I must warn you not to let your emotions rule your head, or the police will know it is a crime of passion, perpetrated by someone who knew the victim and they will investigate further to narrow down possible suspects, why are you inviting more trouble to yourself when you can make it look like a burglary gone wrong and the police will concentrate their efforts to look for a robber and not somebody who knew the victim.

You are right Ricardo, I don't know how I will react when I see the bitch, but I know in my heart you are right and I shall endeavor to be in control of my emotions.

Yes, Oscar, you need to be quick and surgical, just yank your face mask off and shoot her between the eyes, two bullets, one from you and the other from me, and then stage the scene to make it look like a burglary and get out without being noticed. You will be happy to know you were the last person she saw when she took her final breath, what a gratification!!

The two guys checked the guns and the ammunition then stood at attention in front of each other, one hand holding a gun and the other raised in a Nazi salute, and after they hailed the Fuehrer they walked out into the cold, wet air. There was a light snow but it was not sticking to the ground.

Ricardo drove off on I-94 West and Oscar jumped in the SUV rental they picked up the night before and headed East on I-94. He then turned north when he reached the Southfield exit aiming for the heart of Dearborn. The appointment time was getting closer, and the snow was getting heavier but the roads were still passable as he turned into the subdivision where Ingrid lives. Oscar looked in the rear view mirror to make sure nothing unusual was behind him.

Ingrid was up early in the morning. She made half a pot of coffee since Greg was gone for the official inauguration of their son in New York, and then she took Goldie for a walk round the block. When she returned she decided to have a hot bath and get dressed since Father O'Malley was expected soon. She put Goldie in the garage, and turned on the TV to watch the live broadcast of her son's inauguration, regretting now that she'd made this appointment with Father O'Malley at the same time. She really wished she was well enough to attend in person; she was so happy and proud David had made a name for himself and attained the highest office in the state. Ingrid checked out the window to see if it was still snowing; she hoped it wouldn't build up and block the driveway. She hates to get stuck inside and not able to leave as she no longer has the strength to shovel the snow and Greg won't be back until tomorrow evening to do it.

The local TV station broke into their scheduled programming to air the inauguration of Detroit native David McKay as the new Governor of New York. Ingrid turned up the volume and sat on the couch to watch. The TV cameras turned on David as soon as he walked in, hand in hand with Nancy and little Daniel trotting behind. Her heart melted to see her grandson dressed in a suit and tie, he looked so adorable standing at attention like a grown up man. She also recognized a copy of the Torah in Nancy's hand, the very copy she gave her son when he came to see her in Detroit at Christmas, and now he will take the oath of office with his hand on the holy book of the Jews. Tears came to her eyes, but she was distracted as she noticed the white SUV approaching the driveway. Oh, darn, it must be Father O'Malley, she told herself, as the tall priest exited the vehicle and walked towards the entrance. She went to the foyer to answer the doorbell.

Meanwhile Ricardo was going over the last detail of the murder plot in his mind while driving on the freeway. I will blast the nigger's head off when I come face to face with the ugly coon and nobody will give a damn, he thought. Their time will come after we finish off the Jews; all of them will be shipped back to Africa where they belong, they have out-lived their usefulness and must be given a one-way ticket out of here. This country belongs to the Aryan people and there is no room for these apes.

Oscar, dressed like the priest shook Ingrid's hand when she opened the door and followed her to the living room.

"You'll have to excuse me, Father. My son is about to take the oath of office. Please join me to watch for a few minutes."

The TV was showing David standing in front of New York's Chief Justice who will administer the oath of office. Nancy rested the holy book on both of her hands and the ceremony began. "Please repeat after me," the supreme judge ordered David. "I, David McKay, do solemnly swear that I will perform the duties of the office to which I have been elected..."

But suddenly, Oscar stood up and quickly yanked the mask off of his face. Ingrid didn't understand what was happening at first and she nearly fainted when she recognized the man standing in front of her. She could hear her son repeating the words behind the judge... "and to faithfully perform the duties of the office of Governor..." Her mind froze in time, "Oh, my God, he is going to rape me again," as images of the first attack were flashing back. Then she heard his unmistakable voice.

"You thought I was dead, didn't you? You fucking whore!"

She gasped when he slapped her across the face, stunned and sobbing hysterically. "Don't do that to me Hans, I haven't done anything to you!"

"You fucking Jew bitch want to snatch Karl from me! This is my boy and he will never marry your filthy daughter you slimy fucking Jew! And which is it, Rachel or Ingrid? You can hide your sleaze from the world but you cannot hide it from me. Your people killed my grandfather and threw him out in the street. Now the great German warrior's grandson is here to avenge his murder and the murder of our Fuehrer. All Jews should be thrown in an oven to burn and I will delight to see their skin crackle in the flames!"

"Please Hans; I am dying from cancer, please! My son helped you when you needed him, I beg you..."

Oscar slapped her again, punched her in the stomach and ripped her dress. She screamed with agony. "This is my other son you are looking at! You tainted his Aryan blood with your filthy Jewish blood. Now he is an ugly Jew, just like you, pure filth!" He dragged her by the hair and threw her to the floor, then jumped on top of her and with all his power he started to beat at her face. Blood was gushing from her mouth and she could hardly breathe with his weight on top of her. Heaving with pain, she was vaguely aware of the dog barking loudly in the garage. Oscar stood up and pulled the gun out of his pocket, anxious to finish the job and get out of there before the neighbors hear the commotion.

Karl was pleased Father O'Malley agreed to help. He jumped in Brandon's car and drove immediately to Dearborn, he decided to drive by Ingrid's house to check nothing was out of the ordinary, he nervously looked at the time, it was 11:45 am. Brandon sat in the passenger seat with Father O'Malley behind the wheel of his own SUV and they drove as fast as he could to the monastery to pick up Sonia. She and Sister Annabelle were waiting when the priest arrived, and they got in the back seat.

Karl approached the house and drove round the block a couple of times and after he determined everything was normal, he decided to pick up a cup of coffee and then return and park the car on the street few houses away and wait until father O'Malley arrives, but when he got there he noticed the white SUV in the driveway, that is odd, he told himself, I wonder who is there visiting, he parked his car on the street; he didn't want to block the path of the vehicle in the driveway. He decided to approach the house on his own to see if everything is fine and also attempt to talk to Ingrid on his own. He thought if he told her how much he loved her daughter and how sorry he was for what his dad had done in the past, he might convince her to leave with him. Before he rang the bell, he heard the dog barking incessantly; he found the door unlocked and entered with gun in hand.

Oscar looked up from over Ingrid's body. "What are you doing here, son?"

"Dad, please drop the gun. Please, please I beg you, Dad!"

"You are so naïve son! You don't know what the Jews have done to you, to your father and your grandfather, and you don't know how they conspired to kill our Lord!"

Karl realized his father was dangerously unstable. "Dad, please I beg you to drop the gun. Killing this poor woman will not achieve anything, please listen to me, Dad."

"I hate the Jews, can't you understand! This bitch has to go, she is a great threat to you and your family, can't you see it boy?"

"Dad, there are other ways we can deal with this; please drop the gun. I am begging you, Dad!"

"I must kill this fucking filthy whore and cleanse the world of all Jews, they are the scum of this earth and they have to go, one by one and I will start with this bitch!"

"Stop! Stop, sto..."

The gun fired, but before Oscar took aim again, Father O'Malley rushed in the open front door. He was trailed by Brandon, Sonia, and Sister Annabelle. They all stopped abruptly as they saw Karl taking aim at his father and Oscar pointing the gun at Ingrid. Karl fired first and the large hulk of Oscar came crashing to the floor.

He looked up at his son in disbelief. "You shot your own father to save that whore? I will disown you! You are a traitor to your race; you are a traitor to your family and the proud German people! He then tried to reach for his gun but Karl took aim again. He pleaded with his injured father to leave it, but Oscar was adamant. He wanted to finish the job and kill his nemesis, but before he pulled the trigger at Ingrid, Karl fired again. Oscar rolled up on his side first, and then slumped motionless onto his back.

Sonia was out of her mind at the sight of blood pouring from her mother. She ran over and put her arms round her, crying and praying at the same time, her habit drenched. Brandon immediately called the police.

Ricardo was driving along the freeway singing, thinking to himself, I bet Oscar must have finished the job by now, I'll be glad when it's all over. I look forward to getting drunk tonight and toasting our great Fuehrer, two miscreant creatures will be terminated today, and good riddance! He saw the turn off approaching and signaled to exit.

Marvin Cline was already waiting in front of the vacant building when Ricardo pulled in; he got out of the car to introduce himself. "Hello there, I am Marvin Cline, pleased to meet you."

"I am Roger Clarke. Pleased to meet you. Marvin. Would you please follow me in your car? I would like first to show you the house where I believe my wife is hiding and after that we can stop for a cup of coffee to discuss the case and our options."

"Sounds like a plan. You lead the way and I'll be right behind you."

Detective Cline felt a little uneasy when he followed Ricardo. The man said his name was Roger Clarke, but he speaks with a clear German accent and the name doesn't sound too German. Then he noticed the small rental sticker on the back bumper of the van, and what about the van? This is odd, he thought; why would anybody drive for a meeting all the way from Kalamazoo, 140 miles away in a cargo rental van? All of these things are the hallmark of a robbery. Criminals are known to lure their victims to abandoned areas to kill and rob them and then using their ID to steal from their homes. So when Ricardo turned into a dirt road, Marvin followed him cautiously. When the van pulled over to the side, Marvin pulled in behind him. Nervous, he took the gun out of the glove compartment and released the safety pin and put it inside his coat pocket, firmly holding it in his hand. He sensed something sinister was going to happen; maybe this is why the guy baited him to this deserted area, maybe he plans to kill and rob him. As he got out of the car he noticed Ricardo had his back to him and was fumbling inside his coat. The hair on the back of Marvin's neck stood up when he saw Ricardo in the van's large side view mirror pulling a gun. When Ricardo turned to shoot, the ex-policeman was faster and shot first.

Ricardo fell to the snow face down. Marvin approached him slowly and used his foot to flip him over on his side. The single bullet went into his heart.

Her face was badly beaten, but Ingrid's bullet wound was not life threatening; she was hit in the arm. Sonia and Sister Annabelle escorted her to the hospital once the ambulance arrived. Oscar's lifeless body was taken to the morgue and an autopsy ordered to determine the cause of death. The police arrested Karl on the spot against Ingrid's pleas. "No, don't take him, he is a good man! He didn't mean to kill his father. I witnessed everything; please leave him alone!"

Sonia stayed with her mother in the hospital, and Greg and David came rushing to Detroit after they were notified about the murder attempt. Greg was beside himself with guilt for having left his wife alone and allowing such a horrible thing to take place in their home.

"No, my dear, you could not have known this would happen. You had to be in New York for David, for both of us." Ingrid was adamant that her husband should not feel any remorse. "But please, you and Sonia need to go get some sleep. I'll be fine, and I need you to make sure Goldie is okay."

"Alright, but I'll be back first thing in the morning." He kissed her on the cheek and turned to leave the hospital room. "David? Are you coming now?"

"No, Dad, I think I'll stay here with Mother for a while; you and Sonia go ahead."

"I love you, Mother. See you tomorrow," said Sonia as she hugged Ingrid goodnight.

Once they were alone, David pulled up a chair closer to Ingrid's bed. "Can we talk about this?"

"What else do you need to know, son?" Ingrid was guarded.

"Well, of course I'm aware of all the details from the police report, and I was able to speak with Karl on my way back…"

"How?"

"There are certain advantages to being a Governor, Mother…"

"Oh, of course. So Karl told you…his father found out I was Jewish and didn't want him to marry Sonia?"

David considered her explanation. "But you knew him during the war, didn't you?" Ingrid turned her face away to hide the tears. "Mother…Mom… tell me. Sonia and Karl said you recognized him from some pictures?"

"Yes. He was one of them. He was afraid I'd turn him in. That's all." Ingrid still wouldn't look at her son.

"Mom, you were a victim. A survivor! People know about the horrible things that happened there; maybe if you talk about it? Mom? You're safe now."

At this, Ingrid broke down. "Oh, David, I never wanted you to know, I never wanted anyone to know."

David got up and took his mother in his arms, hugging her closely as she sobbed on his shoulder. When she quieted a bit, he asked softly, "He was the one who did these things to you, wasn't he?"

"Mm-hmm" she murmured.

"Well. Okay." David was gathering his thoughts as he continued to rock her lovingly. "A lot of terrible, brutal things were done to women." With some hesitation, he finally decided it was best to get it out in the open. "Mom, did he rape you?"

She shuddered in his arms and backed away. "Oh, David, I never wanted anyone to know. I was so ashamed!"

"What? Why should you be ashamed?"

"I loved you so much, I always loved you. It didn't matter…" She was crying into her hands, hiding her face.

"Mom? Mother? What didn't matter?" Then as he tried to understand her anguish, it dawned on him. "Me? He was my father?" David slumped back in his chair. "What, why didn't you tell me? Oh, my God, why did you keep this to yourself for so long?"

Ingrid was nearly exhausted with emotion. "It was just something you didn't talk about…back then. And later, I worried about Greg, and Sonia, and your career. Oh, David, I didn't want to bring this shame to our family!"

There was that word again; he couldn't comprehend why she would suffer like this over something she couldn't control. "Oh, Mom! No! There was never anything for you to be ashamed of! You never did anything wrong. You were attacked for the simple reason that you were Jewish and the whole world knows about the atrocities that happened in Germany. But I know,

Mom, I know you always loved me! And I always loved you and always will!" He took her in his arms again.

"Oh, David, I'm so sorry for this!"

"Stop saying that. Everything is okay. I'm glad you told me. It's alright, Mom," he consoled her. "But I think it's time for us to tell Dad and Sonia. Tomorrow morning, okay? I'll help you."

Ingrid was released after a few days and Sister Annabelle authorized Sonia to stay with her at home during her recuperation.

Karl was let out of jail when the district attorney determined he was acting in self-defense, and his actions don't constitute a felony since he was attempting to prevent a murder from taking place. He came to Ingrid's house to pay respects and apologize to her in person. Sonia answered the door when he arrived. She was still wearing her nun's habit even while at home.

She was surprised to see Karl. "Hello Mr. Silva," she addressed him. "Please come on in."

"How are you Sonia? It is so good to see you my love. Please call me Karl."

"Hello Karl, good to see you. Did you come to see my mother?" she answered in a serious voice.

"Of course, I am here to see your mother and to see you, too. I don't seem able to stay away from you. You are part of me, Sonia, and I'd like us to talk."

"Please follow me," she replied coolly, as she led the way to her mother's bedroom. Ingrid was still in bed recuperating after she was discharged from hospital, and her arm was still bandaged.

"Good afternoon Mrs. McKay. How are you doing, ma'am? I hate to see you suffering like this. He bent down and gave her a kiss on both cheeks.

"I am fine, son. You saved my life and I am eternally grateful. I don't know why your father had so much hate in his heart, Karl, but he is gone. What a waste of life. I had hoped things would have ended differently but I guess the Lord decided otherwise."

"I don't know why my father had so much hate, but I am terribly sorry for all he has done. I wish it had been different, but unfortunately I have to deal with it for the rest of my life. Please have it in your heart to forgive him."

"Yes, Karl, it is easier said than done. Your father had done so much to me, I will have to work on my heart. Maybe time will take care of my wounds and in the future all will be forgotten and hopefully forgiven."

"Thank you, from the bottom of my heart," he answered. "I hope you don't mind, Mrs. McKay, but right now I have to say something that should not wait." Then he looked at Sonia who was seated on the opposite side of the bed.

"I love you Sonia, and I vowed not to marry another woman if you don't marry me. In front of your dear mother, I want again to ask for your hand in marriage. I have in fact made a stop to see Father O'Malley before I came here and I expressed to him my deep love for you and my sincere desire to marry you. He told me the church will not be in your way if you want to marry me."

At this point, Karl stood up and walked to the other side of the bed and went down on his knee. "So will you marry me, Sonia? We've been waiting too long."

After a brief silence, Ingrid interrupted. "Sonia darling," she addressed her daughter, "I know in my heart this man who saved my life is a good and sincere man. You have my blessing if you want to marry him."

Sonia, who was fighting back tears, looked at her mother and nodded, then she stood up and threw her arms round him. "I love you too Karl Silva! I love you with all my heart. Yes! Yes!"

They shared a long and passionate kiss, and Ingrid gave a big shout to show her happiness and approval.

Karl and Sonia drove to the monastery the following day to say goodbye to the wonderful women there. Sister Annabelle was expecting the couple; she rose to her feet to greet them and gave Sonia a big hug.

"We will miss you my child. You have been a wonderful sister and we will always pray for you and your family. All the Sisters stood at the gate waving to the couple as they drove off, both Karl and Sonia holding hands and crying with happiness.

CHAPTER 66

When Oscar's body was released to the family following the autopsy and police investigation, they had it shipped to Porto Alegre for the funeral. Elsa was there dressed all in black. She took Karl to the side and expressed her sympathy and then she told him how much she regretted what she had done.

"I am sorry Karl for your loss and I take full responsibility for the death of your dad."

"Thank you Elsa, but I don't understand; what are you talking about?"

"I am sure you don't Karl. I loved Mr. Oscar; he was always so good to me. But I loved you more Karl, I loved you from the day I saw you sitting in your crib with your arms flailing, wanting to be picked up. And when you rested in my arms I brought you to my bosom and hugged you so tight; from that day I vowed not to let anybody hurt you. I nursed you when you were a baby and fed you my milk; you are the son I never had. You brought so much joy and happiness to my soul and to my heart. And I was only trying to protect Mr. Oscar. But I could not stand it when I heard him and Mr. Ricardo planning to kill Ms. McKay." She was crying openly now. "I never thought things will turn out the way they did."

Karl realized at that moment who was behind the anonymous warnings. He hugged Elsa, "Oh, Elsa! Elsa, you don't ever have to apologize, my dear, you have done the right thing, and I love you for it. But please, tell me who the caller was?"

"My brother-in-law. He called from his motel in Arizona, after I pleaded with him and my sister, and he told me he was so nervous when he spoke to you." As Karl gave her his handkerchief, she regained some composure.

"Yes, he sure was, but the message was well received, thank you!" Karl embraced her, kissing the top of her head. "I love you Elsa as much as you love me, if not even more! You were like a mother to me when I was a baby but you are like the big sister I never had. I will always love you and will look after you for as long as I live, may the Lord bless your heart and soul.

All you have inside is pure love and I am so thankful my dear for what you have done."

Karl was seated next to his mother and grandmother in the first pew. David and Ingrid sat on the other side, and when the music started Karl stood up and walked towards the altar where Father O'Malley was standing. Sonia, wearing a beautiful white gown and a white satin veil over her golden hair walked down the aisle, arm in arm with her father. As they reached the altar, Greg handed his daughter over to the man of her dreams.

When Father O'Malley finally told the groom, "You may kiss the bride," Karl lifted her veil and the whole church erupted in cheers and applause. Ingrid got to her feet with difficulty, clapping weakly with tears pouring down her face. But words couldn't possibly describe her happiness.

Father O'Malley continued. "And now ladies and gentlemen, I would like to welcome our Carmelite sisters who wish to offer their congratulations for the holy union we just witnessed, and bless the groom and the beautiful bride who was one of their own!" Sister Annabelle led all the sisters in a prayer to bless the marriage:

We thank you, O God, for the Love you have implanted in our hearts. May it always inspire us to be kind in our words, considerate of feeling, and concerned for each other's needs and wishes. Help us to be understanding and forgiving of human weaknesses and failings. Bless our Marriage O God, with Peace and Happiness, and make our love fruitful for your glory and our joy both here and in eternity.

There wasn't a dry eye in the hall when they finished; not even David's tough looking security detail, who stood in the back of the church and were seen removing their dark shades to wipe their eyes.

It was quite a sendoff for Karl and Sonia.

Though Ingrid was so weak she could hardly stand up, she insisted on bidding her daughter goodbye at the airport before she and her husband went to LA to live at their residence there.

Ingrid couldn't be happier and she looked at her daughter with pure love and affection. "You are leaving the nest, my baby girl. I am so very happy for you; please give me many grandchildren, lots of them. I want to see them all before I go to my grave."

Sonia was very emotional, and she hugged her. "Yes, Mother, I will."

The following morning Greg kissed his wife before he went to work, and asked her if she needed anything. "No my dear, all I want is to see you happy and content. I love you, I always loved you Greg McKay. I couldn't have possibly found a better man. You will always remain in my heart till the day I die."

Soon after her husband left for work, she got up to go to kitchen. She felt very weak and had to lean on the wall for support. Goldie came to check on her; when she found Ingrid lying on the floor, the dog sniffed and walked round her again and again, and then she came and curled up next to her mistress, with her head lying on her shoulder. When Greg called as he always did around lunch time, he was concerned there was no answer. He came home and found his wife and her dog in that same position, in their eternal sleep.

ABOUT THE AUTHOR

Basil Taher is a graduate of California University, he worked in real estate and construction in different parts of the world. Writing has been a passion and the David Connection is his first novel, he lives in Ontario, Canada.